"On-screen!" Riker snapped.

With a tap, Keru relayed a signal to the main viewscreen—

Just in time for everyone to watch a vortex of darkness tear Paris to shreds.

The Eiffel Tower collapsed into twists of iron that blew away like leaves. The Palais de la Concorde, the seat of the Federation's government, disintegrated like dust falling into a star. The Federation Council building was swept away seconds later.

The sensors from Paris went black.

The computer switched to the San Francisco feed.

The city's skyline flew apart. The Golden Gate Bridge broke into pieces and fell into the bay. Beyond the bridge, a surge of fire and dark energy obliterated Starfleet Command and Starfleet Academy, leaving behind nothing but scoured, smoldering dirt—

The feed went dark.

Faster than Sarai could keep track, the great cities of Earth were erased: New York. Tokyo. London. Mexico City. Nairobi. Shanghai. All gone within a breath.

Then the only remaining view of Earth was the one from Luna.

The storm swelled, metastasized out of control, and swallowed Earth whole. Spacedock and McKinley Station were consumed.

Darkness hit the Luna feed. Then the Mars feed. Jupiter Station went silent.

The last Sarai saw of the Federation's capital was a long-range FTL sensor image . . . which captured the moment the temporal storm devoured Sol itself.

Half a minute later, the tempest dissipated and vanished . . . and the Sol system was gone. The star, all its planets, its asteroid field, its Oort cloud . . . everything.

Not destroyed—*erased.*

As if they had never been.

STAR TREK™
CODA
BOOK III
OBLIVION'S GATE

David Mack

Story by
Dayton Ward & James Swallow & David Mack
Based on
Star Trek and *Star Trek: The Next Generation*™
created by
Gene Roddenberry
Star Trek: Deep Space Nine™
created by
Rick Berman & Michael Piller
Star Trek: Voyager™
created by
Rick Berman & Michael Piller & Jeri Taylor
Star Trek: Discovery™
created by
Bryan Fuller & Alex Kurtzman
Star Trek: Picard™
created by
Akiva Goldsman & Michael Chabon
&
Alex Kurtzman & Kirsten Beyer

GALLERY BOOKS
New York   London   Toronto   Sydney   New Delhi   La Barre

G

Gallery Books
An Imprint of Simon & Schuster, Inc.
1230 Avenue of the Americas
New York, NY 10020

First Gallery Books trade paperback edition November 2021

GALLERY BOOKS and colophon are registered trademarks of Simon & Schuster, Inc.

For information about special discounts for bulk purchases, please contact Simon & Schuster Special Sales at 1-866-506-1949 or business@simonandschuster.com.

The Simon & Schuster Speakers Bureau can bring authors to your live event. For more information or to book an event, contact the Simon & Schuster Speakers Bureau at 1-866-248-3049 or visit our website at www.simonspeakers.com.

Interior design by Kathryn A. Kenney-Peterson

10 9 8 7 6 5 4 3

Library of Congress Cataloging-in-Publication Data is available.

ISBN 978-1-9821-5967-2
ISBN 978-1-9821-5968-9 (ebook)

In memoriam:
Yvonne Mack, 1941–2020
Neil Ellwood Peart, 1952–2020
Dave Galanter, 1969–2020

By the test of our faith, the highest standard of civilization is the readiness to sacrifice for others.

—David Lloyd George
Queen's Hall, London
21 September 1914

What we do now echoes in eternity.

—Marcus Aurelius
Meditations

PREVIOUSLY . . .

2376

- Captain Benjamin Sisko returns from his sojourn with the Bajoran Prophets, which began a year earlier, after the end of the Dominion War. (*Star Trek: Deep Space Nine*, "What You Leave Behind")
- Bajor joins the United Federation of Planets. Members of the Bajoran Militia are integrated into Starfleet. (*Star Trek: Deep Space Nine* novel *Unity*)
- After being critically wounded, Kira Nerys experiences a vision from the Prophets in which they refer to her as "the Hand of the Prophets." (*Star Trek: Deep Space Nine* novel *Warpath*)

2378

- In the alternate universe, the Terran Revolution succeeds with help from Memory Omega, a secret organization created a century earlier by Emperor Spock. The victorious rebels establish the democratic Galactic Commonwealth. (*Star Trek: Mirror Universe* novels *The Sorrows of Empire*, *Saturn's Children*, and *Rise Like Lions*)
- Wesley Crusher accompanies the Traveler, with whom he's been learning to grow and focus his emerging abilities, to his mentor's home planet, Tau Alpha C. There, Wesley is "reborn" and becomes a Traveler. (*Star Trek: The Next Generation* novel *A Time to Be Born*)
- Kira Nerys resigns from Starfleet and becomes a Bajoran religious novice. (*Star Trek: Typhon Pact* novel *Rough Beasts of Empire*)

2379

- Federation president Min Zife, guilty of arming the independent world Tezwa with illegal weapons that contribute to millions of deaths, is covertly removed from office by a group of Starfleet admirals after they are briefed by Captain Jean-Luc Picard. Unknown to Picard, Zife is assassinated by Section 31. (*Star Trek: The Next Generation* novels *A Time to Kill* and *A Time to Heal*)
- Shinzon, a clone of Picard created to replace the captain as a Romulan spy within Starfleet, seizes control of the Romulan Star Empire in a *coup d'état*. Picard and his crew thwart Shinzon's plan to

attack Earth and cripple the Federation, but Data dies in the battle, sacrificing his life for Picard's. (*Star Trek Nemesis*)

- William Riker marries Deanna Troi and takes command of *U.S.S. Titan*. Troi is *Titan*'s counselor and first-contact specialist. (*Star Trek: Titan* novel series)

2380

- Picard marries Beverly Crusher. (*Star Trek: The Next Generation* novel *Greater Than the Sum*)

2381

- The Borg launch a massive attack on the Federation, annihilating numerous planets and sixty billion lives before Starfleet achieves victory with help from a mysterious and powerful alien race known as the Caeliar, forever ending the Collective's persistent threat. (*Star Trek: Destiny* novel trilogy)
- A female Caeliar named Sedín is revealed to be responsible for a failed symbiosis with humans in the distant past, resulting in one possible origin for the Borg Collective and its Queen. (*Star Trek: Destiny*, Book III: *Lost Souls*)
- During the Borg Invasion, Ezri Dax, serving as *U.S.S. Aventine*'s second officer, takes command when her captain and first officer are killed.
- Riker and Troi have a daughter, Natasha Miana Riker-Troi, named in memory of slain *Enterprise*-D shipmate and friend Natasha Yar, and the deceased sister of Aili Lavena, *Titan*'s helm officer. (*Star Trek: Titan* novel *Over a Torrent Sea*)
- Picard and Crusher have a son, René Jacques Robert François Picard. The boy is named for Picard's nephew, René, and older brother, Robert, and for Crusher's first husband, Jack Crusher. (*Star Trek: Typhon Pact* novel *Paths of Disharmony*)

2382

- Breen spies steal the plans for Starfleet's quantum slipstream drive. Starfleet sends Doctor Julian Bashir undercover to a Breen planet with his old flame Sarina Douglas, another enhanced human and, unknown to Bashir, a Starfleet Intelligence infiltrator inside Section 31. (*Star Trek: Typhon Pact* novel *Zero Sum Game*)

- Andor secedes from the Federation over issues related to the Andorians' now-critical reproductive crisis. (*Star Trek: Typhon Pact* novel *Paths of Disharmony*)

2383

- Breen and Tzenkethi forces attack and destroy Federation station Deep Space 9. Over a thousand lives are lost. (*Star Trek: Typhon Pact* novel *Raise the Dawn*)

2384

- Data is "reincarnated" when his memories are transferred from his brother B-4 to a new android body built by their creator, Noonian Soong. Data's new android body is the one Noonian made to house his own consciousness after faking his death in 2367; Noonian sacrifices his immortal life for his son. Driven by the same passion that inspired his father, "Data Soong" does whatever he must to "resurrect" his android daughter, Lal. (*Star Trek: Cold Equations* novel trilogy)

2385

- Federation station Deep Space 9 (II) is declared operational, positioned like its predecessor near the Bajoran wormhole. At its commemoration, the Federation president is assassinated. Federation Council member Ishan Anjar of Bajor is appointed president pro tempore. (*Star Trek: The Fall* novel miniseries)
- Bashir defies Starfleet and President Pro Tempore Ishan to bring the Andorian people a cure for their reproductive crisis. He succeeds with help from Captain Ezri Dax. They are both imprisoned. (*Star Trek: The Fall*, Book III: *A Ceremony of Losses*)
- President Pro Tempore Ishan is exposed as a criminal. Andor rejoins the Federation. An Andorian wins the Federation's presidential election and pardons Bashir and Dax. (*Star Trek: The Fall*, Book V: *Peaceable Kingdoms*)

2386

- Bashir accepts a mission from Section 31 to stop the Breen from stealing jaunt-drive technology from the alternate universe. (*Star Trek: Section 31* novel *Disavowed*)

- Bashir learns Section 31 is run by a malevolent, centuries-old artificial superintelligence known as Control. The ASI uses Sarina Douglas as a weapon against Bashir and forces her to take her own life after Control is defeated. Traumatized, Bashir retreats into a semi-catatonic state. (*Star Trek: Section 31* novel *Control*)
- Journalist Ozla Graniv, with help from Bashir and Data, exposes Section 31's entire history and all of its illegal activities spanning more than two centuries. All known Section 31 operatives are arrested. Picard is implicated in the organization's 2379 assassination of Federation president Min Zife. (*Star Trek: Section 31* novel *Control*)

2387

- Exonerated from the fallout caused by the revelations about Section 31, Captain Picard and the *Enterprise*-E crew prepare to resume their mission of exploration in the Odyssean Pass. (*Star Trek: The Next Generation* novel *Collateral Damage*)
- Wesley Crusher warns Captain Picard that a mysterious enemy is deliberately collapsing entire timelines. Working with the *Aventine* crew, Wesley and the *Enterprise*-E crew seek out who is behind this terrifying new threat. Their investigation reveals their old foe the Devidians are to blame, but both crews suffer heavy fatalities, including Lieutenant T'Ryssa Chen, Lieutenant Taurik, and Captain Ezri Dax. (*Star Trek: Coda, Book I: Moments Asunder*)
- As the Temporal Apocalypse worsens, Picard faces unexpected resistance when Riker opposes any direct conflict with the Devidians. Shunned by Starfleet, Picard and his inner circle seek help from Data. Meanwhile, Captain Sisko and his former DS9 crewmates reunite in the wake of a cryptic message from the Prophets. At terrible cost, the new DS9 is sacrificed to destroy the Bajoran wormhole and slow the Devidian advance—but the war is far from over. (*Star Trek: Coda, Book II: The Ashes of Tomorrow*)

AND NOW . . .

PRELUDE

THE SECOND SPLINTER

1

Devidian Temporal Collider—Intertime

This was the end. There was nowhere left to run.

Inside the shimmering blue orb of the transphasic attenuation field, the floor was littered with charred and broken corpses. They filled the hexagonal platform's smoky air with a charnel stench, revealing the chroniton reactor core's vast chamber to Captain Jean-Luc Picard for what it had become in the space of just a few minutes: an abattoir.

His pulse raced as he put his sweat-soaked back to the towering, conical core housing and tightened his grip on his phaser rifle. His wife, Doctor Beverly Crusher, and their son, René Picard, backpedaled toward him, each clutching their own rifle. Crusher's auburn hair, dark and heavy with perspiration, clung to the sides of her face. René's blue eyes were wide with fear.

On the far side of the reactor core stood Captain Benjamin Sisko and Doctor Julian Bashir, their overtaxed phaser rifles veiled in ripples of heat. Both men were exhausted. They heaved weary breaths, and their faces were spattered with blood both alien and their own. Sisko cast away his drained weapon and drew a Klingon *mek'leth* with which to finish this fight.

Data stood between the pair and the trio, all of them behind their only cover, a ring of four curved, waist-high consoles that surrounded the core like a low retaining wall. He held a quantum communicator in his left hand while making changes to the reactor's calibration as dictated over the comm by Commander La Forge, in the rare moments that he could hear his old friend over the blood-curdling clamor that had filled the cavernous reactor complex.

A cold rush of foul-smelling air warned Picard that the next round of the assault was imminent. Terrifying shrieks echoed through the wind-fields they were wreathed in miragelike distortion, a field effect related to their phase-shifting and temporal-disruption powers. Also like the leviathans, they each emitted a toxic aura of death and decay.

The portable devices that generated the away team's defensive field whined in protest as the serpents assaulted the barrier and breached it.

The creatures' hideous shrieks of pain bled together and quickly drowned out the straining of the generators that gave Picard's team their last and only measure of defense. Inside the attenuation field, the Nagas' phase-shifting and temporal-disruption abilities were negated, but they still had huge fangs as well as tremendous strength and speed.

Behind the Nagas, the avatars went from a slow march to a manic charge.

Picard raised his voice to address all his people at once. "Brace yourselves."

He looked over his shoulder and saw Bashir wearily lift his rifle into position against his shoulder. Sisko gave his friend a reassuring pat on his shoulder, and then he took his place at the doctor's side and raised the *mek'leth* above his head. "For Worf!"

Bashir took aim at the dark tide of avatars bearing down upon him. "For Worf!"

Both men broke from cover and charged toward the edge of the barrier, whose crackling surface danced with white lightning where a Naga was forcing its way inside.

The same spectacle played out in front of Picard. It would be only a few more seconds until the battle resumed with full fury. He looked back at Data, who continued to key data into the reactor core through a panel of Devidian glyphs. "How much longer?"

The android replied with preternatural calm, "Almost there . . ."

Despite the commotion that surrounded him, Picard heard constant, high-pitched phaser blasts over Data's quantum communicator. La Forge was in trouble, just like they were.

The specter of failure haunted Picard: *If we fall before we finish this, it's over.*

Using the Naga snared in the attenuation field for cover, three avatars entered the barrier zone in front of Picard, and three more breached the field on the far side of the core.

Picard raised his weapon. "Fire!"

The Picard family attacked as one. Beams of brilliant orange light sliced into avatars and Nagas. One of the Nagas flared white, erupting in an act of self-immolation that momentarily overwhelmed the away team's transphasic-field generator.

In the fraction of a second that it took for the barrier to recharge, three more Nagas pushed forward onto the platform, along with more than a dozen avatars.

Crusher and René pivoted with frantic speed, picking off avatars just before they could unleash their handfuls of silvery death upon the team at the core controls. One avatar got behind them. As it prepared to hurl its assault, Sisko severed the automaton's arm, and then its head, with two strokes of his *mek'leth*.

Crusher fell back half a step as she checked her rifle. "Running low."

Picard shared her concern. Wesley's modified transphasic-disruption setting for the rifles was effective against the Devidians' creatures, but it drained power cells at a frightening rate. "Conserve fire. Aim for the heads." He tried to mask his fatherly worry as he looked at René. "Are you all right?"

"I'm okay, Papa."

The reactor room resonated as Sisko bellowed, "Attack!"

He and Bashir raced to meet a new wave of avatars. Sisko's *mek'leth* danced in fearsome arcs, and the sword—newly enhanced with a monomolecular edge—cut the hooded horrors down, hewing synthetic flesh from bone with merciless grace.

Bodies crashed to the deck at Sisko's and Bashir's feet, spilling dark blood in steaming torrents. As fresh corpses landed with wet thuds atop those that had fallen before, the next rank of avatars breached the energy barrier behind them, emerging this time all but on top of Sisko and Bashir. Undaunted, the two men roared and pressed their attack.

At Picard's side, Crusher fired again, as did René, vaporizing more avatars en masse.

A Naga lurched through the gap between two avatars' fading phaserghosts and sprang at Picard as he fired his rifle. The beast flared orange white in midair and vanished, just centimeters shy of rending Picard to bloody bits.

He trembled with unbridled terror as more avatars penetrated the barrier. His voice was raw as he shouted over his shoulder, "Data! We can't hold them!"

"Almost ready, Captain!" Data cradled the quantum comm between his head and shoulder, freeing up both his hands to enter the final sequences from La Forge.

Picard saw that victory was almost in reach—and then it was torn away.

On opposite sides of the chroniton core, Nagas snared in the attenuation field exploded in blinding pulses of white light. The protective blue shield retracted, leaving the bridges open and the platform vulnerable to attack. Only a tight blue sphere of protection remained, hugging the chroniton core itself. Avatars raced over the bridges to the platform, a flood of black-robed nightmares filling the air with lethal silvery beams thrown like daggers.

One struck Data in the back of his neck. He collapsed to the floor behind Picard, sparks flying from his ears and nostrils, his face a slackened mask of death.

Picard thrust himself between his family and the avatars. Caution abandoned, he unleashed a steady beam of phaser energy at full power and swept it in a broad arc from left to right, mowing down anything in its blazing-hot path.

Outside the energy barrier, Sisko and Bashir slew three avatars before a fourth punched a shot of death energy through Sisko's chest.

Sisko staggered and then fell on his back.

Bashir grabbed Sisko's *mek'leth* and sank the blade into the skull of the avatar that had shot his captain, but then he couldn't pull the weapon free. He let it go and retreated, raising his transphasic rifle. He shot down several avatars inside the perimeter—but on both sides of the core, more avatars and Nagas were already pouring off the bridges.

Crusher slapped her hand onto Picard's shoulder. "Jean-Luc! Finish the calibration!" She tilted her head, urging him toward the core. "Go!"

Everything Picard was, all he'd ever been, told him not to abandon Crusher and René, but she was right. Someone had to finish what Data had started, and he was the best one to do it.

He handed her his rifle. "I'll be quick."

She slung his weapon over her shoulder. "You'd better be."

Picard grabbed the quantum comm from the deck. "Geordi? Are you still there?"

The engineer's voice betrayed effort and alarm. *"Barely, Captain!"*

It took all of Picard's will to ignore the new attacks transpiring to either side of him and focus instead on the chroniton core's interface panel. "Data locked in the channel! Send the calibration pulse!"

La Forge's reply was drowned out by the whine of the transphasic-field generator and the primal shrieks of Nagas forcing their way into the team's last sphere of defense.

Picard increased the gain on the quantum comm. "Geordi! Repeat your last!"

Before the answer came, avatars breached the final sphere.

Then two more Nagas exploded.

The beasts sacrificed themselves in blinding eruptions of temporal energy, disrupting the last remnants of the platform's attenuation field—and this time the field didn't snap back. Flames and smoke belched from the portable generator. The protective field that had negated the space- and time-warping talents of the avatars and the monstrous Nagas was gone.

Massive pulses of ghostly death energy shot into the cavernous reactor room.

To Picard's right, Bashir fell, dead on impact a meter shy of cover.

On his left, a Naga lurched over the nearest console and slammed Crusher and René backward, against the core.

Picard disintegrated the Naga, but a fraction of a second too late. In shock, he fell to his knees, dropped his rifle and the quantum comm, and reached out for his wife and son.

"Beverly . . . ? René . . . ?" He tried to cradle them, hoping one or both of them might have enough time to say good-bye . . . only to see them turn to dust in his arms.

The woman whose love had changed his life in countless ways for the better, and the son he had never dared to dream he might have, were both gone. Ripped from the world, from time, from *him* . . . forever.

Somewhere beneath the smoke and bodies, La Forge's voice squawked from the dropped comm—and then came a scream and a burst of static, followed by a grim silence.

Picard sat on the floor, dazed and spent, his back to the chroniton core.

Around him a throng of avatars gathered, no doubt come to sup on the dying neural energy of the human who years earlier had dared to strike a bold but ultimately futile blow against the time-traveling parasites known as the Devidians, whose collective appetite for death had now reached cosmic levels.

Inside their billowing black robes, the silent reapers that surrounded Picard glowed brightly in anticipation of his imminent demise and their long-awaited feast.

An avatar holding a jeweled rod stepped forward. Extended a bony hand.

And proceeded to rip out Picard's soul.

Picard shivered, helpless as they leached the vitality from his body. It would be only a matter of moments now. Just a few more seconds until the end, after which the Devidians would be free to go on devouring more timelines, to feed their insatiable hunger for the kind of terror produced only by sentient beings made to suffer violent deaths.

Only once before had Picard ever tasted such a bitter defeat.

Never again, he had vowed after being freed of assimilation by the Borg.

But here he was, all his gambits countered, all his stratagems foiled.

His strength waned, and he stared forlorn at the dust in his hand.

His body was broken. His spirit was vanquished.

As he felt his life slip away, he was consumed by a fathomless sorrow.

I sacrificed all I'd ever had . . . and everyone I loved . . .

. . . only to see the courage of heroes fail.

PART I

ONLY MOMENTS
BETWEEN

TWO DAYS
BEFORE
THE END

2

U.S.S. Defiant NX-74205

As quiet as the grave. The stillness that surrounded Captain Benjamin Sisko on the bridge of the *Starship Defiant* made him painfully self-conscious, too aware of himself. He couldn't relax.

The bridge was steeped in shadow because the ship was operating in low-power mode. Sisko had taken that step to minimize the compact-but-powerful starship's sensor profile, and to maximize the effectiveness of its cloaking device, both of which were essential to keeping it and its fugitive crew hidden from the Starfleet armada that was hunting them.

Most of the ambient light on the bridge came from the image of fiery chaos that filled the main viewscreen. Great tornadoes of burning plasma sprang from radiant seas of golden fire, twisted hypnotically, and vanished without warning, creating vacuums that acted like vortexes.

This was the Badlands, a perilous place to hide. Sixteen years earlier, not far from these coordinates, the *Starship Voyager* had vanished. For years the Badlands had been blamed for that calamity; only years later did Starfleet learn *Voyager* had been abducted to the far side of the galaxy, to a remote sector of the Delta Quadrant, by a strange entity known as the Caretaker.

Sisko set his elbows on the arms of his command chair, folded his hands together in front of his chest, and closed his eyes. He noted that time seemed at once to be both rushing and dragging: hurtling with increasing speed outside his ship, racing toward the ultimate catastrophe, while feeling slowed to a crawl within it.

In the past Sisko might have tried to lose himself in the tedium of logs and reports, but he feared that would be a wasted effort now. The universe was coming apart; he would find no more solace in Starfleet's seemingly endless litany of routines. No escape in the minutiae of duty.

So he opened his eyes and bided his time.

The worst part of the long wait was having time to think. He was haunted by thoughts of Jake, his adult son from his first marriage, and Jake's wife, Korena, whom he had left to fend for themselves. The last news he had heard of them was that they had been part of a throng of refugees fleeing Bajor, a tide of souls rushing away from their homes, into the unknown. Korena's wide-eyed gaze when he had told her and Jake to evacuate from Bajor was one Sisko would never forget. It reminded him of a truism he had often heard while growing up in New Orleans: *Frightened eyes never lie.*

At least Kas and Becca are far away from all this.

His wife, Kasidy, and their young daughter, Rebecca, were still on Cestus III. There had been no reports of disturbances there—at least, none that Sisko knew of—but he could only hope that his family might be spared whatever horrors the Temporal Apocalypse still held in store.

When he made the effort to push Kasidy and his children from his thoughts, he still found himself burdened by concerns for his shipmates and his friends aboard the *Starship Robinson*, and all those he had known on Deep Space 9, before its tragic last hour had arrived.

He recalled the flash of detonation that had whited out *Defiant's* viewscreen. The new starbase had gone to its doom barely two years after it had officially opened for service, sacrificed in an antimatter-fueled act of self-immolation to permanently destroy the Bajoran terminus of the Prophets' stable wormhole to the Gamma Quadrant.

Guilt gnawed at Sisko, so he bit back at it. *There was no other way. We had no other choice.* He kept telling himself that, hoping that a time would come when he believed it.

Such was the nature of war. Decisions made, by necessity, in haste. And then, for those lucky enough to be called survivors, a lifetime to reflect upon those choices. Decades of regret.

Frustration led Sisko to grind his teeth. *If only stopping the Devidians hadn't meant losing the Celestial Temple.* But it had, and nothing could change that. He suspected the Devidians might have utilized the Prophets' stable wormhole as their point of interdimensional access not just because it represented a path of least resistance, but because they had known that destroying it was a decision that would come at a terrible cost.

Sisko set his hands on the arms of his chair and refused to let himself make fists. He told himself to stop fixating on what had been lost, and remember what—and who—remained with him, here in exile aboard *Defiant*. They were all fugitives now, on the run from Rear Admiral William T. Riker and the rest of Starfleet after defying Starfleet Command and the Federation Council in a desperate bid to halt the Temporal Apocalypse unleashed by the Devidians. Voices of cautious authority had urged Picard and the *Enterprise*-E senior officers to stand down, to be patient while more information was gathered.

They had answered that demand with a resounding "no."

With help from Tom Paris and his wife, B'Elanna Torres, Picard's crew had staged the theft of the *Enterprise*-E from Earth Spacedock—but only as a diversion for their bold hijacking of the damaged but still spaceworthy *Starship Aventine* from a nearby orbital repair facility.

Aboard the *Aventine*, Picard and his team had tracked the Devidians' incursion into this timeline to the Bajoran wormhole, setting in motion a sequence of events that had culminated in the sacrifice of the recently commissioned new Deep Space 9 station—as well as the lives of Ambassador Quark, Captain Ro Laren, Captain Nog, and Command Master Chief Petty Officer Miles Edward O'Brien—to close the wormhole forever.

If only that had ended the Devidian threat, rather than merely delaying it.

Even before the heat radiation of the station's destruction had faded, Riker had come to take Captain Picard and his officers into custody—only to discover too late that Sisko, with help from his shape-shifting friend Odo, had beamed Picard and a handful of his people off the *Aventine*, onto the cloaked *Starship Defiant*. Now they were all co-conspirators in mutiny, in the eyes of Starfleet Command. Which meant that, from here on, they would be on their own.

At the front of the bridge, sitting at the wraparound helm console, was Data Soong. The reincarnated android—Sisko was still unclear on the details behind *that* particular sequence of events—only partly resembled his former self, whom Sisko had once met on the old Deep

Space 9. This new incarnation of Data looked fully human. According to Picard, Data's new form had been based on that of his creator, Doctor Noonian Soong, as a young man. This remade Data had come aboard *Defiant* yesterday with his resurrected android daughter, Lal. She stood at the bridge's aft duty station, her posture stiff and her movements oddly birdlike, while she monitored the ship's master systems display for any signs of malfunction or damage.

Sisko's former crewmate Commander Worf monitored the tactical station. Until a few days earlier, Worf had served as the *Enterprise*'s first officer under Captain Jean-Luc Picard, and he had been on the cusp of a promotion to captain and his first command. Now all of that was gone, along with so much else taken by the Temporal Apocalypse.

Picard had ensconced himself portside, opposite Worf, at the bridge's engineering console. He kept busy reviewing reports sent up from main engineering by Commander Geordi La Forge, formerly the chief engineer of the *Enterprise* and now the top tool-pusher on *Defiant*.

Wesley Crusher—a bearded, fiftyish, human-born man who had developed extraordinary powers related to time and space after maturing into a being known as a Traveler—sat aft of Picard, at the controls for the cloaking device, to Sisko's left. Like Data, Lal, and Sisko himself, Wesley wore simple, civilian clothing. Crusher's outfit consisted of dark trousers, black shoes, a long-sleeved linen shirt, and a weathered brown leather field jacket whose hem fell thirty centimeters below his waist.

Across from Crusher and aft of Worf, Doctor Julian Bashir sat at the comms duty station, on Sisko's right. Deep Space 9's former chief medical officer was dressed in tattered civilian garb. His black hair, once kept trim, had turned gray and unruly, like his mad bramble of a beard. Quiet but tense, like a coiled spring, Bashir watched the plasma storm churn across the main viewscreen, its fires reflected in the fierce glint of mania that shone in his brown eyes.

Because Bashir had lost any vestige of his bedside manner, Doctor Beverly Crusher—who was Wesley Crusher's mother as well as Captain Picard's wife and the chief medical officer of Picard's now-former command—was in sickbay, tending to personnel who had suffered minor injuries during *Defiant*'s battle against the Devidians' phase-shifting, space-borne serpentine killing machines, the Nagas, in the Bajor system.

Berthed in the aft guest quarters were Worf's son, Ambassador Alexander Rozhenko, and Doctor Crusher and Captain Picard's son, René.

Vedek Kira Nerys had locked herself and the Orb of Time in cargo bay 1.

Which left the ship's highest-ranking VIP passenger standing behind Sisko on the bridge. Ambassador Spock loomed just beyond Sisko's peripheral vision, but the half-Vulcan diplomat's presence was palpable, as if he radiated calm and confidence to everyone around him. Sisko wondered if it was Spock's soothing demeanor that made it possible for everyone to endure with such equanimity this seemingly interminable wait for contact.

In my youth, I might have been foolish enough to ask. Now I'm happy to let it be.

As if in reward for his composure, the image on the main viewscreen shifted.

A distortion of spacetime took shape outside *Defiant*, displacing a circular region of swirling plasma like a whirlpool in a sea of molten gold.

Soft alert tones chimed from the comms console. Bashir silenced them and checked his displays. "Incoming signal via my quantum communicator, Captain. Audio only."

Sisko hesitated to reply. Bashir had promised Sisko and the others on *Defiant* a safe haven beyond the reach of Admiral Riker and his growing armada—in the alternate universe. Using a quantum communicator gifted to him years earlier by mysterious agents from the other side, Bashir had reached out to request their aid, and they had agreed.

But could they be trusted? How could Sisko know for certain?

He buried his doubts and summoned his courage. "On speakers."

Bashir patched the message through, and from the overhead came a woman's voice, distorted and awash in static. "*Starship Defiant, this is the Commonwealth jaunt-ship* Enterprise. *We have opened a passage for you to our universe. We can hold it open for no more than thirty seconds. If you are ready to proceed, enter at quarter impulse.*"

"Acknowledged, *Enterprise*. Prepare to receive us. *Defiant* out." Sisko signaled Bashir with a gesture to close the channel, and then he regarded the tunnel yawning before them on the viewscreen. "Mister Soong, take us into the wormhole, one-quarter impulse."

Data entered commands into the conn. "Ahead one-quarter impulse. Aye, sir."

Sisko couldn't swear to it, but it felt to him as if he and the rest of the bridge crew were all holding their breath as the ship plunged into the wormhole's chasm of fire and shadow.

Inside the Einstein-Rosen bridge of the interdimensional wormhole, the vermilion hues of the Badlands gave way to a spinning vortex of blue and white light. *Defiant's* hull shuddered for a moment, but then the noise abated. Sisko closed his eyes and attuned himself to the ship, imagined its superstructure as an extension of his own body, and felt it gliding through this passage between universes with an almost unnatural ease.

Not certain he should trust his senses, Sisko opened his eyes. "Helm, report."

Data's reply was calm. "Holding at one-quarter impulse, sir. Cloak intact."

Sisko looked at Worf for further assurance. "Tactical?"

It took Worf only a moment to respond. "All systems nominal."

On the main viewscreen a pinpoint of light grew larger—and then it bloomed open like a flower made of light and vapor, unfolding to eject *Defiant* back into normal space . . . in a universe not its own. The constellations all looked the same, but Sisko could tell there was something amiss in the weakened flickers of starlight that graced his ship's viewscreen.

They were in the alternate universe, a place he had visited on more than one occasion, and that he had come to think of as being synonymous with treachery, betrayal, and senseless cruelty. Every time he had dared to cross into this benighted reflection of the universe he called home, he had found it violent beyond reason and been deeply relieved to escape from it.

Now he was here on the advice of Doctor Bashir—seeking, of all things, refuge.

An alert tone beeped softly at the comms console. Bashir checked the signal's data, and then looked up at Sisko. "The jaunt-ship *Enterprise* is hailing us, sir. Audio only."

"Speakers."

Bashir opened the channel. Once more from the overhead speakers came the stern female voice. *"Defiant, this is the Commonwealth jaunt-ship* Enterprise. *Please disengage your cloaking device, and we will do the same."*

A primitive part of Sisko's brain told him not to trust the denizens of this universe, to order radio silence, to run and not look back. He silenced his fears and replied in a steady voice, "Acknowledged, *Enterprise*. Deactivating cloak."

Sisko confirmed the order with a nod at Wesley Crusher.

The lights on the bridge brightened, and several auxiliary systems that had been dormant hummed back to life. The life-support systems resumed normal ventilation, and the first wash of cool air from the overhead vents kissed the sweat on the back of Sisko's neck.

Then, as promised, their hosts' vessel appeared on the main viewscreen.

The Commonwealth jaunt-ship *Enterprise* was a sleek, silvery update of the classic Vulcan ringship. Its main fuselage was like a needle. Its broad stardrive ring was located roughly one-quarter of the ship's length in front of its stern, where its impulse engines were located. The ring, which was connected to the main hull by three spokes that were wide at each end and slimmed at their midpoints by elegant curves, housed both the ship's quantum slipstream drive and its artificial wormhole generator—also known as its jaunt drive.

Regarding its image on the screen, Sisko couldn't help but think it looked fragile, like a delicate toy that would snap at the first sign of stress. From reports he had read of the ships' performance in combat, he knew them to be fast, maneuverable, and durable.

Another alert warbled from Bashir's console. He muted it. "They're hailing us."

Sisko straightened his posture in the command chair. Lifted his chin to project strength and pride. Circumstances dictated that he ask for help—not that he look weak while doing so. Centered and focused, he put on a subtle but confident smile.

Time to look our hosts in the eye.

"On-screen, Doctor."

The image of the *C.S.S. Enterprise* was replaced by a view of its bridge. It was a compact space, brightly lit from above, with a great deal of functionality built into a confined area. Most of its consoles were simple in design, with bright green holographic controls on dark panels. The crew wore simple dark-gray jumpsuits with colored bands on their jackets' sleeve cuffs and insignia on their right collars.

Standing in the center of the frame, gazing with wonder at Sisko, was a bearded doppelgänger of Jean-Luc Picard. At his right stood a majestically tall and formidable woman of mixed human and Klingon ancestry. She and Picard wore the same division colors.

The moment the pair appeared on-screen, Sisko noted a shift in Worf's posture. Worf pivoted toward the screen, tense and hyperalert. For a moment Sisko thought Worf might stand from his seat, but the Klingon's discipline kept him silent and at his post, off-screen.

"Greetings," said the alternate Picard. *"I'm Captain Luc Picard of the jaunt-ship* Enterprise. *This is my first officer, Commander K'Ehleyr. We welcome you in peace, on behalf of the Galactic Commonwealth."*

Sisko stood. "Captain Benjamin Sisko, commanding the Federation Starship *Defiant.*"

"Indeed." The alternate Picard smiled. It was clearly a warm and welcoming reaction. *"Your counterpart was quite the celebrity on our side, Captain."*

"I could say the same of yours."

"So I've heard."

Out of the corner of his eye, Sisko saw his own Captain Picard scowl as he looked upon his cross-dimensional twin. The last thing Sisko wanted to deal with was fallout from a diplomatic incident. He decided it would be best to move things along.

"Captain, on behalf of myself and my crew, I formally request asylum in your Galactic Commonwealth. And I should note that we have a matter of great urgency to discuss as soon as possible with your civilian leadership—and with the group you know as Memory Omega."

Just as Bashir had told Sisko to expect, the alternate Picard turned cagey at the mention of Memory Omega. The organization was the true power behind the Galactic Commonwealth. It was a secret cabal of scientists and scholars assembled more than a century earlier by Emperor Spock, for the express purpose of archiving the history, culture, and knowledge of the Terran Empire before it fell. Its mission after the empire's destruction had been to help organize a resistance and, later, a rebellion, followed by a revolution; and, now, to advance the causes of freedom, justice, and parliamentary democracy in the new society that it had raised from the ashes of the empire.

As quickly as the alternate Picard had lost his composure, he recovered it. *"Your request for asylum is granted. As for the audiences you've requested"*—he shared an anxious look with the Klingon woman at his side—*"a representative of Memory Omega is already aboard and waiting to speak with you."*

"Understood."

"Are you in need of any repairs or medical assistance?"

"Our ship sustained heavy damage before we reached the Badlands. We'd be grateful for any help you could provide."

Alternate Picard nodded. *"Very good. I'll send over my chief engineer and a repair team as soon as you're ready to receive them."*

"Thank you, Captain. We'll be in touch. *Defiant* out." With a tap at the comm controls on the arm of his command chair, Sisko closed the channel. He took in the reactions of his comrades on the bridge. "Just as you promised, Doctor: a warm welcome."

Behind his wild beard and unkempt eyebrows, Bashir narrowed his eyes. "You still don't trust them, do you?"

"I don't trust *anyone* right now." Sisko was not one to indulge conspiracy theories, but being hunted by other Starfleet ships had left him questioning everything he had ever thought was true. Now the countless warnings flashing on the master systems display at the aft end of the bridge reminded him he didn't have the luxury of paranoia.

"Captain Picard. Get an updated damage report from engineering, and then arrange transport for *Enterprise*'s repair team."

"Yes, Captain."

"You have the bridge until I return. If we can't keep up with *Enterprise*, ask them to take us in tow while we make repairs."

"Yes, Captain." Picard stepped into Sisko's path to waylay him. He lowered his voice for the sake of discretion. "Is everything all right?"

"I don't know." Sisko breathed a heavy sigh, dreading what he knew was to come. "I need to go see an old friend."

The silence was heartbreaking.

Not from *Defiant*—Vedek Kira Nerys sensed the ship bristling with power around her. The hum of the life-support system filled the cargo bay, and she felt the vibrations of its impulse drives resonating through the deck upon which she knelt. On the decks above her, the crew was vibrant and resolute, in spite of all they had recently suffered and lost.

No, the restless quiet that weighed upon her *pagh* was that of the Orb of Time—one of the nine sacred Tears of the Prophets, sent from the Celestial Temple to guide the faithful of Bajor to a fuller understanding of their deities. For millennia it had burned with a magenta glow, an eerie supernatural radiance that had ushered many a supplicant on metaphysical journeys through the past and the future, so that they could better grasp the will of the Prophets.

Now the Orb of Time, like all of its kind, sat dark and cold.

Bereft of light, robbed of any trace of the divine.

Resting upon the shroud within which it had been delivered to Vedek Kira, the Orb of Time now was nothing more than an hourglass-shaped hunk of crystalline rock.

Like the Prophets themselves, the Orb was dead.

Kira placed her palms against the cold facets of crystal, and then she leaned forward and pressed her forehead against the top half of the Orb.

She felt nothing from it. No vibrations, not a hint of warmth.

Tears fell from her closed eyes.

How can they be dead? The question tore at her *pagh*; it threatened to devour her from within. *They were outside of time. Beyond it. More than the sum of the past and future.*

It seemed impossible. Nothing the ancient texts had ever said about the Prophets, nor any of the prophecies of the end times, had ever suggested they could be destroyed.

And yet here was the proof—cold, hard proof—in Kira's hands.

Her gods were dead. Slain. Sacrifices on the altar of time.

The fount of wisdom and insight that had guided her world for millennia . . . the oracle of truth that had given her hope for salvation during the darkest days of Bajor's revolt against the Cardassian occupation . . . the ancient tradition that had given her life meaning, and whose teachings had shaped Kira into the person she had become . . . was gone.

The final moments of Deep Space 9 replayed themselves in Kira's memory, a self-inflicted torment she felt powerless to halt. To thwart the Devidians—who Picard and his people insisted were planning to feast upon the neural energy released by the simultaneous mass slaughter of countless sentient beings—it had been deemed not just necessary but unavoidable that the newly built Federation starbase be sacrificed to destroy the Bajoran wormhole, which had been identified as the Devidians' key point of access to this timeline.

Because the decision to destroy the Celestial Temple was one with staggering cultural ramifications for the Bajoran people, Kira had chosen, as the "Hand of the Prophets," to bear the weight of that cataclysmic sin, and her dear friend Miles O'Brien had pledged to assist her. But after she had irrevocably triggered the countdown, their planned retreat nearly failed when Ops was breached by attacking Nagas, venting the compartment's air into space—and O'Brien discovered that the deck hatch for the emergency escape gangway was no longer airtight.

To give Kira a fighting chance to reach a runabout, O'Brien had stayed behind to quickly weld shut the faulty hatch, halting the loss of air from the gangway.

Leaving O'Brien behind as she fled the station had been one of the most heartbreaking things Kira had ever done, but with her grief still heavy on her *pagh*, she had been intercepted mid-retreat by the Prophets, who entrusted her with the Orb of Time.

The Orb had sparkled with nascent power when Kira looked upon it. Then, as Deep Space 9 exploded, and the wormhole collapsed, the Orb went dark, snuffed out like a candle.

Faith lay bleeding in my hands . . . and then I watched it die.

It felt unreal. Impossible. Kira couldn't make herself accept the idea that the source of her life's inspiration was gone forever, extinguished in a moment of desperation and fury. But here in front of her sat the Orb, as gray and cold as a smothered ember.

The cargo bay's access hatch opened with a soft pneumatic gasp. Next came low, steady footfalls. Kira recognized that cadence. She knew without looking back who had intruded upon her sorrow. She palmed the tears from her cheeks, reflexively adjusted the devotional chain she wore on her right ear, and fought to compose herself. "Have we reached the other universe?"

Sisko's deep voice resounded in the emptiness of the cargo bay. "We have."

Unable to bear another moment of looking upon the ashen dullness of the dead Orb, Kira wrapped the massive crystal in its shroud. She wished the Prophets could have given it to her inside its ark. Then at least she could truly shut it away, out of sight.

She willed herself into a guise of calm before looking at Sisko. "Did they speak to you?"

He seemed confused. "Who?"

"The Prophets. Before we destroyed the Celestial Temple."

Guilt and regret transited Sisko's face like the shadows of passing clouds. "No."

His admission felt like another wound to Kira. Another shred of hope torn away.

"I'd hoped they might have left their Emissary with some final words of wisdom."

A dark melancholy settled upon Sisko. "I gave up that role. Long ago."

Leaden silence filled the space between them. Then Kira's guilty conscience slipped its reins, and she sobbed as tears poured from her eyes. "Benjamin . . . what have we done?"

Sisko got down on his knees beside her and wrapped an arm around her shoulders in a gesture of comfort. "We made a sacrifice." The strength of his embrace felt like the return of order to a life that had spun into chaos. "We did what we had to."

She couldn't dam up the flood of her grief. "What if we were wrong?"

"Then we'll have to make it right."

"How can I, Benjamin? I betrayed my gods. My people. My whole world."

He relaxed his embrace and shifted to sit beside her. "We don't *know* that, Nerys. I have to believe that if they'd wanted us to do something else, the Prophets would have *told* us."

"Maybe they tried." She looked at Sisko. His clean-shaven face was a kaleidoscopic blur to her tear-stained eyes. "Maybe we weren't listening."

Sisko enfolded her hands in his, cupping them together as if in a tandem gesture of prayer. "Then listen for them." He looked into Kira's eyes, his expression one of hope. "As the Emissary, I learned that the Prophets exist in many dimensions at once, and in many timelines. Possibly *all* of them. Not *versions* of them, but truly *them,* the same in every cosmos." He reached out and with the back of one hand gently brushed the tears from Kira's cheeks. "Trust in the Prophets, Nerys. My heart tells me this is all far from over . . . and that before the end comes, we're going to need them—and you—more than we know."

His words buoyed her, and his rich voice, so full of unconditional love and hope, made her forget her sorrow, if only for a moment.

She mustered a sad smile. "Thank you, Benjamin."

He opened his arms, and she accepted his unspoken invitation to rest in his embrace, her head upon his shoulder. Before his visit she had been weary beyond words, fearful that she had forgotten how to hope—but now, safe in the company of this man whom she loved like a brother, she dared to think herself worthy once more of the privilege of sleep, and of the gift of faith.

3

——————

C.S.S. *Enterprise*—Mirror Universe

Commander Worf knew, even before the transporter beam took hold of him aboard *Defiant*, what he expected to see when he rematerialized aboard the jaunt-ship *Enterprise*. What would happen after that, he had no idea.

Mellifluous noise filled Worf's ears as *Defiant*'s transporter enveloped him in sparkling light that swiftly erased his surroundings. Then *Enterprise*'s transporter room took shape around him, like a mirage becoming reality.

Worf tensed as the beam faded. *I must be calm. I mustn't let my emotions betray me.*

As if to spite him, his eyes opened wide and his jaw slackened at the sight of her, standing just a few meters in front of him: *K'Ehleyr.*

He understood, on a rational level, that the imposing woman standing beside the jaunt-ship's Luc Picard was not the K'Ehleyr he had once known. This woman was a denizen of this alternate universe, and her history—most notably, the fact that she was still alive—meant she had lived a very different life from that of the first woman Worf had ever loved in his own universe. A woman who also happened to have been the mother of his only child, Alexander.

This is not her. She can never be her.

Worf repeated his private warning to himself, but a part of him that still loved his K'Ehleyr refused to believe it, because here she was, *in the flesh.* Seemingly untouched by the passage of decades, her half-Klingon, half-human countenance was as proud as ever. The glint in her eyes, as bright as moonlight on the edge of a blade, promised wit and mischief. Every bit of her was just as he remembered: fierce, bold, and beautiful.

Caught up in his adoration of her, he was slow to note her reaction. She met his bewitched gaze with a glare. Even from a distance Worf felt her hatred of him. Her contempt.

Shamed, he averted his eyes and pretended to adjust his chain-mail baldric as he and the rest of *Defiant*'s motley away team—Captain Picard, Doctor Bashir, Wesley Crusher, Data, and Ambassador Spock—stepped off *Enterprise*'s transporter platform to meet their three hosts. Of the six visitors, only Worf and Picard were in uniform. The others wore civilian garb.

Luc Picard stood front and center, flanked, from Worf's perspective, on the right by K'Ehleyr and on the left by an elderly Vulcan woman whom Worf didn't recognize.

Picard was met by his counterpart. The jaunt-ship captain wore a Vandyke-style salt-and-pepper beard, and the back of his neck was replete with scars. His uniform and those of his shipmates were similar to those of Starfleet, aside from the presence of a sheathed combat knife secured to each person's belt just above the hip.

Picard nodded at his twin. "Permission to come aboard, Captain."

Luc shook Picard's hand. "Permission granted, Captain." He let go of Picard's hand and continued making introductions. "May I present my first officer, Commander—"

"K'Ehleyr," Picard cut in, sounding almost as amazed by her as Worf felt.

She responded to Picard with sly curiosity. "I take it we know each other?"

"We did . . . once. Long ago." He offered her a genial smile. "A pleasure to meet you again, for the first time." Turning toward his companions, Picard continued. "This is my first officer, Commander Worf. My stepson, Wesley Crusher. My dear friend Data Soong. And I've been made to understand you and Doctor Bashir are previously acquainted."

"Dramatically so, yes." Luc shook Bashir's hand. "Welcome back, Doctor." He furrowed his brow at the sight of Bashir, who remained long-haired, wild-bearded, and generally disheveled. "Forgive me, but it would seem the years have not been kind to you."

Bashir's voice was courteous, but his eyes were haunted. "No. They have not."

Everyone turned toward the only two persons not yet introduced, to find them standing only centimeters apart, each with their hands folded reverently in front of themselves.

The elderly Vulcan woman bowed her head. "We are honored to receive you, Spock."

Spock nodded once in reply. "The honor is mine . . . Saavik."

As he spoke her name, she looked up. Despite her practiced mask of calm, Worf was sure he caught a glimmer of joyful surprise in her eyes at being acknowledged by Spock, as if she hadn't expected him to recognize her, but was glad that he did.

A pang of envy darkened Worf's mood. *If only K'Ehleyr were so pleased to see me.*

Perhaps sensing an awkwardness in the sudden silence, Luc spoke and pulled the room's attention back upon himself. "As I'm sure you all know, Spock is something of a celebrity here in our universe, one who needs no introduction. But for all of you except the good doctor, allow me to introduce Saavik, the director of Memory Omega."

Saavik faced the group. She approached them in measured steps, clearly a creature of patience. Hands folded at her waist, she stopped in front of Picard. "Doctor Bashir's message requested both asylum in the Commonwealth, and assistance from Memory Omega. The former has been arranged, but before I consent to the latter, I must know what kind of aid you seek."

Apprehensive looks passed from one member of the away team to another, with no one quite certain who was best suited to answer her request. After a moment, Wesley stepped forward. "We're trying to stop a species known as Devidians from killing the universe."

Saavik processed that without any external reaction. "Could you be more precise?"

This time, Data took the lead. "Devidians are humanoids that feed on the neural energy of other sentient beings—specifically, the fear that many experience at the moment of death."

Wesley continued, "By harnessing a species known as ophidians, the Devidians learned how to travel through time and space. For most of their history, they've been simple scavengers, seeking out times of plague or mass casualty events on which they could feed."

Luc appeared intrigued but also concerned. "But something changed."

His guess earned a nod from Data. "Yes. But we have yet to learn what that was."

Saavik's eyes narrowed, and the creases in her brow deepened. "How serious a threat are these Devidians?"

From a pocket inside his long brown leather jacket, Wesley produced a small metallic rectangle, a device he called an Omnichron. Barely as large as his weathered hand, it combined the functions of a quantum receiver and a powerful tricorder, and was capable of scanning across time and space using techniques known only to Travelers. "They're collapsing alternate timelines that branched off from ours, and feeding on the death-energies of countless sentient beings."

Somehow, without a word or a movement, Wesley commanded the device to open. A seam appeared on its smooth surface, bisecting it. The two halves of the lid lifted open, revealing the slender gadget's intricate innards. A tiny crystal embedded inside the device projected a holographic image of countless parallel lines, which vibrated before they unraveled and vanished—a few at first, then many at a time. "The more timelines they destroy, the stronger they get. We think they found a way to store some of the neural energy released during these engineered temporal implosions."

Wesley waited until the last line of his projection trembled and then disintegrated. "If they get strong enough, they might be able to devour all of time—and all life with it."

He turned off his Omnichron. A sepulchral silence filled the room.

Data struck a plaintive tone. "This is why we need your help, Director. Doctor Bashir told me your society possesses a technology known as a quantum window. Is that correct?"

"It is. But its workings are a jealously guarded secret, and its use is restricted."

Ambassador Spock moved to stand beside Saavik. "The peril facing us threatens your universe, as well. The logical course of action is to unite against it."

"I shall have to confer with my peers." Saavik faced Picard. "It will aid our deliberations if you could share with us all available intelligence concerning the Devidian threat."

"Of course, Director." He gestured at Wesley. "Mister Crusher can provide you with everything you'll need."

"Acceptable." Saavik faced the jaunt-ship's officers. "Captain, ask *Defiant*'s commander to let us take it in tow while they make repairs.

Commander, please show our visitors to guest quarters." She looked back at Wesley. "Mister Crusher, I will call on you shortly. Please be prepared to share all of your intelligence regarding the Devidian threat."

"Yes, ma'am."

The Vulcan woman made a small pivot toward Spock, and bowed her head once more. "I shall look forward to speaking with you again soon, Ambassador."

"And I with you, Director."

Pleasantries dispensed, Saavik headed for the door. It slid open ahead of her with a muted *whoosh*. She made her exit to the corridor, turned right, and passed from view.

K'Ehleyr stood near enough to the doorway that its sensor detected her and held the door open. "Distinguished guests," she said with a slightly mocking tone, "let me show you to your cabins." She led the away team out of the transporter room, and down the corridor to the left.

From the rear of the group, Worf saw K'Ehleyr steal a glance at him—and instantly her jaw clenched in anger. Her antipathy for him was nakedly apparent.

I will have to hope my accommodation is not an airlock.

U.S.S. *Titan* NCC-80102

A force both malign and chaotic held hostage the bridge of the *Starship Titan*, prowling from one post to the next while the command crew stood paralyzed and mute, uncertain how to react. To the great dismay of Captain Christine Vale, the presence cowing her and her personnel was her own supervising officer, Rear Admiral William T. Riker.

He forced himself into the personal space of security chief Lieutenant Commander Ranul Keru and shouted in the burly Trill's ear, "How can they just be gone?"

Keru flinched at the verbal assault, and Vale saw the man's lips narrow into a taut frown behind his dark beard. "We tracked them to the Badlands, Admiral. But once they went inside—"

"Not good enough!" Riker made no attempt to effect a pretense of civility as he stalked away from Keru and cornered senior science officer Lieutenant Melora Pazlar at the aft systems display. "There must be something you can do! Scan for comm signals? Changes in the flow of plasma inside the Badlands?"

Pazlar tensed. "Sir, we've detected no comm signals coming or going. As for tracking the flow of plasma currents *inside* the Badlands, there are far too many variables for—"

"Enough!" Riker stormed away from Pazlar, who slumped with relief and exhaustion in spite of the support she received from her close-fitting powered exoskeleton.

The admiral headed to the forward duty stations, visibly seething every step of the way. He grabbed the back of flight control officer Lieutenant Commander Aili Lavena's chair and bent forward to loom over the slender Pacifican woman. "How did they outrun us? They didn't have that big of a head start!"

Lavena's anxiety was telegraphed by a quick flurry of small bubbles inside the fluid-filled breathing mask she wore over her pale-speckled dark-green face. Her melodic voice flowed from the universal translator module built into the front of the mask. "*Defiant's* engine-to-mass ratio is far greater than ours, sir. Though our propulsion system is more advanced, it is unable to compensate for the—"

"Forget it." Riker let go of Lavena's chair and sidestepped to strike a gargoyle's pose in which to haunt the ship's senior operations officer, Lieutenant Commander Sariel Rager. The brown-skinned human woman, who in recent months had begun wearing her hair in long, elegant cornrows, met Riker's arrival with a proud lift of her chin and a refusal to make eye contact, choosing to fix her gaze on the main viewscreen instead.

In a blatant breach of both protocol and basic courtesy, Riker poked at Rager's console, summoning information from several of the ship's departments at once. "Why haven't we deployed our runabouts and warp-capable shuttles to search the Badlands?"

The muscles in Rager's jaw bulged as she briefly clenched her teeth. "Because I deemed the conditions inside the Badlands too hazardous to risk deploying them. Sir."

"Then have them patrol its perimeter! Set up a tachyon grid! Do something!"

"I *am*, sir. I'm coordinating the collection of long-range sensor data

from ships, stations, and relay beacons throughout the sector, and helping Commander Keru analyze them for—"

"Just say it: you've got *nothing.*" Riker turned away from Rager to
face the rest of the bridge. He was manic in a way that Vale had never
seen before. "Useless! Every damn one of you! All you had to do was
catch *one* little ship." His tone became one of petulant, bitter mockery.
" 'Oh, but she's too fast, Admiral!' 'What could we do, Admiral? She has
a cloaking device!' 'We can't go into the Badlands, sir. It's too *dangerous.*
We might get *hurt.*' " He sneered, and his next words to Vale dripped
with disgust. "Your crew is a disgrace."

That, apparently, was the affront that crossed whatever arbitrary
line Commander Deanna Troi—who, in addition to being the ship's
diplomatic officer, was also the admiral's wife and the mother of his
child—had decided would constitute a step too far. The half-Betazoid,
half-human woman put herself between Riker and the rest of the crew.
"That's enough, Will."

He became desperate. "*Et tu,* Deanna? Don't you see what I'm up
against here?"

"What I see is a man who has lost control."

He answered her with a derisive *harumph.* "I should've known you'd
take their side. You're soft. Always have been." He looked past her, at
Vale. "But I expected better from *you.*"

Troi moved in close to Riker, near enough that she could whisper
to him without being heard by the rest of the bridge crew. Her expression was stern as she admonished her husband, whose face reddened—
though whether from anger or from shame, Vale was uncertain.

Riker backed away from Troi. He trembled with suppressed fury. "No
more excuses, dammit! Bad enough we had to release that Changeling
Odo because alien heads of state have diplomatic immunity. We won't
let Picard slip through our fingers, too." He hurried toward the turbolift,
his shoulders hunched like those of a man whose pride had suffered a
fatal blow. As he passed Vale he muttered angrily, "Find that ship."

The turbolift's doors parted at Riker's approach. He stepped inside the
waiting car, then pivoted around to face the bridge as he said, "Deck four."

The lift doors slid shut—and the moment they were closed, Vale and
her bridge crew heaved a collective sigh of relief at the admiral's absence.

Vale stood and stepped forward to stand with Troi. The captain dropped her voice to a confidential register. "Commander? A word in private, please?"

Troi followed Vale off the bridge, into the captain's adjacent ready room. Once the door was closed behind them, Vale motioned for Troi to sit on the room's short sofa while she settled into a guest chair. "Deanna, I trust you know what this is about."

"I do." Troi crossed her arms and her legs—body language that Vale recognized as defensiveness, or perhaps a reaction to anxiety. "Something's been affecting Will's behavior since shortly after the Devidian crisis started."

"Not just his behavior, Deanna—his memory, too. Yesterday, he forgot that I'm *Titan*'s captain. He addressed me as 'Number One.'"

Troi frowned, then nodded. "Yesterday, he thought we had more than one child. And that was just one of many verbal slips."

Vale could tell that Troi knew something important. "What's going on?"

Troi looked around, as if she were fearful someone was eavesdropping from one of the small compartment's corners. When she spoke, her voice was barely above a whisper.

"Remember that holo-comm from Captain Picard? He mentioned symptoms—mood shifts, anger, paranoia, confused memories of 'shadows'—that all sound like what's happening to Will. And he sent a file that says Worf was affected by something Doctor Crusher calls 'temporal multiple-personality disorder.' With all the same symptoms."

As far-fetched as such a condition sounded, Vale had seen stranger things during her years in Starfleet and, before that, as a civilian police officer on Izar. If nothing else, this new information about the recent holo-comm from Picard explained why Riker had been willing to cut it off before they could finish tracing its origin point. But the part of Troi's report that troubled Vale most was the fact that this syndrome had overtaken Worf, one of the strongest and most disciplined officers with whom she had ever served. "Is Worf all right?"

"He's recovering, thanks to a mind-meld with Ambassador Spock. And Picard's crew found a way to protect against the syndrome."

Vale found that encouraging, at least. "Did Picard happen to share their findings?"

Troi nodded. "They did, along with some parameters for diagnosis and protocols for treatment." Her hope turned once more to concern. "If this *is* what's affecting Will, we might not have much time. We need Doctor Ree to examine him right away."

"Agreed. Unfortunately, I don't see the admiral cooperating in his current state. So we might need to do this on the sly—and depending upon what we find, be ready to act quickly."

Troi's manner turned grave. "You mean be ready to relieve Will of duty."

"Yes. But relieving a flag officer is tricky business, so we need to be *very* careful. As the old saying goes, 'If you take a shot at the king, you'd better not miss.'"

C.S.S. Enterprise—Mirror Universe

Walking the corridors of the jaunt-ship *Enterprise* beside the other universe's Spock filled Saavik with an uncommon feeling: nostalgia.

Hers wasn't a reminiscence tinged by longing or regret, nor was it infused with misplaced affection for an idealized past. It was, rather, an inescapable consequence of sharing with this Spock her memories of his counterpart, who had sponsored her application to the Imperial Academy over a century earlier, and who, decades later, had entrusted her with control of Memory Omega. But she wondered if her state of mind might not be at least partly the result of the attention that Spock paid to her every word, as if he knew her better than she realized.

They moved forward, toward the ship's officers' lounge, as Saavik continued to share the history of what Spock's alternate had wrought in this universe. "It wasn't long after he used the Tantalus device to assassinate Empress Sato III that Emperor Spock set his reforms into motion. At first, his efforts were clandestine. He focused on organizing the people of Vulcan through a telepathic campaign of recruitment."

Ambassador Spock barely raised an eyebrow. "Interesting. Tell me more."

"In the years that followed, he sued for peace with the Terran Empire's neighboring powers, and he made a number of concessions that his rivals called foolish and naïve. During this period, I became the captain of the *Enterprise*."

That turned Spock's head. "A prestigious achievement."

She couldn't look him in the eye to accept his praise. "It was a role in which I was called upon to do . . . terrible things. My emperor assured me that what I did was in the best interests of peace, but choices I made . . . actions I took . . . plagued my conscience for many decades afterward."

The duo readied themselves to shoulder through an approaching gaggle of young officers. The moment the officers saw them, however, they stood aside, their backs to the bulkheads, every one of them silent at attention as Saavik and Spock passed by. He noted the officers' behavior with a curious expression.

Saavik took advantage of the distraction to abandon her confession and return to her account of history. "Less than three decades into his reign, Emperor Spock issued a proclamation that transformed the Terran Empire into a republic, liberated its slaves, and abdicated his throne. Shortly after this transformation of the body politic, rivals of the former empire conquered the Terran Republic . . . and for his nobility, Consul Spock and his wife, Marlena, were executed on the floor of the Common Forum."

"A most unfortunate end."

"But a necessary one." Saavik's heart, which was half-Romulan and therefore prone to bouts of sentimentality, swelled as she remembered the recordings of that terrible day. "As Regent Gorkon and Legate Renar forced Spock and Marlena to kneel, Spock declared, 'I regret nothing. I concede no defeat. I admit no failure.'" Grief and reverence tightened her throat and made it hard for her to continue, but she did nonetheless. "His last words were, 'With the fall of my civilization begins the end of your own. Freedom will overcome. Tyranny cannot prevail.'"

Spock took a moment to absorb that. "A most remarkable gamble."

"A sacrifice, in a chess match that he knew would unfold over decades." Saavik gestured at the ship around them. "All of this technology, and the philosophy to guide its use in ways both wise and peaceful— that was Spock's legacy. The inheritance he bequeathed to those brave enough to carry on the struggle he set in motion." Her narrative waned as she remembered the hard times. "There were years, decades even, when no one inside Memory Omega was certain this would work.

We hid in our bases, buried deep inside lifeless planetoids, plotting and waiting. When the first inklings of the Terran Rebellion began on Terok Nor, we dismissed them. Our projections said the Alliance would smother it in its crib. . . . But something happened. New contacts with people from your universe. And then the rebellion that no one thought could survive became something greater. It sparked a revolution."

She and Spock arrived at the officers' lounge, which was half-full. They were less than two steps inside when someone on the far side of the lounge barked, "Atten-*hut!*"

In a flurry of motion, the gathered officers were on their feet, facing Saavik and Spock, all of them standing at attention like the officers in the corridor.

Spock noted the scene with a nod. "Clearly, you command great respect."

She turned toward him, surprised. "This isn't for *me*, Spock—this is for *you*." Studying his face, she realized he did not understand. "To my people, you are more than just another distinguished visitor." She leaned closer and whispered, "To them, you are the Consul reborn. When they look at you . . . they see *him*."

Spock's eyes opened wide, and his eyebrows arched high toward his steel-gray hair. But after a long pause, all that he said in his gravel-hard voice was, "Fascinating."

At the end of a long and deeply strange day, the last thing Commander K'Ehleyr wanted to deal with was presenting a command-level briefing to the *Enterprise*'s guests from the counterpart universe. But orders were to be obeyed, and Luc had made it clear that he wasn't merely *asking* her to do this. And so it had fallen to her to narrate information that could just as easily have been disseminated in a written report while she caught up on her sleep.

The six guests watched her with keen focus while she stood at the head of the conference room's long table, speaking and making occasional perfunctory gestures at the information being shown on the bulkhead display behind her. "As you see, the latest reports indicate that repairs to your ship are nearly complete. We expect our engineering teams to finish their fine-tuning sometime later this morning, around oh-three-hundred."

She looked over her shoulder to make certain she was in sync with the vid presentation. "We've also received permission from Memory Omega to grant three of your personnel supervised access to the quantum window." She looked at the counterpart Picard. "Captain, do you know which of your personnel you mean to send?"

"Mister Crusher, Mister Soong, and Commander La Forge."

"Good. We'll jump to Memory Omega at oh-six-hundred. I'll make the arrangements on our side." To the rest of the room she added, "All other personnel are asked to return to *Defiant* before we make our jump." She switched off the bulkhead display. "Are there any questions?" Restrained headshakes indicated there were none. "Good. My apologies for the late briefing, and my thanks for your patience. Meeting adjourned."

She wasted no time getting out the door. Even from across the room K'Ehleyr had seen the early warning signs of trouble—a gleam in the Klingon's eyes, and a squaring of his shoulders that together suggested he was mustering his courage to confront her.

Not that. Anything but that.

The very thought of it quickened her steps.

Three strides shy of the turbolift, she heard his hurried footfalls closing in behind her. In that moment, she knew she had only two options: surrender to fear and sprint for the lift, and hope that he didn't chase her down anyway; or, halt, turn, and confront him on her own terms.

She stopped and pivoted to face Worf.

Her move caught him off guard, and he almost collided with her before stopping himself. All the same, he ended up mere centimeters from her, well within her personal zone. She felt his breath caress her face. Revulsed, she leaned sharply backward, her nose wrinkled in disgust. "What do you want?"

"I wish to speak with you."

"Is *that* what you want?"

Her question seemed to offend him. "What did you *think* I wanted?"

"Frankly, I don't care."

He seemed annoyed. "My intentions are honorable."

The sound of his voice filled K'Ehleyr with primal anger. "I'm sure you think so."

Worf backed up a step. "If I have offended you, I apologize."

"You . . . apologize?"

Who is this man? The version of Worf that K'Ehleyr and so many others in this universe had hated and feared would *never* have spoken those words. Was it possible for his counterpart to really be this different? *Could it be that I've misjudged him?*

Without sacrificing his pride, he somehow struck a humble note: "If my presence offends you, I will leave and *not* come back. But I ask for only a few minutes of your time. To talk."

K'Ehleyr was wary. Every time she looked at Worf, she saw the despot she had known—but every time he spoke, he sounded like a decent man.

With a tilt of her head, she invited him to follow her. "All right. Talk."

Worf caught up to her and matched her stride. "May I ask a question?"

"Why not."

"You look at me with hatred. Why? Do you know my alternate in this universe?"

She tried but failed to mask her appalled shock at his ignorance. "Are you *kidding*? *Everyone* knew you in this universe."

He accepted that in stride. "I presume I was more *infamous* than famous?"

"That would be the understatement of the century." She studied his face, to see if perhaps he was shining her on. There was no trace of guile in his manner. "Do you really not know?"

He frowned. "Knowledge of your universe is restricted in ours. I have had *little* access to it." He reciprocated her searching look. "Who do you see when you look at me?"

K'Ehleyr stopped, and he paused with her. She looked into his eyes.

"A monster. Regent Worf was legendary for his cruelty. And his sadism. He reigned over the slaughter of millions. Women. Children. Entire worlds turned to ash. Of all the regents ever to rule the Klingon Empire, he was the most feared. And the most hated."

Worf nodded. "Was?"

"The Terran Rebellion captured him in seventy-five. In seventy-nine, a few months after the revolution ended, Smiley O'Brien released him. Gave him back his *d'k tahg*—"

"—with which he committed ritual suicide," Worf said, intuiting the end of the story. "To reclaim his honor in death, after being taken prisoner."

"Exactly."

The light of hope she had seen in Worf's eyes seemed to have dimmed with the receipt of this new understanding. To K'Ehleyr's surprise, she felt a pang of guilt over it.

And when she remembered how intent he had been on making contact with her, she realized that, in spite of her better judgment, she was more than a little curious as to why.

"And if I might ask . . . who am I to you?"

There was something in Worf's eyes—fear? No, that wasn't it. She looked deeper while the man summoned his courage. It was sorrow. No, deeper than that—*grief.*

"You were the first . . . the *greatest* . . . love of my life. And the mother of my son."

His truth hit her like a wave crashing into her at night, its force greater than expected and all the more overwhelming for having sprung from the darkness.

His first love?

Mother of his son?

Worf looked at her, his eyes full of hope, but all K'Ehleyr felt was horror.

She retreated, backpedaling quickly and clumsily, with one arm outstretched to warn him not to follow. He called her name, begged her not to go, but all she heard was her pulse pounding inside her head, a roar like the sea breaking against a cliff.

Him? How could any version of me ever love any version of him?

Stunned, she fled, pursued by questions she couldn't answer, and truths she couldn't bear.

4

—•—

Memory Omega Headquarters—Mirror Universe

At the heart of a secret Memory Omega base concealed deep inside an asteroid, there resided a classified research facility defended by massive blast doors and the most advanced biometric security in the known galaxy. This, Saavik had explained, was the dimensional observation lab.

The chamber was twelve meters across and less than four meters from floor to ceiling. Its perimeter walls were packed with computers more advanced than any Geordi La Forge had ever seen. In any other circumstance, he would have found it difficult to tear himself away from a close study of their sophisticated components and elegant software. This occasion, however, had presented him with an even more compelling sight.

In the center of the room stood a machine unlike any La Forge had ever encountered. It resembled a gyroscope built around a harness seat large enough to accommodate an adult humanoid. The contraption floated inside an antigrav field, within which it was free to spin, roll, or yaw without resistance. Fused to the frame of the harness seat was a holographic projection matrix that wrapped more than 270 degrees around the occupant on both the x and y axes.

While the machine was active, it was encased in two spheres of transparent aluminum, one nested inside the other. Repulsor emitters lined the interior surface of the outer sphere to keep the inner sphere suspended in place while also permitting it to pitch, yaw, and rotate freely. Precisely ten centimeters of empty space separated the two hollow orbs.

At the moment the machine was dormant, and its two encasing spheres had been parted into hemispheres and retracted into alcoves above the ceiling and beneath the floor. Saavik had departed after making the necessary introductions, permitting La Forge, Data, and

Wesley to speak directly with the lab's supervisor, Doctor Tsemiar, a tall Efrosian man with a wild mane of loose white hair, and his most experienced quantum observer, Jesi Mullins, a human woman of average height. She wore her long dark hair in a simple ponytail, but her forehead was covered by bangs that compelled La Forge to notice the woman's large and profoundly expressive pale-blue eyes.

Tsemiar stroked absent-mindedly at his long, elegantly drooping snowy mustache. "That pretty much covers all there is to know about the unit's core functions. But as I'm sure Jesi will tell you, focusing the quantum frame while you're inside the machine is more art than science."

Mullins seemed eager to rebut. "I wouldn't say *that*. But focusing the machine *is* more about intuition and feeling your way through space-time than it is about hard coordinates."

Her boss used his padd to project a hologram of shifting data sets into the air for all to see. "One issue is that each quantum reality has a unique resonance pattern. Sometimes, the interference pattern created by the interaction of our dimension's quantum resonance and the next is negligible. Other times, it's scrambled. To cancel out the—"

La Forge raised his hand to interrupt. "We've had some experience with this kinda thing, Doc." He looked at Wesley and hooked a thumb toward the machine. "Want to go for a spin?"

The invitation made Wesley smile. "Don't mind if I do."

Mullins looked and sounded worried. "No offense, guys, but no one knows this machine like I do. You sure you wouldn't rather I guide the quantum frame?"

Data adopted a friendly smile and did his best to sound diplomatic. "Quite sure. Mister Crusher possesses a unique spatio-temporal perception that we think will make him well suited to using the frame. That said, we'd be most grateful if you'd stay and share your expert advice."

She shrugged in good-natured surrender. "Okay, if that's what you want."

La Forge felt impatient. "Ms. Mullins? Would you mind helping Wes strap in?"

Her smile looked a bit forced. "My pleasure." With a gentle touch on Wesley's arm, she moved toward the quantum frame. "Follow me." Wesley walked with her to the machine.

Doctor Tsemiar became visibly anxious as La Forge and Data moved to stand at the room's master control panel. It was easy for La Forge to intuit the reason: this was clearly Tsemiar's post. Now a pair of strangers had just usurped it, but there was nothing he could do because this entire affair had been granted by the imprimatur of Director Saavik herself.

As Data keyed in new settings, guilt nagged at La Forge. *I guess I ought to throw our host a bone.* "Doctor Tsemiar? Would you mind double-checking our settings before we start?"

"With pleasure!" The Efrosian bounded across the lab to stand behind and between La Forge and Data. On tiptoes he peeked over the two men's shoulders and observed their adjustments. "Be careful not to overcorrect the phase-variance cancellation."

Data answered without looking up. "Yes, it could trigger a temporal feedback wave."

Tsemiar sounded surprised. "That's exactly right."

In the middle of the room, Mullins finished securing Wesley inside the quantum frame's harness seat. As she retreated from the machine, its nested hemispheres of transparent aluminum converged from above and below, guided by precision repulsor beams. At the moment of contact they fused, and any hint of a seam vanished. Seconds later, the gyroscope inside the spheres began to roll, turn, and pitch in a seemingly random fashion.

La Forge opened a closed-circuit comm channel to Wesley inside the machine. "Wes? How you doin' in there?"

"I'm all right." The comm imparted a faint echo to Wesley's voice. *"Give me a few seconds to get the hang of this thing."*

"No problem. Let us know when you're ready." La Forge muted the comm and looked at Data. "Are we set?"

"I believe so."

Tsemiar leaned in. "I don't understand these settings. What are you looking for?"

Data pointed out details on the master panel. "A major temporal variance, one strong enough to weaken this timeline to the point that it became vulnerable to the Devidians' temporal attacks. It is my hypothesis that if we can identify the trigger event, we might be able to use it to find the Devidians' base of operations—and perhaps divine a way to reverse the damage."

The Efrosian scientist recoiled in disbelief. "Are you mad? You'd have to observe and compare hundreds or even thousands of parallel realities at once to detect such a variance!" He cast a worried look at Wesley. "What makes you think your man can survive such a thing?"

La Forge looked out at Wesley, remembered the awkward youth he had once been, shortly after they both had arrived on the *Enterprise*-D . . . and marveled at the strong, confident figure he had become in the decades since then. "Because, Doctor—Wes is no ordinary man." He smiled at Tsemiar. "He's a Traveler."

Data keyed in a final string of commands, then looked up. "Ready."

La Forge opened the comm channel to Wesley. "We're set. How 'bout you?"

"Fire it up."

With the press of a single icon on the master panel, La Forge activated the quantum frame. He felt a galvanic tingling on his skin. Next came a low but powerful hum that he felt in his bones and his teeth. The lights dimmed as the hum became a deafeningly loud droning.

An unearthly glow radiated from inside the spheres. Azure, then crimson, followed by violet, gold, and viridian. Moving flashes of color enveloped Wesley, as if he had been swallowed by a kaleidoscope. Through the blinding glare of colored lights pulsing faster than La Forge could track even with his enhanced cybernetic vision, he caught momentary glimpses of the gyroscopic frame inside. It was spinning, toppling, yawing madly.

La Forge winced and raised a hand to block some of the light. *I hope that thing has inertial dampers, or Wes is gonna be sick as a dog when he gets out of there.*

Data monitored a flood of information racing sideways across the master panel's display. Moving with superhuman speed, he pulled out strings of numbers, snippets of formulas, and other random bits of intel.

The multicolored sphere of illumination surrounding Wesley blanched and brightened, becoming a flood of white light. La Forge faced it head-on, letting his cybernetic eyes mitigate the glare. Mullins and Tsemiar huddled behind him, shielding their eyes with their hands.

Then everything was darkness.

The hum of the machine, which had become a roar, dwindled to silence.

After a few seconds the chamber's work lights gradually brightened.

Even before La Forge thought to ask, Mullins rushed out to the machine. Its inner and outer spheres separated into hemispheres and were pulled by tractor beams into the alcoves. The gyroscope slowed its chaotic rolling, and Mullins used a manual override to halt it. She climbed onto the machine and conferred quickly with Wesley, who was disoriented but conscious. After a few seconds, Mullins looked back at La Forge, Data, and Tsemiar and gave them a thumbs-up, indicating that Wesley was unharmed.

La Forge felt his shoulders relax at that bit of good news.

Then he noticed Data, his fingers a blur on the panel, his positronic mind racing a trillion times faster as he analyzed the information gleaned from Wesley's spin in the machine.

Mullins helped Wesley out of the machine and back to his friends, with his arm draped across her shoulders. When Wesley arrived at the master panel, the deep creases in his face made him look as if he had aged a decade in a matter of moments while inside the quantum frame.

"Wes? Are you all right?"

The weary Traveler regarded La Forge with a haunted expression. "No. None of us are."

Before La Forge could ask Wesley to explain, Data finished his calculations and leaned back from the master control panel, his eyes wide. "Wesley is correct."

Caught between a pair of newly minted doomsday prophets, La Forge felt his temper rising. "Someone tell me something I can use. Wes, *what did you see?*"

Wesley answered in the flat monotone of a person in shock. "How it began. How it ends."

Frustrated, La Forge looked to Data. "Do you know what he's talking about?"

Data's cast took a turn for the grim. "Unfortunately, I do." He downloaded the results of the experiment into his positronic matrix with a single touch on the panel, and then he faced La Forge. "We must return to *Defiant* to brief the captains, before it is too late."

U.S.S. Defiant NX-74205—Mirror Universe

Less than an hour after his mind-bending ride inside the quantum frame, Wesley was still out of sorts. Data and La Forge had spirited him out of the observation lab as quickly as they had been able, and before Wesley had realized what was going on, they had been beamed back aboard the jaunt-ship *Enterprise*. Once they and Saavik were aboard, the ship's crew had wasted no time making the jump to their planned rendezvous.

Then all that had been left for them to do was to go back to *Defiant*.

Wesley had put it off for a few minutes, in the interest of regaining his composure. The strain of extending his awareness into so many thousands of timelines at once, so that he could act as Data's conduit for sensor information from all of them, had left him plagued by a persistent dizziness and the proprioceptive delusion that he wasn't so much walking the corridors of *Defiant* as he was floating through them, like some kind of phantom.

Have to get myself right. Need to focus.

There were so many possibilities for which he might have been prepared. But what he had seen, and what he had instantly known it meant . . . was something he wished he could forget. But now that he knew, there was no way he could ever be free of this gnostic burden.

The words of T. S. Eliot's "Gerontion" intruded upon his thoughts, as unbidden as they were inescapable: *After such knowledge, what forgiveness?*

Data and La Forge were on the bridge, briefing Captain Sisko. No doubt, Wesley and others soon would be summoned to the jaunt-ship *Enterprise* to share their findings, and with them, their conclusions and recommendations.

Anticipating that meeting filled Wesley with dread and despair.

He walked until, at last, he felt his feet on the deck. Until he felt solid again. Looking up, he saw that his wanderings had carried him to the door of the guest quarters assigned to his mother, Doctor Beverly Crusher, and his half brother, René Picard. He approached the door, and it opened. The quarters on the other side were dark, but from inside Wesley heard the soft, steady breathing of two sleepers.

Wesley entered the cabin with care, making sure to tread softly. He didn't want to wake his mother or René. They would ask what he had learned at Memory Omega, and he would either have to lie or break his own heart telling them the truth.

He let the door close behind him before he reached for the compartment's manual lighting controls on the bulkhead. He nudged the lights on, just barely, to five percent strength.

His mother was stretched out on the lower bunk to his right, still in her uniform. René had adopted a semi-fetal curl in the upper bunk on the other side of the cabin.

In slow steps Wesley drew closer, wishing now that he was a ghost, intangible and silent. He squatted beside his mother's bunk. Looking upon the saintly calm of her sleeping face filled his eyes with tears. The part of him that was a Traveler knew that time was an illusion; that the past and the future had always existed, and continued to exist, and it was just an artifact of human consciousness that it could perceive only the ever-transient now. That aspect of his mind, which could see space and time as they truly were, knew that his mother had always been, would always be, and that there was no reason to mourn.

But the part of him that was still human had seen how his mother would die.

He fought not to let racking sobs escape his chest, even as tears fell from his eyes. He choked down his grief like a child taking bitter medicine.

I've seen what happens if I try to warn you. . . . I'm sorry, Mom.

He leaned down and gently kissed the top of his mother's head. Even unwashed and heavy with dried sweat, her hair smelled sweet to him.

Then he stood and turned, his soul breaking apart.

His half brother lay sleeping, prematurely aged from six to nineteen by the glancing touch of a Naga. Wesley had done all he could to help the youth adjust to his new reality by merging his mind with an echo of the consciousness of an older version of him from another timeline. At the time he had thought it the merciful thing to do. Now he wasn't so certain.

All I did was make him conscious enough to know what's about to happen to him. Maybe I should have left well enough alone.

Wesley reached out and rested his hand, as gently as a beam of light, atop René's.

I've watched you grow up in a hundred different timelines, and I've loved you in all of them. He pulled his hand away, heartbroken. *But you were never meant to be, little brother.*

Picard was the last to reach the bridge of *Defiant*. He stepped through the open port-side hatchway to find Captain Sisko had already dismissed the rest of the bridge crew and commandeered the cramped space for this hastily convened private discussion. Data, Wesley, and Commander La Forge stood behind the situation table, which ran parallel to the bridge's aft bulkhead. The steady ambience of feedback tones from the duty stations had been muted, making the hum of the ventilation system more audible.

Sisko noted Picard's arrival with a request: "Lock the door, please, Captain."

Resisting the temptation to ask why, Picard closed and secured the port hatch. Then he returned to stand with Sisko and face the other three men. "What have you learned?"

La Forge, Data, and Wesley all wore the same look of weary dejection.

Wesley was the first to speak. "The Devidians didn't *cause* the instability in the branching timelines. They're just taking advantage of it, and making it worse for their own gain."

Something about the trio's manner struck Picard as cagey, perhaps even evasive. "If the Devidians didn't set this in motion, who or what did?"

The guilt in La Forge's voice was almost palpable: "*We* did."

With a few quick taps on the situation table's control panel, Data summoned a three-dimensional hologram in the air between himself and the captains. It was a complicated diagram; the most prominent elements were two parallel lines, each entwined with an oscillating wave. They were linked by angled and perpendicular lines—some intersecting, some not. A third parallel line lay between them, but it ended at one of the transverse lines connecting the main lines. To make the pieces more easily distinguished, they were rendered in a variety of colors.

Annotations appeared as Data highlighted a set of connecting lines. "The original divergence event was triggered in 2373 by the Borg, who attempted to use a chroniton attack upon the *Enterprise*-E while it was transiting the Borg's temporal vortex."

Picard's memory flashed upon those events. The Borg attack on Earth. The cube he had helped destroy. The time-traveling Borg sphere that he and the *Enterprise*-E's crew had chased into the past, to 2063, to prevent the Borg from interfering in Zefram Cochrane's first warp flight, and humanity's subsequent—and consequent—moment of first contact with the Vulcans.

Most of all Picard remembered the Borg Queen.

But Data's report left him confused. "Data? I don't recall any chroniton attack during that mission."

"We were not aware of it at the time."

La Forge reached up to highlight a different portion of the temporal schematic. "Do you remember the transformed Earth we saw, *before* we went into the past?"

This time, Picard nodded. "Our entire world, assimilated. Nine billion life signs . . . all Borg." It was a memory that filled him with horror, even now, nearly fourteen years later.

"Well," La Forge continued, "that's where the attack came from. Even though we were shielded from being erased from history because we were caught up in the wake of the Borg sphere's temporal vortex, the Borg on Earth's surface knew we were there. Until we weren't."

At once Picard began to understand. "They saw us go back in time. To 2063." Doubts continued to plague him. "But we *prevented* that version of 2373."

A frown presaged La Forge's rebuttal. "Not exactly. We kept it from supplanting the Prime timeline, but that's not the same thing as making it never have existed."

Data selected a connecting line and traced it back to the earliest intersection point in the diagram. "While we worked in the past to unravel *their* history, the Borg used a temporal disruptor to hold open the 2373 end of the temporal vortex, even after the 2063 aperture had closed. Later, when we reversed our arrival vector and replicated the Borg's temporal vortex to make our return, the Borg on the assimilated Earth of 2373 intercepted our vortex and tried to sabotage it with a chroniton surge while we were in transit."

Sisko looked perplexed. "To what end?"

Wesley reached past Data to activate a simulation linked to the schematic. It depicted a tunnel-like temporal vortex, spinning madly. "The Borg must have thought a chroniton surge inside the vortex would trigger an anti-time event, undoing the *Enterprise*'s mission to the past, and preserving their timeline." The simulation ended with a flash—and the division of the vortex into three identical tunnels of light and shadow. "Instead, they caused a major temporal fracture."

La Forge highlighted the second of three prominent parallel lines in the schematic. "The first consequence of the fracture was that it spawned a *stable* quantum-branching timeline that extended both forward and backward parallel to the Prime timeline. From the Borg's perspective, their plan worked, because that timeline still exists—parallel to the Prime timeline instead of in place of it. For our purposes, let's call this the Borg timeline."

Wesley highlighted the third parallel line. "The second consequence of the fracture was the creation of this *unstable* quantum branch, the First Splinter timeline. Generally intact, though susceptible to the occasional temporal glitch, it later spawned innumerable branching quantum timelines of its own—each one more unstable than its parent."

Picard took a cautious step forward, entranced by the strangeness of temporal mechanics. "And those inherently unstable timelines are what the Devidians feed upon?"

"Like sharks on chum," La Forge said.

Sisko moved forward alongside Picard. "All right. How do we get to this First Splinter timeline?"

His question prompted uncomfortable looks among the trio on the other side of the situation table. Somehow, their silent consensus placed the obligation of a reply upon Data. "I think you might have misunderstood our presentation, Captain." Data highlighted the last parallel line in the diagram. "*We* are the First Splinter timeline. Every moment we have lived since the *Enterprise*-E returned from its mission to 2063 Earth has transpired in this new temporal reality. And the longer it goes on, the more it diverges from the Prime timeline."

The implications of Data's statement filled Picard with dread. "Diverges? How?"

Wesley turned off the holo-projection. "Like all timelines do. Life is just an infinite number of chaotic possibilities that eventually collapse into finite outcomes, so the likelihood that any two universes would turn out exactly the same is so remote as to be nearly impossible. Of course, the closer the timelines are to one another, the more events they'll have in common. But when you factor in branching events happening at the quantum level, and then extrapolate outward to the macro level, even closely parallel timelines become different very quickly."

Sisko held up his hands, as if to signal the trio to slow down. "I'm confused. At the Academy, I was taught that quantum branching is a natural phenomenon, a normal part of the creation of parallel timelines."

That drew a nod from Data. "It is."

"So what caused the instability in our First Splinter timeline and its quantum branches?"

"The Borg's chroniton attack. Because our First Splinter timeline was produced by a catastrophic artificial temporal fracture, it lacks the inherent stability of a natural branching quantum path. Consequently, each subsequent branch that splits from ours, or from one of our sub-branches, is less stable than the one before it, weakens the one from which it departed, and threatens the general integrity of the twelve-dimensional temporal mesh that unites them all."

Sisko pinched the bridge of his nose, as if to fend off a headache. "Then why isn't the Borg timeline unstable like ours?"

La Forge shrugged. "Best guess? Maybe it merged with a stable, natural quantum branching timeline during the divergence event. Or maybe it was always meant to exist. But whatever the reason, it lacks the inherent instability of the First Splinter and its subbranches."

Hands in his coat pockets, Wesley stepped around the situation table to stand with the captains. "The progressive weakening of our timelines is what attracted the Devidians. They live attuned to two things: the time stream, and the neural energy released by dying sentient beings.

They saw this weakness as an opportunity, and they exploited it. But once they got a taste of what it means to kill an entire timeline *at once*, and devour an *infinity* of dying beings' neural essences . . . their appetite became an addiction. They started destroying more timelines. Soon they learned how to bank large portions of the energy they harvested from each dying universe. With each timeline they kill, the stronger they get."

La Forge emerged from behind the situation table, on the other side of the captains. "Sirs, if the Devidians succeed in killing *our* timeline— the First Splinter—they'll become unstoppable. They'll have enough power to go after *stable* timelines. Maybe even *all* of them."

Unwilling to surrender hope, Sisko asked, "Is there really no way to negotiate with the Devidians? No way to make them see reason?"

Remorseful, Wesley shook his head. "Maybe if we'd caught this sooner? Maybe not. But all they know now is their insatiable need, their hunger for *more*. You can't reason with that."

Picard added, "We can't allow them to go on. We must stop them, at any cost."

Sisko bristled at that proclamation. "Hang on. What does that mean?"

Wesley stepped forward to face him. "We have to erase this threat from the time stream. And the only way to do that . . . is to make sure the First Splinter never happens."

Now Sisko was furious. "That is *not* the mission I agreed to support!" He pivoted toward Picard. "How can you even *consider* such an option?"

Picard struggled not to respond to anger in kind. "With great reluctance, I assure you."

Not satisfied, Sisko moved in quick strides to supplant Data at the situation table's controls. "There must be another way. Some option we've missed."

Dubious but trying hard not to sound insubordinate, La Forge asked, "Such as?"

Jabbing at the controls, Sisko grew more agitated. "I don't know! Something that doesn't entail erasing ourselves and everyone we love from history?"

Data struck a diplomatic tone. "To be fair, Captain, we would not be erased from history, per se. The original versions of ourselves in the Prime timeline will continue to exist."

That only vexed Sisko further. "So? What difference does *that* make? You already said their lives and ours diverged years ago!"

Data conceded the point with a nod. "That is true."

"Well, I want to protect the life I fought for *here*, in *this* timeline. The choices I've made here. The people I've loved. The ones I've lost. *All* of it, for better or for worse. *This* is the reality I swore to defend."

Cautiously, Picard sidled toward Sisko. "Benjamin. I understand your pain. But the reality we swore to defend is the one that existed *before* the Borg created this one by force."

The rationalization seemed to appall Sisko. "Does that make this life any less important?"

"No, it doesn't." Picard reached out and took gentle hold of Sisko's upper arm. "I know what you're feeling. I have the same fear." He waited until he saw Sisko's questioning look, and then he lowered his voice, and bared his soul. "I've also fathered a child since the temporal fracture. I feel the same terror you do—the fear of losing my son. Of erasing him from time."

Tears of desperation welled in Sisko's eyes. "Then help me find another way! Help me *save* this timeline, before it's too late!"

"Benjamin. Listen to me." He took Sisko by his shoulders. "This is no time to let selfishness guide our hand. As Starfleet officers, we have a duty to serve the greatest possible good. Which means we need to think on a grander scale than the fate of any one universe and its entangled dimensions. Our mission now is to save the countless universes that remain—to save time itself—even if it means sacrificing *this* timeline."

The mania that had possessed Sisko abated. His shoulders slumped, and his head drooped forward in surrender to the inevitable. "Is that even possible?"

"I don't know." Picard looked to his friends. "Is it?"

Data traded a look with La Forge, and then he said, "I think it is, sir." He called up the temporal diagram once more and pointed out junctions as he continued. "Because the First Splinter was created by a chroniton attack that originated on the Borg-timeline Earth of 2373, any plan to sever this damaged timeline from the Prime timeline must begin there."

Worry lines deepened on La Forge's brow. "Of course, if we do it wrong, we might send shockwaves through time that would destroy every cosmos and unravel time itself across the multiverse. To undo this entire timeline and stop the Devidians permanently will mean finding their intertime base of operations, wherever and *when*ever it's hidden, and then somehow coordinating a cross-temporal, multidimensional recursion—all before they deliver this universe's death blow, which could come at pretty much any moment, with no warning whatsoever."

Sisko clung to denial. "Is that really the only way to stop them?"

"Unfortunately, yes," Wesley said. "We have to undo this timeline without damaging any others in the process. It was the flaws in our timeline and those it spawned that drove the Devidians to break from their natural pattern as cross-time scavengers and become timeline-slaughtering fanatics. The only way to fix this is to rid the multiverse of this temptation without giving more power to the Devidians in the process."

After a long, heavy silence, Sisko nodded. "So be it."

Picard regarded his friends and Sisko with a combination of exhaustion and apprehension. He felt then as if a great emptiness had opened up inside of him, a sinking feeling at the prospect of what would have to come next.

And then Wesley put Picard's growing dismay into words: "Does anyone know a *non*-terrifying way to ask Memory Omega to help us retroactively destroy the universe?"

5

Clandestine behavior did not come naturally to Doctor Shenti Yisec Eres Ree, chief medical officer of the *Starship Titan*. He had been raised, like any good Pahkwa-thanh, to be forthright in all matters personal and professional. Even his physiology betrayed a predilection for action over skulduggery: massive, bipedal, and reptilian with powerful jaws, muscular legs for running, and a prehensile tail. His was a species for which subtlety had never been a virtue.

That was why Ree had invited Doctor Huilan Sen'kara, one of the ship's junior counselors, to join him for this session of covert observation. Huilan was a male S'ti'ach, a diminutive species of blue-furred humanoids with enormous eyes, sharp fangs, and lethal claws. Although many larger humanoids at first found S'ti'ach "cute," they soon learned that the compact creatures were densely muscled as a result of their having evolved on a high-gravity world whose surface was mostly covered in oceans. The S'ti'ach were aquatic hunters who survived by stealth, speed, and guile. As a fellow carnivore and medical professional, Doctor Huilan had become one of Ree's closest friends on the ship over the past several years.

Now Ree needed his friend's medical expertise as much as his discretion.

Ree stood behind the crescent-shaped standing desk in his office adjacent to the main sickbay, and Huilan stood upon it. As a caution to anyone who might seek to interrupt them, Ree had engaged his office's privacy mode, which soundproofed the space and turned its transparent-aluminum walls temporarily opaque from the perspective of those outside.

Two clusters of holographic displays were projected above Ree's desk. The first was divided into several smaller images, each showing a different angle of view from inside the private quarters of Rear Admiral William Riker, the flag officer in charge of *Titan's* exploratory group. Riker was seated at his dining table, reviewing reports recently uploaded to his padd. His wife, Commander Deanna Troi, and the ship's commanding officer, Captain Christine Vale, sat on the other side of the table, both facing him.

The next group of displays above Ree's desk showed biometric readings being taken in real time, measuring all manner of vital activity inside Riker's body and brain.

Huilan stared in wonder at the vid feeds and bio-readouts. "How did you set this up?"

"Troi did most of the work. With a bit of help from Captain Vale." Ree keyed in a few commands to amplify the sensitivity of the medical scans. "I asked you here because I want your medical opinion on the admiral's EEG."

The S'ti'ach psychiatrist stood up on the toes of his tufted paws so he could lean in to study the waveforms. "These readings are . . . peculiar."

Ree remained still, but blinked his eyes' inner nictating membranes. "How so?"

Huilan almost touched his flat nose to the hologram. "Is the signal garbled?"

"No. I ran a diagnostic. There is no interference."

"Hardware malfunction?"

"Again, ruled out by the diagnostic." Ree selected one of the brain-wave scans and magnified it with a simple two-handed gesture. "Look closer."

"I'm looking." Huilan squinted at the enlarged image for several seconds. Then, weary and annoyed, he faced Ree. "Can't you tell me what I'm looking for?"

"I don't want to bias your conclusions. I need to know whether your independent diagnosis reaffirms mine, contradicts it, or simply provides a plausible alternative to it."

Huilan returned to his seat and flumped onto it. "What motivated this study?"

"Behavioral changes. Several parties, including Commander Troi and Captain Vale, have reported unusual actions and statements by Admiral Riker. Orders that might suggest cognitive impairment, memory loss, or otherwise warrant concern for the stability of his mental state."

The S'ti'ach side-eyed Ree. "Those are serious allegations, Shenti."

Ree flicked his forked tongue and tasted sickbay's antiseptic air. "Yes, they are."

Huilan switched his focus to the vid feeds of the ongoing meeting of Riker, Vale, and Troi. "Has the captain invoked Regulation 121 or Starfleet Order 104-C?"

"Not yet. She's waiting on our results before she throws down that gauntlet."

The counselor turned slowly toward Ree. "You know what I need to ask next."

"I would prefer not to guess."

Blue paws gestured at the holograms. "Is any of this legal? Or admissible?"

"It is. The captain has plenary authority to conduct investigations aboard her own ship, and Commander Troi personally consented to the placement of surveillance devices and medical sensors inside her and the admiral's shared quarters." Ree pointed at the medical readouts with his scaly index finger. "Look again. Tell me what you see. What you think these mean."

This time the counselor studied the EEG data for several seconds. "The patterns seem to stutter." He looked over his shoulder at Ree. "Does that make sense?"

"Continue. Tell me what you mean."

Huilan selected a segment of the EEG and isolated it from the live readout. "I have an idea. Maybe it's crazy. But I think the 'stutter' could be canceled out if we assume that there are two signals here instead of one. They're incredibly close together, almost synchronous—but just far enough off to cause disruptions." He keyed in some commands, which resulted in regular, alternate intervals of the pattern being selected. "But if we remove the highlighted set—"

With one tap on the desk's control interface, Huilan segregated the highlighted parts of the brainwave into another holo-frame. Then, with a few more taps, he closed up the gaps in both the original pattern and the separated one. "Each of these looks like a normal, healthy brainwave pattern. And what's more"—he called up archived medical scans from Admiral Riker's service record and compared them against both edited brainwave patterns—"they both register as a match for Admiral Riker's healthy baseline waveform."

Ree nodded his long, reptilian head. "I made the same finding. But tell me, Doctor: If both of the isolated patterns match that of Admiral Riker, what conclusion can we draw?"

Huilan initiated a simulation and ran it parallel to Riker's real-time brainwave scans. "The data seems to suggest that there are two distinct neural identities active inside the admiral's brain, that they are competing for control of his actions . . . and that both are Admiral Riker." The S'ti'ach's large eyes were fearfully wide. "But how can that be possible?"

"I don't know. But I reached the same conclusion an hour ago."

The tiny counselor met the unknown with bared fangs. "What do we do now?"

"I'll make my report to the captain. What happens after that . . . is up to her."

Listening to her peers debate the fate of her husband felt surreal to Deanna Troi. She had set this process in motion, but now that it was moving forward, she was plagued by guilt and regret.

Captain Christine Vale—her shoulder-length hair dyed in ombré layers of midnight blue, magenta, and forest green—had summoned Troi, along with Doctors Ree and Huilan, to her ready room. Ree, because of his reptilian Pahkwa-thanh body, was not suited to using the guest chairs. Huilan, being less than a meter tall, was obliged to stand on his to see over the desk's edge. Troi, for her part, remained at a distance from the proceeding, with her back to the bulkhead beside the door to the bridge.

The captain scrutinized the information on her padd. "Walk me through this, Doc."

Doctor Ree tapped with a claw at his own padd. "Doctor Huilan and myself both reached the same conclusion after reviewing Admiral Riker's brainwave scans. There appear to be two versions of his psyche competing for dominance over his brain and body."

Vale raised a hand to interrupt. "Did I hear you correctly? Did you say there are two versions of the admiral's personality living inside his head at the same time?"

"Yes."

The captain looked at Huilan. "And you concur with this finding?"

"Yes, Captain." Cued by a nod from Ree, the counselor elaborated. "Doctor Ree and I both noticed, independently, the oddity of the interference pattern in the admiral's EEG waveform. Close review of that waveform, coupled with a comparison to recordings of his brainwaves that are stored in his medical records, led us both to separate the admiral's current brain activity into an opposed pair of oscillating waves, each representing a distinct version of the admiral. We think the interactions of these competing waves are causing the admiral's mercurial moods, as well as his recent lapses of memory and degraded impulse control."

Vale set her padd on her desk. "What's the diagnosis? How'd this happen?"

"After ruling out biological and environmental factors," Ree said, "we concluded that the diagnosis suggested by Commander Troi was likely the correct one: temporal multiple-personality disorder. The admiral's symptoms, behaviors, and other factors are consistent with those reportedly experienced in the past forty-eight hours by Commander Worf."

The captain absorbed that news with subtle, pensive nods. Her subdued reaction caught the attention of Doctor Huilan. "Pardon me if I'm out of line, Captain, but you don't seem especially surprised by our diagnosis. One might surmise you were *expecting* it."

"One would be wise to keep such speculations to one's self, Doctor."

"Yes, Captain."

Vale stood and walked to her ready room's only viewport. She looked lost in thought while she gazed out at the warp-streaked stars. "If there are two versions of the admiral living inside him, how do we find out which is the right one?"

The two medical doctors both looked at Troi, who stepped forward to join the discussion. "I might have a perspective that could help."

The captain pivoted away from the window. "Explain."

"Will and I share a special connection. One that has its origins in my Betazoid heritage."

Huilan perked up. "You mean an *imzadi* bond?"

"You know of it?"

"Indeed, I do!" The S'ti'ach counselor's manner became noticeably animated as he continued. "Part of the Starfleet Medical curriculum regarding the psychology of telepathic and empathic species focuses on the unique nature of Betazoid romantic bonding. It's remarkable for many reasons, not least of which is the fact that Betazoids can form such profound psionic bonds not only with non-Betazoids but even with members of predominantly non-telepathic species."

Vale made a circular gesture with one hand. "Getting back on topic, please?"

Troi hesitated. To tell others of things she knew about her husband only through their decades-long emotional harmony felt like a betrayal—not just of their marital vows, but of the very foundation of trust they had vested in each other. But these were not ordinary circumstances, and whatever was afflicting Will, it was corrupting him, changing him with each passing hour into someone she recognized less and less as her *imzadi*. She had to speak.

"I feel the struggle inside his mind. It's happening even now. Something damaged him, but I don't know what it was. All I know is that it's left a terrible wound in his psyche. When I open my empathic senses to him, I'm overwhelmed by the intensity of his rage, and the depth of his grief." She remained disconcerted by what she had found in the soul of the man she loved. "There's a cold shadow haunting his mind."

Vale returned to her desk and sat down. "We're agreed that something is clearly not right with Admiral Riker. Based on the evidence, temporal multiple-personality disorder seems the most likely culprit. Doctor Ree? Has Commander Troi shared with you the treatment protocols given to her by Captain Picard?"

"She has."

"Do you think you can implement them effectively to help the admiral?"

"I don't know. The admiral began showing symptoms at roughly the same time as Commander Worf did on the *Enterprise*. But the admiral's condition has progressed much further than Mister Worf's did. I can't guarantee the same treatment regimen will succeed—or, if it does, to what degree the admiral might recover, or how long it will take."

Doctor Huilan looked aggrieved by Ree's equivocation. "But surely you would still recommend we attempt treatment rather than allow his syndrome to continue unchecked?"

"Well, naturally."

Vale sounded convinced. "Then that's what we'll do. Doctor Ree, do you officially support my recommendation of an invocation of Starfleet Order 104, Section C, with regard to the flag command of Rear Admiral William T. Riker?"

"I concur, Captain."

"Commander Troi? As the ship's senior counselor, and as the admiral's next of kin, do you concur with our recommendation that we should temporarily relieve your husband of his command of this exploratory group?"

"I do."

"Then the only question that remains is: Where and when do we do this?"

Ree suppressed a rattling noise emanating from deep inside his throat before he spoke. "In this case, I think an excess of discretion is warranted."

Huilan tilted to one side, as he sometimes did when confused. "Why? Are we worried about crew morale?"

"Partly. The present crisis has the crew on edge. But my chief concern is that the admiral is in a volatile, agitated state of mind. There's really no telling how he might react to being confronted. Given his recent outbursts, I would suggest we approach him in as collegial a manner as possible, in a space where he feels comfortable—his quarters, for instance."

Troi nodded, seeing the wisdom of Ree's proposal. "I agree. It should be just the three of us"—she nodded at Vale and Ree—"so that Will doesn't feel ambushed." She faced Huilan, who looked up at her with his huge, dark eyes. "Would you make sure that T'Pel knows to keep Tasha at day care for a few extra hours? If this business with Will becomes adversarial, I don't want our daughter caught in the middle of it."

Huilan nodded. "Of course, Deanna. I'll take care of it."

A host of worries seemed to weigh upon Vale. "Deanna? Be honest: Do you think Will's gonna stand down quietly? Or is this gonna get ugly?"

"I don't know. If it's my Will Riker we're dealing with, he should be able to see reason."

"And if it's *not* your Riker?"

Troi remembered the shadow haunting Will's soul. "That's what frightens me."

An invisible knife of guilt and fear twisted inside Troi's gut as she led Doctor Ree and Captain Vale inside the quarters she shared with Will Riker. The three of them were doing their best to appear calm and nonconfrontational, but the harder Troi worked to seem relaxed, the worse her mounting anxiety became. Struggling not to betray herself, she forced an innocent look onto her face as they approached Riker, who sat at his desk, in a nook just off the suite's main room.

He looked up as they approached. To Troi's surprise, her husband's response was jovially self-deprecating. "Don't tell me I forgot another meeting? Ssura will never let me hear the end of it."

She smiled to hide her dread. "Not at all." Halting beside him, she turned back toward Vale and Ree. The captain was holding a padd, which she kept tucked behind her back. "We need to discuss something time sensitive with you—if you can spare a moment."

"Of course." He stood and motioned toward the L-shaped sofa across the main room. "Captain, Doctor: please make yourselves comfortable." Riker led the way. He planted himself in the corner of the sofa, reclined, and crossed his right ankle over his left knee.

Troi and Vale settled onto the sofa—the captain to Riker's left, Troi to his right. The doctor, as usual, crouched lower to the deck—a stance that only made the reptilian physician look more like a jungle predator poised to spring forward in attack.

Sounding like a man without a care in the world, Riker asked, "What's up?"

Vale activated her padd with a tap on its screen. "We're having a problem with one of our officers. His performance is deteriorating, and we're afraid it's starting to harm crew morale."

"I see. Have you tried reprimanding him?"

Troi chose her words with care. "That's not really an option in this case."

The admiral seemed confused. "Why not?"

An awkward moment stretched around the four of them while Riker inferred from their silence where the problem truly resided. He acknowledged it with a pained look. "It's me, isn't it? You're talking about me."

Troi rested her hand on Riker's forearm. "I'm sorry, Will."

Inching forward, Ree held up his empty hands as if it might make him seem less threatening. "If I might be permitted to explain, Admiral?"

"Please, Doctor. I'm all ears."

Ree rambled on for nearly a minute, explaining what was known about the condition of temporal multiple-personality disorder, what he had seen in Riker's EEGs, and the course of treatment he hoped to pursue, just as soon as they could get Riker to check himself into sickbay.

Riker, for his part, remained both engaged and sanguine during Ree's medical briefing, and he maintained his equanimity while Vale recounted the several recent incidents that had led her and Troi to fear that Riker had been afflicted by this mysterious new malady.

At the end of it, another silence fell. Riker pondered what had been said. Sitting so close to him, Troi felt her husband's worry, his embarrassment, and his effort to remain cool and professional. When she tried to sense the "shadow" that had so troubled her, however, she found nothing at all. *Will is being defensive about his thoughts. He's shutting me out.*

He sighed. With a frown of contrition, he asked Vale, "Can I see my EEGs?"

The captain looked at Ree, who nodded his long head in assent. Vale called up the scans from Riker's medical records and then handed him the padd. "These were all made today."

Poking at the padd, Riker squinted. As he pored through his medical file, his look of dismay deepened. "Can we wait until *after* I've been treated to share this with Starfleet?"

Vale shrugged. "I don't see why not. Doctor?"

"That would be acceptable to me, as well."

"Great. Glad to hear it. As for my treatment"—he keyed a final command into the padd with a flourish—"that'll have to wait until after you two get out of the brig."

The captain stiffened. "Excuse me?"

Troi sensed Riker's deception a moment too late to stop it.

Riker's demeanor turned dark, and he yelled, "Now!"

The door to the corridor slid open.

The first person through it was Lieutenant Ssura, Riker's unfailingly loyal personal aide de camp. The dark-furred Caitian had come ready for trouble, his large furry ears flat against the patches of white on the back of his head, and a type-2 phaser in one paw.

Four members of *Titan*'s security division entered the room behind him: Lieutenant Pava Ek'Noor sh'Aqabaa, a tall and powerfully built Andorian *shen*; Lieutenant Gian Sortollo, a notoriously suspicious human man from the Earth region known as Sicily; Lieutenant Feren Denken, a strapping Matalinian man with an imposing cybernetic right arm; and Ellec Krotine, an enlisted Boslic woman with golden skin, a tightly knotted ponytail of violet hair, and dramatically angular cheekbones and brow ridges.

In the moment that Vale, Ree, and Troi all spent stunned by Riker's brazen abuse of power, the admiral sprang to his feet and began giving orders. "Mister Ssura! Arrest Doctor Ree and Captain Vale for attempted mutiny. Place the captain in the brig. Confine the good doctor to his quarters under guard until further notice. No one is to speak to them, and they're to have no visitors. Is that clear?"

Before Ssura could reply, Troi snatched the padd from Riker's grip and thrust it into the Caitian's free paw. "Don't listen to him, Ssura! Look at the brainwave scans on the padd. They clearly show that something's *wrong* with him."

Ssura tapped the padd. Eyed its screen. Twitched his whiskers. And then he handed it back to Troi. "Forgive me, Counselor, but I see no scans of the admiral's brainwaves."

"Of course you don't," Riker cut in. "Doctor Ree and Captain Vale made them up. As you can see, their ruse was quite convincing. They even had my wife believing them."

Troi heard Vale mutter, "He deleted the scans."

Riker raised his chin and struck an imperious pose. "Take them away."

Ssura delegated the order with a nod to the security team. The guards slapped magnetic manacles onto Vale and Ree, and then marched them out of the suite at phaser-point. Once they had left, Ssura holstered his weapon and faced Riker. "Admiral, shall I inform Commander Sarai that she is now in command?"

"No. Inform the crew that I'll be taking command of the ship, effective immediately."

"Aye, sir." Ssura skillfully avoided meeting Troi's pleading stare as he pivoted on his tufted paws toward the door and made his exit.

When the door closed, leaving Troi alone with her husband, she looked up at him through eyes brimming with rageful tears. "What have you done?"

"What I had to do." There was no remorse in his voice. He took the blanked padd back from Troi and flung it away. "One of the perks of being an admiral: I can classify and delete pretty much any information I want." He walked back to the desk where she had found him minutes earlier, and eased himself into his chair. "By the way, I found your hidden sensors. They've been removed."

Bitter fury welled up inside of Troi. "We only wanted to help you."

"How? By locking me up? Erasing my memories? No, thank you."

"You won't get away with this. I won't *let* you."

Riker leaped to his feet, sending his chair tumbling backward. He seized Troi by her shoulders hard enough that she was sure his fingers would leave her marked with bruises. There was a madness in his eyes, but also a sorrow, a desperation unlike any she had ever sensed in him before. "Damn it, Deanna! I'm doing this for *us*. Don't you get that?"

All she could do was stare up at him in horror.

After a moment, perhaps seeing himself in her eyes, he relented. His mania abated, and he let go of Troi, who backed away as Riker retreated to the sloping viewports of the main room.

When he dared to look at her again, she was almost to the door. She heard it open behind her, but she kept her eyes on him. Even from across the room, she felt his anguish, his fear . . . and his sincerity as he said, "I'm doing this for our *family.*"

Then, like a devil emerging from mists primordial, she felt the cold shadow that lurked within him. His features darkened with anger, and a promise of violence turned his voice sinister: "But as much as I love you, *Imzadi* . . . don't ever do anything like this again."

Troi hurried away, sparing the admiral neither a word nor a backward glance.

Whoever that is, he is not my Will Riker.

6

C.S.S. Enterprise—Mirror Universe

Doctor Tropp, the perpetually irascible chief medical officer of the jaunt-ship *Enterprise*, held up to an overhead light the thin, slim-profile black wristband that Doctor Beverly Crusher had given him. "So how does this gizmo work?"

Crusher and Doctor Julian Bashir stood on one side of a biobed in the *Enterprise*'s sickbay. On the other side stood Tropp and this universe's Lieutenant Commander Reginald Barclay, the ship's chief engineer. From the foot of the biobed, Director Saavik observed the meeting with typically cool Vulcan detachment.

Crusher did her best not to be annoyed by the ill-tempered Denobulan, even though he lacked any semblance of the bedside manner that had been the hallmark of his counterpart in her universe, on her *Enterprise*. "It's a temporal discriminator," she said, in her friendliest voice.

Tropp sounded unimpressed. "And that means what, exactly?"

"It protects the wearer from extratemporal influence, such as becoming imprinted with the psyche of one's parallel self from another timeline."

A scowl deepened the lines on Tropp's face. "Does that happen a lot?"

She answered his question with a shrug. "At the moment? Thanks to the Temporal Apocalypse, my best guess is that it affects maybe one person in a million."

"If it's that rare, is this really necessary?"

Bashir chimed in, "We also think it will shield the wearer against the fear-based neural attack the Devidians' avatars project ahead of themselves before engaging with enemies."

"I guess that's useful enough to merit mass production." Tropp fiddled with the discriminator. Turned it one way, then the other. Scowled at it. "Where's the damned interface?"

Perhaps sensing Crusher's impatience with Tropp, Bashir took it upon himself to explain the device to their host. "The discriminator requires no interface. Upon activation, each one is programmed with the archived medical profile of its subject. From then on, its protection of its subject is automatic."

Barclay extended his open palm to Tropp. "May I, Doctor?"

Grudgingly, Tropp handed over the wristband-shaped device to the engineer. Barclay studied it intently, even though there was little to see on its smooth, glossy black surface. "This is amazing!" He looked up at Bashir. "Your work?"

"I had a hand in its design, but it was, as they say, a 'team effort.'"

"Of course." Barclay ran his fingertips along the band's thin edge. "I presume it's a selenium-powered chroniton stabilizer, coupled with a temporal capacitor that adjusts to its subject's unique quantum resonance, and a medical scanner specialized for EEG isolation?"

His assessment caused Bashir to arch an eyebrow in surprise. "Correct. Most impressive, Mister Barclay."

Tropp folded his arms and *harrumph*ed. "Don't let him fool you. I'll bet he looked up the specs when he saw that your doohickey was scheduled for prioritized fabrication on every ship in the fleet."

Crusher fixed Barclay with an accusatory stare. He withered like a weed in the desert sun, and then he shrugged and mustered a crooked, embarrassed smile. "Is it a crime to do the reading before a test?"

"I'm not going to dignify that with a response." Crusher turned her attention to Director Saavik. "These are the only defense we have against temporal multiple-personality disorder. How soon can we have them distributed to all starship personnel and political leaders?"

"A matter of hours. I've already given the order to disseminate your report on TMPD and the replicator pattern for the discriminator throughout the Commonwealth, and also to our galactic neighbors, regardless of any past or current rivalries."

Crusher smiled with relief to hear that something finally was going as planned. "That's excellent news, Director. Thank you."

"You are more than welcome, Doctor." Saavik's demeanor took a dark turn. "Though I would be thankful for some candor in return."

Crusher looked at Bashir, who mirrored her confusion. Reluctantly, she met the piercing stare of Saavik. "In regard to what, Director?"

Saavik shifted her gaze toward Tropp and Barclay. "Give us the room, please."

Tropp's face flushed with anger. "This is *my* sickbay."

One sharp look from Saavik relieved Tropp of that illusion. Seconds later, he and Barclay had made a hasty departure, and the door slid shut after them.

Director Saavik confronted Crusher and Bashir. "It has been several hours since we granted your shipmates access to our quantum observation lab, but they have yet to share their results with us. What did they find?"

The director's demand left Crusher at a loss for how to respond. "I'm sorry, but I have no idea what they learned. If you want to know, you'll have to ask them."

That did not seem to satisfy Saavik, who trained her stare upon Bashir. "You were the one who requested asylum, for yourself and your friends. Do they not tell you of their plans?"

"In this case? No." He pulled his hand over the front of his beard. "I've suffered some reversals in recent years. Emotional trauma. It left me . . . compromised." He sighed. "I suspect my captains consider me something of a wild variable at the moment."

Saavik folded her hands in front of her—an affectation Crusher had observed in other Vulcans, including the late Ambassador Sarek. After a pensive moment, the Vulcan woman returned her attention to Crusher. "If our partnership is to succeed, it must be built upon a foundation of trust. And trust comes from candor and truthfulness."

"We completely agree," Crusher said. "If we've been slow to share our findings, I have to believe it's because Captains Picard and Sisko want to be in accord before presenting a plan of action—and that whatever they recommend will be in our mutual best interest."

"Then let us hope they reach that accord quickly"—Saavik picked up the temporal discriminator from the biobed and held it up as if it were a token freighted with significance—"while we still have time to rage against the dying of the light."

U.S.S. *Defiant* NX-74205—Mirror Universe

The inside of the *Starship Defiant* looked more like a vessel under construction than under repair. K'Ehleyr moved through its corridors in gingerly steps, taking care not to kick apart tenuously connected optronic cables as she passed. Engineers from *Defiant*'s crew mingled freely with those from her ship, collaborating on a variety of sensitive tasks. The degree of trust shown by *Defiant*'s officers both impressed and surprised her.

I'd think twice before I let them help fix our jaunt drive. But what does that really say? That I'm too suspicious? Or that they're too trusting?

Some corridors she traversed had all of their interior bulkheads removed, in order to grant the damage-control teams access to the myriad systems packed together behind them. One fact of starship design, at least, seemed to be shared by the counterpart universe and her own: there was no tolerance for wasted space inside a starship. Life-support, data cabling, EPS conduits, emergency force-field generators, fire-suppression systems, internal sensor packages, and hundreds of other systems ranging from the primary to the absurdly redundant lived packed together inside the superstructure of every starship. Space might be infinite outside the ship, but within its hull, space was most definitely limited.

Because *Defiant* was presently docked to her *Enterprise*, K'Ehleyr had come aboard the Starfleet ship through its forward airlock, which served as its main access point, and found herself on deck three. She followed the starboard corridor to its midship turbolift, only to find it marked as "temporarily offline." For a moment she considered returning to the bow of the ship so she could come all the way back amidships in the port-side corridor, and then she thought better of it. Remembering that this vessel's predecessor had served as the template for her universe's gunship *Defiant*, she reasoned that it likely had the same emergency gangways located just one section aft of the turbolifts.

She shouldered her way through a knot of enlisted mechanics who were busy rebuilding the turbolift's magnetic braking system, and found the hatch for the gangway. As she expected, it was unsecured, so she opened it, grabbed the rungs of the ladder, and started climbing.

In less time than it would have taken her to walk to the bow and back, she reached the alcove at the top of the ladder and emerged onto deck one just forward of the transporter room. Down the corridor to her left, a row of officers' staterooms lined the starboard bulkhead. Checking the occupants' names listed beside each compartment's door, she made her way forward until she found the one she sought.

Without succumbing to doubt or hesitation, she pressed its visitor signal.

A gruff voice called from behind the closed door, "Come."

She stepped forward, and the door slid aside with a *swish*. Commander Worf looked up as K'Ehleyr entered his stateroom. He was standing, in uniform, and holding a padd, from which he was reading. When he looked up, he seemed mildly surprised. He straightened his posture. "Commander. I was not expecting you."

"Good. It's not much of a surprise if you expect it."

"Excuse me?"

K'Ehleyr sighed. Like so many Klingons she had met, Worf seemed resistant to the charms of her wit. "Just a little joke." She sauntered farther inside and treated herself to a long look around. The room was gray and utilitarian, devoid of decoration or distraction. "I love what you've done with the place."

Worf cast an appraising look at their surroundings. "I just moved in." He paused until she looked at him. "I have not had time to paint."

She smiled in spite of herself. *So he does have a sense of humor. Interesting.*

His manner was polite but direct. "Why are you here?"

The moment of truth. She gathered her courage. "I came to apologize."

Worf seemed perplexed. "For . . . ?"

"My behavior on the *Enterprise*." She waited to see if Worf would reply right away. When he didn't, she continued. "I'm not usually so . . . emotional. Especially not with people I've just met." She looked down in search of the right words, then faced Worf once she'd found them. "It was unprofessional. 'Conduct unbecoming an officer,' as my captain would say."

Worf was pensive, and then his manner took a turn toward modesty. "You owe me no apology, Commander. It is I who should seek *your* forgiveness." The shift in his expression was subtle, but K'Ehleyr could tell he was struggling to master powerful emotions. "I should not have confronted you. It was clear you did *not* wish to speak with me. I should have respected that. Please accept my apology."

There was more than formality and decorum behind Worf's act of contrition. K'Ehleyr saw it in his eyes, and she heard it in the micro-tremors of his voice. In her heart she felt his shame, his regret . . . and his profound sorrow. Once more she fought to keep her own turbulent emotions under control. She smiled at Worf. "Let's consider each other forgiven, shall we?"

"Agreed."

She gestured at the padd in his hand. "You seemed pretty focused on that when I came in. Are you always so riveted by damage reports and duty logs?"

"Hardly." He turned the padd to show her its screen. It was a de-classified Commonwealth dossier, and the image of its subject took K'Ehleyr by surprise: it was her universe's Regent Worf. "I thought I should learn more about my counterpart. His crimes. His victims." Worf regarded the information on the padd with a strange apprehension. "He was what you said: a tyrant who found a better death than he deserved." He set the padd on his desk, and then seemed almost ashamed to look at K'Ehleyr. "If that is who you see in me, I understand your hate."

She moved closer to Worf. She wanted to resist the urge, but she felt compelled—irresistibly drawn, like iron to a magnet. "I also did some reading. From *your* ship's files, about *my* alternate. She was a scholar. A warrior. An ambassador. And she was taken from you far too soon—the kind of death no one deserves." She could tell that her words had res-urrected old memories inside of Worf, along with a grief more terrible than any she had ever known. When he looked at her, she saw the years of buried pain scribed into every line on his face. She took his hand. "I also know that you avenged her. Like a *Klingon*."

He nodded. Whatever he was thinking, it was too fraught with feel-ings for him to express in words. Unsure of what she was feeling herself, K'Ehleyr turned to leave.

"Wait."

She turned back. Worf seemed to be grappling with conflicting desires. He avoided eye contact with K'Ehleyr as he took a cautious step toward her. "I wish to ask a favor of you."

It wasn't hard for her to guess his desire. "You want me to meet your son."

He looked almost relieved to have been so easily revealed. "Yes."

"I'd be happy to." Once again she turned toward the door, only to halt when he spoke.

"I am sorry my other's life caused you such pain."

She looked back at Worf and no longer saw the man she'd once feared; instead, she saw herself anew, through his eyes. "I'm sorry my other's death hurt you so deeply."

Words spoken now lingered in their shared silence, and for a moment K'Ehleyr wondered if maybe there could be such a thing as fate, after all . . .

Then Captain Sisko's voice issued from the overhead speakers. *"Attention, all senior officers: meet in conference room one aboard the jauntship* Enterprise *in five minutes."*

Worf sighed and joined her at the door. "Duty calls."

She led him out the door with a bittersweet smile. "As always."

C.S.S. Enterprise—**Mirror Universe**
Six guests from *Defiant* sat together on one side of the conference room's table: Sisko, Jean-Luc Picard, Worf, Data, La Forge, and Wesley Crusher. Facing them in the room's dimmed light were the *Enterprise's* Luc Picard, K'Ehleyr, chief engineer Barclay, and chief of security Lieutenant Commander Deanna Troi.

Standing at the head of the table, leading them all through a presentation being holographically projected behind her, was Director Saavik. While Luc would not deign to speak for his fellow *Enterprise* officers, he gathered from their reactions—and those of their guests from the counterpart universe—that they were all feeling the same existential horror at the evidence Saavik was presenting.

The elderly Vulcan woman gestured at the hologram. "Using our quantum observation frame, we have documented the destruction of several close parallel timelines. These are alternate universes we have observed many times before. And now . . . they're gone."

Her words drew gasps from Luc's crew, but only grim silence from the visitors.

Saavik pressed on. "I want to clarify that I am not saying that planets we have monitored have been destroyed, or that these other timelines have reached some grim final state. When I say that they are gone, I mean that they have been *undone.* Wiped from history. As if they had never existed." She looked at Sisko. "Just as you had warned."

She called up vids of other realities, including some in which the Terran Empire, instead of falling in the late twenty-third century, had persisted to the end of the twenty-fourth and beyond. "Our records of those realities still exist, but only because we use temporal shielding to defend our archives from paradoxical erasure. Without that, we would be blind to the fact that thousands of parallel universes have been annihilated over the past several years."

With a wave of her hand, Saavik changed the hologram to a diagram of branching timelines, whose elements she manipulated like a conductor leading an orchestra. "We now know that all of the quantum branches that have ever diverged from our present timeline have been consumed by the Devidians, precisely as our guests said. Ours is now the last of the destabilized temporal branches that calved off of the Prime timeline some fourteen years ago."

Confusion knitted Worf's brow. "Do you mean *this* universe, or *our* universe?"

Saavik saw the eagerness in Wesley's eyes. "Would you like to explain, Mister Crusher?"

"My pleasure." He faced Worf. "This universe and ours are actually the same timeline."

Worf remained lost. "I do not understand."

"Think of our reality and this one as the twin strands in a double helix of DNA. Each strand is unique, but they're inextricably tied together." For the rest of the room, Wesley added, "Technically speaking, our two universes are entangled dimensions within the same temporal reality. No matter how separate they might seem, their fates are eternally linked."

Barclay arrived at understanding, and just as quickly looked like he wished he hadn't. "So when you say the Devidians are now targeting *your* universe—"

Troi cut in, "They really mean *our* universes, plural."

La Forge nodded. "Afraid so."

Saavik dismissed the hologram, which faded like a warm mist. As it disappeared, the overhead lights brightened, revealing the conference room's pristine white-and-aqua color scheme and the gently curved styling of its furniture. "It is clear that the Devidian threat is every bit as dire as you've said, Captain Sisko. Less clear is what information your people acquired from our quantum observation lab. While I appreciate their respect for the chain of command, if you still want our help, I must insist you share any relevant intelligence immediately."

Sisko leaned forward and rested his folded hands atop the table. "Of course."

Everyone sat in silence, waiting for someone else to speak.

K'Ehleyr's patience expired first. "*Talk.* How long do we have?"

With varying degrees of subtlety, the visitors shifted their attention toward the android, Data Soong. "With regard to how long we have before the Devidians initiate the collapse of our timeline, my best estimate currently stands at twenty-nine hours and eleven minutes."

A sick feeling snaked through Luc's gut. "How do we stop them?"

His intuition for calamity was confirmed by Wesley's matter-of-fact answer.

"We don't. Our mission isn't to save ourselves, it's to save the Prime timeline. But to do that, we'll have to *unmake* our own timeline, retroactively, before the Devidians kill it."

Barclay and Troi traded stunned looks, and then the chief engineer asked, "How the hell are we supposed to do *that* in twenty-nine hours?"

Across the table, La Forge frowned. "When we figure *that* out, we'll let you know."

7

U.S.S. *da Vinci* NCC-81623

There had barely been time for Captain Sonya Gomez of the *U.S.S. da Vinci* to process the news of the last cosmic-level disaster detected by the ship's long-range sensors when Lieutenant Commander Mor glasch Tev, her Tellarite second officer, turned quickly from his station, his eyes wide and his composure shaken. "We've got another one, Captain."

"On-screen, Tev." Gomez felt her pulse quicken, not with excitement but from anxiety. In just the last hour and a half, her crew had reported the impossibly accelerated evaporation of a massive black hole in the next sector, and a star system whose entire coterie of seven planets had spontaneously broken apart, as if gravity had reversed itself inside their cores and sent their debris flying away toward interstellar space. At last count, they had seen four different stars go dark and three more that had erupted into supernovae, all within fifty light-years of *da Vinci*'s current position, thirty-one light-years coreward of the Denab system.

Now the main viewscreen switched, from a view of the binary star pair they had been monitoring, to a computer-enhanced image of a distant phenomenon. Tev edged toward Gomez's command chair. "Captain, we're looking at something that should not be physically possible."

"That's all we've seen for the last ninety minutes, Tev. Be more specific."

The tall, bald Tellarite cleared his throat. "A cloud of debris is defying the laws of physics and reassembling itself into a pair of rogue dwarf planets that collided in deep space." Annotations appeared as an overlay to the sensor images. "By tracking the movements of the smaller bits, I was able to simulate the original collision. Based on their current rate of motion, I estimate the two dwarf planets will be fully re-formed in approximately three hours."

Gomez stared at the miracle on the viewscreen, transfixed by both its beauty and its impossibility. Before she could ask Tev for more details, she noticed her first officer, Commander Domenica Corsi, now stood on the other side of her command chair.

The lanky athletic blonde's face was a study in fear. "What the hell is happening?"

"I wish I knew, Dom." Gomez swiveled her chair toward her senior tactical officer. "Shabalala? Any response yet from Starfleet?"

The broad-shouldered lieutenant checked his console and shook his head. "Not yet, Captain. But I'm picking up distress signals on all channels, from all sectors." He swallowed hard, obviously working to maintain his composure. "*Hundreds* of them, sir."

Nausea churned in Gomez's gut—a sensation of imminent disaster unlike any she had felt in over a decade, when the *da Vinci*'s mission to Galvan VI had taken a tragic turn that ended up costing the life of her romantic partner Kieran Duffy. Not even the terrors of the Borg Invasion had filled her with such a primal fear. Being asked to hide the planet Troyius from a Borg cube with less than two hours' notice seemed, in retrospect, a trifle compared to watching the physical laws of the universe begin to unravel on a galactic scale.

Tev leaned close to Gomez and lowered his voice. "Captain, may I make a suggestion?"

It was clear to Gomez that whispering did not come naturally to Tev. Like most Tellarites, he found it difficult to keep his rich baritone from filling the room.

She let his failure of discretion pass without comment. "By all means, Tev."

"I think we should take our primary sensors, comms, and the main computer offline for level-one diagnostics."

Corsi bristled as if Tev had suggested ejecting the ship's crew into space. "What? Cripple three key systems at once? Why would we do that?"

Tev straightened his posture to match Corsi's stance. "Because I think we might be the victims of a hoax. Numerous thermodynamic miracles occurring at once? Hundreds of distress calls? Tell me you don't find that the least bit *suspect*, Commander."

"Of course I do. But if we were being spoofed, I'd think at least *one* of our people would've noticed it by now."

"Prove it. Have Soloman and Faulwell analyze all our recent comms and sensor data for signs of artificial generation or modification."

Gomez raised a hand to halt the debate. "Tev, she's right. Putting a hoax past any Starfleet crew would be a stretch, never mind a ship full of S.C.E. specialists." To salvage Tev's delicate pride, Gomez asked Corsi, "But just for the sake of argument: What if he's right?"

Corsi remained dubious. "It would have to be the most widespread, brilliantly coordinated hoax in the history of hoaxes."

"Not necessarily," Tev cut in. "If we are the target, then the architect of the hoax would only have to gain access to our main computer. Once that's compromised, any system on the ship could be manipulated to make us see whatever they—"

Something powerful rocked the *da Vinci* and threw Tev and Corsi to the deck. Gomez white-knuckled her chair's armrest to keep herself in place, while Lieutenants Haznedl and Wong found themselves pinned against the forward consoles. Shabalala was nearly launched over the tactical console to Gomez's left, while security chief Vance Hawkins and engineering officer Maxwell Hammett tumbled across the deck on her right, hurled forward from their stations.

As her officers picked themselves up, Gomez called out, "Helm, what hit us?"

Wong poked at his console. "Gravimetric shock wave, Captain. The binary pair we've been monitoring? It just separated."

"Come again, Lieutenant?"

"The stars in the binary pair have ceased orbiting each other, Captain."

Wong nodded at Haznedl. The operations officer updated the image on the main viewscreen, which showed the red giant and its white dwarf companion speeding away from each other, as if repelled by an irresistible force.

Gomez shook her head, a prisoner of denial. "That's not possible."

Tev pulled himself to his feet, using Gomez's chair for balance. "*That's* what I'm saying. A deliberate overload to our inertial dampers could've simulated the gravitational disruption of the stellar pair being pulled apart, and our brief power failure would have been easy to simulate."

"One way to be sure." Gomez stood. "Corsi, Tev: with me."

The captain led Corsi and Tev off the bridge, into her ready room. Before the door closed behind Tev, Gomez planted herself in front of the small viewport behind her desk and looked out at the endless void salted with stars. Blindingly bright and monstrously large because of its proximity, the white dwarf—which, just a few hours earlier, they all had observed orbiting the red giant and siphoning off its outer layers—was hurtling away into the void, utterly alone.

She turned and faced Tev.

"Hack the computer and you can fool the sensors. But how does hacking the computer fool our *eyes*, Tev? Or are you gonna tell me you're not seeing the same thing I am?"

Corsi and Tev pressed closer to Gomez so they could look past her. Outside the ship, the white dwarf continued to speed away, diminishing in size and brilliance with each moment. Far beyond it, across the curtain of night . . . one by one . . . the stars began to blink and go dark.

Bewildered, all Corsi could mutter was, "What the hell?"

Tev's jaw fell open in horrified awe. "How can we be seeing so many stars go dark at once? They're hundreds or even thousands of light-years from here. This makes no sense."

"Maybe it does," Gomez said, surrendering to the sickening premonition that had taken root in her thoughts. "Whatever this is . . . it's the beginning of the end."

Corsi turned a fearful look at her friend and captain. "The end of what?"

"*Everything*, Domenica." Gomez felt numb as she confronted the inevitable. "I think this is the end of everything."

U.S.S. *Titan* NCC-80102

Commander Dalit Sarai watched Admiral Riker settle into the command chair on *Titan*'s bridge. Sitting in her own chair to Riker's right, Sarai mustered all of her hard-won self-control not to show her white-hot rage at Riker's betrayal of Captain Vale and Doctor Ree. *I can't let him know how I feel. If he thinks I'm against him, I'll end up in the brig just like the captain.*

For his part, Riker looked perfectly at home in the captain's chair. He ran his hands over the armrests with a look of satisfaction. There was no remorse in his expression, not a hint of regret in his voice as he issued orders. "Mister Keru, initiate long-range scans for *Defiant*. Go sector by sector. Conscript other ships as needed. I want that vessel found."

Keru's suspicion was evident from his expression, but the Trill security chief kept his voice neutral as he replied, "Yes, sir. Initiating long-range sensor sweep."

An alert chirped from the operations console. Rager muted it, checked the details, then looked over her shoulder at Riker. "Admiral? We're being hailed by Starfleet Command."

Riker seemed almost amused. "Take a message."

His insolence clearly troubled Rager. Apprehensive, she added, "Sir? It's a direct comm from Admiral Akaar *and* President zh'Tarash."

That seemed to spark Riker's interest. "Oh, *well*. Why didn't you *say* so? On-screen."

The image of interstellar space on the main viewscreen was replaced by the larger-than-life visages of Admiral Leonard James Akaar and Federation President Kellessar zh'Tarash, sitting together in Akaar's office inside Starfleet Command on Earth. Behind them, through floor-to-ceiling windows, stretched the blurred but still recognizable cityscape of San Francisco illuminated by golden hues of sunset.

The admiral was a large, thickly muscled Capellan man, with snowy hair that flowed over his broad shoulders; his features looked as if they had been hewn from sandstone. The president was the model of a classic Andorian *zhen*—slender of frame, with cobalt-blue skin, eyes of pale gray, delicate antennae, and elegant bone-white tresses that stretched down her back.

Both wore frowns of stern disapproval.

The president spoke first.

"Admiral Riker? What in the name of Uzaveh do you think you're doing?"

"I'm sorry, Madam President. Could you be more specific?"

Admiral Akaar took over the conversation. *"In the past half hour, you've issued commands tasking half of Starfleet with the hunt for* Defiant.*"*

"Yes, I have."

"Are you aware that you lack the authority to issue such broad directives?"

For a few seconds Riker was quiet. Sarai hoped this might be the moment he saw reason. Then he shrugged and said to Akaar, "Are *you* aware that I don't give a damn?"

Akaar lifted his chin in prideful fury. *"Excuse me?"*

Not cowed at all, Riker sprang from the command chair and prowled toward the enlarged images on *Titan*'s viewscreen. "You heard me. I don't give a damn. This universe—this entire timeline—is falling apart. Do you even get what that *means*? Because I don't think you do." Riker paced in front of the viewscreen like a caged beast that wished it could hurt the spectators beyond its bars. "Right now, the only thing that matters—the *only* thing—is *finding that ship*. Because the key to stopping all of this, to finding the source of it, and to saving our *entire goddamned cosmos*, is on *Defiant*. Every second we spend on *anything* else isn't just a waste, it's an act of self-destruction."

The longer Riker talked, the more awkward the atmosphere on *Titan*'s bridge became. Sarai felt the crew's discomfort escalate with each word Riker spoke. As an Efrosian, her empathic talents were nowhere near so sensitive or precise as those of Betazoids, but it didn't take a master telepath to detect the embarrassed distress of her shipmates.

"So believe me when I tell you," Riker continued, "that I don't give a damn about your orders, or your protocols, or your regulations. I'm fighting for our goddamned lives, all of them, yours included, and I will use any and every resource I can find to *get this done*."

Akaar's blue eyes blazed with righteous anger. *"Admiral, up until now I have been patient with you. Your long and decorated record earned you a measure of slack. But your actions today have been inexcusable, bordering on mutinous."*

"If you're trying to tell me I'm fired, save your breath. I don't accept your authority."

President zh'Tarash, despite her apparent fragility, spoke with a voice of steel. *"Then respect* mine, *Admiral. Rescind your orders to the fleet and stand down."*

"With all due respect, Madam President? Go to hell."

Across *Titan*'s bridge, gasps of shock were quickly muffled. Sarai looked on, appalled, as Riker rebelled against his commander-in-chief.

Akaar shook his head sadly. *"Will, you've just signed your own court-martial. If any other officers on* Titan *can hear my voice right now, I am—"*

His order was cut off by an emergency siren.

Outside the windows of Akaar's office, the radiant glow of sunset dimmed and went dark. Apocalyptic strokes of lightning bent across the sky as junior officers and members of the president's protection detail rushed into the office yammering about "subspatial disruptions" and "temporal distortions." In a matter of seconds they gathered up Akaar and President zh'Tarash and hurried them out of frame—just as a burst of static filled the viewscreen, which quickly reverted to the image of deep space.

Sarai didn't wait for Riker to give orders, partially because she was afraid he might not care enough to do so. "Keru! Tap into Earth's sensor network. Show us what's happening."

"Working on it." The muscular Trill worked swiftly, keying in commands. "Got it. Patching in a live feed from Luna." The image on the viewscreen changed to an image of Earth, engulfed by a violent storm of shadows and fire.

Riker raced to Keru's side. "What's happening?"

"Hang on," Keru said. "Maybe I can—yes, I've got feeds from the surface, but they're weakening fast—"

"On-screen!" Riker snapped.

With a tap, Keru relayed a signal to the main viewscreen—

Just in time for everyone to watch a vortex of darkness tear Paris to shreds.

The Eiffel Tower collapsed into twists of iron that blew away like leaves. The Palais de la Concorde, the seat of the Federation's government, disintegrated like dust falling into a star. The Federation Council building was swept away seconds later.

The sensors from Paris went black. The computer switched to the San Francisco feed.

The city's skyline flew apart. The Golden Gate Bridge broke into pieces and fell into the bay. Beyond the bridge, a surge of fire and dark energy obliterated Starfleet Command and Starfleet Academy, leaving behind nothing but scoured, smoldering dirt—

The feed went dark.

Faster than Sarai could keep track, the great cities of Earth were erased: New York. Tokyo. London. Mexico City. Nairobi. Shanghai. All gone within a breath.

Then the only remaining view of Earth was the one from Luna.

The storm swelled, metastasized out of control, and swallowed Earth whole. Spacedock and McKinley Station were consumed.

Darkness hit the Luna feed. Then the Mars feed. Jupiter Station went silent.

The last Sarai saw of the Federation's capital was a long-range FTL sensor image . . . which captured the moment the temporal storm devoured Sol itself.

Half a minute later, the tempest dissipated and vanished . . . and the Sol system was gone. The star, all its planets, its asteroid field, its Oort cloud . . . everything.

Not destroyed—*erased.*

As if they had never been.

Horrified shock settled upon *Titan*'s bridge. Only the automated feedback tones of the computers broke the grief-freighted silence.

Sarai forced herself back into action. "Ops. What *was* that?"

Rager looked horrified. "Based on the levels of triolic waves and antichronitons, it must have been a major temporal implosion." She looked back at Sarai. "If the readings I'm seeing are correct, more events like this one are coming—and they'll happen more frequently the longer it goes on."

An alert chimed on Keru's console. He silenced it, then checked his panel. When he looked up, his manner was grim. "Temporal implosions have started on Trill and Romulus."

Riker absorbed the news with what Sarai considered to be a frightening degree of sangfroid. Calm, collected, and confident, he returned to the command chair and sat.

"Helm, set a course for deep space, away from populated star systems. Mister Keru, inform all Starfleet vessels that Earth is gone. And not just Earth—Starfleet Command, the Federation Council, and the president are lost, as well. As of this moment, I am assuming operational command over all remaining Starfleet vessels, resources, and personnel. I want all ships in this sector to rendezvous with us as soon as possible. Make sure every starship commander in Starfleet knows: Our primary objective is to find the *Starship Defiant*. All other priorities are rescinded." He tugged his tunic flat against his chest. "The hunt is on."

8

U.S.S. *Defiant* NX-74205—Mirror Universe

Smooth facets of crystal, once bright with life, were cold and dark beneath Vedek Kira's fingers. Sitting alone on the gray metallic deck in *Defiant's* cargo bay, she held the Orb of Time in both hands. Robbed of its inner light, severed from its sacred source . . . what was it, really? Just another hunk of crystal? A rare but meaningless ornament? A defunct artifact of a dying faith?

A short sleep had restored Kira's body, but her spirit languished in sorrow and regret. She had meditated upon Benjamin Sisko's sage advice. He seemed to believe that the Prophets continued to exist, and that they would guide him—and her—when the time was right.

But we're running out of time—literally. What if that moment never comes?

She closed her eyes and forced herself to reject despair. There was nothing to gain by losing hope, nothing to win by turning her back on her faith. Her belief in the Prophets, in their wisdom and their goodness, had sustained her through a childhood of privation and abandonment, through an adolescence spent waging a brutal guerrilla war against the illegal Cardassian occupation of Bajor, and an adulthood whose early decades had been marked by further trials: the loss of Kai Opaka, the horrors of the Dominion War, and then the struggle to manage her people's assimilation into another interstellar power, albeit a more benign one—the United Federation of Planets.

Through all of her life's many tribulations, her faith had never wavered. Even when Vedek Yevir had expelled Kira from Bajor's ranks of the faithful by declaring her Attainted, she had remained devout, and her trust in the Prophets had been steadfast. Clad in the armor of true belief, she had resigned her military commission to become a member of the clergy, in order to bring her life and her *pagh* into closer harmony with the will of the Prophets.

And then I betrayed them.

More silent recriminations flooded her thoughts: guilt, shame, and revulsion at the part she had played in the destruction of the Celestial Temple.

What if Benjamin is wrong? What if destroying our version of the Temple destroyed them all? The very notion seemed insane to her, impossible. The Prophets' experience of time was nonlinear, recursive, multidimensional, nuanced, and capable of both resisting and incorporating paradoxes with ease. How could beings so dynamic, so beyond her limited understanding of space and time, ever be destroyed?

Kira set the Orb of Time on the deck. It had a flat base and could stand on its own if placed on a level surface.

Once, long ago, Kira had heard the voices of the Prophets. They had come to her—or perhaps they had brought her to them; she had never really been certain—and shown her a vision of what once had been, on Bajor centuries earlier, and of what then had been yet to come, Bajor's inevitable confrontation with the fiery faith of the Ascendants.

She strained to hear those voices now.

She cleared her mind of conscious thought.

Freed herself of desire and regret. Let go of speculation and blame.

All she found were the whispers of the ship's life-support ventilators and the steady thrumming of its impulse reactor through the deck beneath her.

I'm trying too hard. Have to stop thinking. Just breathe.

Of all the lessons she had faced since becoming a vedek, the hardest had been mastering the skill of existing without conscious thought— the challenge of simply *being*. It sounded like such a simple idea, but in practice she had found it exceptionally hard to clear her mind of all conscious thought during meditation. One idle notion, a stray moment of free association, any reaction to stimuli beyond that of passive sensation, would break the spell and consign her once more to the prison of her own mind.

At the other end of the spectrum, it was possible to become too disconnected from one's senses during meditation. More than once she had jolted awake and felt a sudden flush of shame at having drifted off. The purpose of meditation was to achieve mindfulness without cogitation, to learn to experience existence in the present moment free of analysis or judgment.

And to stop thinking about what meditation means, she scolded herself.

Everything suddenly felt futile. All the prayers. Hours of concentration, meditation, self-negation . . . all for what? For the pleasure of sitting cross-legged on cold duranium, staring at a hundred tiny reflections of herself in the Orb's perfect facets? How many times would she bow her head to this dead hunk of crystal? What was the point of peering so deeply into its occluded heart, only to find nothing but shadows and doubts?

Kira recalled with bitterness all of her fellow resistance fighters who had suffered savage, humiliating deaths at the hands of the Cardassians. What good had faith done them? Where were their rewards for trusting the will of the Prophets? Had the great powers of the Celestial Temple ever given the slightest sign that they knew or cared about all those who had died believing in their promises of better lives, but doomed never to receive them?

What if the Prophets never promised us anything at all? What if the vedeks of old just made it all up? What if they lied? What if everything they've ever taught us . . . was a lie?

It was too awful a notion to consider. Besides, Kira had felt the touch of the Prophets. She had interacted with them, received visions from them. If she could be found worthy of their inspiration, why not others before her?

She imagined as she exhaled that she was purging every last iota of negativity from her being. *I will not despair. I will not surrender. The Prophets will show me the way.*

With her eyes closed, Kira placed both her hands upon the Orb.

She let go of her fears, and then her hopes. Time became fluid as she focused on her pulse. Finally, she felt at peace, unburdened by consideration. She existed in that moment without projection or memory, and for a moment she understood what it meant to let go of her sense of self, to know that her energy and matter were one with all of the waves and particles and extradimensional strings that surrounded her.

A new sensation pulled her back into her shell of self-awareness: a growing warmth in her hands. She opened her eyes—

—to see the Orb of Time ablaze with magenta light, bathing Kira in its radiance and flooding the cargo bay around her with an uncanny glow.

Tears of joy fell from Kira's eyes, and she sobbed even as she smiled.

Inexplicably, here in this long-maleficent parallel universe . . . the Prophets were alive, and once more their power was flowing through the Orb.

She lifted it from the deck and stood. It no longer felt as heavy to her as it once had. Now it felt as light in her hands as the breath of the dawn.

It felt like hope.

There were two science labs aboard *Defiant*, and neither was large enough to hold comfortably the group that had gathered in the dimly lit starboard lab, around the reawakened Orb of Time.

Closest to the scintillating mass were Kira and Sisko. To Picard, the duo seemed reverently protective of the rekindled artifact. He, Data, and La Forge had crowded in for a closer look, only to be kept at arm's length by Sisko and Kira.

Their actions made perfect sense to Picard, considering their shared ties to the Bajoran faith and to the nonlinear entities known as the Prophets. *I barely understand what this object is. How could I ever hope to comprehend what it means to them?*

Predictably, La Forge and Data analyzed the Orb of Time with tricorders, as well as with the full suite of sensors built into the ship's science lab. They both worked quickly, as if they were desperate to keep up with the flood of new information.

Data's fingers continued to work in a blur as he admired the artifact. "It really is quite remarkable. We are detecting what appears to be the spontaneous generation of both chronitons and antichronitons inside its energized crystalline matrix."

His observation put a boyish grin of excitement on La Forge's face. "What's more, they're localized—chronitons in the lower half, antichronitons in the upper, and they're colliding in the neck." He paused his frantic work to look at Picard. "It's like a temporal warp core, Captain. A miniaturized reactor for making and unmaking time."

Wesley Crusher replied, "It's *more* than that. A *lot* more." He stood the farthest from the Orb, just a meter behind Picard. When everyone else in the lab looked his way, he continued, his manner almost professorial. "It can be a beacon across time and parallel dimensions. It can be a power source for a temporal event. It can move a person through time, or time through a person. What we're looking at here . . . is a skeleton key for time itself."

Anger hardened Kira's stare. "What you're looking at is the last gift of the Prophets to the people of Bajor. The Orb of Time is a *sacred* artifact. Not some toy for your time experiments."

Hands raised, Picard adopted the tone of a supplicant. "We apologize, Vedek. I assure you, no disrespect was intended, and we regret any offense we have given."

At first Kira appeared unwilling to relent. Then Sisko laid his hand with care upon her shoulder and said quietly, "Nerys. Please."

Her fury melted away, and an air of melancholy resignation took its place. "Sorry."

Picard shifted his focus to his old friends. "Geordi? Data? Is there some way the reawakened Orb can help us stop the Devidians?"

The android and the engineer traded hopeful looks. La Forge answered, "I think there is, Captain." He stepped to a console and called up a simulation on one of the bulkhead displays. "We know that we need to undo the creation of our own unstable quantum branch—"

"The First Splinter," Picard interjected.

"Right. And we need to do it without harming the Prime timeline, from which we deviated in late 2373. The trick is creating a temporal resonance between the original disruption event—the ODE, or 'Ode,' in the Borg timeline—and our present moment in *this* timeline."

Data stepped around Picard as additional information augmented the complicated temporal schematic on the screen. "Our two challenges will be maintaining a stable temporal link between the two timeframes as we disrupt the Ode at its point of creation, and triggering an anti-chroniton event of the same magnitude from our present." He looked back at the group to add, "We believe the Orb of Time can help us achieve the first of those two objectives."

Encouraged but still not convinced, Picard studied the schematic. "How?"

Wesley interrupted, "By acting as a beacon."

La Forge nodded. "That's right. The temporal signature of the Orb of Time is both unique and powerful enough that we can lock onto it before we undo the Ode. It can help us create and maintain a temporal bridge between the Ode in Borg-timeline 2373, and our inverse, corrective disruptive action, or 'Coda,' in the present of our native dimension in this timeline."

Data added, "It can also help us calibrate the Coda, to ensure the safe and complete retroactive termination of this timeline."

Sisko noted a look of worry from Kira before he spoke. "As a plan, that sounds fine in theory. What I want to know is: How do you plan to pull it off?"

Looking and sounding a bit cocky, La Forge asked, "Which part?"

"Start at the end. How do you plan to trigger this 'Coda'?"

The question gave La Forge pause, so Data answered for him. "We will need to locate the Devidians' intertime base of operations, capture whatever technology they use to collapse timelines, and repurpose it to our task of safely undoing our timeline before it is destroyed."

Kira rolled her eyes. "Oh. Is *that* all? And where will the Orb be when this happens?"

Data gave his head a slight, birdlike tilt to the left. "Ideally, the Orb will be with you, inside this dimension's Bajoran wormhole, where the beings you know as the Prophets can help defend it from counterattack by the Devidians." To Picard he added, "Situating the Orb of Time inside the wormhole should also amplify its potential as a beacon and as a calibration signal."

His matter-of-fact explanation had stoked Kira's temper. "And what if the Prophets don't want to take part in this fight? What if they don't want to be caught in our cross fire?"

"That's why we want you to stay with the Orb," La Forge said. "You understand it better than anyone, and you're one of the few people we know of who's ever made contact with the"—he hesitated half a second, as if rethinking his choice of words—". . . with the Prophets."

"Mm-hm. Sure."

Hoping to lower the group's rhetorical temperature, Picard struck a diplomatic chord. "Let's not get ahead of ourselves. Before we commit to an irrevocable course of action, we should make certain we haven't overlooked anything." He made a point of eyeing Data and La Forge as he said, "For instance, do we have any way of disrupting the Devidians' control of their avatars, or the Nagas?"

The question left La Forge looking deflated. "Not yet. But I've been building portable transphasic-field attenuators, to give us a fighting chance the next time we square off against them. TFAs should neutralize the avatars' and the Nagas' death-touch, prevent both them and their masters from popping in without warning, and force them all to turn and stay solid within a limited range of each device."

Picard nodded. "Anything else?"

Data noted, "We did catch a glimpse of the Devidians' temporal-collider station while observing the death-pulses of dying timelines through Memory Omega's quantum frame. Unfortunately, we have not yet found a way to reach its intertemporal dimension."

Wesley took a careful step forward, shouldered past Picard, and dared to plant himself directly in front of the artifact. Its magenta light cast sinister shadows on his bearded face. "I think the Orb can help us with that, too, Captain."

Picard wasn't sure he followed Wesley's reasoning. "Are you suggesting we somehow connect the Orb to the ship's sensors?"

"Not at all." A cryptic smile formed behind Wesley's beard. "This won't be a job for sensors or computers. I'll need something *far* more sensitive and powerful for this." He looked up at Sisko and Kira, and his smile broadened. "I'm going to need the two of you."

On the walk back down to cargo bay 1, Kira had insisted she be the one to carry the Orb of Time, and that no one else was to touch it. In no mood for an argument when he knew that he was about to need her help, Wesley had been more than happy to agree to her terms.

Sisko locked the cargo bay's entrance while Kira set up the Orb in the middle of the empty compartment. She took special care to unfold and smooth the fabric of its shroud so that it created a sanctified square upon the deck, and then she placed the Orb in its center.

Wesley focused on the purgation of negative energies from his mind and body. When Captain Sisko arrived at his side, Wesley asked him, "Are you ready to begin, sir?"

"Absolutely."

"Vedek Kira?"

"First, tell me what we're doing."

"We're going to project our linked minds through the Orb, and ask the Prophets to help us look beyond linear time for clues to the location of the Devidians' intertime base." Wesley offered Kira his open hand. "Ready?"

She trained a skeptical look at his hand, then at him. "Are you serious?"

"You have a better idea?"

"Yes—don't treat the Prophets like some kind of cosmic tech-support team. These are my people's *gods* you're talking about."

"They're also living beings who have a special, nonlinear relationship to spacetime—as I do, and Captain Sisko does. They've also formed a unique bond with you, which makes you more likely to merit their interest and consideration than if we tried to do this without you." He folded his hands in front of his chest and softened his tone. "Please, Vedek. We're out of options. And I have to believe it was no accident that the Prophets restored the Orb of Time *now*, when it was in *your* hands. Just as it was no coincidence that they gave it to you in the first place. I think they meant for this moment to happen, maybe even knew that it *had* to happen."

Once again Wesley proffered his open hand to Kira. "Please."

Kira looked to Sisko, who nodded. "I think he's right, Nerys. The Prophets gave you the Orb for a reason. Trust them." Like Wesley, he extended his hand to her. "Trust *me*."

She took his hand in hers. "I hope you're right about this, Benjamin."

"So do I."

As Wesley clasped Kira's and Sisko's free hands, they shifted to occupy equidistant positions around the Orb, which continued to coruscate with hypnotic magenta light. Beams of intense white light shot out of the Orb at odd intervals, in seemingly random directions, as it brightened. An eerie, musical sound filled the cargo bay as the spreading brilliance swallowed details, surrounding Wesley, Kira, and Sisko in blinding light and numinous melodies. . . .

Silence fell like a curtain.

The cargo bay vanished.

Wesley, still grasping Kira's and Sisko's hands, stood upon a beach of powdery white sand. Overhead, a dome of stars crept across the sky. It took Wesley a moment to realize the waves were behaving abnormally. Sheets of water rushed up the beach, swelled and curved, springing up from great washes of spume . . . to become waves, not breaking against the shore but unbreaking from upon it, then retreating to the sea.

Tiny loose fronds leaped from the wet sand to fuse themselves to the ends of branches on the palm trees fronting the tropical forest that covered this island paradise.

Kira and Sisko turned their heads and drank in the strange wonder of their setting.

At once, they were no longer alone. Three new Presences had appeared, one standing behind each of them. Wesley didn't recognize the stout, shorter middle-aged Bajoran woman in vedek's robes who attended Kira, or the white-haired, white-bearded elderly Caucasian man in a Starfleet commander's uniform who stood at Sisko's shoulder.

But his own host's form he knew at once. The Prophet who stood at his side, sizing him up, wore the image of Wesley's father, Jack Crusher. He was dressed in the same midcentury Starfleet uniform Jack had worn while recording a holo-message for Wesley shortly after his birth, but which Wesley hadn't seen until he was almost a man himself. As Wesley's old Traveler mentor had long ago taught him to expect when conferring with noncorporeal entities, the Prophets had taken this image from his memory.

Wesley tried to hide his awkwardness and anxiety with a crooked smile. "Hello."

He saw the other two Prophets speaking to Kira and Sisko, but he was unable to hear what they were saying. The one who had come to interact with him studied him as if he were a specimen beneath an electron microscope. When it spoke, its voice was flat and monotonal.

"Nominally human. But evolved. Nonlinear."

"I'm a Traveler."

The Prophet shifted from side to side. Wesley imagined the entity wanted to circle him, and that the others had similar impulses toward Sisko and Kira, but the trio's linked hands prevented it. It had been a simple bit of psychological sleight of hand, but Wesley was glad now that he had insisted upon it. By linking hands before embarking on this mystical journey into a nonlinear dimension of time, he, Kira, and Sisko had formed a united circle of defense, one that would, he hoped, prevent them from becoming divided and overwhelmed.

The stars faded from the sky overhead, and the ocean retreated from the shore before sublimating into vapor. The palm trees shrank and vanished back into the sand from which they had grown, and then the beach itself flew upward, a reverse deluge of dust.

Wesley concentrated on removing himself from the Prophets' framework, on finding an objective vantage point. With a bit of effort, he forced himself, Kira, and Sisko into a void-like space, from which they observed the backward flow of sand through a planet-sized hourglass.

But the sand in the top chamber continued to diminish, as if it were falling naturally through the neck into the lower chamber. Instead, all the sand vanished into the center.

The Prophet stared, unblinking, at Wesley. *"No beginning. No end."*

The hourglass shattered in a flash. Wesley shut his eyes until the painful glare abated. When he opened them, he beheld the birth of the universe, the moment when time and space broke free of a singularity to expand into the black. Clouds of gas congregated and ignited into stars. A red giant hurtled toward the trio, and even though Wesley knew in his conscious mind that this was only a mental projection, the more primitive parts of his brain raged and scrambled like animals trapped in cages while watching a wall of flames race inexorably closer.

The trio plunged into the fiery corona of the red giant—

—but instead of scorching heat, all Wesley felt was numbing cold.

Then the explosion of creation receded, retreated into itself, into a point that vanished.

"No beginning," the Prophet said. *"No end."*

Bitter wind slashed at Wesley's face, hurling flakes of snow and tiny daggers of ice into his eyes and caking his beard with frost. His hands still held on to Sisko's and Kira's. Their two Prophets continued to whisper into their ears as a blizzard swirled around them.

Wesley wished he could lift his hands to protect his face, or at least his eyes, but he didn't dare let go of Sisko or Kira. There was no telling what might happen if he let them wander into the Prophets' temporal labyrinth without his extratemporal senses to guide them home.

He shifted his feet, tried to pivot so he could look for his Prophet. His shoes slipped on what he realized was dark ice. A gust of wind blew past with such force that it scoured the frozen sea clean of snow and sleet, revealing a surface so perfectly black and pristine that Wesley saw his reflection staring back at him.

Massive ice sheets cracked with a sound like the breaking of a giant's bones. Three cavernous fissures shot across the ice, all converging at once— and then a spire of black crystal pierced the surface and climbed into the leaden sky. It was impossibly slender—it looked so narrow that a stiff breeze could snap it in half. But it kept rising, until its apex receded into the clouds. When Wesley looked closer, he saw in the spire's details echoes of the mysterious death-energy collection towers the Devidians had built in the distant past and the far faded future.

Now the Prophet that spoke to Wesley had taken on the visage of the first Traveler that Wesley had ever met, many years ago. The Prophet-as-Traveler gazed up at the long-passed-from-sight top of the spire. "No beginning."

The world turned upside down.

Sisko, Kira, and Wesley were launched into the air—fumbling, kicking, flailing with their legs, but still hanging on to one another's hands with fierce determination. For a disorientating few seconds, they fell toward a sky that was suddenly beneath them—and then they plunged toward the mirror-perfect icy surface that was now above them.

Their reflections rushed to meet them—

—and then they smashed through the mirror together, into a fury of white light.

Gravity reasserted its hold and slammed them down onto a surface of immaculate white marble. Without letting go of one another, the trio got up onto their knees and surveyed their new surroundings. Perfect white stone stretched away as far as Wesley could perceive, but right in front of them yawned a narrow, circular opening in the otherwise perfect horizon. From it came the most beautiful, reassuring light Wesley had ever seen.

The trio shuffled toward the pit's edge and looked over.

Beyond its point of no return lay an abyss beyond measure, flooded with light.

Wesley's Prophet and the others all spoke then in unison, and he heard them all:

"No end."

The white light of the chasm overflowed, washed over them as it turned pink, and then it flared magenta—

—as the reverie ceased, jolting the trio with such force that they finally let go of one another's hands. They fell backward to the cargo bay deck, away from the Orb of Time, which went on spilling out its otherworldly light as if nothing had happened.

After a moment, the trio collected themselves and sat up.

Kira looked shell-shocked. "No beginning."

Sisko seemed to be looking at something a hundred kilometers away. "No end."

Wesley stood, and then he offered his hands to Sisko and Kira, who accepted his aid this time without question. He helped them stand. "We need to assemble the crews, quickly." He walked toward the exit, and Sisko and Kira followed him.

As they left the cargo bay and hurried down the corridor, Sisko sounded like a man afraid to embrace hope. " 'No beginning. No end.' Do you understand what that means?"

Wesley sounded worried. "I think so. But if I'm right, we're almost out of time."

Kira's doubts sounded like anger. "And if you're wrong?"

"Then we're already dead. We just don't know it yet."

9

C.S.S. Enterprise—Mirror Universe

A low murmur of anxious voices filled the *Enterprise*'s auditorium. Most of the jaunt-ship's senior officers had assembled in a hurry, and the officers and crew of *Defiant* had joined them. The two ships' personnel had segregated themselves—*Enterprise*'s officers to one side, *Defiant*'s complement to the other. The only mingled seating Saavik observed was hers, beside Ambassador Spock. The one thing all the assembled personnel had in common were their temporal discriminators—thin, narrow black bands each person wore around one wrist.

Captain Luc Picard and Commander K'Ehleyr were the last to arrive. As they descended the center stairs that divided the auditorium, Commander Worf moved to the front of the low stage and filled the wedge-shaped theater with his rich bass voice. "Attention. Please take your seats." He paused as the gathered personnel fell silent and sat down. "Thank you."

The stoic Klingon exited stage right as Wesley Crusher, the Traveler from the counterpart universe, climbed a short stair at stage left to take Worf's place in front of the audience. "Thank you all for coming on such short notice. Captain Sisko, Vedek Kira, and I have already briefed both Captains Picard, as well as Director Saavik. So, with their permission, I'm going to dive right in and bring the rest of you up to speed."

Wesley looked for Saavik and the starship captains in the front row. Saavik nodded her assent first, and the captains did the same.

"For those of you who haven't heard, we have just one chance to stop the Devidians from rampaging through an infinity of timelines. To do that, we need to prevent the creation of the unstable timeline that made this psychotic scheme of theirs possible in the first place.

"As it happens, that unstable timeline . . . is ours."

A somber hush settled over the room before Wesley continued. "To retroactively prevent the creation of our timeline without harming the Prime timeline from which we came, we need to do three things.

"First, we have to commandeer the original disruption event that caused our timeline to splinter from the Prime timeline, and change its parameters to protect the Prime timeline.

"Second, we need to capture whatever tech the Devidians are using to kill timelines, and use it to collapse our timeline *before* it forms.

"Third, and last, we have to create a temporal bridge between those two events, and trigger them in unison across that bridge."

From the *Enterprise* crew, chief engineer Reginald Barclay raised his hand to interrupt. "Excuse me, but . . . how the hell are we supposed to do that?"

Vedek Kira stood and answered Barclay. "Using the Orb of Time. It can act as a beacon and as a standard against which we can calibrate our efforts."

Saavik held up a Memory Omega quantum communicator. "We will also use these to generate synchronicity fields across space, time, and parallel dimensions, including intertime."

Onstage, Wesley reclaimed the room's focus. "There's also bad news."

K'Ehleyr grumbled, "I thought that *was* the bad news."

"If only. To undo the original disruption event, we have to send *Defiant* to the 2373 of *another* alternate-timeline Earth, one assimilated by the Borg. At the same time, the jaunt-ship *Enterprise* will have to cross over to our native dimension to find the Devidians' hidden base."

Commander Troi, *Enterprise*'s chief of security, lifted her hand. "Are you suggesting we search an *entire universe*?"

"Good question. On this, at least, I think we caught a break. The Devidians, as far as Traveler lore can tell, are native to the Milky Way, so I think the access point to their intertime base will be somewhere in our galaxy. Specifically, I need to find a rift in spacetime, near or on the event horizon of a black hole on the order of several hundred thousand solar masses."

The next question came from La Forge. "That sounds fairly precise, Wes. Can you tell us where that info came from?"

Wesley sighed. "Geordi, we're about to try to erase our own timeline before it happens. This is the craziest thing we've ever been asked to do.

So if I tell you this intel *came to me in a dream*—would it make any difference?"

La Forge took a second to let that marinate. "Good point."

"Thank you. Just so you all know, there *is* good news. Based on previous fights with the giant space-borne serpents I call Nagas, we've learned how to modify starship phasers with transphasic disruption to improve our chances of doing real damage to these things. Those specs have been shared with your jaunt-ship fleet. And since your ships already use transphasic torpedoes and shielding, you should have no trouble modifying your shield-nutation specs to provide additional defense against the Nagas' disruption attacks."

That information seemed to buoy the room's collective spirit—until Wesley pulled it back down again.

"Now for the last bit of bad news. We have less than twelve hours before the Devidians collapse this timeline and eat our neural energy as we die. We need to go now: *Defiant* to the past in the Borg timeline, *Enterprise* to what I call home but your side calls the 'counterpart' dimension, and Vedek Kira with the Orb of Time to *this* dimension's Bajoran wormhole."

Saavik took that as her cue. She and Spock stood and moved in opposite directions along the front row of seats, passing out handheld quantum communicators to the senior officers. "These are all the quantum comms we have on hand," she explained. "They have already been synchronized for this mission."

Spock handed comms to Sisko, Jean-Luc Picard, and Data. "Director Saavik tells me these units have been further modified, with chroniton regulators that enable them to maintain synchronous open channels even when they are separated in time."

"Try not to lose those," K'Ehleyr said, as droll as ever.

"Last but not least"—Wesley held up a mysterious silvery gadget—"I've already used the Omnichron to program *Defiant*'s helm for its trip through the temporal fracture, to the Borg-timeline Earth of 2373, and also for its return jump, to its original home dimension."

From the second row of seats, Doctor Bashir asked, "What if we don't make it home?"

It was clear that Wesley had expected that question. "Then the *Enter-*

prise will have to finish the hunt for the Devidians, and destroy their time tech, on its own." He raised his voice to address the entire room. "Any questions? Just kidding, we don't have time. Get ready to ship out. We deploy in fifteen minutes. And for those of you I won't get to see again: thank you."

With that, he walked off the stage.

A buzz of nervous voices filled the auditorium.

Saavik threaded a path through the suddenly chaotic mass of people and returned to Spock's side. "Ambassador, you and I need to go to Deneva, to address the Parliament."

He sounded curious. "To what end?"

"Given our abbreviated deadline, I think it would be wise to send as many jaunt-ships as possible to assist *Enterprise* in its hunt. But to do so will require their permission."

"Given our exigent crisis, might they waive such formalities?"

"Regretfully, no. In recent years they've come to resent Memory Omega's habit of giving orders to the jaunt-ship commanders, without the Parliament's consent."

"I see. In hindsight, that policy would appear to have been ill-advised."

"Yes, Your Excellency. So I have gathered." She started up the stairs, then turned back and gestured toward the exit. "Our transport awaits."

Asking for no further explanation, Spock followed Saavik out of the auditorium.

People were leaving the auditorium at a quick step. Luc felt the urgency in the room; he was sure that everyone did. It was a heady sensation, a brew of excitement, fear, sorrow, and pride—the overwhelming awareness that one was going into battle. Going to war.

Wesley the Traveler emerged from the shifting wall of people and headed straight to Luc. "Captain, thank you for agreeing to help me search for the Devidians' base."

"*De rien.* We're the only ship that can cover that much distance in the time we have left. Though I should warn you, my crew is struggling with the sensor upgrades you requested."

The haggard, weary-looking Traveler smiled. "No worries. I'll talk them through it once I—"

He was cut off by the phlegmy growl of K'Ehleyr clearing her throat behind him. She wore a plaintive look as Wesley and her captain faced her. "Excuse me—Captain?"

"Number One?"

She shot an embarrassed look at Wesley, but then she pressed on. "I'd like to request a transfer, sir. To *Defiant*."

Her request went through Luc like an assassin's blade, straight to his heart. K'Ehleyr had for years been his right hand, his confidant, his most trusted friend. The thought of going out to meet what might well be the end of everything without her steady courage and sage advice to call upon shook him to his bones.

But I dare not tell her that. She would laugh and call me soft.

He masked his pain and fear with a frown. "Why, Number One?"

Then he saw it, behind her own façade—an ineffable need, a long-ing . . . desperation. But she was half-Klingon, and that part of her heritage would never admit to serving her human side. "I can't explain it, Captain. But there's something I—" She stopped, shook off whatever she had been about to say. "Forgive me, sir. But I *need* to do this."

What could he say? It was obvious, to him, that she had felt the touch of fate. She had never asked him for anything. Who was he to deny her now, on the verge of Armageddon?

He reached out and clasped her hands. "Godspeed, Number One."

"Thank you, sir." For a moment, he thought he saw a hint of tears in her eyes. She turned away before he could be certain, and then she was away, sprinting up the stairs and out of the auditorium, racing toward whatever destiny awaited her.

Then he remembered his new VIP passenger, whose conversation had been so abruptly halted. He turned back toward him with a smile. "My apologies, Mister Crusher."

"None required, Captain. Now, as I was saying, I could—"

A hand on Crusher's shoulder interrupted him. "Wes?"

Wesley turned, permitting Luc to see a stunning, tall red-haired woman who was, he estimated, some twenty years his junior. Next to her was a sullen, lanky young man in drab civilian clothing. The woman nudged the auburn-haired youth toward Wesley. "Wes, I need you to take René with you aboard the *Enterprise*."

René brusquely shook off the woman's hand. "I don't need a babysitter, Mom. I'm not a kid anymore." He eyed Luc with suspicion. "And I'm not going with *him*."

"You'll be going with your brother—"

"Half brother," René corrected her.

All that Wesley could do was shrug. "I don't know if he'll be any safer with me than with you, Mom. Once we go back, it's a good bet Riker's gonna be hunting us every step of the way."

"I don't care, Wesley. I'm not taking your little brother—"

"*Half* brother," René cut in.

"Shut up," Wesley and his mother snapped in unison at René.

All at once, the red-haired woman became aware of Luc Picard's gaze. She smiled and held out her hand. "Sorry, where are my manners? Doctor Beverly Crusher." She tilted her head toward Wesley. "I see you've met my older son. This is his younger *half* brother, René Picard."

Hearing his own surname sent a jolt through Luc.

He felt exposed and awkward. "Picard? You mean—? His father—"

"Is your counterpart from my universe." Doctor Crusher held up her left hand to show Luc her engagement ring and wedding band on her third finger. "He's my husband."

"I see." Feelings of responsibility and obligation overwhelmed Luc when he dared to look at the young man. René, for his part, made a point of avoiding eye contact with him. Luc swallowed hard to contain his surprise and conceal his sudden fascination with the idea of the life he might have led in the other universe—the life his counterpart *had* led.

He looked at Doctor Crusher and focused on not losing himself in her beauty. "Doctor, I give you and your husband my word: while your son is aboard my ship, I shall treat him as if he were my own—and my crew and I will defend him with our lives."

Crusher stepped past her sons to stand in front of Luc. She looked into his eyes as if she had the power to peer through them into his soul. Then she placed her palm against his cheek, and in a voice that resonated with trust and compassion, she said to him, "I know you will."

He was so awed by her that all he could do was stand there as she turned away, kissed both her sons goodbye, and left the auditorium with the other *Defiant* officers.

Wesley studied Luc's befuddled state and grinned. "You all right, Captain?"

Luc was shocked to find himself at a loss for words.

Wesley nodded. "Yeah. She has that effect on you. I mean on *him*. I mean—" Amused, he shook his head, gathered up his half brother René, and led the brooding lad toward the stairs. "Forget it. See you on the bridge."

A minute later, Luc Picard was the last person left in the auditorium.

And he still had no idea what he wanted to say.

Merde.

S.S. Sleipnir—Mirror Universe

Points of starlight stretched into circles, the cosmos into a kaleidoscope, and then it all snapped back, this time in new configurations—that was how it looked to Kira as the *C.S.S. Enterprise* engaged its jaunt drive and made an instantaneous transit through an artificial wormhole, from a remote region of the Cardassian Sector to coordinates less than a million kilometers from Deneva, the capital world of the recently formed Galactic Commonwealth.

Through it all, the *Sleipnir*, Director Saavik's personal transport ship, remained docked to the *Enterprise*, as was *Defiant*. Kira sat in the rear of the *Sleipnir's* cockpit, behind Saavik and Ambassador Spock. At the *Sleipnir's* helm sat a human woman in her late thirties who wore her hair pulled back tight, a style that called attention to her long, slender neck and angular jawline.

Kira had secured her small duffel of personal possessions and the reverently shrouded Orb of Time in her quarters, a VIP guest cabin that Saavik had set aside for her.

All her life Kira had traveled light, first as a guerrilla fighter, and later as an officer in the Bajoran militia. Material possessions had never been important to her, nor had she ever thought of herself as sentimental. Only now, as she considered the possibility that she was mere hours from the end of not only her own life but the end of everything she had ever known or imagined, she wondered whether it might be a sad commentary that her whole life literally fit into a single duffel with room left to spare.

Her reverie melted away as a man's voice issued from a speaker on the forward console. "Sleipnir, *this is* Enterprise *flight ops. Stand by to detach.*"

The pilot opened a reply channel. "Acknowledged, *Enterprise. Sleipnir* is good to go."

Kira took note of the woman's accent. It was one she had heard only once before, in her native universe, in the starport city of Port Shangri-La on Cestus III.

The *Enterprise*'s docking clamps released *Sleipnir* with a jolt Kira felt through the small vessel's spaceframe. A moment later, she heard the same voice from the *Enterprise* say over the comm, "Sleipnir, *you have cleared moorings. Your lane is open, and you are free to navigate.*"

"Thank you, *Enterprise. Sleipnir* out."

The pilot keyed commands into the helm and adjusted the transport's orientation, bringing the glorious blue orb of Deneva into view through the forward canopy. The long slender mass of the *Enterprise* loomed above the *Sleipnir*, and Kira felt a pang of nostalgia mixed with fear and sadness as she watched *Defiant* disconnect from *Enterprise* and ease itself away from the jaunt-ship using navigational thrusters.

Defiant looked like a blocky, ungainly ship, but she was fast, nimble, even graceful. There was an elegance to her. She and the rest of her class had been conceived as gunships, but they had proved to be so much greater than the sum of their parts.

Just like any of us, Kira mused, feeling suddenly maudlin.

Only as she palmed a tear from her cheek did Kira realize she had drawn the attention of Ambassador Spock. His rasping voice was low and full of concern. "Are you all right, Vedek?"

Kira smiled, knowing the only politic response was to lie. "I'm fine, Your Excellency. It's just been a very long week."

"Indeed, it has. For all of us." His expression was enigmatic, but something in his eyes, or perhaps some subtle inflection of his tone, suggested to Kira that he understood her current distress. However, rather than press her further, he resumed facing forward and left her to contend with her emotions, free of an audience.

Outside, *Enterprise* and *Defiant* diverged, each with its own mission to pursue. After a brief bit of routine comm chatter, *Enterprise* spawned a new wormhole and leaped through it in a burst of light. Even before the flash had faded, the wormhole snapped shut and vanished.

Seconds later *Defiant*'s warp nacelles glowed brightly—and then it, too, disappeared in a prismatic burst, speeding at high warp toward Deneva's sun for its jump backward in time, into a parallel universe.

At the transport's helm, the pilot muted an incoming comm. She looked back at Saavik. "Director, Deneva Control has given us clearance to approach."

"Thank you, Miranda. Assume standard orbit, and inform the Parliament that Ambassador Spock and I intend to beam down immediately."

"Yes, Director."

Unsure what Saavik and Spock's plans meant for her, Kira leaned forward to whisper to the old Vulcan woman. "Director? Am I also beaming down?"

"No. You'll stay here on the *Sleipnir*, with Lieutenant Kadohata. Another starship is on its way to pick you up and take you to the B'hava'el system."

"Why do I need another ship? Can't this transport take me?"

"It is capable of doing so. However, should Ambassador Spock and I need to make a swift departure from Deneva, we might need this vessel. Consequently, I have arranged for another ship to take you to the Bajoran wormhole. One better suited to the task."

Outside the canopy, Deneva grew larger and more majestic by the second. Spock and Saavik stood and moved aft, to leave the cockpit and make their way to the transporter nook in the corridor that led to the guest quarters.

Plagued by misgivings, Kira caught Spock's eye. "Ambassador?" She paused until she had his full attention. "How can we be sure we're doing the right thing here?"

"We cannot. Sometimes, we must act despite our lack of certainty."

"Is that wise?"

Her question seemed to intrigue Spock. "If it is necessary, the question is moot."

"Are you suggesting we should proceed on faith?"

She could have sworn she caught the ghost of a smile behind the elderly diplomat's careworn features. "I would not presume to speak of faith to a member of the clergy."

Director Saavik put herself between Spock and Kira. "Forgive me, Ambassador, but we need to go." The pitch of her voice betrayed her impatience as she added, "At once."

Spock placated the director with a small nod. Then he looked at Kira.

"When the time comes, you will know what to do."

"How?"

His lips thinned into a frown, as if he found this particular truth distasteful. "Because it will be the thing you most wish *not* to do—and the only thing you *can* do." He raised his right hand in the classic Vulcan salute. "Live long and prosper, Vedek Kira Nerys."

It hurt the tendons in Kira's hand to mimic his salute, but she did it. "May you walk in the path of the Prophets, Ambassador Spock."

He nodded, lowered his hand, and followed Saavik out of the cockpit.

The door slid closed, leaving Kira alone with the pilot, who seemed to have little to no interest in small talk, which was just fine with Kira. But the abrupt and suffocating silence only served to remind Kira of her loneliness, and of the last thing the Prophets had told her before the end of the Orb vision she had shared with Sisko and Wesley Crusher:

"After you next part ways, you will never see those you love again."

As emptiness yawned within her *pagh*, she knew the prophecy had come true.

PART II

MANY POSSIBLE WORLDS

10

U.S.S. *Defiant* NX-74205—2373, Borg Timeline

Transiting the temporal fracture was unlike anything Picard knew how to describe. It was wilder than the channeled fury of a wormhole, an assault not so much on his senses as on his ability to syncretize his perceptions of the physical realm with his inner conscious awareness of himself as a mind experiencing reality.

It was nothing like the *Enterprise*-E's journey through the Borg-created temporal vortex fourteen years earlier. That trip had been unexpectedly smooth, mercifully brief, and free of turbulence. This headlong flight through a wound in spacetime was an exercise in endurance, one that haunted Picard's memory with echoes of lives he had never lived. Faces strange and familiar sprang into his mind unbidden, only to fade away like ghosts, leaving him disoriented.

If only Wesley were here. He might be able to explain this to me, provide me some kind of context. Are these other lives I might have led? Or echoes of a future that never came to be?

He pondered those questions alone at the aft end of *Defiant*'s bridge, behind the console for its master systems display. The others on the bridge were as mute as stones, absorbed in their duties or, perhaps, as lost in reverie as he had been.

Data was at the flight controls, at the forward end of the low-overhead compartment. Sisko was in the command chair. In front of the captain and to his left, Lal sat at the engineering station, while Worf's son, Alexander, monitored the ship's cloaking device. Occupying the starboard stations were Worf at tactical and K'Ehleyr at the controls for the comms. Seeing Worf and Alexander together on the bridge, Picard noticed that they wore matching baldrics— Worf's over his uniform, Alexander's over his Klingon-style tunic and robe.

Frequent creaks and groans from the ship's spaceframe had everyone on edge.

Sisko sat up a bit straighter and lifted his voice over the rumbling echoes. "Report."

Data muted an alert tone on the flight ops console. "Chroniton distortion waves are increasing in magnitude as we near the fracture's aperture."

"How long until we're out?"

"Eight seconds."

Sisko perked up at the promise of action. "Mister Rozhenko, stand by to engage cloaking device. Commander K'Ehleyr, prepare to jam all known Borg frequencies. Mister Worf—tactical status?"

"Ready."

On the main viewscreen, a fine slice opened in the whirlwind of light and shadow. It expanded swiftly as the ship sped toward it. Then *Defiant* shot out of the temporal fracture, back into normal spacetime.

Picard felt the difference at once: it was like holding one's breath underwater until the urge to exhale becomes too much to bear, and then surfacing in a rush, exhaling in a single gasp, and greedily gulping in new air—only with one's perception of the natural unity of space and time, a sensation that most people took so much for granted that they couldn't even imagine what its absence would feel like.

Data swiveled his chair to look back at Sisko. "We are free of the temporal fracture, sir."

"Thank you, Mister Soong. Keep us in Luna's shadow for a moment. Mister Rozhenko, engage the cloaking device."

Picard realized only after Sisko had said its name that he was looking at the far side of Earth's moon. Rather than recognize its geography, he had failed to identify it at first because all of the cities whose configurations he knew so well were absent. Unlike the Luna beneath which he had lived as a youth, this one was unpopulated. No cities. No bases. Not a single automated observatory. It was just a dead gray orb, an airless rock.

The bridge's already subdued illumination turned crimson as the cloaking device rendered the ship invisible to sensors and the naked eye.

Alexander said, "Cloaking device engaged, Captain."

Sisko folded his hands above his lap, a pose that suggested patient consideration. "Comms: Any chatter on Borg frequencies?"

K'Ehleyr reviewed the readouts at her station. "Some from a trio of Borg cubes on the edge of the system. Nothing about us."

"Very well. Helm, bring us around Luna, quarter impulse. Tactical, look sharp."

It was a slow maneuver, a careful one. Picard respected Sisko's exercise of caution. *In his position, I would likely do the same.*

As *Defiant* edged its way around the Moon, Picard told himself he would be ready for whatever came next.

He was wrong.

As Luna's curve passed from the viewscreen to reveal Earth, Picard felt a cold chill down his spine. In place of the lush blue world he thought of as home, there loomed a dark sphere aglow with vast webs of green light; an Earth long ago assimilated by the Borg Collective. This, Picard realized, was a manifestation of all his darkest fears. Not just the specter of his own death, but the prospect of something greater and more tragic. The loss of humanity's shared identity, its collective heritage, was a crueler fate than mere extinction. To have every trace of human civilization wiped away—art, literature, music, history, and so much more—just to appease an oppressive force whose appetite for domination could never be satisfied, was an affront to every principle Picard held dear, and a loss beyond measure. An evil without compare.

Too late he realized the worst was yet to come. Even from 384,000 kilometers away, he heard the evil whispering of the Collective inside his head, as intimate and invasive as it had been the day he was first assimilated, more than twenty years earlier.

Panic swelled inside Picard, but he forced his face into a blank mask to hide his distress. He fought to shut the Borg out, but he failed. There were billions of them on Earth, and he could sense them all. He was as aware of their existence as he was of his own.

How can this be? The Caeliar purged me of Borg nanites years ago. I'm free of their accursed enhancements—so why do I still hear them?

"Helm," Sisko said, his manner cool and deliberate, "continue on this heading for Earth. Quarter impulse. Comms, stay alert for any sign that we've been spotted."

His order drew a look of alarm from Alexander. "Can the Borg see through our cloak?"

The captain shook his head. "I have no idea. But I learned a long time ago to *never* underestimate the Borg."

The console in front of Picard lit up with reports from the ship's sensors. He made a fast review of the flood of new intel, parsing some of it only as he spoke. "Captain, we're picking up a major temporal distortion in orbit above Earth." He double-checked the readouts. "It's the temporal vortex created by the Borg fourteen years ago—the one through which we followed their time sphere to the twenty-first century."

"On-screen, please." Sisko waited while Picard relayed the ship's live sensor feeds to the main viewscreen. At first the distortion appeared as little more than a smudge above the planet's night side. "Magnify, please."

Picard keyed in the adjustment. "Full magnification."

The temporal distortion filled the viewscreen. It resembled a tunnel of vapor in orbit of the Borg-infested Earth, and trapped inside it was the *Starship Enterprise* NCC-1701-E.

It filled Picard with longing and regret to look upon the ship that had been his home for the last fifteen years. Having had his command so brusquely ripped away by a man he still thought of as a surrogate son had left him filled with rage and sadness. Riker's betrayal stung Picard like the bite of a serpent's tooth, and the loss of his ship had left him feeling incomplete. Hollow. Old.

Now he looked upon *Enterprise* once more, this time with wiser, sadder eyes—and knew that for the sake of his mission, as well as history and all of time itself, he had to let her go.

I've had my time in the sun. Strutted my hour upon the stage. Now calls the curtain.

New readouts crossed his panel. "The *Enterprise* is entering the temporal rift to 2063."

All eyes were on the main viewscreen as Sisko asked, "How long before she returns, triggering the original disruption event?"

Data looked back at Sisko. "In subjective time, our mission to 2063 lasted twenty-five hours, forty-eight minutes, and nine seconds. However, because of temporal dilation inside the Borg's time vortex, the *Enterprise* will return to *this* juncture in nine hours and seven minutes."

"All right," Sisko said. "That gives us very little time to find our target before—"

Picard cut in, "I'm reading a power surge on the west coast of North America." A blinding beam of emerald light shot up from Earth's surface, into the sickly green temporal vortex still swirling in orbit. "It's a high-energy chroniton beam. It's holding the vortex open."

Data checked his console's readouts. "Its properties are consistent with those of the beam I detected using Memory Omega's quantum observation frame. I calculate a ninety-nine-point-nine-nine-eight percent probability that this is the cause of the original disruption event that produced our First Splinter timeline."

"Good enough for me," Sisko said. "Captain Picard, do we have a lock on the origin point of that beam?"

"Affirmative. It's being projected from the San Francisco area. Pinpointing its coordinates now." He waited for the sensor image to update. "Its precise point of origin is on the north side of Golden Gate, east of the bridge."

The other Starfleet officers on the bridge all looked up from their stations, then at Picard. It was Worf who put their collective shock into words. "East of the bridge? But that would be—"

"Yes, Mister Worf." Picard sighed at the dark irony of his discovery. "The precise location . . . of Starfleet Command."

Alexander quipped, "Perhaps the Borg have a sense of humor after all."

Sisko showed no sign of being amused. "Helm, keep this heading and steady as she goes. We can't risk dropping the cloak to use the transporter, so we'll keep it engaged and land as close to the target as seems safe."

"Aye, sir." Data adjusted *Defiant*'s heading, pointing it toward the source of the intensely bright green beam. "Three minutes to target."

"Acknowledged. Captain Picard: please tell Doctors Bashir and Crusher they'll be joining the away team once we reach the surface."

Picard relayed Sisko's order to sickbay via the ship's internal comnet, while an anxious silence settled over the bridge. He imagined the others

116 DAVID MACK

felt the same trepidation he did as they cruised toward an Earth that was no longer their home but an alien, hostile world.

As the dark sphere of the Borg's Earth swelled to fill the viewscreen, Picard couldn't help but wonder what they would find on the surface.

Will we even recognize San Francisco? What if—

Alerts flashed on his panel, and simultaneously on Alexander's and Worf's consoles. They all scrambled to identify the cause. "Elevated tachyon levels caused by the temporal-disruption beam," Picard said, parsing the readouts. "They're disrupting our cloaking field."

La Forge's voice snapped from the overhead comm, *"Bridge, what the hell's going on up there? We're getting tachyon surges in the cloaking device!"*

The bridge team exchanged fearful looks. Alexander spun his chair toward Sisko. "Captain? Do you think—"

"—the Borg can see us?" Before Sisko could answer the question he'd finished, the first barrage of radiant plasma from the surface shot past *Defiant*, grazing its cloak and rocking the tiny vessel stem to stern. "We've been spotted! Drop the cloak, raise shields! Helm, continue approach, evasive pattern Delta!"

Worf replied, "Shields are up!"

At the aft console, Picard found the source of their peril. "We're being targeted by a particle cannon on the surface. Sending coordinates to tactical!"

Worf fed Picard's sensor data to the ship's tactical AI. "Target locked!"

Sisko bellowed, "Hold fire!"

Worf sounded betrayed. "Sir! We can disable that cannon with *one* shot!"

"And confirm our status to the Borg as armed and hostile, Mister Worf. Do that, and we'll have those three Borg cubes on top of us in minutes! Helm, continue evasive maneuvers."

Another fusillade of blazing plasma streaked up from the planet.

Data's hands were a blur at the helm, but no matter what heading he chose, the gauntlet of plasma bursts remained on-target for *Defiant*.

Sisko called out, "All power to shields!"

The viewscreen flared white as a particle beam struck—

A deafening crash of impact, then everything went black. A crush of acute deceleration pinned Picard to his console while the inertial dampers struggled to reset from overload.

Sparks rained from overloaded EPS conduits, bounding off personnel clinging to their stations or sprawled on the deck. The overheated-chemical stench of fried ODN cables and melted circuitry wafted through the compartment on thick plumes of smoke. Picard searched for signs of life, movement, functionality. All he found were consoles and companels stuttering on and off, their adaptive interfaces distorted and confused.

After a few seconds, dull reddish emergency lighting snapped on, from fixtures under the duty consoles and a few at the foot of the bridge's bulkheads. The illumination was faint but enough for Picard to see that everyone else was alive, if worse for wear.

Static and digital noise spat from the overhead speaker. Straining to hear, Picard could tell that it was La Forge's voice, but he couldn't make out what he was saying.

Sisko pushed himself up off the deck and all but threw himself back into his command chair. "Stations! I need damage reports, now."

Picard checked his malfunctioning console, which was operational enough to confirm what he already suspected. "Internal comms are down."

"We have a text-only backup hard line to engineering. Subrelay Gamma, panel two."

As Picard sought the emergency link to the ship's main engineering deck, Sisko continued belting out orders. "Mister Soong, try to relay backup visual sensors to the main viewscreen. Mister Worf, weapons check."

Worf was the first to answer. "Targeting systems offline. Shields weak, but holding."

At the front of the compartment, the viewscreen stuttered back to life—to show the planet's surface spinning and tumbling chaotically in and out of frame as a fiery nimbus of friction-heated air took shape around *Defiant*.

Picard saw the first written reply from engineering on his console. "Captain? I have La Forge on the backup channel. He reports impulse engines are offline."

Sisko's eyes were fixed upon the viewscreen's dizzying spectacle. "How long to fix?"

Picard sent Sisko's query, then read out La Forge's answer. "Ten minutes."

"Mister Soong—can you land us with navigational thrusters alone?"

Data cocked his head, his manner dubious. "In a manner of speaking."

"Meaning what?"

"Do you consider a crash landing a landing, *per se*?"

Sisko tensed, clearly not encouraged by Data's liberal definition of the word *landing*.

"Everyone, brace for impact." He kept his eyes on the cold, hard ground rushing up to meet his ship. "Mister Worf, route all remaining power to the shields. And Picard?" He turned aft and looked Picard in the eye, his demeanor as grave as death itself. "Tell La Forge we need impulse power in *two* minutes, or we're all dead."

11

———

C.S.S. *Enterprise*

The jaunt-ship's crew made the task of moving from one universe to another look easy—maybe even deceptively so, in Wesley Crusher's opinion. Their initial calculations had taken only a matter of minutes, followed by a brief spinning up of *Enterprise*'s jaunt system—in essence, a singularity-driven artificial-wormhole generator. By the time Wesley and Luc Picard had reached the ship's bridge, his offer to help them plot the crossing had become moot. The helm officer had said "Ready," Luc had ordered "Execute," and then the ship jumped.

An eyeblink later, the *Enterprise* cruised smoothly from the mouth of its Einstein-Rosen bridge, which had linked its alternate universe to the one that Wesley called home.

It took him some effort to conceal his surprise. *They plotted that crossing almost as quickly as I could have with the Omnichron.*

The helm officer, a Vulcan woman named Tolaris, checked the ship's coordinates with cool efficiency. "Jump to counterpart dimension complete. All systems nominal, Captain."

"Thank you, Lieutenant." Luc faced the empty chair on his right, quickly masked his disappointment at the absence of his first officer, and then looked the other way, toward Troi at the security console. "Commander, raise the cloak and take us to yellow alert. Monitor all long-range sensors for signs we've been detected."

"Aye, sir." Troi turned away and delegated tasks to her subordinates.

Being back in his home universe made Wesley feel anxious in a way it hadn't when he had been a younger man. He had spent years, subjectively speaking, shifting through various parallel timelines and alternate dimensions, fleeing attacks and ambushes by the Devidians.

Until his relatively peaceful recent sojourn in the infamous alternate universe, however, he had never considered the possibility that there might be someplace where the Devidians and their pet horrors could not follow him.

We weren't there very long, but I didn't sense their presence at all in that dimension. Is it possible they're no longer hunting me?

He looked at the temporal discriminator on his wrist.

Maybe this thing deserves some of the credit. I doubt it would do any good against an avatar's death-touch or a Naga's disruption field, but maybe the same thing that shields me from TMPD makes it harder for the Devidians to find me?

It was a reasonable hypothesis. But a darker possibility gnawed at him.

What if the Devidians backed off because they're so close to their end-game that they don't think they need to hunt me anymore? What if they've gone into hiding in order to prevent me *from tracking* them *back to their hidden base?*

Whatever was the truth, his mission remained the same.

He made his way to the center of the bridge and stood beside Luc's chair. "Captain? How long until we can start the search?"

"As soon as you give us a target, we'll plot the jump. After that, the rest is up to you." Luc trained a skeptical eye on Wesley. "How long will each investigation take?"

"Normally, I'd say hours. But we don't have hours, so I'll say, 'as little time as possible.' " He gestured at K'Ehleyr's empty seat. "May I?"

The captain nodded and motioned for Wesley to sit. "Of course."

Wesley pivoted into the chair and leaned toward Luc. "The first thing we need to do is narrow the search."

He entered search parameters into the command console next to his borrowed seat. "There are roughly ten million black holes in the Milky Way. Fortunately, the vast majority are of the stellar-mass variety, between four and sixteen solar masses. We can rule those out because they don't deform spacetime enough to enable the Devidians to create an extratemporal breach." Satisfied at his first round of winnowing, he continued. "We can also rule out the supermassive black hole Sagittarius A-star at the center of the galaxy. Even the Devidians can't tame that beast. So we're looking for an intermediate-mass black hole."

Wesley perused the remaining targets. "I'd expect the Devidians would have a way to protect their stronghold from the chaos they've unleashed on the rest of the galaxy, so any IMBH showing signs of accelerated evaporation or other temporal abnormality is not a candidate."

He turned the small console toward Luc. "That leaves seven for us to scout." He pointed to the one named, ominously enough, Abaddon. "This one's the closest."

The captain tapped at the console and called up more details about the target. "Over three hundred thousand solar masses. With a huge accretion disk, spun up into a superheated fury." He looked wary. "How close do we need to get for you to do your work?"

"A lot closer than we'll like."

"I'll ask Mister Barclay to reinforce the transphasic shields." Creases on Luc's brow deepened as he scrutinized the details on the screen. "Mister Crusher? This notation on the star chart you gave us—what does it signify?"

Wesley frowned. He knew that Luc and the rest of this ship's crew deserved the truth, especially since their survival would depend upon being prepared for what was coming, but he also knew that the captain was not going to be happy about this news. "That's Starbase April, a designated rendezvous point for Starfleet in the event of a quadrant-level catastrophe."

"You mean such as the disaster unfolding right now?"

"Pretty much, yeah."

Luc shook his head, both worried and annoyed. "How many ships might be there?"

Wesley shrugged. "Dozens? A hundred? There's no way to know."

"Not until it's too late." With a tap and a sweep of his hand, Luc relayed the screen's information to Troi's tactical console. "Deanna. How long will it take a Starfleet battle group to get from Starbase April to the Abaddon singularity?"

She quickly plugged in the variables. "Less than ninety minutes."

That sounded overly pessimistic to Wesley. "Assuming they detect us, you mean."

"Raising shields to investigate the accretion disks will mean disengaging the cloak." The captain aimed a dark look Wesley's way. "But I assure you, Mister Crusher, Starfleet has *already* detected us, the moment we crossed the dimensional barrier. And every time we use the jaunt drive in space they control, they'll be alerted to our position *again*. So I suggest you run your tests at Abaddon with all due haste."

Wesley pulled his hand over the front of his beard, exorcising some of his mounting stress with the self-soothing gesture. "All right, I'll do my best. But if you want faster results, we'll need to get as close as we can to the event horizon. And that's gonna be a rough ride around goliath-sized singularities like these."

"The *Enterprise* can take it," Luc said, sounding to Wesley very much like the Captain Picard he had known most of his life. "But if I could ask a measure of fair warning? How many of these black holes are likely to take us into hostile territory?"

Wesley faced the console so he could see the names. "Kali 531 is deep inside the Romulan Star Empire. Orcus 784 is in unclaimed space between the Federation and the Klingon Empire. Yama is less than half a light-year from a natural transwarp current in the Carina Arm, twelve-point-eight light-years from the galaxy's core."

His report seemed to confuse Luc. "The latter two seem remote enough. What kind of resistance should we expect there?"

"Maybe none. But if Starfleet figures out what we're doing, they might anticipate our targets. If that happens, both Orcus and Yama are close enough for them to attack."

The captain nodded. "I see now." He looked up, his expression that of a man who would rather do anything than fight another battle. "But are they really likely to guess our mission?"

Wesley shook his head, and almost had to laugh. "Captain, this is *Starfleet* we're talking about. I'll be truly surprised if they *don't*."

U.S.S. *Titan* NCC-80102

Sleep was impossible. So was sitting still. Riker teetered on the edge of mania as he paced in *Titan's* ready room, away from the judgmental stares of the bridge crew.

They don't understand. How can they? There's no time to explain. No time to bargain. I'll only get one chance at this, and maybe not even that.

Passing his desk, he scooped up his padd and skimmed through the latest reports from the search for *Defiant*. It had been missing in action for over thirty-six hours. He imagined the little ship and its crew of fugitives evading detection, skirting the edges of civilized space, running out the clock on the death of spacetime.

Even with a cloaking device, they shouldn't be this damned hard to find! Where the hell could they be?

None of the reports on the padd offered new leads. He had put out calls to friend and foe alike, to rivals and galactic recluses, in the hope that someone, anyone, had spotted *Defiant*, or maybe granted it a safe harbor. He'd offered outlandish bribes to the Orions and the Ferengi—it wasn't as if anyone in this universe would live long enough to collect that debt—but neither of the notoriously avaricious cultures had tried to claim the reward.

Likewise, he'd ordered Ssura to promise generous bounties to anyone who offered information that led to the capture of *Defiant*. That offer had gone out to the Klingon Empire, the Romulan Star Empire, the Gorn, and anyone else willing to listen. But nine hours later, there were no takers. Not even scam artists trying to make a quick credit.

Looking out of his ready room's viewport, he understood why. The countless points of fire that filled the universe were, one by one, going out.

All the laws of time and nature had gone haywire.

Cause and effect were reversing themselves in some places; entropy was running amok in others. Planets were reversing their rotations without warning and then, as if gravity itself had abandoned them, they flew apart, not so much exploding as being hurled apart, atom by atom, repelled from one another at the speed of light.

Reality is committing seppuku, *and my only chance of doing anything about it lies in finding that damned ship!*

He scrolled through long-range sensor reports. Fleet activity logs. Stellar observatory records. There had to be *something*. Anything. He ran a search for chroniton particle surges—maybe the Orb of Time wasn't as dead as the vedeks of Bajor insisted it must be, or perhaps Wesley, the Traveler, was disrupting time and space in that peculiar way of his.

There had to be *something*.

He poked and prodded at the data, but it kept adding up to nothing.

He was about to pitch the padd against the bulkhead in a fit of rage when a signal chimed from the overhead speaker, followed by Commander Sarai's voice: *"Admiral? Commander Pazlar has something."*

"On my way!" He lobbed the padd onto his desk and headed for the door.

He stepped onto the bridge and was met by the muted ambience of feedback tones and low chatter. He walked at a quick step, heading toward Pazlar at the aft science station.

Commander Sarai left the command chair and fell into step beside Riker. "Sir, still no contact with any of Starfleet's auxiliary command centers, or any word on whether any member of the executive chain of succession survived the loss of Earth."

"In other words, I'm still in command of the fleet."

"Yes, sir."

"Good." They arrived at Pazlar's station and flanked the Elaysian woman with their shoulders against the bulkhead. "Pazlar? Sarai says you have a lead?"

Pazlar shifted awkwardly. Her discomfort reminded Riker that the science officer disliked being crowded because of her full-body mechanical exoskeleton, which, as a native of a low-gravity world, she needed in order to function in an environment with standard Earth gravity. He backed up a bit, giving her some room. "Sorry."

"Thank you, sir." She pointed at one of her console's readouts. "A few minutes ago, the Mainzer FTL Observatory picked up some off-the-chart energy readings and gravimetric distortions just one sector away from Starbase April, near the intermediate-mass black hole known as Abaddon." For comparison, she pulled up another set of sensor readings—and at a glance, the profiles appeared nearly identical. "These readings were taken just over four years ago, originating in the Tirana system. Starfleet Intelligence says these were made by something called a jaunt drive. Basically, a singularity-powered artificial-wormhole generator."

Memories teased Riker from the depths of his consciousness. Fuzzy, half forgotten, never really his to begin with, but slowly becoming his with time. They came into focus as he stared at the intel on Pazlar's display. *The ship that made this . . . isn't from our universe.*

Sarai's manner turned apologetic. "I'm sorry, Admiral. I know you want leads to *Defiant*, and this clearly isn't that. Should we continue to monitor—"

"Alert the fleet," Riker said, before he knew why he was saying it.

His order had surprised Sarai. "And tell them what, sir?"

A sensation like déjà vu overcame Riker. All of this seemed strangely familiar to him, as if he had already fought this battle. He stared at the display and struggled to focus.

Why is a ship from the alternate universe coming here now? And why so close to a black hole that big? What are they—

A memory of another life, another place, gave him the answer.

They're looking for the Devidians' base. Which means maybe there's still a chance. A way to stop them without sacrificing this reality and everyone in it.

His doubts fell away, and he felt flush with righteous strength.

"Commander, I want every Starfleet vessel in that sector to converge on Abaddon, right now. Whatever ship they find there, I want its crew captured alive. Something tells me their arrival so soon after *Defiant's* disappearing act is no coincidence." He left the science station and strode to the command chair. Planting himself upon it, he confronted the dying cosmos on the main viewscreen. "Helm, set course for Abaddon, maximum warp. Engage!"

The crew snapped into action, crisp and professional. Seconds later, the increasingly sparse starfield on the viewscreen stretched and spun as *Titan* leaped to high warp.

Ensconced in the center of it all, Riker remained a desperate man, but now he recalled how it felt to have a glimmer of hope—and he would do anything to keep that spark alive.

Anything.

I've already lost everything once. Not again. Never again.

C.S.S. *Enterprise*

"Transphasic shields holding, Captain, but the emitters are taking a beating."

Luc acknowledged the report from operations officer Pog with a distracted nod. "Maintain power levels. If they start to fall, alert me at once."

"Aye, sir."

So far all had gone to plan, but Luc remained on edge. This was not his universe, no matter how similar it might appear. He was keenly aware that he was a pilgrim in a hostile land, an interloper tempting fate. *It would pay to be cautious here.*

His crew and Wesley Crusher had begun working on their detailed sensor analysis of the black hole's event horizon as soon as *Enterprise* jumped into the system. As promised, Abaddon had proved to be a true terror of nature: a singularity of greater than three hundred thousand solar masses, it sported an accretion disk nearly three hundred million kilometers in diameter.

Up close, the accretion disk resembled an endless sea of fire. Condensed gas and planetary debris, hyperaccelerated into a superheated slurry, blazed as brightly as a star. At its core sat a lightless sphere of annihilation encircled in bent starshine.

And riding the wild edge between its crushing grip and its event horizon was the *Enterprise*, racing at nearly a quarter of the speed of light, fighting to resist the incredible gravity of the intermediate-mass black hole.

Luc left his chair, too wound up to remain still. He headed aft toward the science stations, where Lieutenant Kell Perim, the ship's senior science officer, worked with Wesley Crusher to search for . . . well, on that point, Luc was not entirely clear.

He had been placed into command of this vessel years earlier by Memory Omega not because he was in any way qualified to command a capital starship, but because he had achieved a measure of notoriety that would enable him to act as a symbol to inspire others. During his first few years in command of *Enterprise*, Luc had relied on the expertise of his first officer, Commander K'Ehleyr, to make him look competent and keep the ship running.

Since then he had grown more comfortable and sure-footed in his role, but now, without K'Ehleyr at his side, he felt her absence most keenly.

She could explain technical jargon better than anyone. If only she were here.

Now he would need to trust Lieutenant Perim to fulfill that role. He approached Wesley and the thirtyish Trill woman carefully, making sure they saw his approach. He didn't want them to feel ambushed. When he was close enough, he spoke to them in a quiet voice.

"Lieutenant. Mister Crusher. Have you found anything?"

A look from Crusher signaled Perim that he intended to let her answer. She faced Luc. "Not yet, sir. But we need to make at least a few more orbits of Abaddon before we'll have enough sensor data to run exclusionary chronospectrograms for signs of temporal anomalies."

Luc acted as if all that had made any sense to him. "I see." He cast a skeptical look at Wesley. "Are you sure you know what you're looking for?"

The tall, bearded Traveler smiled. "Quite sure, Captain."

"Very well, then. Continue." He walked away, feigning an urgent need to attend to some other vital aspect of ship's business that would, conveniently, take him away from them and back to his command chair.

He arrived at his customary seat to find it occupied.

His counterpart's son, René, looked up at him. "I guess you want the chair."

"You guess correctly."

The young man stood and stepped aside. Lurking beside the command chair, René was a portrait in gangly limbs, imbalanced hormones, and simmering resentment. He eyed Luc, his mien doubtful. "So, what am I supposed to call you? Uncle?"

"*Captain* will suffice." Luc pulled his command panel closer to his chair and called up a flight ops report so he could estimate how much longer they would be orbiting Abaddon. Then he noticed the lad was still idling beside his chair. "Do you need something?"

René shrugged. "Something to *do*, maybe."

Luc was too busy to entertain a fool's delusions of adequacy. "Unless you possess advanced training no one's told me about, I doubt you'll be of any use on my bridge."

René's eyes narrowed in anger. "Well, I'm not just gonna sit in my quarters."

Challenged, Luc took René's measure. "You feel as if you want to fight, but you've nowhere to aim the fury that burns inside you. . . . Sound familiar?"

René gave a grudging nod.

All at once, Luc felt as if he understood the lad. "I remember that feeling well. Growing up, rage was all I knew. It was my constant companion."

The young man leaned in, his curiosity engaged. "What did you do?"

"I learned to channel it. Harness it. Absent that control, our passions enslave us; yoked to our better natures, they become a source of strength, an inspiration."

To Luc's surprise, René regarded Wesley Crusher with sadness. "And what do I do with the knowledge that I'm a substitute—and a disappointing one at that?"

He had spoken to a pain Luc remembered all too well from his own childhood. Luc stood and led the teen across the bridge, farther from his half brother, and lowered his voice in the interest of discretion. "I had an older brother when I was young. His name was Robert. He was . . . my father's favorite. To save himself and Robert, my father sold me into slavery, to a Cardassian named Gul Madred. As it happened, Madred had children of his own, and *their* accomplishments were all *I* ever heard about." He searched the youth's face for any warning signs of something darker hiding behind his words. "Have your parents ever hurt you?"

"No." René looked almost ashamed. "But I *always* hear Mom talking about Wesley when she thinks I'm not listening, or in the other room. She's always wondering where he is, what he's doing, when she'll see him again. He's all she cares about."

"I don't believe that." Luc did his best to sound reassuring. "I've never met a mother who didn't love *all* her children."

René cocked an eyebrow. "All of them *equally*?"

Such a knowing question from so young a soul.

"Love is not so simple, René. It has no unit of measurement. It's possible to love different things, or different ideas, or different *people*, to the same degree but . . . in different ways."

Apparently unpersuaded, René curled his mouth in disdain. "Sounds like a lot of words just to say my mom loves him more than me." He sighed and looked away. "Which explains why she dumped me here with you and him: to get rid of me."

How am I to dissuade him from such self-destructive petulance?

"René, I won't pretend to know your family's situation. But if your father and I have anything in common beyond the superficial details of our names and appearance, I can assure you that your parents did not 'dump' you out of spite or a dearth of affection. If anything—"

Alert signals chimed from Troi's tactical console. She muted them quickly, checked her panel, and then looked toward Luc. "Captain, long-range sensors show an incoming Starfleet battle group, en route from Starbase April at warp nine-point-eight."

"ETA?"

"Sixty-three minutes."

"*Merde.*" Luc returned to his chair, leaving René behind without a thought. "Mister Crusher, Lieutenant Perim, how long until you finish your scans of the event horizon?"

The pair conferred quickly sotto voce, and then Perim answered, "Seventy-five minutes."

It was not the number Luc had hoped for. He steeled himself for battle. "Find a way to hasten your results, Lieutenant. Or else those extra twelve minutes might prove to be our last."

12

Galactic Commonwealth Parliament, Deneva—Mirror Universe

Spock had accompanied Director Saavik to the Commonwealth Parliament expecting to be welcomed by a solemn body of elected officials gathered in serious deliberation.

Instead he found a tableau of mayhem, as if one of the nightmarish murals of Earth-born painter Hieronymus Bosch had sprung hideously to life. Hundreds of people shouted over one another with no one listening and no one willing to hear any voice but their own.

Projected above them were holographic images of panic and destruction. Worlds being torn apart by invisible forces; desperate calls for help interrupted midsentence, leaving only static followed by silence and emptiness; star charts that diminished as points of light vanished one after another, taking countless billions of lives with them into oblivion.

Larger than life overhead, a woman's face, her eyes bloodshot from crying, shrieked for aid—until she dissolved into a spreading cloud of fading energy, as if the strong and weak subatomic forces that had bound her together, along with everything else in the universe, had simply given up.

As each vision of existential annihilation faded away, another took its place.

Spock stood, transfixed by the titanic holograms.

Never did I expect to witness the end of all existence within my own lifetime. Confronted with it now, I find it almost too horrific to believe—even though I know it to be true. He could not help but reflect upon events from more than a century earlier—the last time he had ever seen his foster sister. *I wonder if this was how Michael felt while she was fighting to save all life in the galaxy from the first omnicidal artificial superintelligence known as Control.*

Saavik took his arm, breaking Armageddon's spell over him. "This way, Ambassador."

She led him off the floor of the Parliament's main hall, back the way they had come in. A pair of armed security officers, who had been tasked with protecting him and Saavik, met them and led them down a curved passageway, and then into a turbolift.

Inside the lift car, Saavik leaned close to Spock and said in Vulcan, "I was not aware the situation had grown so dire."

Spock replied in their native tongue, "I did warn you: as my universe falls, yours will fall with it. But yes, our time is running out sooner than I had expected."

The doors opened. The two guards left the car first, confirmed the corridor outside was clear, and motioned for Spock and Saavik to step out.

As they followed the guards down a drab institutional-looking hallway, Saavik said to Spock, again in Vulcan, "We've had only a few years to develop the command-and-control hierarchy for the Commonwealth. I am concerned this crisis might be too much for it to handle."

"If it is, we will know soon enough. For now, let us remain hopeful."

The curve in the passageway became more acute, signaling that they had reached one of the ends of the oval-shaped Parliament hall. On the inner edge of the curve's apex was a pair of doors. The guards reached them first and entered a series of signals and codes that Spock could neither see nor hear. As he and Saavik arrived, the doors opened ahead of them, swinging inward toward the spacious office on the other side. They entered, and the guards stayed outside.

The room was long and wedge shaped, narrowing as one moved deeper inside. At the far end the wall was one long window that looked down upon the Parliament hall.

A tall, fair-skinned balding human man with a squarish jaw stood at the window, behind a large plain desk. He looked down upon the unfolding chaos with his hands folded behind his back, his head bowed—though whether in shame or from fatigue, Spock could not tell at first.

As he and Saavik moved closer, however, Spock saw the strain in the man's clenched jaw and the tensed muscles of his shoulders and neck. He looked as if he were bearing an impossible weight upon his back— one that Spock recognized as the terrible burden of responsibility.

They halted in front of the desk. Saavik said, "Please forgive our intrusion, Mister Prime Minister."

He faced them. Lines of worry creased his forehead, and the hair on his balding pate had gone white. "Director Saavik." When he looked at Spock, he froze, and his eyes widened.

After a moment, he recovered his composure. "Forgive me, Mister Ambassador. I was briefed regarding your visit, but it's still . . . *unnerving* to find myself face-to-face with the counterpart of the man who changed the political trajectory of local space. The inspiration for the revolution himself! It's a bit much to process all at once."

"Understandable, Prime Minister Eddington."

Eddington gestured toward the guest chairs in front of his desk. "Please, sit." He took to his own chair while Saavik and Spock settled into theirs. "What do you need, Director?"

She volleyed the question to Spock with a sidelong look. He replied to Eddington, "We need your fleet of jaunt-ships to aid our search for those responsible for this cosmic holocaust."

"Our jaunt-ships?" Eddington looked stunned. "They're the only vessels we have that are fast enough to respond to all the distress signals we're receiving."

Saavik's manner was hard and calculating. "To what benefit, Prime Minister? The jaunt-ships are fast, but none has the capacity to evacuate an entire planet. Their speed is irrelevant when they are unable to address the tragedies to which they race."

"So you'd have us give up the only assets we have?"

Spock folded his hands and leaned forward. "Permit us to suggest, sir, that they would be of greater help in my native dimension, rooting out the authors of this crisis."

Eddington's face reddened. "But our people—!"

"Are already lost," Saavik interrupted. "As are Spock's. I sent his people's report ahead. Did you read it?"

Her question dispirited Eddington. "I did." He frowned and slumped a bit lower, as if the ponderous weight upon his shoulders had grown that much heavier.

Spock stepped into the rhetorical breach. "Then you know that our timeline is unstable, and therefore a threat to the timestream. The only question that confronts us now is whether we persist in a futile effort to prolong the inevitable—or leverage the value of our own self-sacrifice to save countless other iterations of spacetime."

Eddington shook his head in what seemed an expression of denial and desperation. "The other ministers will *never* consent to release the jaunt-ships. In the last two hours we've lost Earth, Kaminar, Bolarus, and a dozen other worlds. Our people want their best ships *here*, defending *them*."

Director Saavik seemed sympathetic. "We understand. But we need you to be the voice of reason. We need you to persuade them to release the fleet."

"I don't think I can." He cast a pitch-black look at Saavik. "But why the pretense, Director? We both know Memory Omega loaned those ships to the Commonwealth after the Great Revolution. You could take them back any time you want. So why don't you?"

Saavik regarded Eddington like a teacher considering a bright pupil who had just made an embarrassing error. "Because the jaunt-ships were not *loaned* to the Commonwealth, Michael, they were *given*. They are no longer Memory Omega's to command. We will not violate our pledge to respect and uphold the sovereignty of the Commonwealth by usurping control of its military assets."

Eddington looked ashamed. "Forgive me, Director. I didn't mean to impugn your integrity, or that of Memory Omega." He stood and turned to look out the window, down at the continuing hysteria on the Parliament floor. "But I just don't see a way to persuade this many frightened people to give up the most powerful defense they have, to carry out a mission I don't know how to explain, to achieve an end in which all of us die."

His dilemma seemed to flummox Saavik, but Spock answered without hesitation.

"Tell them, Mister Prime Minister, that nothing we do or fail to do at this point will prevent the imminent demise of our cosmos. The only questions that remain before us now are: Shall we cling to selfishness and die in vain? Or shall we take up the mantle of heroes, and die so that others may live? Any questions beyond those are now, I fear, entirely moot."

Eddington looked stricken. "I don't know if anyone down there is ready to hear that."

Saavik's mood turned dour. "No one ever is."

U.S.S. Defiant NX-74205—2373, Borg Timeline

Smoke and drooping tangles of ODN cable choked the corridors of *Defiant*. Main power was still offline, along with most of the overhead illumination. Debris cluttered the decks. Every step of the way from the bridge down to main engineering, Picard found it hard to keep pace with Sisko, who, despite his greater height and body mass, ducked and sidestepped with ease through the crash-inflicted obstacle course inside his ship.

Picard caught up to Sisko in front of the turbolift. "Is it working?"

Sisko tapped at the manual interface next to the lift doors. It didn't respond to his touch, not even to cough up a dysfunctional chirp of malfunction. "Looks like we're climbing down."

Again in the lead, Sisko led Picard to the compartment for the emergency gangway. Its door was already open. The two captains paused on either side of the ladder, looking down.

Beyond the first meter, all Picard saw below was darkness.

Undeterred, Sisko grabbed the top of the ladder, set his feet on the nearest rungs, and climbed down. He looked up at Picard as he descended. "Give me a few seconds' head start."

"Very good." Picard watched Sisko sink into the shadowy gangway, and then he took hold of the ladder's top section, which extended well above the deck, and eased his feet into place on the rungs below.

The climb down was not difficult, but in the near-total darkness Picard worried about the cost of a single misstep. To his relief, a faint orange glow of emergency lighting filled the deck-two gangway compartment, and some of it spilled into the gangway beneath him.

He reached deck two and stepped off the ladder to find Sisko waiting for him. "This way," the other captain said, leading Picard into the port-side corridor.

It was only a handful of long strides from there to main engineering, which had been transformed into a jungle of twisted metal fogged with noxious vapors. In the midst of the wreckage stood La Forge. He gave orders to enlisted mechanics and advice to senior engineering officers, in between answering questions and spraying bursts of chemical flame retardant onto a smoldering plasma conduit that was threatening to ignite again at any moment.

The bedraggled chief engineer looked ready to collapse by the time the captains reached him. Sisko slapped a reassuring hand against La Forge's shoulder. "How are you holding up?"

"Couldn't be better, sir."

Sisko looked around at damage in every direction. "I certainly hope that's not true. Because if we can't improve upon *this*, we're in serious trouble."

La Forge let out a tired huff of amusement. "I said *I* couldn't be better. This engine room? That's another story." He ducked under a fallen stanchion to reach inside an open bulkhead panel and rip out a capacitor that was vomiting sparks. "The good news is, once we get some antigrav lifters in here, we can put the heavy stuff back in place pretty quickly."

Sisko seemed placated. "All right. What's the bad news?"

"Everything else."

Picard gave him a look that said, *Not very helpful.* "Care to elaborate, Mister La Forge?"

The engineer pointed every which way as he delivered his damage report. "Ventral hull breaches from nose to midship. Three of four landing struts broke off when we hit the surface. Deuterium lines to the main warp reactor are broken, and the dilithium crystal articulation frame is bent. Primary comms are fragged, and power isn't reaching the backup system—we don't know why yet. Magnetic containment on the impulse reactor failed, so I had to take it offline, which means we're on battery power 'til further notice. Oh, and pretty much the entire shield emitter grid is fried, which means our only remaining defense is the ship's ablative armor."

Sisko's pained look resembled one that Picard had seen on his own face too many times over the years. It was the expression of a captain internalizing his ship's suffering. Sisko tried to hide his anxiety by filling his rich voice with confidence. "How long to get her up and running?"

"Depends. With or without the landing struts?"

"Let's say without."

La Forge looked one way and then another, appraising the ship's prognosis. "If you need her combat ready? Ten hours."

"The cosmos will be gone by then. Do better."

"I can have her warp capable in eight."

"Make it seven. And no extra points for neatness. Understood?"

"Five by five, Captain."

"Good. Carry on." Over his shoulder, Sisko added to Picard, "With me."

He led Picard out of the mangled mess of the engineering deck, back to the gangway. They climbed down again, disembarking this time on deck three. They walked quickly, heading forward. They arrived at the nose of the ship, outside the main airlock.

The inner airlock doors were open, and five people were inside, four of them attired in all-black Starfleet special-operations uniforms, the likes of which Picard hadn't seen since the Borg Invasion. Each of the four carried a phaser rifle that had been modified into a transphasic-disruption weapon using specs adapted from Wesley Crusher's custom-made armament, and rendered inconspicuous with a matte-black finish.

Added to the spec-ops uniforms were tactical vests, which provided numerous pockets filled with plasma grenades, tricorders, compact hand phasers, and spare power cells to satisfy the increased energy needs of the modified rifles.

Near the front of the group were Data and Lal. Behind them, Picard saw Doctor Bashir and Beverly Crusher, who were vetting the emergency medical kits that had been loaded into their low-profile backpacks.

Moving among the team, checking their gear and weapons, was Worf, still in his duty uniform and baldric. He noted Sisko's arrival and stepped forward, at attention. "Sir. The away team is ready, as ordered." He nodded toward a nearby cargo crate, atop which rested two folded, all-black combat uniforms, and two modified rifles. "For you and Captain Picard, sir."

"Thank you, Mister Worf. I'll take it from here."

"Sir—" Worf seemed conflicted, as if he knew that what he wanted to say would not be well received. "I wish to join the away team."

Sisko shook his head. His voice was calm but firm. "I'm sorry, Worf. I need you here. La Forge has seven hours to get *Defiant* off the ground. Until then, I need *you* to defend my ship from the Borg. Understood?"

Worf accepted his mission with pride. "Understood."

"Good. Dismissed." Sisko watched the Klingon leave the airlock and head aft, and then he turned to Picard. "Suit up."

Sisko started briefing the away team while he and Picard removed their outer layers of clothing. "Visual scans indicate we crashed somewhere near the Ridge Trail on San Bruno Mountain, south of what used to be San Francisco."

Picard added, "That puts us approximately twenty-three-point-five kilometers from our target, across hard terrain and a Borg-infested landscape."

Sisko pulled on a black tunic, and then he reached for its matching jacket. "The good news is, with main and impulse power knocked out, it's possible we dropped off the Borg's scanners before we hit the surface. They might think we were destroyed, or fell into the sea."

Picard's new combat uniform had the slightly harsh chemical odor of freshly replicated matter. He winced but ignored it as he tugged its jacket smooth against his torso. "To avoid triggering a Borg search for this ship, it's imperative we proceed with discretion. Which means avoiding both detection *and* combat, at all costs."

Crusher shot a teasing look at him. "In other words, do *not* engage?"

He smiled at her inversion of his preferred bridge command. "Exactly."

After checking the settings on his rifle, Sisko faced the group. "Keeping a low profile out there will also mean avoiding the use of tricorders and comms, unless absolutely necessary. Anything with a signal might attract the Borg—and that's a mistake we can't afford."

The group's members nodded their understanding.

Picard wanted to end the briefing on an optimistic note. "Fortunately, most of us are at least passingly familiar with the city of San Francisco. This, plus the fact that our target is shooting a blinding beam of green light into the sky, should help us find our way in the dark."

The away team reacted with mild chortles, which abated quickly.

Sisko handed the last rifle to Picard. "We have seven hours to reach the target, complete our mission, and then get off this planet and back to our universe for our showdown with the Devidians. Are we ready?" Everyone nodded in assent. "Mister Soong, take point. Doctor Bashir and I will bring up the rear. Move out."

The six of them fell into formation with Lal, Crusher, and Picard in the middle of the group, and they entered the airlock. The inner door closed behind them, and Data switched off the interior emergency lights, plunging the entryway into darkness.

Then he opened the outer door.

At first, Picard saw nothing outside but more blackness. But as he crossed the threshold and set foot on the dusty ground of San Bruno Mountain, he saw the sickly green glow of a Borg metropolis spread out as far as the eye could see, along both the peninsula and the mainland. Ugly grids of piping, catwalks, blocklike structures, and barren swaths of ground. Much of it was steeped in shadow, while the rest was awash in harsh acetylene light.

Nearly everything that had ever made San Francisco beautiful was gone, erased by the Borg's hideous, utilitarian city of metal. All of the classic architecture, the marvelous skyscrapers, the cultivated parklands . . . they had all been paved over and buried in steel.

The only remnants of the fallen city were to be found in the shapes of the street grid, the arc of an old highway cutting across the peninsula . . . and, to the north, barely visible in the night, limned by the emerald glow of the Borg's infrastructure, the Golden Gate Bridge.

Picard thought it remarkable that the Borg had left it intact. Then he realized that it must serve some function for them, perhaps offering an energy-efficient way to move materials across short or intermediate distances. *Or maybe they just like it because it's large and metallic.*

As the away team hiked northward, toward the city, Picard suspected he would find out soon enough what the Borg saw in the bridge.

Not that I'm in any hurry to—

An inhuman chorus roared through Picard's thoughts, raw and unstoppable, like an ocean wave cresting a sea wall. It was both distant and omnipresent, subtle yet overwhelming. He tried to shut it out, to pretend he was imagining it, that he couldn't really hear it, or it him, but he knew that was a lie. It was a trillion whispers in the dark, a pulse in his temples like the beating of a billion wings against a window-pane. . . .

He prayed he didn't hear the name. Told himself it had been centuries since these Borg had last heard it. He hoped that time and distance had wiped him from their shared memory.

But does the Collective ever really forget?

Lurking beneath the whispers, rustling like a predator creeping through dead leaves, the name was still there. He felt it. And the closer he got to the Borg's soul-crushing sprawl of cybernetic machinery, the more certain he became that they soon would hear it, too. And when they did, they would smash down like a tsunami upon him and the away team.

It would take just one word, one name, to seal all their fates in this hellish place.

Locutus.

S.S. *Sleipnir*—Mirror Universe

Kira had hoped that losing herself within a state of silent meditation would help her to quickly pass the time until her next transport arrived. Instead, it had served only to make her keenly aware of the tension in the *Sleipnir*'s cockpit.

The human woman at the helm—Kadohata, Saavik had called her—had kept her back to Kira since their brief exchange of words following Spock and Saavik's departure. As far as Kira could tell, the other woman had not spared her a single look, nor spoken a single word.

Yet a cold disquiet filled the small compartment. It troubled Kira, because she felt as if it existed because of her, but she was reluctant to broach the subject with Kadohata.

What if I'm wrong? What if I'm just projecting my own discomfort at being back in this universe that's tried so many times to kill me?

She concentrated on clearing her mind—only to find a tide of anxious thoughts flooding in to fill her consciousness.

Why did I let everyone leave without me? I should have asked someone to stay behind, just to watch my back. Especially since this place seems so fond of sticking knives in it.

Her faithful nature wanted to cast off doubts and suspicions, but her cynical side knew the terrible price of showing weakness—not just in this universe, but in any place, at any time. No matter how cathartic she imagined it might be to invite Kadohata to speak her mind and air any grievances she might harbor, the part of Kira that had spent so long as a leader in the Bajoran Militia and then as a senior officer on Deep Space 9 knew that one of the surest ways to inflame a conflict was to make a gesture intended to prevent it. Her whole life had been a study in the grim costs of unintended consequences and the ways that people resented good deeds.

There's no time for mistakes. I have to play this safe.

So she kept her eyes closed and her thoughts to herself.

Her reward, after what felt like the slowest two hours of her life, was a brief comm chirp from the forward console, followed by a masculine voice. *"Hey, Miranda. You there?"*

Kira returned to full wakefulness as Kadohata answered the hail. "Go ahead, Rennan."

"Sorry we're late. Hope your passenger isn't too upset."

"She'll live. How far out are you?"

"About a hundred meters, give or take. Stand by."

"Copy that." Kadohata looked back at Kira. "Grab your stuff. Your ride's here."

Kira picked up the swaddled Orb of Time, tucked it under her arm, and moved forward to stand behind Kadohata's shoulder. All she saw outside the broad forward viewport was the northern hemisphere of Deneva and a spray of swiftly expiring stars. "Where are—?"

Her question died on her lips as she saw the stars ahead ripple, distorted by the telltale mirage of a cloaking field being terminated. Seconds later a familiar starship appeared: *Defiant.* Or, to be more precise, the duplicate of *Defiant* that the Terran Rebellion had built several years earlier, using schematics stolen from the computers on the old Deep Space 9.

Even though she knew this wasn't the ship on which she had served, she smiled.

Aren't you a sight for sore eyes? I think I'll call you Defiant II.

Rennan's voice flowed from the comm. *"Vedek Kira? If you'll head back to* Sleipnir's *transporter pad, we'll beam you right over."*

Kira leaned forward to reply, and noticed as she did that Kadohata flinched and leaned away from her. "Negative, *Defiant*. I have cargo that doesn't play well with transporters. I'll need to come aboard through the airlock, please."

"Not a problem. Give us a minute to come around and set up the docking bridge. Defiant *out."* The channel closed with a soft *click*.

Straightening and taking half a step back, Kira studied Kadohata. "Are you all right?"

The woman answered without looking at Kira. "Fine."

"Are you sure? Because you seem a bit tense when I—"

"Your *counterpart*." Kadohata glowered up at Kira. "She killed my family. My parents, my sister, my husband, my children. She only let me live so she could sell me as a slave to some Cardassian." An angry sigh. "I know you're not her. But I wanted to see her die, more than anything, and I never got the chance. And I know it's not fair, but when I see you—"

"I get it." Kira adjusted the shroud of the bundled Orb and headed for the *Sleipnir*'s port-side hatch. "I met her. And not a day goes by that I wish I never had."

A gentle bump reverberated through the deck beneath her feet as *Defiant II*'s airlock bridge made contact with *Sleipnir*'s outer hull and locked into place. A second later, the air pressure indicator on the outer hatch changed color to confirm the airlock passage was secure.

Before she opened the hatch, Kira looked at Kadohata. "Would it help if I say I'm sorry?"

Kadohata stewed in void-black bitterness. "Why would it?"

Kira frowned. That was what she had figured.

She opened the hatch and carried the blanket-wrapped Orb of Time into the airlock passageway in the nose of *Defiant II*. As she crossed *Defiant II*'s first threshold, its hatch and the *Sleipnir*'s hatch both closed behind her. Then *Defiant II*'s inner airlock hatch opened, revealing her one-woman welcoming committee.

Standing with arms crossed and a playfully wicked smile on her lips . . . was Ezri.

"Vedek Kira! It's been far too long. Welcome aboard my ship."

Kira slowed her pace. Barely a week had passed since the death of

Captain Ezri Dax in her universe. It felt like an expression of the cosmos's perverse sense of irony to confront her with her friend's living ghost so soon afterward.

This version of Ezri had a tousled mop of multicolored hair with a dramatic undercut on the right side of her head—a wild counterpoint to the staid, dark-gray uniform of the Commonwealth Starfleet. The svelte, petite Trill woman nodded at Kira's bundle.

"Doesn't like transporters, eh?"

"Hm? Oh. No, it doesn't."

Kira wasn't really sure if that was true. It had long been a tradition on Bajor not to move the Orbs using matter transporters, and Starfleet had always honored that practice—mostly because its sensors were only partially effective in analyzing the Orbs. Some scientists estimated the Orbs existed only five percent within the four-dimensional universe, with the remainder of their energetic nature existing in as many as twelve dimensions. It made the prospect of moving the Orbs via transporter incredibly risky.

The only person Kira had ever known who had even considered beaming an Orb was her double from this universe, the Intendant Kira, who years earlier had tried to steal the Orb of Prophecy and Change from Deep Space 9 and bring it back here by way of an interdimensional transporter. Kira had never been sure whether that would have worked, but she had been grateful not to have found out.

Ezri regarded Kira with curiosity. "That all you got?"

"I'm traveling light for the apocalypse."

"Smart." Ezri tilted her head in invitation. "I'll show you to your stateroom."

Kira fell in behind her. "Thank you, Captain Tigan."

"Dax. It's Ezri Dax, now. I was Joined about eight years ago, at the end of the revolution." When Kira didn't reply, Dax peeked over her shoulder. "I'm sorry, is this weird for you?"

"Which part?"

"My counterpart was some kind of therapist, right?"

"Once upon a time."

"And the last time we met, I was a wild-child rebel, and you were a straight-edge officer. Now you're a holy woman and I'm a starship commander." She flashed a winsome smile. "Must be strange seeing me as a captain."

Kira bit down on her grief and held back her tears.

"Not as strange as you might think."

U.S.S. *Defiant* NX-74205—2373, Borg Timeline

No thrumming of the impulse reactors, no pulse of the warp core. Even the subtle breath of *Defiant*'s life-support system had been stilled.

The gunship Worf had once thought of as home now felt like a tomb. Smoke thick with particulate lingered along the overheads and snaked through open hatchways, lit only intermittently by weak flickers of chemical-powered emergency lighting or plasma-torch flames.

He had started his review of the ship's status on the bridge, which he had left in the care of Commander K'Ehleyr. No one had told Worf before they embarked on this crazy jump back in time that she had requested a transfer to *Defiant*. Or that Captain Sisko had approved it.

No word of warning. No consultation with him or Alexander.

What was the captain thinking?

Seeing her on *Defiant*'s bridge had felt to Worf like a slap in the face, a splash of ice water followed by an electric shock. *I thought I had left her behind. Instead, she haunts me.*

En route to the port gangway, he stopped to check the access nook to the ship's open top hatch. Two of the ship's security personnel were stationed there, taking turns on watch.

Worf nodded first to the human woman who stood at the bottom of the ladder, in the standby position. "Lighton." He leaned past her and whispered up to the man at the top hatch, "Sulok. Any movement?"

The Vulcan lowered his holographic binoculars and looked down at Worf. "Negative, sir. All quiet since the away team left our sight line."

"Use infrared. The air is cool tonight, and Borg implants run hot."

"I remember, sir. Running full IR sweeps every minute."

"Good. Carry on." Worf briefly clasped Lighton's shoulder in a gesture of encouragement. She nodded her thanks, and Worf moved on down the corridor.

Near the gangway compartment, Worf encountered a pair of mechanics. One was busy removing debris from the corridor; the other had been tasked with pulling meter after meter of fried ODN cable from behind the bulkhead that led to the ship's dual computer core.

"Gallegos. How long until this corridor is clear?"

The petty officer paused and sleeved sweat from his swarthy brow. "Another hour at least, sir. Maybe less if I can get another set of hands up here."

"I will ask Commander La Forge if he can spare anyone." Worf pivoted to the chief petty officer who was coiling endless lines of optical cable over her left shoulder. "Visaggio? When will the main computer be back online?"

"Above my pay grade, sir. Tonight I'm just a spool with legs." She nodded toward the gangway. "Lieutenant Scardas is in charge of core repair on deck two."

"Understood. Good work, both of you. When you finish, get some water, and some rest."

Chief Visaggio looped more cable around her shoulder. "Copy that, sir."

Worf stepped around them, into the gangway compartment. He leaned forward, grabbed the top of the ladder, and then let himself slide down with his feet along the outside. When he reached deck two he stuck out his foot and caught the edge of the deck to stop himself. A push and a step, and he was in the corridor, surveying the work underway in main engineering to his right, and in the computer core silo to his left.

There were more than a dozen engineers, mechanics, and computer specialists working around one another down here, all of them light and fast on their feet in spite of the smoke and the darkness. Beams from palm beacons slashed through one another as teams tackled several jobs at once. There was no shouting, however. All of the conversations were quiet, calm, and precise. It filled Worf with pride to see the crew of *Defiant* strive to maintain Starfleet's intrinsic professionalism even when they all knew, down to the last enlisted crewman, that they were on what was very likely to be their final mission.

Doing his best not to get in the way of those who had their hands full, Worf shouldered around fallen beams and warped bulkheads to find Lieutenant Scardas, as promised, directing the repair of the ship's computer cores. The lanky Saurian had an uncommon pigmentation for his species, bright orange mottled with dark brown, and large golden eyes. He stood in the middle of the silo, between the inert core towers, issuing directions with quiet confidence. He noted Worf's approach with a quick tilt of his chameleon-like head. "Commander! I expect to have the cores reconnected in four hours."

"Good. Comms and navigation?"

"That will depend upon the extent of damage in the relays—but we cannot test them until the cores are rewired and main power is restored."

"Very well. Keep me posted."

"I will, sir."

"Carry on." As soon as Worf started back the way he had come, Scardas resumed issuing orders to his technicians in the core silo. Echoes of their chatter followed Worf all the way to main engineering, where he threaded a path through a cluster of grimy, sweaty engineers to find Commander La Forge hunched over the misshapen remains of the dilithium crystal articulation frame. La Forge was trying to straighten it and fuse the cracks in its outer housing. His steady string of muttered profanities suggested to Worf the work was not going well.

"Geordi."

La Forge set down his particle fuser with an exasperated sigh. "Worf?"

"Any progress?"

"You mean since the last time you asked, fifteen minutes ago?" He waved in one direction, then another. "You tell me. I've got tool-pushers elbow deep in every part of this ship. Most are trying to fix things by touch 'cause they can't see anything below deck three."

"Is there anything I can do to help?"

"Got a spare palm beacon?"

Worf took his handheld light off his belt and offered it to La Forge.

"Great. Take it up to Chief Tong in deck one aft. She'll be the one upside down in the dark, trying to build new feed lines for the deuterium tanks."

Worf put the light back on his belt. "I will drop it off on my way back to the bridge."

"Yeah, right. Speaking of the bridge—why aren't you *on* it?"

"Internal comms are down, and I need updated reports."

La Forge skewered Worf with a doubtful look. "That's why we have runners, Worf."

Worf wondered how many of his secrets La Forge could suss out with his cybernetic eyes, reading Worf's galvanic skin response, or tracking the fluctuations of his body heat. "I prefer to gather my own information."

A knowing smile lit up La Forge's face. "I think you prefer to keep your distance from our newest crewmember." Before Worf could deny it, La Forge continued, "C'mon, Worf. I see the way you look at her, and she at you."

"You do *not* understand." Worf lowered his voice; his personal business was not for the crew's ears. "When I see her, it is like looking at a ghost."

La Forge did his best to keep his own voice down. "Really? You think I don't get that? How do you think I felt when Data came back a few years ago? Even with all the changes he went through, it was still damned odd. He was dead, and then he wasn't. He was Data again—but he also *wasn't*. I won't lie to you, Worf—that kind of threw me for a loop."

"How did you deal with it?"

A shrug. "I decided my friendship with Data was too important to give it up out of fear. I let my love for the parts of him I recognized be greater than my fear of the parts of him that had changed. And in time I learned to see past the changes—to see that he really is still Data."

Worf nodded slowly. "You are a wise man. And a good friend."

La Forge clutched Worf's shoulder. "I hope you still feel that way after I tell you we need to go into the Borg city to scavenge for spare parts."

"You are not serious."

"It's our only way off this rock—and if we don't get it done before the Borg come looking to salvage what's left of *us*, we'll be as good as dead."

13

C.S.S. *Enterprise*

Troi looked up from the tactical console. "Sixty seconds until they reach targeting distance!"

Luc felt every second bleeding away. *Enterprise* was already at red alert, with its transphasic shields raised against the superheated plasma orbiting the black hole Abaddon. He wanted to arm the ship's phaser banks and precharge their emitters, but he needed every drop of energy in the shields. If they faltered now, in this hellish place, even a momentary failure could vaporize his ship and scatter its atoms into Abaddon's event horizon.

But doing nothing was just as likely to be an act of suicide.

"Helm! Increase to warp point-eight-five, and take us two hundred kilometers deeper into the plasma stream."

The flight controller looked at Luc, her face drawn with doubt. "Sir? Are you sure?"

"That's an order, Lieutenant Tolaris. Make it so."

Luc waited until he saw the Vulcan woman enter the commands into the helm, and then he left the command chair to head aft, so he could check on his visitor's progress. On his way to the science stations, he was intercepted by Troi, who seized his arm. "Taking us deeper into the plasma? Is that wise?"

He pulled his arm free, with perhaps a bit more force than had been needed. "The effect on our shields is the same as when we skim the surface. But deeper in the stream, the enemy's phasers will be diffused, and their torpedoes are more likely to lose their targeting lock, or to melt down before reaching us."

Deanna seemed primed to argue, but then she backed off. "I hadn't thought of that."

He gave her upper arm a paternal squeeze. "You would have, I'm sure." He gestured with his chin toward René, who lingered near the aft science consoles. "Have security escort our young guest to sickbay for his own safety—and tell them to make sure he *stays there*."

"Aye, sir."

As Troi returned to her station, Luc felt grateful that, in K'Ehleyr's absence, he still had Troi to depend upon. They had been together a long time, the two of them, since well before the Great Revolution. They had survived so much while watching each other's backs that for years he had thought of Troi as the daughter he had never had.

Now, as he continued aft, he studied René, the son he had never sired but might have, in a universe where everything had been different. René stayed close to his older half brother, Wesley Crusher. The shaggy human-born Traveler worked with great focus and fierce intensity alongside Lieutenant Perim, scanning the black hole's event horizon for . . . to tell the truth, Luc *still* wasn't sure what they sought, or how they'd know when they found it. All he knew, and all that he had to know, was that it was his job to keep them safe and alive until they found it.

He sidled up to Perim and Wesley, who both were too engrossed in their work to note his arrival. Their hands moved across the panel's holographic interface faster than Luc could track as they adjusted their search parameters and scanning filters with each new batch of data.

"Isolating the icospectrogram readings," Perim said.

Wesley kept working. "Masking the foreground radiation."

Luc listened a few seconds longer while the pair traded jargon, and then he cleared his throat. "Lieutenant. Mister Crusher. A Starfleet battle group is inbound. Are you done yet?"

Wesley pleaded with eyes opened wide, like those of a puppy. "Almost, Captain. We just need a couple more minutes."

From the tactical station, Troi announced, "Starfleet battle group is locking weapons."

Luc confronted Wesley. "What you *need* is irrelevant. Wrap this up. Now."

"Another minute," Wesley begged. "Please."

A pair of security officers entered the bridge from the aft starboard turbolift and moved straight toward René. The young man tried to retreat from them, but Luc caught René's arm and held him fast. "René, these officers are here to take you to sickbay, for your own safety."

As the officers tried to take René into custody, the lanky youth broke free and backpedaled toward Wesley. "No! I'm staying with my brother."

There was regret in Wesley's voice as he told René, "It might be for the best. Sickbay is almost always the safest area of the ship."

"I don't care. I'm not—"

His protest was interrupted as the security officers each took one of his arms, lifted him off the deck, and carried him, thrashing and cursing like a lunatic, off the bridge.

Wesley cocked an accusatory eyebrow at Luc. "Was that *really* necessary?"

Before Luc could answer, Troi called out, "Torpedoes inbound!"

Luc resigned himself to standing his ground, consequences be damned. "Helm, set jump coordinates for Kali 531. Sixty-second countdown. Engage!"

Tolaris answered as she keyed in the commands: "Sixty seconds to jump. Confirmed."

Troi raised her voice, no doubt partly in alarm: "Torpedoes closing! Five seconds out! Four . . . three . . ." Low rumbles of detonation resounded through *Enterprise*'s hull, and the deck trembled beneath Luc's feet. His command-chair terminal confirmed that two of the five incoming torpedoes had detonated prematurely upon hitting the black hole's high-velocity river of superheated plasma. A third veered wildly off course, plunging deeper into the plasma stream and off *Enterprise*'s sensors.

Then the last two torpedoes struck the ship's transphasic shields.

It sounded like the ship had slammed into a mountain, and the shock of the blast was enough to push the inertial dampers past their limits, throwing Luc and his bridge crew forward. Launched from his chair, Luc landed on his hands and knees. The skin of his palms tore and scraped from the friction.

Pushing himself off the deck, he stood and looked at Troi. "Damage report!"

"Shields holding. Overloads in the aft emitters. Compensating."

"Helm! Evasive pattern Echo Red."

"Evasive Echo Red," Tolaris replied, confirming the order by repetition. "Engaged!"

Troi scowled at new bad news on her console. "More torpedoes inbound."

"Maintain evasive pattern," Luc said, doing his best to sound confident and reassuring. But his console showed the torpedoes closing rapidly. "Mister Crusher! Time?"

"Thirty seconds and we'll know for sure."

"How sure can you be right now?"

Wesley traded a befuddled look with Perim. "Maybe ninety percent? But, sir, if the intertime anomaly we're looking for is in that last ten percent, and we miss it—"

"Enough said, Mister Crusher."

On his command console, five high-yield torpedoes were tracking *Enterprise* by shadowing its maneuvers while remaining above the stream of superheated plasma. Luc had seen this tactic before, and it did not bode well for his ship.

The moment one of those warheads locks onto us, all five will dive into the plasma river—and converge on us at the speed of light. And it might happen any second now.

He looked at the jump timer in the upper corner of the main viewscreen.

Twenty seconds. Nineteen . . .

"Six more inbound," Troi said. "Blocking our escape vectors."

"Acknowledged." *Seventeen seconds . . .*

Luc felt almost brazen enough to hope his ship might escape this snare unscathed—and then the torpedo cluster above *Enterprise* accelerated and began its dive into the plasma.

Merde.

He put himself back in his command chair and gripped the armrests. With a tap on one armrest key he opened an internal comm channel, and said all he had time to say:

"All decks—brace for impact!"

U.S.S. *Titan* NCC-80102

I've got you now, you sonofabitch. You won't get away this time. Riker watched a series of flashes with satisfaction as quantum torpedoes detonated inside the black hole's swirling plasma stream. Each hundred-megaton blast made white-hot liquefied gas erupt from the stream like a geyser. One would find its mark. One would find the intruder and force it out of hiding, straight into his grasp.

Come on . . .

Around him, *Titan*'s bridge officers were strangely quiet. There was usually an undercurrent of chatter during combat, subtle sounds of cooperation. Today he heard nothing. His officers all were doing their jobs, but no one was talking. He found it troubling.

Damned odd, is what it is.

He shot a look back at the security chief. "Keru, has the intruder changed course?"

The Trill answered without looking up from his console, as if he were deliberately avoiding eye contact with Riker. "Negative. They've begun evasive maneuvers."

"Order the fleet to open fire. Box the target in. Give them nowhere to run." Riker had hoped to capture the extradimensional intruder himself, but a scenario such as this was precisely why he'd brought backup. Credit no longer mattered, only results.

A few dozen streaks of fire ripped across *Titan*'s viewscreen, all racing toward the black hole. Three dozen quantum torpedoes in six clusters sped toward the accretion disk of fiery plasma, and then they diverged to create a sphere of destruction that would envelop the target.

Riker smiled with dark anticipation. *That deep in the plasma, they must be using transphasic shielding to keep from getting cooked. And in that soup, they've got to be at their limit. Hit them with enough quantum warheads at once, and that'll be all she wrote.*

The flight of torpedoes—long out of visual range, and represented now only as dots on the tactical console beside the command chair—formed a constellation of death around the vessel from the alternate universe, the one on which Riker was sure he'd find Jean-Luc Picard.

Then, as the torpedoes converged to close the trap—the target vanished.

Thirty-six warheads detonated as one, forming a short-lived sun that within seconds was absorbed into the relentless flow of the black hole's accretion disk.

Riker's temper turned volcanic. "Tactical! What the hell just happened?"

Commander Tuvok worked quickly, collecting and analyzing data as he acquired it. "The target vessel appears to have escaped by means of an artificial wormhole."

"To where?"

"Unknown, Admiral." Tuvok noted the arrival of new sensor data. "The wormhole's mouth was deep inside the plasma stream. Consequently, we were unable to identify its far terminus."

Fueled by frustration and rage, Riker sprang to his feet and looked around at his bridge team. "Is that all we've got? Tell me *one* of you has something better than that!"

Lieutenant Commander Pazlar stepped away from the sciences console. "I think I might have something, sir." She lifted a padd from its pocket on the outer part of her exoskeleton's left thigh, and used it to control a quick presentation. Images of ripples moving through Abaddon's superheated accretion disk appeared on the main viewscreen. "When we arrived, I started recording the target's sensor activity. In addition to tactical sweeps watching for us, they were conducting intensive scans of the black hole's event horizon."

Once again feeling the itch of an old memory struggling to make itself known, Riker asked, "What kind of scans?"

Pazlar highlighted different results with unique colors. "Chroniton bombardments. The frequencies suggest they were using them to look for nonrandom tachyon scatter patterns and elevated levels of antichroniton decay."

"Which would suggest *what*, Commander?" The truth felt so close that Riker almost thought he could taste it.

The blond Elaysian woman tapped her padd again, and a crude schematic of a pocket dimension appeared, imposed as an overlay upon the black hole's event horizon. "They're hunting for an inverted twelve-dimensional temporal recursion."

Riker scowled.

Pazlar took the cue and simplified her answer. "They're looking for a pocket universe of null-time, one that exists outside of this universe but remains linked to it. Basically, a kind of intertime dimension parallel to our own. An infinity that can exist between picoseconds."

This sounded familiar to Riker. "Just the kind of place the Devidians might use to launch an attack on multiple linked branches of time."

"Yes, sir."

"And is there a reason they were looking for it here?"

The science officer nodded. "This kind of temporal recursion would be hard to create in normal spacetime. But along the event horizon of a singularity, many of the rules of spacetime break down. It would be an ideal point at which to bridge our universe to an intertime pocket."

"Would any black hole serve that purpose?"

"No, sir. They'd need an intermediate-mass black hole—one big enough to distort spacetime sufficiently to facilitate the bridge, but not so massive as to render it unstable."

"Good work, Melora." Riker returned to the command chair. "Tuvok. If we're looking for a stable, intermediate-mass black hole comparable to Abaddon, how many are there in this galaxy?"

"A handful at most."

"And what's the nearest one to here?"

It took Tuvok only seconds to find the answer. "Kali 531, in the Romulan Star Empire." After a moment of consideration, he added, "But there is no reason to think that was their next destination. A wormhole drive such as theirs could take them nearly anywhere."

"True," Riker admitted. "But let's assume that the greater the distance, the more involved the calculations. And they were in a hurry to get away from our torpedoes. They'd want to make the fastest, simplest jump they could."

The Vulcan nodded. "Logical."

Riker faced Keru. "Tell every ship and starbase: watch the black holes like this one, and report any sign of artificial wormhole activity.

The moment we pick up anything? Send out the coordinates on all Starfleet frequencies and get me every last ship we've got."

"Aye, sir."

As Riker settled back into the command chair, first officer Commander Sarai, who had observed most of the battle without comment, leaned toward him. "Admiral, if your assumption that the jaunt-ship leaped to Kali 531 is correct, should we alert the Romulans?"

Riker weighed the pros and cons of that course of action. "Don't bother." He couldn't help but crack a sly smile. "I'd bet they already know."

14

———

San Francisco, Earth—2373, Borg Timeline

A hundred boots marched in lockstep on the catwalk above the away team. Crouching in the misty shadows beneath a labyrinth of pipes, Jean-Luc Picard focused on the mental image of a silent void to hide his presence from the Borg drones overhead.

The away team had been walking for hours, traversing narrow passages between structures and using the murky fog and darkness to their advantage.

Past experience had taught Picard that the Borg were hard to anticipate. Sometimes they ignored intruders, treating them as irrelevant unless and until the interlopers actually inflicted damage substantial enough to warrant the Borg's response. At other times the Borg had proved fanatical in defending their ships and installations from trespassers. Not knowing what to expect from the Borg that presently infested what once had been San Francisco, the away team had agreed that discretion was the preferable tactic.

The last of the Borg drones rounded a corner on the catwalk, but still the echoes of marching feet resounded off every nearby structure. At the front of the team, Data—barely a silhouette in the damp gray haze that blanketed the city and its bay—held up a hand with his fingers spread, and then he folded them one by one into a fist, counting down to zero. Then he pointed forward, signaling the team to resume its northward hike.

After leaving the foothills of the San Bruno Mountain State & County Park, the away team had found its way to the city's long-defunct Highway 1, known locally as 19th Avenue. The streets Picard had remembered from his Academy days had been lined with beautiful, early-twenty-second-century homes and residential complexes, most of which had been built during the Global Reconstruction era following the Third World War and Earth's civilization-altering first contact with the Vulcans on April 5, 2063.

Now the old road was flanked by featureless, multi-story black buildings bestrewn with pipes and wires, all of it reduced to faint outlines by the omnipresent fog. Everything stank of petroleum products, chemicals, and overheated metal. A maze consisting of at least three different levels of catwalks linked the various drab structures.

Since leaving the hills and entering the city, Picard had not seen a single native life-form. Not one animal, not a blade of grass. Not a single creeping insect or skittering rat. The Borg, it seemed, had purged Earth of every life-form that served no purpose in the Collective.

If there had been one discovery that Picard could think of as a saving grace, it had been the realization that the Borg's ugly mechanical sprawl was almost entirely bereft of exterior lights and surveillance technology. No external sensors, no antipersonnel systems of any kind. It was enough to make him wonder why the Borg were so lax about security.

Perhaps the Borg have conquered so much of local space that they no longer expect to face intruders this deep inside their own territory.

It was as reasonable a hypothesis as any Picard had heard. But there would be no time to test it. The away team was on too tight a schedule to worry about that.

Despite the apparent absence of intruder-detection systems, the away team had taken no chances. Their spec-ops uniforms had been designed to mask their life signs from most sensors, as well as their heat signatures. As long as they maintained comm silence and avoided being spotted by Borg drones on maneuvers, there was a decent chance the Collective was, so far, unaware of their presence and movements.

The first moment that Picard felt as if he recognized something of San Francisco proper was when the away team reached what once had been Golden Gate Park. The greenery was long gone, and the majority of the park's footprint was naked, dusty ground scoured by cold winds in the night—but he knew the curves of Crossover Drive by heart, and its eastward fork onto Park Presidio Bypass. Those roads, at least, remained intact.

After leaving Golden Gate Park—or, to be more precise, the barren acreage once known as a park—the away team continued north until it reached the hilly grounds of the Presidio. Like the remains of Golden Gate Park, the once-pristine acres of the Presidio had been laid bare and stripped of their natural beauty. Whether the Borg had done it out of necessity or out of malice, Picard was unable to say.

Using the terrain to conceal the away team's movements, Data led the group northeast, in a slight detour toward the coastline, and then north, away from the Borg-modified towers and infrastructure of the Presidio, until they reached a rocky slope at the northern tip of the city, west of the Golden Gate Bridge.

Barely visible at the water's edge, on the east side of the bridge, were the crumbling ruins of Fort Point, a nineteenth-century seacoast fortification constructed before the American Civil War. Once a site of historical interest, it now was little more than a heap of weathered stone.

The away team kept to the shadows as they surveyed the approach to the bridge, which was shrouded in Borg technology: maglev cargo-movers, power couplings, and a host of other systems about whose purposes Picard could only speculate, all crowded into continuous masses that covered what had once been the bridge's main roadway.

Beverly gazed up at the defiled marvel. "I can't believe it's still standing."

"As has often been the case," Data said, "the Borg found it convenient to build their infrastructure on top of what was already available."

The sight of it drove Sisko into a black mood. "It's an abomination."

Data replied, "It is also our only way of reaching the Borg's temporal disruptor, which is located on the far side."

Staying low, Bashir searched the coastline with a pair of holographic binoculars. "Data, there must be another way. A rowboat. A raft. Something."

"I am afraid not, Doctor. Sensors detect no watercraft in the vicinity."

Lal cocked her head in the same way that Picard remembered Data tilting his, many years earlier, when lost in thought. "Given our deadline, and the local geography, we don't have time to go the long way around on foot." She turned a worried look at the bridge. "We must find a way across, as soon as possible."

Picard extended his hand to Bashir. "Doctor? May I borrow those?"

Bashir seemed hesitant to give up his holographic binoculars, but he handed them to Picard, who looked through them to reconnoiter the situation on the bridge.

What he saw was not encouraging.

"There are hundreds of Borg on the roadway. Several appear to be heavily armed. And between their infernal machines and the old solar panels, there's barely room to move."

Data crouched next to Picard and gazed intently at the bridge. "I think I see a way, Captain." He pointed at the bridge's underside. "The framework beneath the bridge is also packed with Borg devices, but not so tightly as on the main roadway. Also, because of an abandoned effort in the mid-twenty-first century to add a lower roadway to the bridge, there are several catwalks and long runs of cable that span the length of the crossing. And, best of all—"

"No drones," Picard observed, studying the bridge's underside through the holographic binoculars. Troubled, he lowered the device. "But navigating those catwalks in the dark will be treacherous, Data."

"I know, sir. Just as I know that if we wait for daylight, we will miss our deadline—and be spotted by the Borg, no matter where we are."

Picard told himself this was the best course of action. The prudent choice. But all he heard was the abyssal roar of Borg drones' minds surrounding him, an endless sea of broken consciousness, nine billion cells of awareness representing one diabolical entity: the Borg Queen. Until now he had been able to keep his distance. But traversing the bridge would mean passing within mere meters of hundreds of Borg drones, any one of which might succeed in piercing his mental defenses should he find himself distracted, even if just for a few seconds.

Pushing onward, into the clutches of the Collective, felt like a suicide run. A foolhardy risk of not just his own life, but that of every member of the away team, including his wife.

But doing nothing because he lacked either courage or conviction would summon a fate worse than death for himself: inaction would condemn every other sentient life-form in creation to be slain by the Devidians in the name of a selfish, pointless feast of souls.

He bade his mind to be still.

Awash in his inner silence, he knew what to do.

He clapped his hand to his friend's back. "Mister Data . . . make it so."

C.S.S. *Enterprise*

There were truths about the universe that Wesley Crusher intuitively understood: that space, time, matter, energy, and thought all were manifestations of the same thing; that what most beings considered to be reality was merely the accumulated permutations and attenuations of twelve-dimensional forces, vibrations of invisible strings knotted in four dimensions as m-brane sheets; that there was no "true" timeline and no "true" universe; that so-called "dark matter" was a sentient force unto itself, and not at all one with a sense of humor; and that spacetime expanded forever into both the future and the past, a phenomenon with no beginning and no end, one that embodied its own finite infinity, unbound by any Alpha or Omega.

But for the life of him, he failed to understand how Luc Picard of the jaunt-ship *Enterprise* could be so impervious to reason.

"There is no way to speed up the scans, Captain. We'll need at least four or five near-warp orbits of the singularity before we can finish analyzing its event horizon."

Luc's mood grew darker by the minute. "We barely escaped Abaddon with our lives, Mister Crusher. That's not a mistake we can afford to repeat."

"Sir, if there was a way I could speed up the process, I would, but—"

Perim interrupted by clearing her throat. "We have auxiliary craft that can generate transphasic shields. They can't go as deep into a plasma stream as we can, but if they skim along just above the stream, and relay their sensor data back to us in real time—"

Wesley was impressed by the simple elegance of her idea. "That could work. How many ships do you have that fit the bill, and how long would it take to deploy them?"

The Trill woman looked up the information on her console. "We have five outriders that can take this kind of heat. They can all be fueled and launched in about twenty minutes."

Wesley checked the technical specs for the outriders by looking at Perim's screen, and then he faced Luc. "That would cut our scan time to two passes."

The captain looked pleased to hear that. "Splendid. Lieutenant, make it so. Coordinate with—" A red-alert siren cut off his order. The overhead lights dimmed and a crimson glow suffused *Enterprise*'s bridge as Luc hurried back to his command chair. "Deanna! Report!"

"Two Romulan warbirds, *D'deridex* class, decloaking above us on our aft flanks."

"Range?"

"Thirty-five thousand kilometers. They're locking—"

Explosions buffeted the jaunt-ship, and the quaking in the deck nearly knocked Wesley off his feet. Perim caught him as he stumbled and set him upright. Then they both grabbed the edge of the aft console as another barrage struck *Enterprise*'s shields and momentarily overloaded the inertial dampers.

Troi muted multiple alarms on her console. "They're recharging disruptors."

Manic fervor replaced Luc's black mood. "Helm! Take us out of the plasma stream. Once we're clear, evasive pattern Romeo White—keep the warbirds above us. Tactical, transfer shield power to—"

"Incoming!" Troi cut in. "Torpedoes! Two volleys!"

Luc opened a shipwide channel with a tap on his chair's armrest. "All decks, brace for impact! Damage-control teams, stand by!"

Anticipating the strike, Wesley flinched—and then a bone-rattling detonation left him clenching his jaw with his eyes squeezed shut while a whipsaw of shifting gravitational effects tossed him around the bridge. He slammed into a guardrail, felt a rib crack on his left side. Landed on his back. Rolled—and then flew up, off the deck, and slammed into the overhead. For just over a second, the bridge was upside down, with everyone sprawled on the overhead—and then the artificial gravity corrected itself, and everyone fell like sacks of meat to the deck.

Wesley opened his eyes to find the bridge drowning in bitter black smoke. He pulled himself to his feet even though he could barely breathe, much less speak. Beside him, Perim was scuffed and bruised, but otherwise she seemed all right.

Luc rose from the deck, sporting a bloody wound on the left side of his head. He surveyed his ravaged bridge, then looked toward Troi. "Deanna, report."

"Transphasic shields are down. Romulan boarding parties are beaming into decks twelve, six, and three. And the warbird *Kerithrex* is hailing us."

"What do they want?"

Troi touched her ear to block out the wild chatter on *Enterprise*'s internal comms, listened for a moment, then looked Luc in the eye. "Commander Shulor orders us to surrender and submit to his boarding parties."

Luc smirked. "That'll be the day."

Before Wesley could ask what Luc meant to do, the captain turned and headed aft, bellowing orders. "Perim! You have the conn." He stopped at Troi's console and with one tap opened a general-address internal comm channel. His voice resounded through the deck and bulkheads as he spoke: "All decks! This is the captain! Repel boarders!" Another tap, and he closed the channel. "Deanna, with me."

As Luc and Troi headed to the aft bulkhead, Perim moved swiftly to the command chair. As she settled in and reviewed tactical readouts on the console next to the chair, Luc and Troi opened a disguised panel on the aft bulkhead, revealing a well-stocked weapons locker. From it, Troi took a rifle.

The captain grabbed a pistol with his right hand—and a bandolier of grenades with his left. He smiled at Troi. "Let's give our visitors a proper welcome, shall we?"

She mirrored his confident swagger. "With pleasure, sir."

A relief officer took Troi's place at tactical as she and Luc strode to the aft turbolift. He draped the bandolier across his torso as the lift doors closed, and then they were gone.

Meanwhile, at the center of the bridge, Perim started giving orders of her own.

"Tactical, raise standard shields and arm all weapons. Helm, resume evasive maneuvers, at your discretion." She aimed a pitying look over her shoulder at Wesley. "Hang on to something heavy, Wes. This is gonna get rough." Then she settled back into position, checked her readouts, and pointed at the warbirds on the viewscreen. "Lieutenant Ries! *Destroy those ships.*"

Luc led his team through the darkened corridors of deck three, stalking the moving song of battle. After so many years commanding the *Enterprise*, he knew its melodies and its rhythms by heart. Overtures of disruptor fire. The percussion of stun grenades detonating in close quarters. An aria of troops bellowing as they charged. The minor chords of the wounded and the dying. It was all music to his ears, and today he would be its most ruthless conductor.

Troi was close behind his left shoulder. Trailing her were a dozen members of the ship's security division, each armed with the latest small-arms technology from Memory Omega.

Pistol in hand, Luc halted shy of an intersection. Raised a fist to halt his people behind him. Took a knee and listened.

Bright chords of violence rang out from the corridor beyond the turn.

I know this tune. Let's change its key.

Using hand signals, he organized Troi and the troops behind him into staggered ranks, with those in front kneeling, the middle ranks crouched, the rear ranks standing.

He shaped his thumb and forefinger into an L-shape, the signal to lock on enemy targets.

Then he swung his arm forward in a chopping motion—the order to fire.

Muzzle flashes lit up the corridor. Smart projectiles left crimson trails that arced around the corner ahead of the strike team—and found their Romulan targets in the midst of a bloody scrum thanks to target discriminators that distinguished intruders from *Enterprise*'s crew.

Luc raised his hand. "Again!" Another fast chop of his arm—

Red tracers seared the air above his head.

Then came the screams of Romulans riddled by bullets from shooters they couldn't see.

That's enough prelude. Luc pulled a munition from his bandolier and faced his strike team. "Charge!"

He was the first around the corner.

An opera of carnage greeted him. Green blood stained the bulkheads in broad sprays and wild spatters. Corpses lay two deep on the deck, dozens of them Romulans, but just as many were from his crew. Ahead, at the next junction in the corridor, a squad of six Romulans stood in a circle, all of them facing outward, alert to danger. On their body armor and visored helmets they all wore the insignia of the Tal Hansu, the Romulan Star Empire's elite commandos.

Two who faced Luc fired, filling the corridor with green disruptor pulses.

Luc ducked into a recessed doorway, and his people behind him did the same. The doorways were at best shallow defilades, but any protection was better than none.

He armed his munition with a press of his thumb on its trigger, and hurled it down the corridor with a hard jerk of his wrist against the door frame.

Half a second later he was rewarded by a tooth-rattling blast that scoured the corridor with shrapnel and smoky bits of debris. He leaned out of his doorway just long enough to fire a half dozen quick shots into the hot, billowing smoke. Though he couldn't see his foes, his pistol's smart bullets found the Romulans anyway, and pierced their ablative armor—which was designed to block energy weapons rather than hard projectiles. Seconds later came the muffled grunts and strangled cries of alarm from Romulans who realized only too late that they'd been shot with bullets designed to fragment inside soft targets, to damage the most tissue possible.

Beyond the smoke, hoarse voices shouted orders in *Rihan*, the ancestral tongue of the Romulans. Boots running on metal decks filled the corridors with sharp echoes. Then Luc heard the anxious whispers of desperate Tal Hansu arguing about what to do next.

He drew his combat knife. *Let me make that decision for you.*

Luc broke from cover, treading lightly to muffle his steps. He whistled a few short notes, a code that Troi and the other *Enterprise* personnel would know meant *stealthy advance*.

They prowled into the dense smoke like assassins.

Luc kept his back to the left bulkhead, and he knew Troi was advancing along the right. The smoke only grew heavier and more toxic as he pushed ahead. He pulled up the collar of his shirt to cover his nose and mouth, took a breath, and then held it as he continued.

The Romulans' whispers were intimately close, but all Luc saw was gray fog. Even so, he knew from their hushed voices that they were within arm's reach.

There was no way to coordinate with Troi, or with the rest of his team. The smoke was too dense, the corridor too dark—and any sound he might make would give him away.

He fixed his grip on his knife, putting the flat spine of the blade against his forearm while keeping the cutting edge and tip ready to block or strike at anything in front of him.

If I attack alone, this will be a short fight. Luc shook off his doubts. *Deanna has never failed me before. She won't abandon me now. I'll bet she's just waiting to hear me strike first.*

He cleared his mind and steeled his will.

A quick stab of the blade into the misty veil—and he felt its tip sink into flesh. Rather than pull back, he slashed sideways, and a warm spray of green blood freckled his face.

As his victim gurgled, Luc heard from across the corridor the wet sounds of a blade finding flesh, and he knew that Troi was with him.

Fearing nothing and no one, Luc waded into the midst of the Romulan commandos.

Now for my finale.

He heard the scrapes of their boots on the deck, the huffs of their breathing, the rustling of their uniforms, and from those he deduced where each of the Tal Hansu was in relation to himself. He adjusted his hold on his knife to a simpler grip and set his thumb on the back of the blade, just ahead of the handle.

Then, with cold, mechanical efficiency, he started cutting.

He severed the flexors in their wrists, the tendons in their ankles, the ligaments in their elbows and knees. Within seconds he heard weapons clatter to the deck, followed by the heavy thumps of the wounded. Quick strikes to their temples with the pommel of his knife stunned them and brought the battle to an end.

A gust of air cleared the smoke from the corridor, revealing Luc, painted in the green blood of his enemies while standing tall above them, knife in one hand, pistol in the other.

He sheathed his blade and moved to a nearby bulkhead with a companel. He keyed in a command code to unlock the panel, which had been taken offline by the intruder alert. Once it was restored to normal operating status, he opened an internal comm channel.

"Picard to bridge. Report."

"This is Perim, sir. Enemy ships destroyed, boarding parties on decks twelve and six neutralized. What is your status?"

"Deck three secure. Did those warbirds send out any signals about us?"

"None that we know of—but if they alerted their chain of command before engaging us, there might be more like them heading our way."

"Assume for now that there are. Restore the transphasic shields as soon as possible, then deploy auxiliary craft to speed up your scans of Kali 531."

"Aye, sir."

"I'll be back on the bridge in twenty minutes. Have a repair update ready when I arrive."

"Twenty minutes, sir? Are you all right? Do you need transport to sickbay?"

Luc regarded his nightmarish reflection in the glassy black surface of the companel. "No, Lieutenant, just a shower. Picard out."

San Francisco, Earth—2373, Borg Timeline

Getting into the superstructure beneath the Golden Gate Bridge had not proved as difficult as Sisko had feared. The marriage of fog and darkness had yielded perfect cover for the away team during its short sprint from its scouting position to the leg of the bridge nearest the hillside.

The real problem, Sisko had realized only after it was too late, was going to be reaching the other side of the bridge, almost three kilometers away, by way of narrow beams and ledges while steeped in misty blackness, without the aid of lights or safety cables, while trying not to look down through occasional breaks in the fog at the icy water nearly seventy meters below.

Everything Sisko reached for here was cold and slick with moisture. Steel beams, wires, pipes—they all were slippery with a mixture of condensation and chemical lubricants.

Regardless, it had seemed manageable until the team arrived at the first wide gap in the bridge's packed underside. Without any warning, they had come to a patch of empty space that was crossed by only one iron girder. It was barely thirty centimeters wide and seemed to appear and disappear at random as banks of fog rolled over it. Two hundred–odd centimeters directly above it ran another girder of the same width. It was close enough that the away team members were able to use it as a handhold—all except Lal, whose reach came up just short.

Data was the first to brave the crossing, with Doctor Crusher tethered to him using a short length of wiring he had torn free of a long-dormant machine. Every step of the way, the two were buffeted by frigid winds. Sisko feared that one strong gust might be enough to send them both plunging to their deaths. *Hitting water from this height would be as devastating as hitting solid ground. Even Data might not survive that kind of trauma.*

Sisko had never been fond of heights—or, to be more precise, of the possibility of falling to his death from a great height. His palms grew clammy with sweat as he watched Data ferry Crusher across the beam. *Steady. One step at a time. Easy . . .*

A drop of something viscous and odorous landed on Sisko's shoulder. He flinched at its impact, then wrinkled his features at its stench. Cursing the Borg, he shifted his stance in the hope of not getting dripped on again.

The next pair to cross the beam were Lal and Picard. Even though Lal was unable to reach the overhead beam, her android balance, strength, and reflexes, as well as her high density, made her well suited to the role of anchor. This time, however, there had been no spare wire, so Picard kept his left hand on Lal's shoulder and his right on the beam above his head as they made their slow, carefully synchronized tandem crossing.

By the time they reached the far side, Sisko was wiping the sweat from his hands onto his trouser legs.

Bashir edged up to the beam, and then he looked back at Sisko. "Are you sure you don't want my help getting across?"

"I'll be fine, Doctor. You go ahead."

"If you insist." Bashir turned and walked across the beam as if he were just out for a carefree stroll through the center of town.

It's so easy to forget he's genetically enhanced, until he does something like that.

From the far side, the away team beckoned.

Sisko took hold of the beam above him. Shuffled forward. He kept his eyes mostly on his hands but stole glances at his feet. *One foot in front of the other. Slow and steady . . .*

Just over halfway across, his right foot slid on a patch of grease.

He teetered on one foot and prayed his hands didn't lose hold of the oily steel beam. He fought the urge to overtighten his grip—that would only make it harder to hold on.

Don't panic. Don't panic. Find your balance.

He shifted his weight, ever so slightly—it would be far too easy to overcorrect up here. His right leg swung awkwardly. And then he steadied himself. Put his right foot back on the beam. He was doing his best not to look down at the water, far beneath the ragged curtain of fog drifting past below him, when a gust of wind struck him like the hand of the Almighty.

The gale swept his feet from under him, tore his hands from the overhead beam.

For an instant prolonged by his fear he felt weightless, suspended in time between the loss of his grip and the surrender to gravity that was about to follow it.

Then he was falling.

Sisko's world became a blur—and then came a streak of motion, racing at him as he plunged past the beam, his limbs flailing without purpose or purchase—

Crushing, viselike pressure seized his left wrist.

His fall was halted with a terrible jolt that dislocated his shoulder and sent scarlet waves of pain into his spine. He wanted to holler, but he knew there were Borg drones just a few meters overhead, so he choked back his shout of pain and clenched his jaw.

When the white heat in his shoulder socket abated to mere agony, he squinted through the foggy darkness at his savior.

Lal lay prone on the lower beam, holding Sisko with one hand.

She whispered, "I'm going to pull you up, Captain. Be advised, it will hurt."

He nodded his understanding. Then she straddled the beam like a gymnast, pushing her torso upright with her free hand, and lifting Sisko with the other. She draped him atop the beam.

"Can you get your leg over the side, Captain?"

"I think so." He mirrored her pose, straddling the beam.

"Good." With preternatural agility, Lal pulled herself up, and perched in a squatting pose atop the beam. Moving with care, she pivoted about-face, then backed up against Sisko. "Lean against me, sir. Put your right arm over my shoulder, as far as you can reach."

He did as she directed, and then momentarily held his breath in alarm as she took hold of his arm and stood, lifting and then bearing his full weight on her back.

She crossed the beam in steady, graceful steps, her hold on Sisko gentle but solid.

When they reached the far side of the beam, Lal handed Sisko off to Bashir. There was genuine concern in Bashir's voice. "Captain? Are you all right?"

"Yes, but I'll need you to take a look at this shoulder once we're back on solid ground." He regarded Data's daughter with humility and gratitude. "Thank you, Lal."

She cocked her head, then smiled back. "You're more than welcome."

Picard gave Sisko an appraising look. "We're a kilometer from shore. Can you make it?"

"Of course," Sisko said, and then immediately regretted his defensive tone of voice. He mustered his strength and recovered his regular demeanor of command. "We've got a long way to go, people, and not much time to get there. Mister Soong—lead the way."

15

Her husband-who-was-not-her-husband had eyes everywhere. Whenever Troi got close to stealing a moment in private with a member of *Titan*'s crew who might be able to help her stop not-Riker's obsessive hunt for *Defiant* and get him into sickbay long enough to bring back the real Riker, *her* Riker, either the admiral or his aide Ssura appeared.

Ssura must be watching me. Tracking my combadge. Troi hated feeling paranoid, but under the circumstances it struck her as the only truly rational response. *I can't risk visiting the captain, or Doctor Ree. So where do I go?*

Waves of suspicion and fear assailed her empathic senses as she moved through the ship, but even without her Betazoid talents she would have known something was off. She heard the whispers behind her back as she passed junior officers. Caught the sidelong looks that were always averted just as she noticed them. *Titan*'s crew knew something was wrong in the upper echelons of command; the lower decks were abuzz with nervous chatter.

The fastest thing in the universe is bad news on a starship.

Unsure where to go, Troi felt as if she were making endless circuits of one deck after another, but she needed time to think—and if her constant movement served to confound not-Riker and his enabler Ssura for even a few minutes, she considered that a bonus.

I know Ssura is on his side. And maybe Keru. If he has both of them, he could put both command and security under his thumb. That's bad. Really bad.

She stepped into a turbolift, ignored the spike in emotional tension she sensed from the pair of ensigns standing behind her against the lift car's wall, and ordered it down one deck.

Seconds later she was out of the turbolift and starting a new set of laps on deck five. Doing her best to maintain a poker face, she resumed considering her options.

Pazlar might be rational enough to see something's wrong, but I doubt there's much she can do to help me. If I want to take away not-Will's control of the ship, I can talk to Doctor Ra-Havreii. But would he be sympathetic? I can't be sure, and that's far too great a gamble.

Every potential answer only left her with more questions.

Then she caught a familiar face out of the corner of her eye. She stopped, took a step back, and looked through the open doorway of the officers' mess. The ship's first officer, Commander Dalit Sarai, was sitting alone at a table in the back of the dining area, picking dejectedly at the food on her tray.

Troi did her best to look casual and unrushed as she entered the mess hall. *Just a senior officer grabbing a quick bite to eat. Nothing suspect about that.*

She made her way to an open replicator. "One sweet-cheese croissant, warm, and a Mexican hot chocolate, seventy-two degrees Celsius." The pair of treats materialized inside the replicator's nook with a prismatic swirl and a musical wash of sound. When the process was finished, she picked up the tray that had been created beneath her snack and carried it across the mess hall, to the table of Dalit Sarai.

Sarai had situated herself at the back corner of the table, facing the replicators. Troi settled onto the table's attached bench, at a slight angle to Sarai, one of the few women on the ship whose sable hair was even darker than Troi's. The Efrosian woman noted Troi's arrival, and then she returned to stabbing stewed vegetables with her fork.

Despite the fact that most Efrosians possessed at least low-level empathic talents, Troi was unable to pick up any cues to Sarai's emotional state. She wondered whether the first officer, in turn, was getting any kind of a read on her. *Can she feel my apprehension? My desire to confide in her? My fear that she might betray me?*

Small talk seemed to Troi like the safest gambit. "Didn't get what you wanted?"

The first officer stared glumly at her meal. "Just not as hungry as I thought."

"Sorry to hear that." Troi took a small bite off the end of her croissant. "I ask only because sometimes the replicators . . . get strange."

Sarai narrowed her eyes. "Strange?"

"You know what I mean. They seem dependable. *Familiar*. And then, one day, it's like it's been replaced by one that *looks* the same but doesn't *work* the same. At all."

Troi sipped her cocoa as Sarai studied her.

"I know what you mean," the XO said. "You spend years getting to know its quirks. And then one day you wake up, and it's like someone *reprogrammed* it. All the buttons are still there, but not all of them work the way you remember." With her fork, she lifted a limp bit of overcooked tomato flesh from her plate. "It's almost enough to make you wonder if you can trust *anything* that comes out of it."

Tearing her croissant in half, Troi said, "If my replicator did that, I'd want to put it through a level-one diagnostic. Just to be sure."

Sarai's head was down, her eyes on her half-eaten meal. "Mm-hm."

Troi didn't have to ask about the abrupt change in Sarai's behavior. Her empathic skills felt the sickly waves of suspicion emanating from not-Riker immediately behind her. She turned and saw him looking down at her, a phony smile plastered on his face.

"What a surprise to find you here, Deanna. Is the replicator in our suite not working?"

She mirrored his insincere geniality. "It's fine. I was just stretching my legs when I had a sudden craving." She held up her mug. "You know me: I can't resist the call of hot chocolate."

"I do, indeed."

He set his hand on her back. "Bring it with you."

It was hard for her to mask her anger. "Am I going somewhere?"

"Things are about to get rough. I'd feel better knowing that you and Tasha were safe in our quarters." His voice took on an edge as he added, "She needs her mother. Right now."

"I see." Troi stood. She grabbed her cocoa but left her half-eaten croissant. She caught Sarai's eye, and then she nodded at the pastry she had left behind. "Would you mind?"

"Not at all. I'll take care of it."

"Thank you."

Walking out of the mess hall, Troi ached to look back, to seek out a wink or a nod or some kind of signal that Sarai had understood her request for help. That her promise to "take care of it" was more than just a pledge to dump her leftovers in the waste processor.

But with not-Riker at her side, she knew there would be no looking back—just as she already knew she had nowhere left to run.

San Francisco, Earth—2373, Borg Timeline

Beverly Crusher had never been so grateful to feel mud beneath her boots than she had when she and the rest of the away team reached the far end of the Golden Gate Bridge.

As soon as they had all arrived on terra firma, Bashir had called for a five-minute break so he could treat Captain Sisko's injuries. Data then led the team into a shallow crevasse just a few meters away from the bridge, below the level of the roadway. Here they had a modicum of concealment. At the very least, they were unlikely to be spotted by any Borg drones that might pass by on the road above, or fly past overhead.

As a perk, their temporary shelter had an unobstructed view to the east, past what had once been a marina, to the grounds where Starfleet Command had never been built. Instead, a monstrous structure dominated several acres—a grotesque biomechanoid cathedral. Shooting upward into space from its tallest crooked spire was a painfully bright beam of emerald light, the chroniton bombardment that had been meant to kill them but instead had spawned an infinite number of unstable quantum timelines—the unforeseen consequence that now threatened to spell the end of every timeline, stable and unstable alike.

It was all too much for Crusher to wrap her head around. At a time when she was being asked to put cosmic needs ahead of her own, all she could think about was how this tragedy was going to affect the ones she loved. Her husband. Her children. Her friends.

Picard nudged her with his elbow. She could barely see him in the dark. His noble profile was limned by the actinic glow of the Borg's temporal disruptor beam. When her eyes adjusted she realized he was offering her a sip from his open canister of energy drink.

She took it with a grateful nod. "Thank you."

"Small sips. It packs a jolt."

She downed a long swig. "It's okay, I'm a doctor. I know what I'm doing."

"Well, that makes *one* of us, at least." There was a ghost of a smile on his lips.

It was hard for her not to be appalled. "How can you be so calm at a time like this?"

"I only *look* calm, Beverly. I assure you, I'm anything but."

She handed him the drink canister. "I can't even describe how I feel. I'm shaking with adrenaline, so ready to do something that I feel like I might shatter. But when I think about what we need to do, I go numb. I feel *dead* inside."

He sipped from the canister. "Denial. Anger. Bargaining—"

"Depression and acceptance. I know the stages of grief, Jean-Luc." She averted her eyes from the Borg's doomsday weapon and looked instead at Data and Lal, who were huddled and sharing a quiet moment a few meters away. Seeing them made her think of Wesley, and then of René. "What if we've made a mistake?"

"What kind of mistake?"

"This whole plan. What if Will Riker is right?"

Picard shook his head. "He isn't. We've seen the proof, done the math—"

"*Forget* all that. What if he's right and we're wrong? What if there *is* a way to save our timeline? One we haven't found because we *stopped looking for it*."

He remained dubious. "I wish there were. But if I believed that, if I thought there was even the *slightest* possibility that might be true . . . I would *never* stop fighting for that chance."

She reached over and found his hand in the dark. Squeezed it for the sake of holding on to what mattered. "Then *fight* for it. Find a way."

He wrapped her hands in both of his. "I tried. There's no way to save our timeline without condemning a multitude of others." He leaned toward her and touched his forehead to hers. When he spoke again, she felt his voice as much as she heard it. "Each of us owes the universe a death, Beverly. Ours have come due. But we have a chance to make them mean something. To spare an infinity of possibilities from sharing our fate."

Hot tears ran from Crusher's eyes. "But at what cost, Jean-Luc?" Her voice faltered as she continued. "Can we really risk losing our son? After all we went through to find our way home to each other, can we really risk losing *us*?"

She caught a reflected glint of green light in the lone tear that fell from her husband's eye. "I don't want to lose any part of our life, Beverly. Not you, not René. Not Wesley." He gestured with his chin toward Data and Lal. "Not our friends." He swallowed hard, clearly fighting to maintain some semblance of composure. "But if there really are an infinity of possible timelines, I have to believe that ours isn't the only one in which we find each other. There must be countless realities where we get to watch René grow up in his own good time. An infinite number in which Data returns and brings Lal back to life. Endless dimensions in which the sacrifices we've made, and all the good that we've done, matter and are remembered."

With the back of his hand, he tenderly stroked Crusher's chin and cheek. "The only thing that gives me the courage to see this through is that I believe that somehow, somewhere, some*when* . . . the love you and I have found together will *live on*."

As her emotions swelled, Crusher knew she had to make a choice, though it was truly no choice at all. There was no time now to break down and sob like a broken soul, so she channeled all her fear, all her grief, and all her hope into one passionate kiss with her husband.

He wrapped her in his arms and let the kiss go on for as long as she needed it to.

Crusher cast out her fears and her sorrows and rooted herself in that moment, in the strength of her husband's arms, the softness of his lips, the warmth of his body against hers.

Our love will live on, she promised herself.

I don't know if I believe that.

But I need to.

So I will.

I will.

It will.

16

U.S.S. *Defiant* NX-74205—2373, **Borg Timeline**

Worf's order was not the worst idea K'Ehleyr had ever heard, but she was sure it was the dumbest. She lowered her chin in disapproval. "Tell me you're not serious."

"There is no other way." Standing beside K'Ehleyr at the master systems display on *Defiant*'s bridge, Worf pointed out systems as he elaborated. "Engineering cannot make further repairs to the warp drive or impulse core without additional parts and materials."

K'Ehleyr's mind raced to find alternatives. "Why not use the industrial replicator?"

"It cannot create the needed components on battery power alone."

She refused to concede defeat. "What about scavenging from our own systems?"

"None contain the needed materials."

She highlighted the small-craft hangars on deck four. "Why not take what we need from the shuttles? They have impulse reactors and warp cores."

Worf shook his head. "All but one were destroyed in the crash. The last one is a type-10 shuttlecraft. Its engine components are too small to be compatible with *Defiant*'s systems."

A sound that was half sigh, half growl rattled in K'Ehleyr's throat. "So much for the safe way. Do we know where to find what we need?"

"We think so." Worf switched the image on the aft console's display to show a map of the area within twenty kilometers of *Defiant*. A handful of locations to the north, within the Borg city, flashed red. Worf pointed at them one by one as he spoke. "Passive sensors indicate the materials and parts we need are at these sites."

She leaned closer to study the map, and was rewarded with a whiff of the commingled sweat, grime, and smoke residue that had permeated

Worf's uniform. Part of her found its odor repellent—but some atavistic Klingon node of her brain stirred at his scent, leaving her secretly and awkwardly aroused. "How much resistance should the salvage team expect?"

"Some." Worf gestured at areas between the targets. "Sensors have detected drones roaming here, here, and here."

The tactical segment of K'Ehleyr's imagination kicked in. "Are the drones following a pattern that we can see? If they're sentries on patrol, they might repeat the same route."

Worf nodded. "There have been repeated sightings at regular intervals."

K'Ehleyr called up the sensor records of the drones' movements, charted their movements relative to one another, and then ran a regression simulation. "I have something. Our projected model, if run in reverse, correctly predicts the recorded movements of the drones. So if we run the sim forward—"

She observed the results, noting the speed and movements of the Borg sentries. It felt right to her. During her years of field work for Memory Omega, she had always had a good sense of which plans were doomed to screw the *targ* and which were likely to succeed. This one felt like the latter. "All right, this looks doable. I can dump the Borg's patrol routes and timing to a tricorder. With that, the salvage team should be able to avoid the drones. As long as they don't get bogged down at some point, they should be fine."

"Good. Because you and I will be *with* them."

That was not what she had hoped to hear. "Excuse me?"

"Mister La Forge will lead the salvage team. It is vital that we send our best security personnel to defend them."

"Worf? You and I are *command* personnel."

"We are also *warriors*. I served for many years as a chief of security. And your file says you spent over a decade as a Memory Omega field agent."

"Oh, *sure*. Hold *that* against me."

His expression darkened. "Without us, the engineers are *not* likely to survive. In which case, our mission *will* fail."

K'Ehleyr rolled her eyes at Worf's humorless scolding. "Fine. Spare me the guilt trip and the pep talk, and tell me you have a plan for getting us all back to the ship in one piece."

"We will need to rely on stealth." Worf gestured toward the curved *mek'leth* sheathed on his back. "The security team will use melee weapons. No phasers, no munitions."

She lifted one elegant eyebrow in disbelief. "Tell me you're kidding."

"I am not."

"Don't the Borg have adaptive shields or some nonsense?"

"Yes, but they only use them against energy-based attacks." He glanced at the grip of his Klingon short sword. "They seem to think melee weapons are not worth defending against." He cracked an evil smile. "I look forward to proving them wrong."

Though the plan sounded borderline insane to K'Ehleyr, the deepest parts of her Klingon nature stirred at the promise of real hand-to-hand combat, a bloody close-quarters battle, and the visceral satisfaction of using a blade to butcher flesh and bone.

But her Memory Omega training asserted its hold over her. Compelled her to cling to her discipline, her reason, her orders. Hiding her growing excitement, she asked Worf, "Who's going to guard the ship while we're off babysitting the salvage team?"

"I will leave Alexander in charge."

"Alexander?"

"Do not judge my son by his size, or his nature. He has faced greater dangers than you will ever know."

She accepted Worf's rebuke in stride. "Fair enough. But putting him *in charge?*"

"As a Federation ambassador, he has the diplomatic rank of a vice admiral."

K'Ehleyr took a moment to imagine all that was implied by that statement, and then she switched off the aft console, as much to conserve battery power as to end the conversation with Worf. "When do we move out?"

"Five minutes. A field-ops uniform is waiting for you on your bunk."

"How thoughtful." She nodded at his *mek'leth.* "Do I get one of those?"

He handed her the blade and its sheath. "Take mine."

As he turned to leave, she asked, "You're not going out there unarmed?"

He paused in the aft doorway, looked back, and smiled. "I am not."

Without explaining himself, he vanished down the darkened corridor, moving at a quick step toward his stateroom.

Tucking the weapon under her belt, she headed aft toward her own quarters, fighting to suppress her growing urge to smile. A truth had just taken her by surprise:

She found Worf . . . *interesting.*

No, more than that—she found him *attractive.*

Kahless, help me.

C.S.S. *Enterprise*

Luc Picard was sure he must have misheard Director Saavik. "What do you mean they haven't decided yet? We need reinforcements."

"Ambassador Spock has yet to address Parliament."

He stood in his ready room, facing a life-size hologram of the elderly Vulcan woman. Rendered by the ship's quantum comm system, her likeness was projected in real time with such fidelity that Luc could catch every nuance of her microexpressions—which meant that his holographic avatar, addressing her in their home dimension, was equally detailed.

"Have you made Parliament aware of the urgency of our request?"

The shift in Saavik's mien suggested that she found his query irksome. *"I assure you, Captain, they know all too well how urgent this matter is."*

His temper got the better of him. "Then why in blazes aren't they *doing* anything?" As soon as the words left him, he felt regret.

To his relief, Saavik did not seem in a reproachful mood. *"If you must know, Captain, the members of our esteemed legislature have been quite busy. Most have been consumed by the pressing business of panicking in the face of catastrophe, and then seeking scapegoats."*

Luc's spirits sank. The government he served was in chaos, rendered impotent by fear at the moment when it was needed most. "Can we bypass them? Make an appeal to the fleet?"

"Nominally, the fleet still answers to the Galactic Commonwealth. On

behalf of Memory Omega, I vowed to respect the Commonwealth's sover-
eignty, especially with regard to control of the jaunt-ships. I will not break
that oath. Not even in the face of annihilation."

Under any other circumstances Luc would have found Saavik's integrity inspiring. Now, however, it was yet another obstacle to the com-
pletion of his mission. "Director, *please*. In the last several hours, my
ship has twice come under assault by superior forces. This dimension's
Admiral Riker is more than a zealot—I fear he's gone mad."

"That sounds like hyperbole, Captain."

"I assure you, it is *not*. He's rallied every surviving ship in his Federation to join the hunt for us, and he's even made his galactic rivals aware
of the price on our heads. There is nowhere we can go in this counterpart galaxy without being harried by fleets of aggressors."

"I was led to think you would be able to stay ahead of them. Was that
incorrect?"

"Regrettably, yes. We've suffered serious damage during our first two
encounters. Mister Barclay is trying to expedite repairs, but the truth,
Director, is that my ship cannot stand many more battles. The nature
of our search leaves us vulnerable—and our enemies have shown a pro-
pensity to attack in overwhelming numbers, and without quarter."

Saavik turned away from Luc—whether to steal a moment to think
without having to consider his presence, or because she was paying attention to something else, he couldn't tell. He could see the weight of
her own troubles bearing down upon her. For a moment she closed her
eyes. When she opened them, she faced him once more.

"Captain, I appreciate the gravity of your predicament. But I cannot,
and will not, usurp the authority of the Commonwealth. In spite of the risk,
I must implore you to be patient."

It was not the answer Luc wanted to hear. "Patience is not always
a virtue, Director. My chief of security is tracking five more Romulan
warships closing on our position as we speak."

"Will you be able to complete your survey by then?"

"I can't say for certain. There are too many variables—not the least
of which is the volatility of Kali 531." He stole a look out of his ready
room's viewport at the swirling violence of the massive black hole looming beyond its fiery event horizon. "If the Devidians' hidden base is

here, we'll be compelled to hold our ground against the Romulans until *Defiant* returns from the past. And if the Devidians *aren't* here, we'll have to fend off another assault before we've had a chance to finish our repairs."

"Then I suggest you expedite your search, Captain. And hasten your departure."

"Easier said than done. Even if we make it to our next survey target, I cannot guarantee we'll be in any condition to finish our search in time. And if our enemy turns out to be there, waiting for us . . . this might well end up being a futile effort."

"There is no such thing as a futile *effort, Captain. It is what we fight for* and *against* that define us. The battles we wage, win or lose, give our lives meaning."*

Luc smiled at Saavik's attempt to placate him with wisdom. "If it's all the same to you, Director, I would much prefer to *win* this battle. And to do that, I'll need assistance. Soon."

"I understand, Captain. Ambassador Spock and I have spoken with Prime Minister Eddington. With luck, we'll address Parliament within the hour. But until then, please remember exactly *what* I *have told you:* I *cannot and will not defy or circumvent the authority of Parliament with regard to the jaunt-ships under its command. Nor can* I *intercede on your behalf with those ships' commanders.* I *am bound by a solemn pledge, and* I *will honor it."* She lowered her chin, as if to challenge Luc in some way. *"Have* I *made myself clear to you, Captain?"*

There had been a subtle change in the pitch of her voice, a modulation of her inflection several times when she had emphasized the pronoun "I," that snared Luc's attention. He thought about all she had told him, and then he considered her cautionary statement.

He acknowledged her with a single nod. "*I* understand, Director."

"See that you *do, Captain."* She let slip a weary sigh. *"I will contact you again as soon as we have an answer from Parliament. Until then, may your efforts be safe and fruitful."*

"Thank you, Director."

Saavik's holographic avatar faded, desaturated, and then vanished.

Alone in his ready room, Luc wished he had K'Ehleyr at his side to offer him advice, or to at least serve as a sounding board for his own desperate schemes. But he had let her leave to pursue something he couldn't understand but which she had assured him was too profound for her to ignore. He thought about confiding in Troi, but then he thought better of it.

If I'm right, it might be best if I played my cards close this time.

He sat at his desk and activated his holographic display. With a few taps on his desk's built-in haptic interface, he summoned the latest long-range scans of the incoming Romulan warships. Then he compared their ETA against Lieutenant Perim's estimate of when she and her team would finish their analysis of Kali 531's event horizon for Wesley Crusher.

If we're lucky, we might be able to jump away within thirty seconds of being intercepted. Then all we'll have to worry about is what's waiting for us on the other side.

What . . . or who.

He switched off his holo-display. It was time for him to make a choice and live with the consequences, for however long or brief the rest of his life turned out to be. Director Saavik had made her instructions clear, but now the choice was Luc's.

He, too, had sworn oaths. *Why should my promises be worth any less than hers?*

At the same time, Luc had learned from hard experience during the Great Revolution that sometimes illegal actions served a greater good. When immoral laws became impediments to justice, being a law-abiding person was the same thing as abetting evil through passive acceptance, while serving the greater good might mean becoming a criminal.

Saavik's words echoed in his thoughts.

It is what we fight for and against that define us.

He resolved himself to what had to be done.

Without hesitation or regret, he set the gears of fate once more into motion.

San Francisco, Earth—2373, Borg Timeline

Shadows in the fog, the black-clad salvage team had sprinted away from *Defiant*, through the night and out of the hills, into the charred remains of what once had been San Francisco. Gone was any trace of the city La Forge remembered from his youth at Starfleet Academy. All that remained was a nightmare wrought from blood and metal.

At the front of the group, Worf raised a fist, signaling the team to halt. It felt strange to La Forge to see Worf without his heirloom baldric. The Klingon had left it behind on *Defiant* to avoid giving away the salvage team with an accidental reflection off its bright metal.

Worf waved his palm toward the ground. The away team kneeled in silence as he pulled his *bat'leth* off his back.

La Forge had no chance to ask Worf what was going on before the Klingon stole away into the darkness, *bat'leth* in hand, with K'Ehleyr prowling a few steps behind him on his right.

Sure, we'll just sit here, Worf. Thanks for not asking.

La Forge had chosen his salvagers as much for their skills as for their speed and stealth. Worf and K'Ehleyr were in charge of guarding the perimeter, with help from *Defiant* security officers Keeso and Slayton. Keeso was stocky and muscular, a Canadian with hair like a hay bale who had learned to fight as a semipro hockey player. Slayton was a dark-haired, sun-browned high-plains marksman from Oklahoma, as accurate with a thrown blade as with a phaser.

More importantly, La Forge had brought his best mechanics into the field. Not engineers—he needed his top technical specialists on the ship, supervising repairs while he made this high-risk grocery run. He had brought a noncom and two enlisted personnel, each of them adept at high-speed component extractions, whether by force or finesse.

Senior among them was Chief Petty Officer Koor, a gangly thin Tellarite who happened to be an artist with a plasma cutter. Following his lead were crewmen Yong and L'Peng, a human male from Coridan and a Vulcan woman who had been born and raised on Mars. The two mechanics had met during basic training a year earlier and ended up posted together on *Defiant*. Since they had first arrived, they had worked as a team, and their tandem speed and efficiency at repairs had become the envy of their shipmates.

Worf and K'Ehleyr returned. He held his curved Klingon sword at the ready while she waved the team forward and added a hand signal that meant *move slowly and quietly.*

La Forge adjusted the sensitivity of his cybernetic eyes to enhance his night vision for better contrast and sharpness. He stayed in front of his mechanics, trusting his eyes' multispectrum sensitivity to reveal any hazards. If there was a cavity beneath the ground—a sinkhole, or a trap—he would see it. Likewise, he could detect the heat signatures left behind by the last Borg drones to patrol this ground. By their rate of heat loss relative to the ambient temperature, he calculated how long ago the drones had passed. Infrared and ultraviolet sensor beams, and even radar sensors, all betrayed themselves to his eyes.

Wrapped in the velvet mists for which San Francisco had once been famous—and would be again, if La Forge had anything to say about it—the salvage team threaded a path through the blackened sprawl of the Borg complex. La Forge monitored the feed from his tricorder, which for the team's safety had been set for silent operation. Its readouts had been switched off and their signals routed directly to La Forge's cybernetic eyes, which rendered the tricorder's data stream as a semi-transparent virtual heads-up display superimposed over his field of vision.

The tricorder simultaneously guided the team toward several of their desired items in a single location, while also generating a scattering field designed to mask the team's life signs and energy readings from the Borg. Maintaining the scattering field was draining the tricorder's power cell far more quickly than normal operations would have. They had, at most, another thirty minutes of cover before the tricorder would become just a hunk of dead weight on La Forge's hip.

The team reached a sealed door on the side of a windowless box of steel festooned with conduits and cables. Overhead, three different levels of intercrossing catwalks became progressively harder to find in the fog. All around the black box masquerading as a building were heaps of industrial wreckage, discarded technology, broken concrete, and, mixed into all that detritus, countless artifacts of humanity's extinct civilization.

A quick, soft whistle from Worf snared the away team's attention. He directed Keeso and Slayton with gestures to circle the target building. Blades drawn, the security officers stole away.

Next he looked at K'Ehleyr, pointed with two fingers at his eyes, then upward at the catwalks. K'Ehleyr nodded and vanished into the mists with a short, curved Klingon blade in her hand. Once she was gone, Worf signaled La Forge to proceed.

With a slap on Chief Koor's shoulder, La Forge sent his team to work.

The trio of tool-pushers converged on the building's only door. Koor dismantled its locks and alarms while Yong and L'Peng broke out fusion torches and cut the door's bolts and hinges with surgical precision and breathtaking speed.

Before La Forge had a chance to ask his people how they were doing, the door fell from its frame. The three mechanics caught it, and then set it aside. They were about to head inside the structure when La Forge stopped them with a raised fist.

He signaled them to back away from the door as he approached. They made room for him. He moved up to the now-open doorway, primed his cybernetic eyes for a fast recon of the structure's interior, and then ducked his head around the corner for a fraction of a second— more than he needed, but as fast as his reflexes allowed.

After he had withdrawn behind the corner, he reviewed the multi-spectral snapshot his eyes had taken of the building's interior. Rendered in infrared, it was a wash of crimson, a wall of dry heat from corner to corner. Filtering the image in ultraviolet, he saw the space inside was mostly one open area, packed with pipes, generators, cables, and other machines—but no sign of Borg drones or detection systems. Acting out of an abundance of caution, he reviewed his snapshot through a tachyon discriminator, to rule out the presence of any cloaked persons or objects.

Satisfied, he waved his mechanics inside. "You know what to take. Go get it."

He was impressed and pleased by his mechanics' alacrity and precision inside what he was now certain was a power relay station. The trio split up, each targeting an item on La Forge's "shopping list" for the repair of *Defiant*. La Forge remained behind, just inside the doorway, watching outside for any sign of trouble.

Trouble arrived less than a minute later.

His first warning was the return of Keeso and Slayton. The Canadian was carrying his shipmate over his shoulder. Most people would not have been able to see Slayton's wounds through the darkness and heavy fog, but La Forge's eyes pierced the vapor to see a flurry of grievous blood-soaked lacerations on the young man's chest, arms, and back.

No one had to tell La Forge what that meant. He had seen it too many times before.

The Borg know we're here. And they're coming for us.

He stepped clear of the doorway and waved Keeso and Slayton past him, inside the power relay station. Once they were inside, La Forge searched above and to either side for any sign of the Borg. He saw nothing, but the sound of heavy-booted footfalls echoed off every hard surface. It sounded as if they were coming from *everywhere.*

If we're surrounded, we're cooked.

The marching steps, with their synchronicity and steady cadence, grew closer and clearer.

A tap on La Forge's shoulder startled him. He turned to see Chief Koor. He wanted to shout, but kept his voice to a sharp whisper instead. "What?"

"Should we get Slayton back to the ship?"

"Not yet. Keep working."

"Sir, he's losing a lot of blood. If we don't—"

La Forge snapped at Koor, "Keep working, Chief. That's an order."

The Tellarite chief petty officer, normally a fan of arguments, apparently sensed that this was neither the time nor the place to test La Forge's patience. He took a step back—"Aye, sir."—and then he slipped away, back to his work of salvaging components that could be used to rebuild *Defiant's* dilithium crystal articulation frame.

Outside the doorway, the percussion of marching feet was loud and clear. La Forge stole a quick look past the corner. Eight drones were coming directly toward the power relay station.

And then he saw Worf and K'Ehleyr. They appeared like phantoms in the mist, behind the advancing squad of Borg drones. Both of them wielded short Klingon daggers—La Forge remembered that kind of weapon was called a *d'k tahg*—as they prowled closer to the rear pair of drones.

Attacking in tandem, like dancers moving to the same music, Worf and K'Ehleyr thrust their short blades forward—through the necks of the two drones at the back of the formation. Perfect, silent kills. The drones went limp. Worf and K'Ehleyr caught them and lowered them to the dusty ground.

The remaining drones continued to close in on the relay station.

La Forge wished he had a phaser, but he remembered Worf's warning from before they had left the ship: the sound and brightness of a phaser beam would draw many more drones than it could kill. Attracting attention out here would be tantamount to suicide.

Outside, Worf and K'Ehleyr skulked to within half an arm's length of the two drones now at the back of the squad. Without a sound, again acting in elegant concert, each of them snaked an arm around a Borg drone's throat, seized its jaw, and with a swift, hard twist snapped its neck.

This time the kills were not soundless—the wet crunch of shattering vertebrae was audible even to La Forge, many meters away.

The second pair of drones stopped, turned back, and faced K'Ehleyr and Worf.

But the first two pressed onward, straight toward the open doorway and La Forge.

The engineer's pulse and mind both were racing, fueled by adrenaline. Worf and K'Ehleyr were skilled combatants, but even they wouldn't be able to take out two drones and reach La Forge before the leading pair of drones arrived.

Need a weapon—something quiet . . .

In the fog beyond the doorway, Worf brandished his *bat'leth*. K'Ehleyr traced hypnotic figure eights with her *mek'leth*. The drones in front of them charged their cybernetic arms' built-in plasma blasters and raised them to fire . . .

. . . as the leading pair of drones stepped through the doorway into the power station—and into the path of La Forge's fusion torch, which had been set to maximum burn.

A white-hot jet of ionized plasma shot from the muzzle of the torch—and disintegrated the two drones' heads in a single burst.

It took the fire-decapitated drones' bodies nearly two seconds to fall to the floor at La Forge's feet—by which time Worf and K'Ehleyr had expertly dismembered the last two drones outside. The duo came running to La Forge, only to halt abruptly in the doorway at the sight of his handiwork, still smoking on the floor in front of them.

Worf noted the carnage, then looked at La Forge. "Nice."

K'Ehleyr cracked a sarcastic smile. "Kudos, Commander."

As much as he appreciated their compliments, La Forge had more pressing matters on his mind. "Any more out there?"

Worf shook his head. "Not that we saw. But more will come."

"I figured. Slayton's hurt. Can you hold the line with just Keeso?"

K'Ehleyr nodded. "I think so." She snapped her fingers, capturing Keeso's attention. "Finish patching him up, then get back outside."

"Aye, Commander."

La Forge gauged his team's progress and opportunities. "If I'm right, we'll be able to get everything we need here, so we can skip Site B."

That got a nod from Worf. "Good. How long?"

La Forge took a second to think it over. "Ten minutes?"

Without a trace of irony, Worf replied, "You have *five*."

La Forge sighed. "Worf, I don't care what anybody says. You were *born* for command."

The Klingon knitted his brows in confusion, and then he looked at K'Ehleyr. "I think I have just been insulted."

She smirked. "I *know* you have."

La Forge patted Worf's shoulder, then said as he walked away from him, "I *like* her. She's a *keeper*." From that moment onward, La Forge felt Worf's stare burning into his back for the rest of the salvage mission—but if anyone had asked, he would have sworn to the Great Bird of the Galaxy that it was worth it just to have seen the look on Worf's face.

The big galoot's in love, and he doesn't even know it.

17

Galactic Commonwealth Parliament, Deneva—Mirror Universe

Beyond the door, hundreds of voices spoke while no one listened; behind the door, one man listened without speaking.

They also serve who only stand and wait, Spock mused, reflecting upon the line from John Milton's famous poem "On His Blindness." While the poet had meant it as an expression of faith that, even after being rendered infirm, his life still had purpose in the designs of a higher power, Spock had interpreted it as a call to patience. Even when action was delayed, he reasoned, merit resided in one's readiness to act.

Hours had passed while he and Saavik had waited for Eddington to bring the Parliament to order, to no avail. In what now seemed to Spock like an overabundance of optimism, the prime minister had brought him to the private entrance to the speaker's podium. Located behind and beneath the tiered dais from which the Parliament's senior members presided, the door led to a platform at the base of a steep incline. Spock had determined, thanks to a cursory examination of the platform, that it was mechanized to scale the slope in a manner similar to a funicular.

He turned at the sound of a door opening in the long corridor behind him. Prime Minister Eddington returned, walking quickly and looking harried. As the tall human drew closer, Spock noted the sweat on the man's high forehead. He spoke as he slowed to a halt, and sounded out of breath. "I'm sorry, Mister Ambassador. It's a madhouse up there."

"So I have heard." Spock turned his head, angling one ear toward the doorway. His hearing was still quite sharp, but even he was unable to make any sense of the din from above. Then he considered the possibility that he and Eddington might see better results with a method designed to overcome the chamber's hubbub. "Mister Prime Minister, I have an idea."

It was a simple plan, and Spock explained it quickly to Eddington.

The prime minister considered Spock's suggestion, and then he nodded. "Yes, we can do that. When should we proceed?"

"The present seems as good a time as any." Spock raised his right hand in a salute. "May you enjoy peace and clarity, Prime Minister."

"I thought the saying was 'Live long and prosper.'"

"Under the circumstances, such a wish seems ill-considered."

"I suppose you're right. Good luck, Mister Ambassador."

Eddington walked quickly back the way he'd come, in a hurry to prepare the chamber above for Spock's address. As the prime minister retreated into shadow, Spock stepped onto the funicular platform and pressed a button on the wall beside it. As he'd expected, it began a smooth ascent, maintaining a level surface as it silently climbed the steep incline.

As the platform neared the slope's apex, Spock squinted against the bright lights that flooded the arena-like Parliament chamber, and winced at the rising clamor of shouting voices. The platform slowed and halted at the top. Standing on the speaker's dais, high above the frantic scrums in the aisles and rows, Spock folded his hands in front of him. And he waited.

For several seconds, the chaos continued around him, unabated.

At first no one noticed as the banks of huge overhead lights that lined the ceiling dimmed. The eerie half-light stopped some of the struggles on the floor, while others soldiered on. Then the great lights went out completely, submerging the hall into darkness broken only by tiny points of light. But even in the dark, shouting matches persisted—

—until a narrow shaft of bright light cut through the sea of black to land upon Spock, a spotlight as bright and hot as the Vulcan sun.

And still he waited with quiet patience, until the sounds of argument below fell away and were replaced by exclamations of disbelief: "It's him!" "It can't be him? Can it?" "It must be!"

Then a single syllable spread like a virus through the arena: *Spock!*

Next came a hush of reverent, expectant silence. Standing at its center, Spock felt the tremendous weight of celebrity and history. In this dimension, his alternate had died over a century earlier, a martyr who had given his life for the very concepts of freedom and democratic government. *What my old friend Jim would have called "a tough act to follow."*

"Distinguished members of Parliament. I am *not* the emperor-turned-consul your people once knew. I am what you would call his counterpart—Ambassador Spock of the United Federation of Planets, in the alternate universe.

"I am here to ask for your aid. Even now, one of your jaunt-ships, the *Enterprise*, is alone in my universe. Its crew seeks the hidden base of the Devidians, the architects of this cosmic disaster. If we do not find them in time, ours will not be the last universe to fall.

"If the Devidians succeed in killing our universe, and harvest the neural energies released at the moment of its collapse, they will become powerful enough to destroy *any* timeline. Unless we stop them now, they will become *invincible*.

"But the *Enterprise* is outnumbered. She is harried by fleets of hostile starships, and struggling to survey more targets than one ship can possibly reach in the scant time we have left. Captain Picard has called for reinforcements. I stand before you now to implore you, on behalf of not just my universe, but infinite countless others, to grant his request." He paused for dramatic effect, and then added in summation, "We must act now, or all will be lost."

His speech was answered first by silence. From the dark he heard the scuffling of feet, an isolated cough or two. Then a woman shouted up at him from somewhere deep in the black:

"If we send away our jaunt-ships, who will protect us *here*?"

The shortsightedness of the question gave Spock pause. "No ship in this universe can defend you now. You, or anyone else. Our impending annihilation is no longer preventable or escapable. The only choice left to us now is whether we will end the Devidians' carnage here, with our own deaths—or permit it to continue beyond us, into eternity."

His declaration was met by a moment of stunned quiet.

Then came a roar of profanities and anti-Vulcan ethnic slurs, deafeningly loud and all directed squarely at him. Small thrown objects caromed off the front of the speaker's dais, falling short of reaching Spock but striking close enough to let him know how his audience felt.

This did not go as I had expected.

Seeing nothing more to gain as the target of the Parliament's ire, he turned away, stepped onto the platform, and rode it down to the door at the bottom, where Eddington stood waiting.

The prime minister was sympathetic. "I'm guessing they said 'No'?"

Spock sighed. "In a manner of speaking." The shouting and epithets from the main hall grew louder. Disappointed, Spock frowned. "Let us hope Director Saavik's advice was better received than mine."

C.S.S. *Defiant*—Mirror Universe

Sequestered inside her stateroom on *Defiant II*, Kira sat cross-legged on the deck, the Orb of Time perched in front of her but still wrapped in its shroud.

The classic metal-and-gemstone tabernacles that for millennia had housed the Tears of the Prophets on Bajor had been crafted to contain the Orbs' mystical emanations. Whether the containment had been the result of the tabernacles' materials, their design, or some combination of the two, Kira had never really known. All she could say for certain was that a swaddling of heavy blankets was enough to mask the Orb's light but not its *pagh*-altering presence.

It called to her, but not in words. She felt its power, saw its magenta light even with her eyes shut. She was *drawn* to it. Ever since she had first encountered the Orb of Time, while transporting it home to Bajor aboard Deep Space 9's first *Starship Defiant*, she had felt a connection with it. That had been why Captain Sisko had entrusted Kira with the task of learning how to use the Orb to bring them home after a surgically disguised Klingon spy had used it to hurl the ship back to the twenty-third century, as part of a misconceived revenge plot.

Now the Orb wanted her to connect with it once more. But why? Was it a conduit for the Prophets? Was it them she heard whispering in the corners of her mind? Were the Prophets in this dimension the same ones she had known? And if not, could she trust them?

Getting ahead of yourself, Nerys. Breathe. Clear your mind.

Around her, *Defiant II* pulsed with power from its warp core—a synthetic heartbeat fueled by matter and antimatter annihilating each other. Cool, odorless air from the ventilation system washed over her bare arms, disturbing the fine hairs on the back of her hands. Each part of the ship was connected to every other, and to her.

Which was how she felt Dax's approach half a second before the door signal buzzed.

Kira sighed in exhaustion. "Come."

The door slid open, and Ezri Dax leaned in holding a padd, her face lit up by the same disarming smile that Kira had so adored in her universe's Ezri. "Am I disturbing you, Vedek?"

"Not at all, Captain. Please come in." Kira stood and then set aside the Orb to make room for Dax, who pulled back the chair from the desk against the bulkhead. Since there were no other chairs in the room, Kira sat on her bunk. "What can I do for you?"

"I just want to bring you up to speed about what to expect once we get to Bajor."

"Has much changed since the last time I was here?"

"More than you might think." Dax activated her padd and called up some data before handing the slender tablet to Kira. "For starters, Bajor has a truce with the Galactic Commonwealth, but so far they've resisted becoming members."

"Sounds familiar so far."

As Kira paged ahead through the report, Dax continued. "Unlike your universe, ours has no station guarding the mouth of the wormhole to the Gamma Quadrant. Mostly because Terok Nor was destroyed about ten years ago during the Great Revolution, and also because we and the Bajorans only became aware of the wormhole's existence a few years ago."

"Been there, lived through versions of all of that. What else?"

Dax waited for Kira to call up the next page of intel. "Because they don't have the resources to build a new station right now, the Bajorans have hired a fleet of mercenaries to guard the mouth of the wormhole, and prevent passage in either direction."

"Mercenaries? What kind?"

"The meanest they could get. Nausicaans. Balduks. Chalnoth. Even a few Gorn."

Kira skimmed the reports from long-range sensors and cloaked scout ships, and saw that Dax was correct. A large force of heavily armed hostile vessels had been massed in a hemispherical formation to blockade the mouth of the wormhole. "Okay, that's bad." She looked up at Dax. "Why do they need all this firepower?"

A thin smile suggested that the question brought up bad memories for Dax. "A little something called the Dominion. Ever heard of it?"

"Once or twice. They've sent ships through the wormhole?"

Dax nodded. "A couple of times."

"And . . . ?"

"Let's just say they aren't welcome here at the moment."

Kira skipped ahead to the end of the report, switched off the padd, and handed the device back to Dax. "Where does all this leave us?"

"Looking down the muzzle of a loaded blaster." The younger woman's demeanor took a grim turn. "Those mercenaries aren't just packing heavy ordnance. They've got state-of-the-art mil-tech they stole from the Klingons and the Cardassians, including a tachyon detection grid."

Now Kira understood the real problem. "They can see through our cloaking device."

"If we get too close, yeah." Dax's mien turned dubious. "But even if they didn't have a tachyon net, we'd have a hell of a time running that blockade. They're grouped so tight, they could see our wake in stray particles from the Denorios Belt. And even if we slip past them, they'll see the wormhole open—which means they'll chase us inside, guns blazing." She looked Kira in the eye. "Getting inside that wormhole is looking like a suicide mission."

Kira almost had to laugh. "It always was, Captain. It always was."

18

San Francisco, Earth—2373, Borg Timeline

An officer with whom Worf had served long ago, on his first posting after the Academy, once told him, "Any away mission that ends with the whole team coming back alive is a good one." At the time, that had struck Worf as a rather low bar for success. More than thirty years later, however, he had come to see the wisdom in those words.

The Borg drone who had attacked Slayton had slashed him badly with a small rotary-saw cyber-attachment, but it hadn't injected the security officer with any Borg nanites.

"Wounded is better than assimilated," Worf had told Slayton, who had gratefully agreed.

With his wounds closed by liquid bandages and his pain dulled by targeted neural blockers, Slayton trudged forward beside Keeso at the front of the away team. Worf could barely see the two security men through the cold fog, which had thickened as the night wore on. Now that they were out of the Borg complex and back in the hills, Worf hoped his point men didn't become careless. The hillsides were barren, but one misstep could send them and other members of the team tumbling a long way back down.

In the middle of the formation were the engineers, toting their salvaged parts and supplies on two medical stretchers. The gear was piled high on each stretcher and crudely lashed down with found bits of wire and cable. To better clear the rough terrain and distribute the burden, each porter supported a pair of protruding stretcher handles on their shoulders. Yong and L'Peng were in front, bearing one stretcher. La Forge and Koor followed a few paces behind them with the other. Aside from the fact that Yong and L'Peng preferred to work as a team, it had made sense to pair them because they were closely matched in height. Likewise, Koor and La Forge were similar in stature, which made for more level portage.

Bringing up the rear were K'Ehleyr and Worf. From their vantage they were able to keep an eye on the entire team while guarding their backs against Borg reprisals. Worf cradled his *bat'leth* with its back against his torso. His hold looked relaxed, but from this position he could defend immediately on his left, or be ready to strike in any direction in a fraction of a second.

K'Ehleyr toted the *mek'leth* in her right hand, swinging casually at her side. Having seen her fight, Worf had no doubt she could attack or protect just as quickly as he could—if not faster.

He stepped a few centimeters closer to her so that they could speak softly. It took him a second to catch her eye. "You fought well."

She side-eyed him with a grudging smile. "You weren't so bad, either."

Her smug teasing reminded Worf of her counterpart, the woman he had once known and loved. "Who taught you to fight?"

"Many people. Martial arts were a big part of my life growing up inside Omega."

"You were raised by Memory Omega?"

The question seemed to stir up bad memories for K'Ehleyr. "I was a child of—" She stopped to reconsider whatever she was about to say. "The child of an Omega agent. She gave birth to me inside a secret Omega base."

"But she did not raise you."

"No. She died when I was very young. I never really knew her."

Worf thought about asking after her father, but then he intuited that she must have avoided mentioning the man for a reason. He decided revelation was the safer course. "I, too, was orphaned as a child. I grew up on Earth, raised by human parents."

K'Ehleyr's interest became more noticeable. "You must have felt like an outsider."

"I did. I was . . . *lonely* as a boy." Feeling suddenly too vulnerable for his own comfort, Worf shifted the subject. "How did you go from Omega to the *Enterprise*?"

She cracked a smile. "By twists and turns. For years I was an Omega field agent. Just me and my tech guy Reg. We—"

"*Barclay?*"

"You know him?"

Worf muzzled his disdain for the engineer prone to borderline in-subordinate holodeck misadventures. "I know *of* him."

K'Ehleyr shrugged. "Anyway, we hopped around the galaxy for about a decade, mixing it up and having fun, until one day the director sends me to find some dusty human archaeologist named Luc Picard, steal him from his patron Gul Madred, and bring him back to Omega so he could take command of the *Enterprise*."

This time Worf found it hard to mask his disbelief. "You *recruited* the captain?"

"The director did. I just got him to the church on time."

"Is that how you became his first officer?"

"That was more about me feeding him his lines until he learned how to improvise. Once he grew into the role, I stepped back."

Worf nodded. "So you and Barclay serve together on the *Enterprise*. Are the two of you . . . ?"

"Involved? No. Never have been, never will be. Besides, Troi won his heart years ago."

The thought of any version of Barclay romantically entangled with any version of Deanna Troi made Worf wince, but he pushed that image from his mind. "Do you have any family of your own?"

That inquiry turned her mood wistful. "Never had the time. Just never 'clicked' with anyone. Know what I mean?"

A solemn nod. "I do."

Perhaps wanting to prevent Worf from digging deeper into her life, K'Ehleyr asked, "What about your son, Alexander? What kind of man is he?"

Thinking about Alexander filled Worf with nostalgia—and regrets. "My K'Ehleyr did not tell me I had a son until he was almost two years old. Soon after I met Alexander, his mother was slain by Duras"—even now, decades later, that name was like poison in Worf's mouth—"and I was all he had left. My parents tried to raise him on Earth, but by then they were too old, and he was too wild. So he came to live with me. I was . . . a poor father. Unprepared. Ill-equipped."

"I find that hard to believe."

"He was too Klingon to live like a human, but not Klingon enough to live among our people in the Empire. When he grew older, he joined the Klingon Defense Force, to prove to me that his heart was truly Klingon. Because he thought that was what I wanted."

"Was it?"

"I wanted him to live for himself. Not for me. Not for anyone else." He sighed. "In time, he did. He succeeded me as the Federation's ambassador to Qo'noS."

"For a boy who had such a rough start, he seems to have turned out okay. The man I met on *Defiant* is smart, brave, and honorable—which I think speaks well of his father."

Worf looked at his feet rather than look K'Ehleyr in the eye. "It does not. My son became a good man in spite of me—not because of me."

K'Ehleyr nudged his arm with her elbow, to make him look up at her. "*That.* That right there is how I know you're *nothing* like my universe's Worf. Humility? Selflessness? Those were traits the regent never had. But you do. You love to beat yourself up and tear yourself down, but I see you as you *are*, Worf: a good man, to your core."

There was affection in her tone, and admiration, and even a note of emotional hunger—and the sound of her voice woke a long-dormant fire deep inside Worf. But could he trust his instincts? He had never been a good judge of what his K'Ehleyr had wanted from him.

"It is odd," he said at last, "that my other and I are so different, but you and yours are so very much the same."

She shot a flirtatious look at him. "Is that a good thing?"

"That remains to be seen." Without waiting to see her reaction, he pushed a few strides ahead, to prevent her from seeing the fear, the grief, and the longing in his eyes.

Teeth gritted, he scolded himself in silence.

My K'Ehleyr is dead—and her counterpart is not her.
This is not the woman I knew. Not the one I loved.
And I must not forget that—for my own sake.

Temporal Disruption Base—2373, Borg Timeline

Cresting the rise, the away team saw it: a towering cathedral of black metal, sharp angles, and weltering light that seemed to have erupted whole from the scorched bedrock, like Athena bursting forth from the forehead of Zeus, fully grown and garbed for battle. The massive structure emanated dark energy in regular pulses that made the ground tremble.

From its highest tower shot a beam of emerald-green light too bright to look at for more than a moment at a time. It reached upward, through the fog, to pierce the ceiling of leaden clouds and spear into the endless black of space.

Picard lay on his stomach, peeking over the rocky edge at the hideous edifice of the Borg's dark temple devoted to the rending of time. Through gaps in its outer walls, he glimpsed what had to be hundreds of Borg drones moving about inside the facility. Outside, several squads of drones walked overlapping patrol routes in front of the entrance.

Lying on the rock to Picard's left, Sisko whispered, "What do you think?"

It was hard for Picard not to give in to despair. "It's a damned fortress."

A single pulse from the facility, louder than the rest, shook the rock face beneath the away team as its jagged exterior gave off a flash of sickly green radiation.

Crusher's blue eyes went wide as the green wave passed over the away team. "What the hell was that?"

Lal checked her tricorder. "The temporal disruptor inside the building appears to be modulating its output by bleeding off excess energy in regular pulses."

That news only agitated Crusher further. "Is it harmful?"

The female android put away her tricorder. "I don't think so. The pulses are fast-decaying temporal distortion waves. At close range, we might experience slight alterations in our perception of time, but only momentarily."

Despite her assurances, Bashir seemed concerned. "What about aftereffects, Lal?"

"Research by the Daystrom Institute suggests even brief exposures might lead to unexpected psychotemporal phenomena during later prolonged or severe exposure to free antichronitons." She eyed the Borg structure. "But I doubt that will be a risk here."

Sisko observed the Borg sentries' movements with intense focus.

"Mister Soong, how long do we have before the Borg trigger that weapon against the *Enterprise*-E?"

"Three hours, seven minutes, and eleven seconds."

"Then I suggest we stop worrying about the pulses and start looking for a way inside."

Nothing about the front of the facility looked inviting to Picard. "A frontal assault is out of the question. We haven't the bodies, the cover, or the firepower."

A nod from Sisko. "We'll flank left and use those rocks for cover. Scout its perimeter for another way in. If we . . ."

Vertigo overwhelmed Picard. The thudding of his own heartbeat in his ears drowned out Sisko's voice and left Picard nauseated, his forehead coated in sweat. He put his face down on the cool, smooth rock, hoping the sickness would pass quickly.

Without warning came the voices.

There were thousands of them. Each alone was nothing more than a murmur echoing in the void . . . but in unison they were the howl of a tempest, the music of the spheres twisted into discordance.

Then a single voice sliced through the din, dominated the innumerable masses, and whispered a single word that hit Picard like a dagger of ice thrust into his brain:

«*Locutus?*»

As quickly as the fugue had seized him it vanished, like a wave retreating from the shore. Picard lifted his head from the stone to see the rest of the away team gathered around him, hands outstretched, their expressions full of concern.

Closest to him was Crusher, who eased him back from the rock's edge, and then helped him sit up. "Are you all right, Jean-Luc?"

"No. I'm not. None of us are." He hated to throw another spanner in the works, but he couldn't let the team take one more step without telling them the truth. "We need to be very careful, my friends." He cast a fearful look at the dark temple. "She's here."

Everyone tensed except Lal, who seemed perplexed. "Who is?"

Data mirrored Picard's grim countenance. "The Borg Queen."

Sisko pulled his hand over his face. "You're sure it's her? Here?"

Picard nodded. "I'm certain."

Crusher took his hand. "The bigger question is: Does she know *you're* here?"

"I don't know. She senses me somehow. But when I heard her voice, it sounded as if she didn't *know* me. I can't explain it."

"Enough," Sisko said. "We stick to the plan."

Incredulous, Bashir asked, "What about the Queen?"

"She's just one more Borg. We'll handle her the same way we handle all the others." Sisko grabbed his rifle and shimmied down the rock. "Let's move."

She's here.

A declaration? A caution? From whom had it come?

The Collective searched itself for the source. Trillions of minds acting as one moved through their shared galactic consciousness like wind over water, like exotic particles raining down upon airless moons, a deluge of dark energy with a sinister purpose.

The answer became clear. Its roots were three centuries deep, buried in the assimilation of the world once known as Earth and now designated Alpha 337521-c. The same event that long ago had necessitated the creation of the temporal disruption cannon had also brought a warning about the future, about this moment.

Two drones from Unimatrix Delta-648—Third Auxiliary Vinculum Repair Four of Twelve, and Tertiary Antimatter Reactor First Defense Six of Six—had been the only survivors of a time sphere sent to this world by the Collective of an alternate timeline, one in which the Alpha Quadrant had come under the sway of a technologically sophisticated political entity known as the United Federation of Planets.

The Federation. The destroyer.

The temporally displaced Borg strike force had prevented a critical event in Earth's history, but in the process it had suffered catastrophic losses, including the death of its Queen's avatar and the loss of her memories. It was months before its two surviving drones, damaged and wounded, finally contacted the Collective, to summon its forces to assimilate Earth, and to warn that they might be pursued from the alternate timeline by a Federation starship.

A ship called *Enterprise*.

And in command of that vessel, the Collective's greatest traitor: *Locutus*.

The two drones' memories of the betrayer were fleeting. Fragmented. Little remained but the faded recollection of a face, the distant echo of a voice all but forgotten . . . until now.

Tonight, that voice, that singular mind, was alive on the surface of Alpha 337521-c. No longer a mere fabrication of shadows and dust, it taunted the Collective. Eluded it. Tasked it. Challenged it to match wits.

It was time for the Collective to respond.

This singular intelligence deserved to be met in kind. The Collective would face this interloper directly, through an avatar of the Borg's core identity.

Through the Borg, *personified*.

Encased in a synthetic duranium skull with a dangling spine that flickered from the inside with viridescent radiation, she watched the self-governing machinery inside the temporal disruptor site lower her toward a waiting headless female body.

Undulating, the metallic spinal column snaked inside the waiting humanoid form. Embraced by nanite tubules and biosynthetic data fibers, the spine fused with its new host, read the quantum chart of its nervous system, and mapped its nodes to the corresponding functions in its ancient, perfected consciousness. The host's eyes snapped open, and its localized awareness fused with the Collective's universal perception.

The Queen was once more manifest, freshly incarnated on Alpha 337521-c.

For over three hundred years the Queen and the Collective had awaited this moment, this opportunity to confront their nemesis from another time, from a universe unknown—and to learn why two drones orphaned from another timeline's Collective had harbored such unbounded hatred and fear of the entity they had known only as *Locutus of Borg*.

U.S.S. Defiant NX-74205—2373, Borg Timeline

Taking a moment for himself felt selfish beyond words, but Worf knew he would be better able to focus if he could get some of the blood and grime off his face and hands before returning to duty; their grit and ferric tang had become distracting.

He and the salvage team had returned to *Defiant* in good time, despite having to make an uphill march in the dark over unfamiliar ground. Once inside, La Forge and his mechanics had absconded aft to engineering with their bounty of parts and materials, while Keeso had enlisted Worf's help to lift the wounded Slayton up the gangway to deck two, and from there to sickbay, where Nurse Nooranvany, the only medical officer still on the ship, had knit Slayton's savaged flesh back together as if she were mending ripped upholstery.

With Slayton in good hands and the engineers back to work, Worf had seized the rare opportunity to return to his stateroom so he could change his clothes and clean up. He knew he wouldn't have long. Soon there would be some urgent matter demanding his attention, and he would be called back to the bridge. It was fortunate, then, that having spent most of his life in Starfleet, he was accustomed to handling his personal needs as quickly as possible.

The black jacket he had worn on the salvage run lay rumpled in the corner. A clean jumpsuit and underclothes lay folded in the storage space beneath his bunk, alongside his baldric. He had always kept at least one spare uniform on hand for situations such as his current predicament, in which there were no replicators available to fabricate new clothing.

At least the refresher still works.

Worf cupped his hands under the faucet, and a weak stream of tepid water filled them. Though the ship was on battery power, it had enough reserves of potable water to last the crew for several days, if used sparingly. He didn't have the option of a shower—not that he had time for one—but he could, at least, wash his face and hands.

It felt good to push water onto his face and over his head. He took a clean cloth from beside the sink and wiped his face clean, taking a moment to pry bits of dirt and sludge out of his facial hair. He regarded his face in the mirror. *Not perfect, but better.*

He stripped off his undershirt as he left his lavatory.

One step into his stateroom, he realized he was not alone. He caught a faint scent of musk in the air, one that resurrected long-buried memories of passion and tragedy.

K'Ehleyr leaned against the frame of his stateroom's open doorway. She, too, had used the brief respite to clean herself up and shed her uniform jacket. The amber glow of emergency lights made her eyes look as soft as candleshine, and the room's deep shadows flattered her face. She looked like Worf's memories brought back to life.

Still, her presence left him unnerved. Like the woman he had once known, this K'Ehleyr carried herself with an intensity that would be impressive even from a full-blooded Klingon. But her human aspect also beguiled him; it spoke to the parts of him that had grown up raised by humans, that had learned to be comfortable living among them.

Somehow, in K'Ehleyr he had found the best of both of his worlds. She . . .

Stop. This is not my K'Ehleyr. I must not—

She strode toward him, her carriage purposeful, her gaze unwavering.

He froze, and his mind went blank. Behind her, the door slid closed.

She was still an arm's length away. He held up a hand. "What are you—?"

Her lips found his, kissing him hungrily. He reveled in the taste of her—then he pulled away, tried to back up. She grabbed his arms. "Take me, Worf."

"Now is not the time. We should be—"

"*Now* is the only time we have." She took hold of his head and pulled her to him, her kiss as irresistible as gravity, holding him prisoner. She bit his lower lip, inflaming his lust.

But guilt tore him apart from the inside. Was giving himself to this K'Ehleyr a betrayal of the woman he'd once loved? Would he just be using her counterpart?

She started undoing his trousers. He grabbed her hands. "I cannot."

Her eyes blazed with mischief. "You *can*." She reached for his waist.

"*Stop.* I cannot pretend you are her."

"I'm not asking you to." She thrust her hands against his chest and dug her nails into his skin, sending ecstatic waves of sweet agony through his core. "Be with *me*." She reached up, her arm faster than a serpent's strike, and cupped her hand behind his neck. "Look at me, Worf."

Like a man bewitched, he stared into K'Ehleyr's eyes, which were wide with desire.

Her breathing turned deep and heavy, and her chest rose and fell with alluring grace. "I feel something for you that I've never felt before. Not for *anyone*, Worf. I've only known you a day, yet I feel like I've waited my *whole life* for you." She pushed herself against him, pressed her face to his chest, inhaled his scent—and overwhelmed him with hers. "I *burn* for you, Worf. And I *know* you burn for me. I can *feel* it. Tell me you feel it!"

Worf took K'Ehleyr by her shoulders and forced her back, to his arms' length. "I do. But I cannot trust my feelings."

His denial drove her to anguish. "Why not?"

"Your counterpart . . . was everything to me. My first love. The mother of my son. I cannot let myself—" Shame and fear seized him by the throat and made him mute.

His silence incensed K'Ehleyr. "Let yourself what? Lay with me?"

Worf forced the truth into the open. "Love you." He looked into K'Ehleyr's eyes, expecting to see pity, disgust, or derision. To his profound surprise, she met his gaze with a tender compassion that coaxed an even deeper admission from him. "I loved my K'Ehleyr as I have loved only one other. . . . Until you."

He let go of her, certain she would retreat from his declaration.

Instead she drifted toward him, and embraced him. But she said not a word.

Worf felt torn. *Do I say more? I have said this much. I should speak the rest.*

"I *do* burn for you. But is my love real? Or does my heart just not know you from her? And if I give myself to you, does that make my love for her a lie?"

She looked up at him, a ghost of a smile haunting her lips. "Worf?"

"Yes?"

She slapped him hard across the face. "You *think* too much." With one strong tug, she pulled his trousers to the deck. "Shut up and be a Klingon."

His blood raged, and passion took hold of him. He kicked away his trousers, grabbed K'Ehleyr, and hurled her across the compartment into his bunk. In a rush he was on top of her, and together they yanked and tore away her clothes, along with what was left of his, and entangled themselves with a primal frenzy he hadn't known since his youth.

It felt like falling in love for the first time, all over again.

He had almost lost himself in the moment, succumbing to the sublime sensation of her teeth piercing his shoulder, when his anxiety intruded upon their tryst once more.

He pulled away, and she exploded in rageful frustration. "What *now*, Worf?"

Despair welled up inside of him. "What is the point?"

"Of what?"

"This. Why find love again *now*?"

"Why *not* now?"

"Why fall in love just *hours* before we erase ourselves from time?"

She stared at him, aghast. Then she slapped him again.

"What's *ever* the point of love, you fool? We're all born to die. What matters is remembering to *live—before* you go to *Sto-Vo-Kor!*"

Every word she had said was true.

Life was short. Death was coming. And true love was a gift given to very few.

Grateful once more to feel the flames of desire, Worf surrendered himself to the first and also the last woman he would ever love.

19

U.S.S. *Titan* NCC-80102

"Dropping out of warp in fifteen seconds, Admiral."

Riker leaned forward in the command chair. "Careful, Lavena. Make sure we're not inside their sensor range." He looked back at Tuvok. "Passive sensors only. No active targeting until I give the order."

The aloof Vulcan double-checked his console. "Aye, sir."

"Ops, take us into stealth mode as soon as we're out of warp. I don't want our power signature to give us away."

"Stealth mode standing by," Rager answered.

Tensions were high on *Titan*'s bridge. Riker felt the crew's anxiety; it mirrored his own. He remained bitter about their quarry's previous escape, and he had made his displeasure known to his officers. Armed with a new lead, he was determined this time to capture the intruder from the alternate universe and make its crew give up the hiding place of *Defiant*.

At the helm, Lavena tensed. "Five seconds."

Riker did his best to sound inspiring. "Look sharp, everyone."

The steady, high-pitched hum of the warp drive ceased with hardly an echo as streaks of starlight on the bridge's main viewscreen retracted into points. As soon as the ship was back at sublight speed, the overhead lights dimmed, along with numerous unstaffed duty stations on the bridge. Any system not in active use or deemed essential to the ship's operations had gone into standby mode, to help reduce its aura of waste heat and electromagnetic radiation.

Searching the image on the viewscreen, Riker grew concerned. He saw the massive dark circle of intermediate-mass black hole Orcus 784, surrounded by rings of gravitationally lensed starlight and girdled by a swiftly rotating accretion disk of fiery, superheated gas and debris.

But he saw no sign of the ship he had come to capture.

Hope we didn't miss the party.

From the seat to his right, first officer Sarai anticipated Riker's next command. "Tuvok, visual scans of the accretion disk, full magnification. Check the inner edge, along the singularity's event horizon. Note any plasma flow disturbances consistent with a starship of the mass and configuration of a ringship from the alternate universe. Keru, see if we've missed any recent flash traffic on the SLF channels."

"Checking." A moment later he said, "We've got something! An orbital path and projected course for the intruder. Relaying coordinates to Commander Tuvok."

Tuvok applied the new data. "Adjusting sensors. Target confirmed."

Riker felt vindicated. "On-screen, Commander. Full magnification."

The image on the forward viewscreen shifted to a view of a narrow sliver of the accretion disk's fiery inner edge. Its innermost ring of ionized plasma betrayed ripples retreating from a moving point—the wake of an object inside the stream, disrupting its natural flow.

Brimming with malicious satisfaction, Riker muttered, "Thar she blows."

Sarai turned a curious look his way. "Excuse me, sir?"

"Nothing." Time was short, and Riker was in no mood to explain *Moby-Dick* to his Efrosian second-in-command. "Mister Keru. Send a coded reply on the SLF: 'Stand by for Signal Alpha.' Helm, intercept that wake in the plasma stream, full impulse. Tactical, precharge our transphasic shield emitters, and get ready to go weapons hot."

Tuvok nodded in confirmation. "All systems ready, Admiral."

Cruising without shields, with weapons at standby, and no active sensors, *Titan* would be like a ghost to the intruder ship hiding in the plasma stream. At least, that was what Riker hoped. After learning of the intruders' encounter with the Romulans near Kali 531, he had felt all but certain they would come here next. Seeing his suspicions borne out gave him confidence.

This time, we'll have them.

After several tense minutes of quiet, he was anxious for an update. "Time to intercept?"

Lavena answered from the helm, "Sixty seconds."

"Tactical, any sign they've spotted us?"

Tuvok shook his head. "None. They are continuing to make high-energy scans of the singularity's event horizon. It is likely that their own active sensors and interference from the plasma stream have rendered them effectively blind to activity outside the accretion disk."

"They think it'll hide them," Riker speculated.

A nod from Tuvok. "Perhaps."

"Thirty seconds," Lavena announced.

Time to finish this. "Red alert! All hands to battle stations. Tactical, raise shields and arm all weapons. Lock quantum torpedoes onto the intruder, full spread. As soon as we flush them out, target phasers on their wormhole drive, in the ring-shaped section."

"Aye, sir."

Crimson panels flashed on the bulkheads as the red-alert siren wailed. Consoles surged to life, and relief officers poured out of the turbolifts and spread out to auxiliary stations around the bridge, ready to take over for any of the senior personnel should they fall in action.

Sarai looked up from her command console. "We're in position."

"Tactical?"

"Weapons locked."

"Fire torpedoes!"

With one tap, Tuvok unleashed a spread of six torpedoes. They streaked across the main viewscreen, sank into the fiery chaos of the accretion disk, and then detonated in unison, a tiny white supernova inside a burning river.

The intruder vessel surfaced and sluggishly came about toward *Titan.* Its needle-inside-a-ring profile all but vanished as it faced the *Luna*-class explorer head-on.

Sarai observed with icy calm, "Looks like they're ready to fight."

It was hard for Riker not to gloat. "Let's show them who they're fighting. Mister Keru, send Signal Alpha on the SLF."

"Sending, sir."

It had been many years since Riker had first learned of super-low-frequency subspace signals, during the *Enterprise*-E's mission to Tezwa. Up until then, the SLF bands had been a closely guarded secret of the Klingon Empire, their means of clandestinely maintaining contact with their fleets of cloaked starships without betraying their positions to their foes.

Today, Riker had made that technology work for himself.

In the space of a few seconds, seven Klingon warships, ranging from birds-of-prey to heavy cruisers and even a pair of battleships, deactivated their cloaking devices and rippled into view—in a formation surrounding the intruder vessel.

Suddenly, the comm channels were flooded with excited chatter, and new alerts sounded at every duty station on *Titan*'s bridge.

"Enemy vessel has halted its approach," Lavena reported. "It's holding position, sir."

Keru added, "All Klingon vessels have shields up and weapons locked. Waiting for your order, sir."

That was the news Riker had been waiting for. *Gotcha.*

"Tactical, do we have phaser lock on their wormhole drive?"

"Confirmed," Tuvok said.

"Good. Mister Keru, hail the intruders. Order them to lower their shields, surrender, and prepare to be boarded. And tell them that if they don't comply within thirty seconds, I'll blast their ship into scrap."

C.S.S. *Enterprise*

I'd hoped it wouldn't come to this.

Luc felt like an island of calm in a sea of troubled minds. Around him, his bridge officers delivered frantic reports, each more dire than the last, none of them telling him anything he couldn't see by looking at the tactical console beside his command chair or at the sobering image of multiple Klingon warships on the main viewscreen.

If the Klingons had been content merely to shadow us as they have since we arrived, I'd have left them in peace. Alas, now they've forced the issue.

He was still weighing his options when he heard the chime of an incoming hail being received at Troi's security console. He watched her reactions as she listened to the message; she seemed to go on a journey that took her from alarm to simmering fury.

When she looked up at Luc, he raised a hand. "Don't tell me. They order us to surrender and prepare to be boarded, or else be destroyed."

She seemed surprised, and a bit offended. "Sorry, Captain. Do you still need me here?"

"You know damned well that I do! Send our mayday on the quantum channel, then stall the admiral with whatever lie he seems most willing to hear."

While Troi put Luc's orders into action, Wesley Crusher took it upon himself to leave his post at the sciences console and instead hover above Luc, who was still seated. "Captain, we need to finish this orbit. We're only forty seconds from completing our last scan."

Luc turned a withering scowl at the younger man. "Mister Crusher, you might have noticed we're in the middle of a situation."

"If we'd stayed inside the accretion disk, we'd have finished by now."

"We would also be *dead*, Mister Crusher. Our transphasic shields started failing after *Titan*'s first salvo. Had we stayed submerged, they could easily have hit us again at least twice—but once would have been more than sufficient to see us vaporized."

Wesley looked ready to argue further, until Perim made the judicious choice to take him by the arm and shepherd him back to her station, far from the captain's chair.

More pings sounded from Troi's station. With her eyes she signaled Luc to check his tactical monitor. He turned it toward himself and skimmed its contents. He quickly deduced that the key to escaping this snare would be timing.

And, of course, luck.

He straightened his back, tugged the front of his uniform tunic smooth, and invested his voice with its richest tones of steady authority. "Helm, stand ready to come hard about and dive! Tactical, on my command, send all power to aft shields until we reach the accretion disk, then transfer power to the transphasic shields. Lieutenant Perim, Mister Crusher: once we're back inside, finish your scan as quickly as possible."

Troi sounded worried. "Should I arm weapons, sir?"

"Negative. Send all power from the weapon systems into the shield grid."

"Aye, sir."

Seemingly unable to help himself, Wesley left his station to once again cast his lanky shadow over the captain's chair. "Are you crazy? The second we move, they'll blow us to bits!"

"I am not in the habit of *justifying* my orders, Mister Crusher."

Troi called out, "*Titan* says this is our final warning: drop our shields and surrender, or they'll open fire." She checked her console. "All enemy ships have armed their weapons."

There was a note of panic in Wesley's voice. "Captain! We're outnumbered, outgunned, and out of time. We can't risk—"

"*Shut up*, Wesley! Get back to your post or I'll have you removed."

Eyes narrowed and brow knitted in anger, Wesley slunk away beneath a figurative cloud of resentment. Strangely, his petulant reaction brought a half smile to Luc's face.

I don't know why, but that felt rather satisfying.

On the main viewscreen, dim pinpoints of light from the enemy vessels' beam weapons and torpedo launchers swelled and brightened. Their barrage would begin in a few seconds.

Why must we always cut these things so close?

Multiple new signals on his tactical monitor told him it was time. "Helm! Hard about and dive! Tactical, aft shields!"

If any of his officers thought him mad, they kept that opinion to themselves. Tolaris pushed the ship into an inverted dive while rolling it hard to starboard, and then she gunned the impulse drive, while Troi put every drop of defensive power they had into the aft shields.

Normally, it would have amounted to nothing more than a stupid, utterly futile gesture. The enemy had enough collective firepower to collapse the *Enterprise*'s aft shields three times over.

Fortunately for the crew of Luc Picard's *Enterprise*, the enemy had other problems.

A dozen ripples appeared beyond and around *Titan* and its Klingon allies. Spacetime swirled and distorted as if it were being spun, pinched, and pulled all at once—and then twelve artificial wormholes erupted into existence and bloomed into a storm of bluish-white energy.

From each wormhole leaped a Commonwealth jaunt-ship of the same class as *Enterprise*, their shields raised, weapons hot, and positions advantageous.

Either oblivious or overconfident, the crews of four of the Klingon ships fired on the *Enterprise* as it plunged toward Orcus 784's swirling ring of fire.

"Aft shields buckling," Troi shouted over the din of disruptor blasts. Luc trusted his fellow jaunt-ship commanders. "Steady."

One look at his tactical monitor rewarded his faith. His allies retaliated on his behalf, and immediately the Klingons and *Titan* broke formation and scattered, all of them forced into defensive postures if not outright retreat as they came under fire by superior forces. Each ship retreated on its own heading, pursued by at least one of *Enterprise*'s sister ships.

Her mood visibly improved, Troi muted the alert of an incoming comm. "Captain, we're being hailed by Captain Madden of the *Intrepid*."

"On-screen."

The image on the main viewscreen snapped to one of a bridge identical to that of the *Enterprise*. Seated in its command chair was Captain Martin Madden, an athletic, bearded man four decades younger than Luc. He flashed a bright smile. *"Luc! Everyone okay over there?"*

"We're fine, Martin, thanks to your timely rescue."

"You're good to continue, then?"

"Affirmative. My people tell me we can finish here in under a minute."

"Okay, then. Do what you came for, we'll cover you."

"Acknowledged. *Enterprise* out." Luc signaled Troi with a gesture to close the channel. "Helm, take us into the disk. Perim, finish that scan. As soon as we confirm this isn't the target, we'll signal the fleet to withdraw and regroup, and then lead them out."

Troi left her console, approached Picard, and squatted beside his chair. In a low voice she asked, "What happens if Mister Crusher confirms this *is* the Devidians' hiding place?"

That scenario, Luc knew, would involve a degree of carnage he found upsetting.

"Let's hope we don't need to find out, Deanna. For all our sakes."

U.S.S. *Titan* NCC-80102

At first Sarai had thought Riker had frozen at the sight of twelve jaunt-ships snapping into position above and around his ambush. It wouldn't have surprised her. She had seen veteran commanders succumb to combat paralysis just as often as newly minted officers. To lose one's advantages and wind up surrounded in the blink of an eye? It could faze anyone.

Just before she was about to step in, Riker recovered his wits. "Hard to port, full evasive!" The tableau on the viewscreen shifted in wild blurs as *Titan* broke away from the Klingon attack group. Thunderous blasts rocked the ship and flickered the lights.

Despite the continuing barrage, Tuvok remained stoic. "Two jauntships in pursuit, Admiral. Closing fast, firing phasers."

"Fire aft torpedoes, wide spread!"

With a single tap, Tuvok fired a cluster of six quantum torpedoes, whose launch resounded through the ship's spaceframe. "Torpedoes away."

"Helm, evasive loop, into attack pattern Kilo."

Lavena was already executing the maneuvers as she confirmed, "Evasive loops, pattern Kilo—aye, sir." The stars on the main viewscreen spun, twisted, and streaked with sickening velocity as the flight controller pushed *Titan* through a looping corkscrew at nearly half impulse, finishing its final roll into an attack position off the starboard side of one of its pursuers.

Riker sprang to his feet, with one fist raised and his eyes manic. "Fire everything!"

It took less than a second for Tuvok to trigger the ship's main phaser banks and launch another volley of quantum torpedoes—but before any of them found the target, the ringship blinked out of sight, gone in a flash followed by ripples of distorted starlight. Crisscrossing phaser beams slashed at nothing, and six torpedoes vanished into empty space.

The admiral's face contorted into a mask of rage. "No!" He spun and pointed at Sarai. "Get me another target, now!"

Sarai was already consulting her tactical monitor. "Tuvok, our second pursuer is on our aft port quarter—"

"Target acquired."

Riker snapped, "Fire!"

"Firing phasers," Tuvok confirmed, pressing the pad.

Now the admiral sounded desperate. "Dammit, Rager! Get it onscreen!"

Lieutenant Rager didn't acknowledge his order; she had done it before he'd finished saying it. On the main viewscreen, more shafts of brilliant phaser energy cut across one another's paths . . . only to find nothing there.

Keru reacted with curiosity to new alerts on his console. "Sir, the jaunt-ship fleet is jumping away. Only three— Correction: two left, bearing— Correction: they've all gone, sir."

Riker gaped at the chief of security. "Even the first one? The one we've been hunting?"

"All of them, sir."

"Well, track them, dammit!"

That demand prompted Keru to trade bewildered looks with Tuvok before he replied, "We can't, Admiral. They vanished through wormholes that aren't *there* anymore. There's nothing to follow."

Riker looked ready to rip out his own hair, set it on fire, and eat it. "Did we even score a single hit? *One* goddamned hit, on *any* of them?" No one spoke up. "You're all *worthless!*"

Gauging the bridge crew's reactions to Riker's tantrum, Sarai found it telling that, for the first time since she had joined *Titan*'s crew, Keru and Tuvok both regarded the admiral with the same expression of aloof disdain. Nothing in Riker's attitude suggested he had taken any note of his officers' collective reproach.

Riker grabbed a padd from a relief officer's hand and pitched it across the bridge. The thin tablet audibly cracked as it struck the far bulkhead.

Shocked silence followed, and to Sarai it felt as ponderous as it was awkward.

Riker pulled his hand over the front of his beard, inhaled, and sighed loudly. "We'll get one more shot at them. Helm, set course for the natural transwarp eddy that'll take us to Yama, maximum warp. The rest of you? Learn to do your damn jobs."

He stalked away to the ready room. Seconds after the door had closed, Sarai and everyone else on the bridge heard the admiral's muffled flood of vulgar profanities, coupled with the erratic thuds of chairs and small pieces of furniture being hurled with wanton violence.

As *Titan*'s executive officer, Sarai was responsible for safeguarding the crew's morale as well as their lives. She reminded herself of that duty as she walked, with reluctance, to the ready room's door. Its panel showed it was locked. She pressed the visitor's signal.

The admiral's voice was flinty with anger as it spat from the panel comm. *"What?"*

"This is Commander Sarai, sir. I thought I heard—"

"It was nothing."

"But it—"

"I'm all right, Sarai. You have the conn. Tell me when we reach Yama."

A light next to the door comm switched off, alerting Sarai that the channel had been closed. Clearly, the admiral was not of a mind to talk about his problems, or anything else.

Standing in front of the closed door, she felt the other officers' eyes on her back.

She walked to the command chair and sat.

I really wanted to be wrong about this, but there's no denying what we all just saw. I don't know what's going on with Admiral Riker . . . but he most definitely is not "all right."

20

C.S.S. Defiant—**Mirror Universe**

Walking the corridors of *Defiant II*, Kira felt as if she had come home, but she also felt like a foreigner. Every detail of the ship's interior was familiar to her. Small bits of signage, quirks of the layout from one deck to the next—they all reminded her of the first *Starship Defiant* that had been posted to Deep Space 9 so many years earlier. Immersed in this replica of that ship, she sometimes forgot that it was only a copy, built from the same shipyard specs.

Then she would pass another member of its crew in the corridor and remember where she really was. Each member of Ezri's crew who set eyes on Kira had the same reaction: a flash of hatred or disgust, followed by the swift aversion of their gaze.

None of the crew spoke to her, but Kira was sure she knew what each of them was saying inside their head: *I know that's not the* real *Intendant Kira, but still . . .*

Then they'd note Kira's steely-eyed stare and flush with embarrassment.

Worst of all, I don't recognize anyone. Not from their counterparts, not from anything. If it weren't for Ezri, I'd be alone among strangers.

She stepped out of the aft port-side turbolift on deck one, turned left, and continued until she reached the door to the captain's ready room. Though on many ships the ready room was connected to the bridge, on *Defiant*-class starships it was set apart, though still on the same deck, just a few steps away.

She pressed the door signal. Over the comm, Dax answered, *"Come."*

The door unlocked and slid open. Kira entered the ready room to find Dax seated behind her desk, looking concerned while reading from a padd.

Kira stopped in front of the desk. "You asked to see me?"

"I did. Please, have a seat."

Kira sat on one of the guest chairs. "What's going on?"

"Funny. I was about to ask you the same thing, Vedek."

Dax's confrontational tone put Kira on edge. "I don't understand."

The petite Trill was irked as she held up the padd. "My orders were simple. Pick you up at Deneva. Take you to Bajor. Get you inside the wormhole." She dropped the padd, which clattered onto her desk. "Now I think there's more I should know—but no one's talking."

Kira straightened her back, signaling she wouldn't be bullied. "Last time we spoke, you sounded ready to fight, risk be damned. What's changed?"

"Ten minutes ago, a dozen of our jaunt-ships went AWOL to *your* universe. Now my long-range scans show the number of mercs at the wormhole has *doubled*, our comms are flooded with distress signals from people saying stars are winking out, and Spock's counterpart addressed Parliament right before it turned into a riot." Dax stood, circled the desk, and planted herself against it in front of Kira. "Something big is going on. As in, cosmically big. So before I start a war by taking my ship into a hot zone and running a blockade, I'd like to know why my crew and I are being asked to play the part of sacrificial pawns."

"And you think I can tell you?"

"I'm willing to bet you can."

No one had sworn Kira to secrecy, but she had no idea how this Ezri Dax would react to the terrible truth of what was to come. "It's complicated."

"Try me."

"All right. But after I tell you, I need you to remember—*you asked*."

Kira spoke quickly and in simple terms, sparing Dax the technobabble when she could. She told her about the Devidians' ongoing temporal holocaust, the slaughter of entire timelines so they could harvest the neural energies released by the deaths of entire realities. Then she explained how it all was traced back to a particular mission, and interference by the Borg—and the chilling realization that the only way to save the Prime timeline and the greater multiverse from the Devidians' insatiable appetite for death was to make the mother of all sacrifice plays.

"And that's the bottom line," Kira said finally. "It's too late to save our timeline—"

"The one you called 'the First Splinter.' "

"Not my name for it, but sure. Anyway, our branch of time is doomed no matter what. In a few hours, all this will not only cease to be, it'll never have been."

Dax looked stricken. "And there's nothing we can do to stop it."

Kira shook her head. "The only choice we get to make now is whether to let this horror perpetuate . . . or to make our deaths mean something by trying to save everyone else."

Dax's temper had lost its fire, and her eyes were widened in horror. It was a look that Kira had seen on her own face, and on many others'. It was the expression of a person who has confronted not only the inevitability of their own death, but its imminence—and, with it, the existential dread of knowing that all of creation, even time itself, would succumb, as well.

It was the stare of a soul gazing into the abyss, hoping secretly that it would be eternal, only to realize they could see the bottom, and it was coming up fast.

It was the face of a person who knew the end was at hand.

Is she going to go berserk? Have a breakdown? Maybe I should've lied.

Dax turned her back on Kira for a few seconds, no doubt in an effort to recompose herself. Kira stood and wondered if she should go to Dax.

How do I comfort her? I don't even know her. She decided to hold her ground.

Dax faced Kira, her demeanor eerily calm and focused. "I have questions."

"Naturally."

There was sorrow in Dax's eyes and a vibrato of suppressed anguish in her voice. "In your universe . . . is Leeta still alive?"

Her question surprised Kira. "Leeta? You mean Quark's ex–dabo girl?"

Tears shimmered in Ezri's blue eyes. "Just answer the question!"

"Okay! Yes, as far as I know, Leeta's alive."

"So there's a chance she's still alive in this 'Prime timeline' you want to save?"

Kira nodded. "That one, and many others." For a moment, she was tempted to ask Dax why she wanted to know. Then she saw the heartbreak in Dax's face, the bitter tears falling from her eyes, and Dax's reason why became perfectly clear.

"You loved her."

Dax nodded as she palmed the tears from her face. "She was my wife." The slender Trill pushed through her pain and lifted her chin, reclaiming her pride.

Then she offered her hand in friendship, and Kira took it. As the two women looked each other in the eye, Dax's smile shone through her grief.

"All right, Vedek. I'm all in. Let's go save *everything*."

C.S.S. *Enterprise*

Looking into the faces of a dozen of his peers on *Enterprise*'s main viewscreen, Luc Picard felt both grateful and humbled. "To be honest, I still can't believe anyone answered my call."

Captain Madden seemed to have been chosen to speak on behalf of the group. *"How could we not, Luc? After all you've done for us, and the Commonwealth. We owe you, sir."*

The other captains' nods of concurrence filled the viewscreen: Benjamin Maxwell on the *Phoenix*; Hans Balfe, commanding the *Independence*; Thadiun Okona, on the *Endurance*; thick-bearded Captain K. D. Hageman of the *Terra Nova*; Kelly Swails of the *Vostok*; Kirsten Perez on the *Vasquez*; Prynn Tenmei in the center seat of *C.S.S. Hope*; her spouse, Andorian *chan* Thirishar ch'Thane of the *Progress*; Lisa Neeley on the *Victory*; Patrick Tomlinson on the *Kearsarge*; and, finally, the one that Picard still found it hard to believe—Mackenzie Calhoun, who had been persuaded to take command of a jaunt-ship on the condition that he be allowed to rename it *Excalibur* and bring with him his entire roster of senior personnel from his previous command.

Luc wished he could thank each of them individually, but there wasn't time. "Please know, all of you, how grateful I am. It was Saavik who encouraged me to defy protocol and solicit your aid. I'd never imagined so many of you would come."

Tenmei shook her head in disappointment. *"When we heard the Parliament turn against Ambassador Spock, we all knew they weren't seeing the big picture."*

"That's putting it mildly," Maxwell interjected.

Captain Hageman nodded. *"About five minutes after Spock left the Parliament, we got word from on high that the answer to his request was a hard no."*

Calhoun cracked a wicked smile. *"We therefore decided to go anyway."*

Wesley Crusher, who had been eavesdropping from behind Luc's command chair, chuckled softly. "Our realities seem to have more in common every day."

"Indeed." Luc took a moment to choose his words. "We have reason to think our next destination, the singularity known as Yama, is likely to be the Devidians' hiding place."

On the viewscreen, more nodding heads. Captain Okona replied, *"We've all read the report from Crusher and Perim, and we agree—their analysis looks solid."*

Perez asked, *"What's the risk, if any, from the natural transwarp current near Yama?"*

"Extreme. The same forces that harassed us at Abaddon and Orcus 784 could use that transwarp current to reach Yama in as little as an hour. They might already be on their way." Luc sighed; he hated delivering bad news. "The greater threat, however, will likely be the Devidians. If we find them—"

"When we find them," Wesley cut in.

Luc grimaced at the correction. "When we find them, I expect they'll put up a fight. One we might not be able to win. My crew and I are committed, but I won't blame any of you—"

"Quit the excuses, Luc," Tomlinson said in a joking tone. *"We didn't come all this way just for the view."*

Maxwell put on his bravest face. *"What Patrick said. We came to help. So let us help."*

It was the answer Luc had hoped for, but he feared they might be offering their pledges without knowing what they were really getting into. "Do you all concur? I ask because this will not be a routine strike-and-jump. None of us will be coming back from this, dead or alive."

Neeley, an intense woman with copper-hued hair pulled back into a ponytail, met Luc's challenge with open eyes. *"We didn't* skim *Crusher and Perim's report, Luc. We all know what it says. And where we're going."*

White-haired before her time, Swails feigned impatience. *"Time's wasting, Luc."*

Balfe chimed in, *"Yeah, let's get this show on the road."*

"All right, then." Luc cued Troi, and she entered a command at her panel. "You all have the coordinates for Yama. Captain Tenmei, we're sending you the coordinates to which we expect this universe's *Starship Defiant* to return at any moment. After they arrive, plot your jump to Yama, and bring *Defiant* with you."

"Acknowledged." Tenmei reacted to someone off-screen, and then she added, *"Coordinates received. Jumping in twenty seconds. See you all at Yama. Hope out."* Tenmei's image vanished from the grid of faces.

"Everyone else, once we reach Yama, Mister Crusher will send you search-pattern assignments. Working together, we should be able to find the Devidians with relative haste. Which is critical because we now have less than two hours before they finish their attack on this timeline."

Tolaris looked back at Luc. "All ships have synchronized their jump solutions, sir."

"Very good, Lieutenant." It was time at last to take this fight to the enemy. Luc stood, pulled the front of his tunic smooth, and did his best to present his fellow captains with an image of unshakable confidence and courage. "Time is precious, my friends. *Engage.*"

21

Temporal Disruption Base—2373, Borg Timeline

Concealed amid debris and defoliated shrubbery on an elevated patch of ground behind the away team, Data and Lal had been tasked by Captain Sisko to watch for any signs of danger. He needed to be warned if Borg drones approached him or any other member of the team, or if Data or Lal detected any alarms sounding inside the Borg stronghold.

Sisko and Bashir were at the bottom of the slope in front of Data and Lal. The two men were scouting the foundation in the rear of the Borg's temporal disruption facility, in search of a means of covert entry. Captain Picard and Doctor Crusher were several meters away, seeking other less obvious ways inside the building, such as thermal vents, abandoned maintenance hatches, or the like.

It was a slow process, but Data had agreed with the tactical assessment that a direct assault would likely be not only ineffective but suicidal. He remained concerned, however, about their dwindling reserve of time. They needed to be ready in just over one hundred minutes to disrupt the Borg pulse intended for the *Enterprise*—the shot responsible for the original divergence event. Even more important, they had to hope that their allies in the timeline they had left behind, as well as its alternate-dimension counterpart, would be ready to do their parts at that same moment, their efforts coordinated across their still-active linked quantum frequencies.

Traces of movement inside an exposed section of the fortress's interior attracted Lal's attention. She whispered, "Father?" Then she gestured with her chin toward the quartet of drones. "Is that the same patrol we saw a few minutes ago?"

"I am comparing my memory file of the drones we saw earlier with my observations of this group." He finished his analysis in under three nanoseconds. "It is not the same patrol."

"Are you sure?"

"I ran comparative analyses of the various drones' kinetic and biomass profiles, and found no commonalities. Ergo, these are not the same drones."

Lal seemed to grow more concerned. "If there's more than one group of drones assigned to patrol that route, the same might be true of other areas inside the facility."

"Yes. We will need to practice extreme caution once we go inside."

They passed a few more seconds making visual sweeps of the area.

"Father?" An uncharacteristic note of guilt in Lal's voice caught Data's ear. "Are we sure we should be doing this?"

"We must find a way inside, Lal. The plan depends upon it."

"I'm talking about the plan. The mission." There was fear in her eyes. "How can we be sure that sacrificing our own timeline is the best course of action?"

Her doubts came as news to Data. "Lal, I helped create this plan based on the best evidence available. I would not have suggested so drastic a measure if I thought a less-extreme solution were possible. The facts in hand tell me this is the way."

"I'm not so sure, Father." She tensed, and her lips thinned in anger—no, not anger, Data realized; it was denial. "I'm starting to think this might be a mistake."

"I assure you, Lal, it is not. We cannot simply reset our timeline, or try to separate it from the multiverse. Its persistent instability would continue to tempt the Devidians, as would the increasingly unstable quantum realities that would once more branch away from our own. The only way to prevent this calamity is to ensure the Devidians never encounter it in the—"

"I'm not talking about that, Father. I concede your point: we have to undo the accident that created the temptation that led the Devidians astray, that changed them from scavengers to predators. That isn't what bothers me."

Data continued to monitor the zone around the away team even as he became alarmed by his daughter's mounting distress. "What does trouble you about this, Lal?"

"Questions I can't answer." Her stare took on a faraway quality.

"After we prune our branch of time from the tree of the multiverse . . . what will take our place?"

Her question had sounded simple, but Data knew that any truthful answer would not be. "I cannot say, Lal. No one can. It is possible that nothing will take our place."

"So we'll all just be gone? Everything we did, everything we fought for—all erased as if we never were?" Her aura of fearfulness deepened. "For what?"

"To protect the Prime timeline and its stable, natural branches from being harvested by the Devidians."

Lal's eyes were bright with tears. "And what makes the Prime timeline so great?"

Data had no context for a reply. "I do not understand."

"We're supposed to change the past so that *our* timeline never existed, all to protect the Prime timeline. But what do we know about it?"

"Aside from the reasonable likelihood of its temporal stability? Very little."

"So we might be doing all this to save an emanation of time that looks nothing like ours. That turned out differently in potentially infinite ways."

"Yes."

"And those differences might be better, or they might be worse." Bitterness choked her as she asked, "How can I know the realities you'd have me die to save will be good ones?"

He felt his daughter's fear of the unknown, and wished he knew how to assuage it. "I cannot promise that, Lal. No one can. But not all changes should be feared. For example, some persons who died in our reality might be spared in the others—"

"—and some who lived might die. And some who came back to life might *stay dead.*"

At last the source of Lal's existential crisis came into focus for Data.

"Yes, Lal. That is a risk. There is no guarantee that you and I are part of the timelines we are helping to defend."

"So why blindly give up *our* reality for *those*?"

"Because we already know ours is doomed, Lal, and the others are not."

She shut her eyes to force back her tears, and clenched her jaw in rage. "It's not fair."

"No. It is not." Data gently lifted Lal's chin with his hand, and waited until she met his gaze. "All I know for certain is that our timeline was never really meant to be—and that whatever realities are saved by our sacrifice deserve to exist as much as ours ever did."

Lal nodded, still fighting her urge to give in to her sorrow.

Data pulled her close and held her until she was calm again.

When they parted, he used the corner of his sleeve to dry her tears, and he gave her a bittersweet smile. "Whatever happens, Lal, I will always love you."

"And I will always love you, Father."

From the bottom of the slope came a short, shrill whistle.

Data and Lal looked down to see Sisko beckon them. With a gesture, he signaled that he and Bashir had found a way in.

Data and Lal quit their overlook position, and then they walked down the slope together in silence, side by side, toward whatever future awaited them.

Steam and stench, endless shadows broken by pulses of green light or firefalls of sparks . . . the interior of the temporal disruption facility struck Sisko as a labyrinth of horrors. Every flickering glow and wafting patch of smoke reminded him of the fires that had choked the corridors of the *Starship Saratoga* during the Battle of Wolf 359—the day the Borg killed his first wife, Jennifer.

Twenty years had passed since that day of blood and fire. No matter how many times Sisko had told himself that its painful memories were behind him, something had always proved him wrong. This day was no exception.

In a grimly ironic twist of fate, he was leading this mission alongside Jean-Luc Picard—who, during his temporary assimilation into the Collective as Locutus of Borg, had led the attack on Wolf 359, destroying thirty-nine Starfleet vessels and killing more than eleven thousand personnel. Sisko found it disconcerting to see Picard in this place. Supposedly, like all other liberated former drones, Picard had been freed of all traces of Borg nanites when the Caeliar had absorbed the Collective into their gestalt six years earlier. But then how was Picard hearing the Borg now? What lingering connection bound him to their inhuman designs? Was part of him still Locutus?

I hated him for so long. Until, finally, I forgave him. And now I have to trust him with my life, against the one enemy that ever truly beat him. Maybe bringing him was a mistake.

Sisko tightened his grip on his phaser rifle and pressed forward, guiding the team deeper inside the maze. He halted short of a four-way intersection. Activating the passive sensors on his rifle, he nudged its muzzle past the corner and watched its display. It showed no movement. No airflow irregularities to suggest stationary sentries.

He gave his team a thumbs-up to let them know the way was clear.

Data, who was right behind Sisko and Picard, signaled they should go left.

Sisko turned the corner. Within ten meters, he regretted it. The heat and humidity spiked, and the air grew heavy with odors of burnt polycarbons, scorched metals, and unwashed bodies—an early warning sign that drones were nearby.

It was a characteristic of the Borg with which few people were familiar, outside of a handful of veterans of the 2381 invasion: they stank. Beneath all their cybernetic enhancements and synthetic garments, they remained organic beings—flesh, blood, and bone.

A drone's link to the Collective overrode most of its executive capacity, but its autonomic functions and reactions remained the same. Under all of their mesh and machinery, the drones perspired. Though they no longer consumed food with their mouths, bacteria still lived in them, generating some of the worst halitosis in known space. And their pallid, mottled skin gave them not just the look of cadavers but also their sickening reek.

Sisko dropped to one knee, and the team behind him did likewise. He signaled Data to look for drones on the catwalks overhead, or on sublevels visible through the meter-wide steel grates that constituted every fourth section of the corridor's floor. The android acknowledged the order and moved up, his movements eerily silent in spite of his dense synthetic structure.

At the rear of the formation were Lal and Crusher. Every time Sisko saw Lal, he had to remind himself that, despite her diminutive stature and innocent visage, she was as strong and nearly as formidable in every way as her father, Data.

I keep thinking she ought to have more protection than just Doctor Crusher. Then I remember that Lal is the one protecting her.

Bashir, meanwhile, squatted with his rifle balanced across his knees. His eyes were wide and unblinking, and he remained perfectly still. His intensity, unkempt salt-and-pepper hair, and ragged beard gave him the affect of a wild frontiersman or a nomadic warrior. Sisko surmised that his genetically enhanced friend was putting his superior hearing to work, listening for any signs of approaching Borg drones.

Seconds became a minute of immobility. Sisko was considering going ahead on his own to check on Data's status when Picard whispered to him, "We should keep moving."

He looked over his shoulder at Picard, but could barely see more than the man's silhouette. "Not yet. Moving without a purpose can be more dangerous than holding still. We need to wait for Data's report."

Picard's hand grasped Sisko's shoulder. The other captain's grip was viselike, and his voice, though still a whisper, gained a desperate edge. "We *cannot* stay here."

"What are you—?" Sisko's vision acclimated, and he saw the fear in Picard's eyes. The man was trembling, as if from an overload of adrenaline. "Picard? Are you all right?"

The tremors worsened to the point that Sisko feared Picard was on the verge of a seizure. He took hold of the captain's arms and tried to compel him into stillness through sheer force of will. "Picard. Talk to me. What's happening?"

Picard's voice quaked. "I hear them. I hear *her*. She's everywhere." He shut his eyes. "They sense me. They know there is something *different* about me." Decades-old trauma filled Picard's eyes with angry tears. "She wants me to surrender. And part of me . . . wants to."

Sisko pulled Picard closer to him, hoping to overwhelm him to such a degree that it might make him forget about the Borg, even if only for a second. "Fight it, Picard. Maybe it's not real. You were purged of nanites, weren't you?"

"I was, but they left their mark. The Collective is like an obsession. It burns patterns into the brain. Rewires it. Changes it for life."

Data returned from his scouting action just as Crusher appeared at Picard's back, her focus sharp but her fear still evident. "Jean-Luc? What's wrong?"

"I shouldn't have come, Beverly." He turned his terrified gaze upward, as if he had just heard the voice of the Almighty passing judgment upon him. "They can hear me."

Data kneeled next to Picard. "He appears to be having a panic attack."

Sisko felt like he'd been sandbagged. *This is* not *how this was supposed to go.*

"Doctor, is there something you can give him?"

Crusher reacted as if Sisko had suggested a course of leeches. "Like *what?*"

"I don't know. Anything. A sedative? Something to stop—"

"There's no time," Picard interrupted. "We need to go. *Now.*" He stood and looked back the way they had come, his focus distant, as if he could see through the walls. "They're coming."

22

U.S.S. *Titan* NCC-80102

Riding a natural transwarp current felt like free-falling while standing still—that was the only way Sarai could describe it. It wasn't a smooth, innocuous transit like that of an artificially created transwarp conduit, such as the ones used for eons by the Borg. For a starship like *Titan*, traversing a natural transwarp current was like riding a whitewater rapid. Sarai felt its influence through the deck, in the bulkheads, in the air around her. It was beyond exhilarating; for her, it felt like being fully alive for the first time in her life.

And no one else on the bridge seemed to notice it.

Couldn't they feel this acceleration in the fabric of spacetime? Were they really oblivious of the special energy the current imparted to every living thing in its grasp? She pondered the possibility that only Efrosians were sensitive to the effects of the current, but to test that notion would entail speaking with and confiding in the ship's only other Efrosian crew member—its abrasive chief engineer, Doctor Ra-Havreii.

Sarai didn't need to know quite that badly.

She checked her command console. *Titan* was eighty minutes out from Yama.

I wonder if the galaxy will still be here in eighty minutes.

Each minute brought more reports of the weird and the impossible from every sector of the Federation, and from every quadrant beyond. Nebulas condensing into the supernovas that had birthed them; sensor data suggesting the universe was contracting back toward the Big Bang within the next two hours; and a report that the ruins of the ancient sentient artifact known as the Guardian of Forever had spontaneously reassembled into an entity that called itself the Guardian of Never—which promptly crumbled to dust six seconds later.

None of it had been compelling enough to distract Admiral Riker from his manic fixation upon long-range sensor data from the Yama system. Sequestered in the ready room, he had demanded updates from Tuvok every five minutes since *Titan* left Orcus 784. Sarai checked the ship's chronometer and winced when she saw the time.

Four . . . three . . . two . . .

The chirp of an internal comm sounded from the tactical console, followed by Riker's voice. *"Tuvok? Any new readings from Yama?"*

"As it happens, sir . . . yes. We have—"

The ready room door opened and Riker jogged out. "On-screen, Tuvok!" He faced the main viewscreen, his hands flexing into fists and then opening, over and over. The admiral could barely stand still; he had the frantic manner of a child with an overfull bladder.

A chart showing Yama, its event horizon, and its accretion disk appeared on the main viewscreen. Several glyphs with supplemental notations surrounded the black circle representing the singularity. Tuvok highlighted the dispersed symbols. "Long-range sensors have detected several high-energy events proximate to Yama's accretion disk. Each showed nearly identical levels of gamma radiation and chroniton particles."

"Like you'd see from artificial wormholes!" Riker pointed at the screen, nodding vacantly. "I was right. I told you they'd go to Yama, and there they are!" He faced Tuvok. "Tell our Klingon allies to be ready to attack as soon as we drop out of the transwarp current. We need to hit those jaunt-ships fast, take out their jump capabilities before they can—"

Riker's mania turned to paranoia. "Why isn't anyone doing anything?" He shot a mad-dog look at Keru. "Hail the lead Klingon ship!"

Keru was steeped in regret. "Sir, the Klingons didn't follow us into the current."

"What? Why not?" No one answered him. Riker searched in vain for someone who would look him in the eye. "Hail them, Keru!"

"They're out of range, sir."

"Then extend our range!" Riker prowled from station to station, haranguing the bridge crew one by one. "Don't you people get it? We need them! We have to get them back!" His fury became tearful hysteria as he raged, "I need them to help fight the Devidians! To save this timeline! To save *my family!*"

A look of horror passed over Riker as he spoke those two last words.

My family. He seemed to realize he had said too much. That he'd shown one card too many.

Then, as if he could smell the coming betrayal, he pivoted toward Sarai. There was murder in his eyes. "You. What have you done?"

She got up, stepped forward, and confronted him. "I told the Klingons to stand down."

Sarai had never seen so many emotions cross a person's face in so short a time. Grief, fear, wrath, desperation, confusion—Riker expressed all of them at once.

Then he slapped Sarai, hard enough to turn her head.

She took the hit, faced Riker, and cracked an evil smile. *Finally.*

"Admiral William T. Riker: pursuant to Article 128 of the Starfleet Code of Military Justice, you are hereby charged with assaulting a commissioned officer. You are relieved of your command. Mister Keru, take the admiral into custody."

Keru left his console and strode toward Riker. "Aye, Commander."

Only then did Riker notice that Keru was already equipped with a pair of magnetic manacles. "What the hell is this? What's going on?"

The port-side turbolift doors opened.

Captain Vale stepped out first, followed by Doctor Ree, Commander Troi . . . and Ssura.

Riker stared in shock at Troi. Then she nodded at Sarai, who returned the gesture, and the admiral suddenly seemed to understand the horrible truth of his predicament. "This is mutiny!"

Vale paused on the way to her chair, to confront Riker. "I'd say court-martial me, but I doubt any of us will live that long." She looked at Ree. "Doctor? He's all yours. Good luck."

Sarai said to Keru, "Take the admiral to sickbay, on the double."

"Yes, sir."

Keru manacled Riker and hauled him away, accompanied by Ssura, Ree, and Troi, while the admiral swore a blue streak that was silenced only by the closing of the turbolift doors.

Vale returned to her command chair and sat. Sarai stood at ease in front of her. "Good to have you back, Captain."

"Good to be back, Number One. I'll need damage and casualty reports ASAP."

"Already updated." Sarai stole a look at the main viewscreen, which had reverted to the forward angle of *Titan*'s journey through the mad wash of rainbow colors that was the natural transwarp current. "Should we reverse course?"

"Not a chance. I don't know what's wrong with Will, but he was right about one thing: whatever happens next, it's happening at Yama— which means *that's* where we're going."

23

C.S.S. *Enterprise*
If I've guessed wrong, I've wasted our final hours on a wild goose chase and doomed us all.

Wesley Crusher stared, glassy-eyed with exhaustion, at one screen after another of multispectral sensor data collected by the jaunt-ship *Enterprise* and its eleven sister ships, which all were orbiting the singularity Yama along the periphery of its event horizon, at intervals of thirty degrees. The other ships were relaying their sensor readings in real time to the *Enterprise*, and that deluge of raw information paraded across Wesley's bank of displays.

Even with his Traveler's powers to accelerate his perception of time—and, consequently, slow the apparent rate of arrival for new information—he had trouble keeping up. There was so much noise, and the signal for which he searched was, he feared, too subtle to be found this way.

What if the Devidians' base was at Orcus 784? Or Kali 531? Or Abaddon, and we just missed it? How can I be sure we checked every variable? The Devidians aren't stupid. They built technology that can destroy entire realities—it wouldn't be a stretch to think they learned how to hide that technology, as well. He paused the flow of updates on his screens, shut his eyes, and covered them with his palms. With his fingers he massaged the ache from his temples. *I made Captain Picard and the others believe I'm an expert, that I know what I'm talking about. But what if I'm just fooling myself? What if I'm just guessing in the dark?*

He couldn't remember the last time he had slept. Or the last cup of coffee he'd guzzled. *I'm running on fumes. I'd give anything for a few hours of shut-eye, but this universe literally doesn't have that much time left.* When he closed his eyes and mentally blocked out the ambient sounds of the bridge, he could reach out with his temporal senses and feel the coming disaster.

It was like standing in an ocean on a moonless night, feeling the rising tide climb up his legs, its numbing chill claiming his flesh by degrees, and knowing that at some point the sea would sweep his feet out from under him, pull him down into its power, and swallow him whole.

And that there was nothing he could do to prevent it.

It's coming. I feel it, like I feel my own breath. It's coming.

His morbid reverie was broken by the bright ping of an alert on Perim's console. He swiveled toward her, encouraged by the look of awe on her angular face. "What is it?"

Her shock turned to hope. "We have something. Look at this." With a sweep of her arm she tossed the new readings from her screens to his, and then she got out of her chair to stand behind him while he reviewed the new information.

One look told Wesley that Perim was right. "This is amazing! Twelve-dimensional spatial folding along the event horizon? That's what we've been looking for. Who found this?"

She pointed out details in the metadata. "*Endurance*, one hundred fifty degrees ahead of us in orbit."

"We need to get there. And until we do, *Endurance* needs to run every kind of scan ever devised on that intertemporal fold. By the time we arrive, we'll need a map of the way through."

Perim met his requests with doubt. "Through to what? Can we operate starships in intertime? Can we *exist* there?"

"I think so."

"You *think* so? That's the best you can do?"

Wesley shrugged with his empty hands raised in front of him, a gesture of supplication. "What do you want from me? I've never seen an interstitial subdimension of time before. Until a few weeks ago, I thought it was strictly theoretical." He paused to collect his wits. "Look, just tell *Endurance* and whatever ship is right behind it—"

"*Vasquez.*"

"Fine, *Vasquez*. Tell Captain Perez to add her ship's scanning power to *Endurance*'s. I'm gonna need all the data I can get on that intertime blister when we arrive."

"Need it? For what?"

"Kell, *please.*"

She relented with a muffled growl of annoyance. "Fine."

"Thank you." Satisfied that Perim was on board with his nascent plan, Wesley left his station and made his way to the side of Luc's command chair. "Captain?"

Luc didn't lift his eyes from the damage report he was reading on a padd. "What now?"

"Perim found something in the readings taken by *Endurance.* I think it's a pocket of twelve-dimensional intertime—the kind of hiding place the Devidians would make to shield themselves from the effects of their attacks on different timelines."

Luc lowered his padd and faced Wesley. "Are you certain?"

"As much as I can be without setting foot inside it."

Luc turned cagey. Having spent many decades surrounded by dissemblers, he clearly sensed that Wesley was not being candid about his agenda. "What do you *want,* Wesley?"

"I want to take one of your shuttlecraft, or any warp-capable auxiliary spacecraft you have, through the intertemporal fold, into the intertime blister."

The captain shook his head. "Absolutely not. You'll be safer inside the *Enterprise.*"

"With all respect, Captain, I'm not sure that's true."

That did not sit well with Luc. "Explain."

"My abilities as a Traveler—sensing pathways through space and time, for one—work better when there's less technology around me. We need a safe route through the intertime rift, or else the fleet will be shredded trying to make it to the other side. Alone, in a small craft, I can navigate a safe path through the rift. Once I'm done, I can send that route back to the fleet."

"You'll also wind up alone on the other side of the rift, at the mercy of the Devidians and whatever they might have waiting for you there."

"True. But that's a risk I'm willing to take—and more importantly, it's a risk you *need* me to take. For the good of everyone."

Luc thoughtfully stroked his facial hair while he considered Wesley's request.

He made his decision quickly. "Very well. I'll have an outrider prepped for you in shuttlebay one. Can you be ready to leave in ten minutes?"

"I can be ready in five."

"Fortune be with you, Mister Crusher. We'll await your signal."

Wesley risked putting his hand to Luc's shoulder in a show of gratitude. "Thank you, Captain. I won't let you down." As he dashed to the turbolift, Crusher called out to Perim, "Keep sending me updates until I reach the other side!"

She consented with a single nod, but said nothing before the turbolift door closed.

Wesley's entire body shook with adrenaline overload. *This is it! I found them!*

Then the rational part of his brain exerted itself, and bestowed a grimmer realization.

This is the beginning of the end.

This is where we're all going to die.

Yama / Intertime Rift

The outrider *Smiley O'Brien* was shaped like a needle, and its controls felt more intuitive to Wesley than those of any other ship he had ever flown. It responded to his will almost as if it could read his mind. He knew his Traveler abilities were not responsible for his seemingly innate control of the ship, because in the past such harmony had required great effort on his part. No, there was something special about the Commonwealth's outriders.

But I'll never know what it is, because this cosmos is going to end before I can ask anyone about it. He pushed away his regrets and self-pity. *There are lots of questions that'll never find answers now. I need to stay focused on the problem in front of me.*

He pushed the outrider to its limits, defying the monstrous gravity of Yama on his port side, and skirting the fiery edge of the singularity's accretion disk to starboard. Even so, the craft felt impossibly steady. He marveled at its integrity in the face of incomprehensible forces. *A Starfleet runabout would be shedding chunks of its hull by now.*

His coordinates confirmed he was closing rapidly on the intertime rift. Even though the navigation computer would do most of the work, he checked his course again. To make it across the rift's spatiotemporal threshold, he needed to intercept it at a precise point, along a heading with an exceptionally narrow margin of error.

If I miss, there's no way to turn back, not against this kind of gravity. I'll have to make another orbit of Yama to try again—and that'll waste half an hour I don't have.

A single bump of turbulence escalated within seconds into a violent jouncing. As soon as Wesley thought of looking for the cause, the dart-like ship's computer presented a summary report on an auxiliary screen to his left. Yama's gravimetric profile was changing, in ways that had never been documented before in any singularity. Whatever was tearing apart the rest of the universe was finally making its way here.

Wesley channeled his Traveler powers through the ship to steady its quaking spaceframe, and then he focused his abilities on guiding the ship through the rift.

Let's do this.

He increased the outrider's speed, then opened a comm channel. "*Enterprise*, this is outrider *Smiley O'Brien*. I'm preparing to cross the intertime rift. Fifteen seconds to target."

He was answered by Luc. *"Acknowledged, outrider. The fleet is holding position at ten million kilometers."*

"Perfect. I'll map the passage on my way through. Wait until you receive my navigational data before you attempt to cross the rift."

"Understood, outrider. Good luck. Enterprise *out."*

The comm channel went silent—and then *Smiley O'Brien* struck a sliver-thin wound in the fabric of spacetime and shot through it like a bullet.

The outrider tumbled and rolled with wild violence.

Overwhelmed by a blur of swirling light and darkness, Wesley felt sick and dizzy. Power to the outrider's inertial dampers fluctuated, whipsawing him between weightlessness and the wrenching pains of chaotic high-g rolls and yaws.

The holographic and haptic controls in the outrider's cockpit blinked out.

Wesley shook off the nausea and disorientation of his rough trip through the rift. The brutal push and pull ceased, which suggested that perhaps his ship had stabilized, or its inertial dampers had reengaged, or possibly both.

Outside the cockpit canopy there was nothing but darkness. No stars. Just *nothing.*

He reached inside his jacket and pulled out a light-stick. It was an ancient design, the lowest of low tech and therefore perfect for emergencies. With just a bit of effort he bent its shell, cracking a more fragile interior casing. That allowed binary chemicals inside the tube to react, producing a bright white light that would last for up to half an hour.

Now able to see his cockpit's controls, he started searching with his hand for the switch an *Enterprise* flight-deck officer had pointed out to him before clearing him for departure: the outrider's emergency restart. He recognized it the moment he touched it. With one push, the slender, silvery hulled vessel purred back to life, from its engines to its control interfaces.

There we go.

He tucked the light-stick back into one of his coat's inside pockets. Then, as he turned his head to check the outrider's latest sensor readings, an icy sensation washed through him.

It wasn't a regular chill, or some psychosomatic manifestation of fear. Its point of origin was external to him and even to the outrider, and its source was one of infinite malevolence. This feeling was unlike any Wesley had ever known, yet he recognized its meaning at once. He was not welcome here, wherever or whenever *here* was.

When he tried to extend his Traveler senses, he realized that the extraordinary perceptions and powers he had spent decades learning to control were no longer there.

He had never before felt so profoundly . . . *alien.*

If my Traveler talents are being suppressed, or if they just don't function in this pocket of intertime, then I can't just pop in and out of here. Either I leave in a ship, or not at all. He tried again to marshal his Traveler senses, just enough to perceive the disproportionate reaction from the uncanny dimension around him. *Definitely a hostile space. In a pinch, maybe I could force my way out with the Omnichron, but the effort would probably kill me.*

He was still waiting for actionable intel from the outrider's computer. Both the short- and long-range sensors were struggling to run routine analyses—most likely because they weren't finding any of the phenomena they had been programmed to detect. No signal beacons for gauging time. No pulsars with which to triangulate position. No gravimetric waves to suggest the proximity of star systems. Wesley interrupted their futile processes and disengaged them.

Just give me a short-range proximity scan, and we'll build from there.

The new scan registered a massive structure, one nearly twice the size and eight times the mass of Earth Spacedock.

And it was just five kilometers away—directly beneath him.

Wesley gently rolled the outrider 180 degrees to port, so that his cockpit canopy faced the gigantic space structure. As soon as the maneuver was complete, he wished he hadn't done it.

Suspended in the starless void was a technological horror. It looked as if it had been grown organically rather than built.

The nightmarish behemoth would have been all but impossible to see against the backdrop of the void except for the countless swirling ribbons of violet light that encircled it, illuminating its dull-black outer hull. Wesley focused the outrider's sensors on the twisting bands of energy. As he expected, it was bleed-off from an enormous temporal collider somewhere inside the station. Even with his Traveler powers suppressed, Wesley felt the temporal collider's nauseating effects. Its distortions of time burned like acid in his veins.

The station's core had exterior structures that resembled an exoskeleton. Asymmetrical extensions from one end of its cylindrical hull evoked for Wesley the idea of mechanized tentacles; they undulated lazily while collecting countless streams of white bioneural energy, which spilled in chaotic torrents from transient microwormholes that formed just a few hundred meters away from the hungry, writhing mass on the end of the station.

Its other end was encircled by a massive ring structure. The ring was connected to the core by three thick spokes, and it rotated slowly around a tower that extended more than twenty kilometers from a colossal dome that covered the top of the main core.

The next thing the sensors picked up was an intense cluster of life signs beneath the station's dome. Distortion made the signal intermittent but was unable to conceal its magnitude. Wesley fine-tuned the sensors until he was certain of what he had found.

Devidians. There must be at least half a million of them packed inside there.

As curious as Wesley was to know what was happening beneath the opaque dome, he couldn't divert his attention for long from the tower that protruded from it.

On a sensor display inside the cockpit, details of the tower's structure appeared. He recognized them at once. Though orders of magnitude larger and more sophisticated, the tower was of the same peculiar design as those he and the *Enterprise*-E crew had discovered deep in the past of Devidia II, and on a barren plain of a desolate world thousands of years in the future. Lambent tendrils of violet energy danced along the tower's entire length as it projected a steady stream of white neural energy into the endless void.

The station must be the master receiver. The one to which all of the Devidians' other towers send the life-forces they've stolen from across time. But where's the energy from this *tower going?* Wesley squinted against the glare of the beam. *Not into the void . . .*

There's something down there.

He trained the sensors on the beam. "Magnify and enhance."

Almost invisible in the eternal starless night of intertime, less than a hundred thousand kilometers from the nightmarish station, was a planet.

It was a rocky world, slightly less massive than Earth. When Wesley scanned it for life signs, he found nothing. Not a single plant, no animals, not even fungi or bacteria. But the sensors detected massive synthetic energy signatures from vast structures beneath its surface, and he presumed the Devidians weren't bombarding the planet with stolen neural energy for no reason.

Let's take a closer look.

He launched a miniprobe from the outrider. The self-propelled autonomous device was smaller than his forearm but packed with the Galactic Commonwealth's most sophisticated sensor equipment. It raced toward the planet, parallel to the energy stream from the tower. When the beam split into multiple paths in the upper atmosphere, the probe locked onto the strongest one and followed it down to the surface, while sending a steady flow of data back to the outrider.

Nitrogen-oxygen atmosphere. Uniform ambient temperature of twenty-one degrees Celsius. Negligible trace elements or pollutants . . . Wesley made a sudden realization: *This atmosphere can't be natural. The structures under the surface must be filtering the planet's air and keeping it warm in the absence of a star for heat. What a remarkable—*

In an instant his wonder turned to horror.

The flow of neural energy led the probe to a vast caldera dozens of kilometers wide and hundreds of meters deep. Flashes of sickly green light seethed around its edges. The barren crater teemed with millions of spectral Devidians, who were attended by legions of their deadly Naga soldiers and countless languid ophidians, all of them shifted two millicochranes out of phase.

Souls fell from the sky like luminous silver rain.

The great horde of ghostly Devidians squatted in the crater's knee-deep blanket of ash, their gaunt gray forms practically motionless, and their scarlike feeding maws turned upward, as they drank the stolen energies of the dead.

Every glimmer of life that fell from the starless sky represented a sentient being's anguish and torment; each spark that rained down was another life stolen, another soul murdered, all to feed a hunger that had grown like a cancer until it became insatiable. Millions of brilliant motes descended on the horde like a blizzard; not a single shining bit ever touched the ground.

The miniprobe sped onward across the dusty moonscape, making rapid orbits of the ghastly gray world. In a matter of minutes it documented several *thousand* craters—each one infested with at least a million phase-shifted Devidians, all of them apparently surrendered to a fugue state while their orbital station deluged them with an endless feast of souls.

My God. There are billions *of them down there.*

Every molecule of Wesley's being told him to run. To flee this pocket universe that clearly hated him. To save himself before the Devidians' temporal collider turned him inside out and spilled his soul with a trillion others onto its dead world of ash and shadows.

But something was amiss—or, to be more precise, was missing.

Why aren't there any Nagas defending the station?

He checked his sensor readouts again. Except for the smaller specimens his miniprobe had sighted guarding the Devidians on the dead planet's surface, there was no sign of the colossal serpents that in the past few days had laid siege to Deep Space 9 and, before that, crippled the *Starship Aventine.* He had expected the Devidians' principal base of operations to be heavily defended by the fearsome creatures. Though he saw numerous possible apertures on the station's exterior from which the beasts might emerge, all of them were tightly sealed. Around the station, the only signs of motion were the swirling bands of violet energy.

Maybe the Devidians sent them all out hunting for us. Or maybe the battle at DS9 took more out of them than we thought. Either way, this is too good an opportunity to waste.

He reset the outrider's sensors for a new task: "Find me a place to land."

As Wesley started his approach, it became obvious the Devidians were not expecting company. None of several large clusters of weapons dotting the base's core reacted to the approach of his outrider. Any one of them was more than powerful enough, he was sure, to vaporize his tiny craft in a single barrage. But they all stood silent and still as he drew near.

Likewise, there were no open landing bays, or anything that resembled docking facilities. As he flew closer and steered a rolling course through the bands of amaranthine light that circled the gargantuan structure, the outrider's sensors detected small gaps in the base's outer shell—openings large enough for him to fly through, into the station's substructure.

He checked his sensor readings of the base's interior. There were signs of an M-class atmosphere: breathable air. He reasoned there must be something holding the air inside. After a quick adjustment of the sensors, he identified the low-power force field that kept the base's exterior together and its air inside.

If I can modulate the nutation of the outrider's shields into a canceling frequency, I should be able to penetrate the force field without disrupting it or setting off any alarms.

It took him a few seconds to alter the shield emitters' output, and then he was ready. He nudged the ship forward, and it glided through the force field like a scalpel through fat.

Within the station's substructure, everything appeared to be at least semiorganic. Parts of the interior resembled massive organs, and the curved, tapering linkages between them made Wesley think of cartilage, muscles, and sinews. Twisted ribbons of violet light danced through the empty spaces between structures. Wesley felt keenly aware that he was a foreign agent invading the body of a leviathan.

I need a place to set down. Fast.

Few platforms inside the base appeared wide or strong enough to support a landing of the outrider. Then Wesley spied a broad causeway linking two enclosed interior regions.

That'll do.

The *Smiley O'Brien* touched down with feathery grace onto the causeway. As it settled and the thrusters cooled with a falling whine, Wesley opened the cockpit's canopy. Cold air tainted with the odor of decaying flesh washed over him. By the time he had pulled himself to his feet, the side of the outrider had reconfigured itself to offer him an exit stairway—a trick the *Enterprise* crew had attributed to the outrider having been built with programmable matter.

He descended from the cockpit. For the sake of stealth and speed, he had only the clothes on his back; his Omnichron and his quantum comm were tucked in his pockets, and his transphasic-disruption rifle was slung across his shoulder.

Wesley took a moment to orient himself. With his Traveler abilities suppressed by the Devidians' insidious technology, he fell back on his Starfleet training and his experiences as an explorer to find his bearings. He studied the shapes and sizes of all of the station's interior structures that he could see, and he compared them against the overall shape of the station he had observed from outside. Within moments, he felt certain that he knew which direction led to the dome and tower assembly that housed all the life signs at one end of the station, and which way led to the chroniton core of the station's temporal collider. Both sites demanded investigation, but time was hemorrhaging away now.

I'll need to delegate.

He reached inside his jacket, pulled out his Omnichron, and released it with a gentle lift of his hand, cueing its AI to make the device hover.

He pointed toward the core. "O.C., scout the shortest route to the master controls of the collider's chroniton core, then meet me back here." He checked his wrist chrono and decided precautions were in order. "If I'm not back in fifteen minutes, take the outrider back to the *Enterprise* and share all the data we've acquired. *Go.*"

At his command, the Omnichron sped away in a silvery blur. Within seconds the metallic marvel had vanished into the endless shadows of the station.

Time to see what all the Devidians are doing up in the dome.

Wesley moved quickly, his transphasic-disruption rifle at the ready as insurance against hostile encounters. Given how tenacious the Devidians had been in their attacks, he had come expecting the same of their defenses. But the cavernous interiors of their hidden station were just as deserted as the intertime space outside it. Not a Devidian or a Naga in sight.

Where the hell is everybody?

He abandoned all pretense of stealth or subterfuge and found his way through the station by instinct. Most of its passages led to the outer perimeter, which made him think that might be the place to seek accelerated transit.

The closer he got to the perimeter, the more certain he felt that his guess had been right. Unearthly sounds meandered down the long, dark passageways—wails like the cries of damned spirits, shrieks that made him think of the mythical Furies. A series of booms, like a million drums being struck at once, reverberated through the gizzard-like corridors around him.

A few steps before rounding a turn, Wesley halted at the sound of marching feet. He ducked into a shallow nook and stole a surreptitious look at a company of avatars as they passed. Nearly a hundred of the black-hooded automatons moved in unison, following a leader who carried a long rod of bleached bone topped with a bloodred gemstone the size of a human skull.

That's more like what I expected. He listened as they passed from his sight and their steps receded. *Wait—they used to fly. Now they're on foot?* After a moment's thought, it made sense to him. *This whole station is one big temporal collider. It must be flooded with antichroniton distortion and chronometric interference. That would definitely mess with their ability to fly, and maybe inhibit their phase-shifting, too. Good to know.*

After they were gone and silence reigned once more, he pressed onward.

At the perimeter he discovered the horrid clamor was being carried down from high above, from the dome, by hundreds of vertical tubes, each many meters in diameter. The demonic howls were the product of air rushing through the shafts—which alternated between streams that surged upward and those that plunged down from the dome, into darkness.

Turbolifts without the lift cars. Gotta give them credit for efficiency, I guess.

He chose a shaft whose currents traveled upward, stepped into it, and hoped he hadn't just made the worst mistake of his life.

Jets of air took hold of him, cradled him, and held him steady as he soared upward. One level after another blurred past as Wesley ascended, gaining speed as he went—and then his rate of climb slowed, just as he neared the top of the shaft. He felt competing streams vying for his commitment: two led over curves at the top of the shaft, one in either direction, but both feeding into what he surmised were downdraft tubes. A third stream seemed made to draw him out of the shaft, into a corridor much like the one he had left seconds earlier. He leaned into that stream and found himself delivered into a graceful, light-footed landing in the passageway.

Here a different song filled the air.

The percussive beat was oppressive here, and a great chorus chanted in time with the booms that Wesley feared might crack his skull even as they shook his guts against his skeleton. He stood across from a tunnel that flickered with sprays of color and white light—a tunnel that led inside the dome.

He forced himself to enter the tunnel and tread softly to its end, where it opened into a vast arena. There he spied the source of the tumult—and his brain went blank in terror.

Sprawling before and beneath him was a scene from a nightmare.

More than half a million Devidians, all glowing and translucent like ghosts, stood gathered beneath the dome, which was composed of the same hideous extruded textures and structures as the rest of the facility. Most of the Devidians populated the vast tiers of stadium seating that ringed the main floor, where tens of thousands more had assembled, crowded in a frenzy, all of them facing the horror in the center of the arena's floor.

A massive circular structure, a fusion of bizarre mechanisms and what Wesley realized must be hundreds of living ophidians—serpents whose ability to generate bridges through time and space had long ago been harnessed by the Devidians into a semisymbiotic relationship. These snakelike creatures were linked one to another in a living Ouroboros, an ancient symbol of a serpent devouring its own tail as a metaphor for eternity and the cyclical nature of time.

No shortage of snake-things here. But still no Nagas.

The circular gateway was built into the base of the massive tower that Wesley had seen protruding from the dome and stretching out into the void.

Half a million Devidians kowtowed to the gateway.

Through the gateway he glimpsed the collapse of his universe: stars snuffed like dying embers. Black holes evaporating like droplets of water striking red-hot lava. Massive galaxies unwinding themselves into smaller galaxies that had collided eons earlier. One tableau after another of the impossible . . . all united by one common factor:

Inestimable sentient pain.

Trillions of quadrillions of lives being ended without warning or mercy. Cosmic eruptions of terror and sorrow. An endless wellspring of suffering and fear.

Before it, the Devidians gorged themselves on the lamentations of the dying and the bereaved, drove themselves into a collective trance, ecstatic frenzy, and omnicidal psychosis.

The gateway framed its next victim, a world whose continents and moons Wesley recognized immediately: Bajor, surrounded now by dozens of bands of the same violet energy that ringed the Devidians' station.

No! He wanted to cry out a warning, but it was far too late for that. Through the gateway he saw hundreds—no, *thousands*—of tiny ships race upward from the planet's surface, their passengers no doubt praying not to share Bajor's imminent fate.

Below him, the great throng of Devidians swayed and chanted, in thrall to the apocalypse they had wrought. Then they shrieked as one, a piercing, blood-curdling sound—

A flash, and Bajor was torn apart.

Billions of souls howled in terror as the Devidians snared them.

Silvery energy poured from the gateway, billions of discrete streams merging into a flood and cascading down upon the horde of Devidians congregated on the arena's floor. The energy shot from one Devidian's elongated head to another's, propagating faster than Wesley could follow it, until the entire horde stood linked, twitching like puppets on tangled strings, devouring every last drop of neural energy that Bajor's people had to give.

Then, as the planet detonated, a single flash of white-hot power erupted from the gateway, a shockwave of neural energy that rushed through the ghostly mob. The spectacle beneath the dome became a feast fed by death, like a vampiric orgy fused with a fascist rally, all for the pleasure of half a million phase-shifted ghouls.

A residual shock wave hit Wesley. In an instant he died a million deaths. Heard thousands of cries for help. Felt the desperation of parents clutching their children. The anguish of lovers vaporized in each other's arms. The silent grief of a billion extinguished species.

He fell to one knee and slumped against a wall. His guts felt as if they had been turned inside out, then back again—abused, raw, and violated. Bile surged up his esophagus, hot and sour. He choked it back down and fought the urge to vomit. *Breathe, dammit. Breathe.*

When at last he'd recovered his equilibrium, he looked up and saw someone—a stranger who definitely was not a Devidian—in a tunnel across the arena.

It looked like a man: human and ancient, with bone-white hair and a ragged white beard. His posture was crooked but his aspect was fierce. Wesley peered intently, studied the man—

—and then he realized the ancient stranger was looking back at him.

As they locked eyes, Wesley realized who the old man was.

That's me.

24

——

Devidian Temporal Collider—Intertime

«*I'm a version of you,*» the old man replied, his thoughts projected directly into Wesley's mind. «*Don't look so surprised. I'm not the first. But I might be the last—in this timeline, anyway.*»

Wesley recoiled at what felt like a violation of his mental privacy, but trying to hide from himself made him feel more than a little foolish. *When are you from?*

«*Several decades ahead, I think. Hard to say. All my reference points are gone.*»

Between them, countless thousands of glowing Devidians packed the vast circular arena. Wesley and his ancient doppelgänger were just over ninety degrees apart, each of them huddled in the shadows of a tunnel that linked the perimeter passageway to a broad ramp between the tiers inside the arena. Hidden machines pounded out a merciless rhythm that shook the entire structure, punctuating the cacophony that poured from the colossal ring-shaped gateway.

More ribbons of light shot from the ring and speared through countless Devidians, all of whom jerked as they were struck and then swayed as if in the throes of ecstasy.

Wesley focused his thoughts toward his older incarnation. *How did you get here?*

He felt Ancient Wesley's impatience and disdain. «*Doesn't matter now. You need to run. Take whatever you've found and get it back to whoever's waiting for you.*»

How do you know I—

«*Stop! I've been where you are. Seen countless versions of you do the same thing, make the same mistakes, over and over. For once, please, just listen to me.*»

His mind reeling, Wesley felt compelled to unite disparate facts, as if they were puzzle pieces. *Are you the version of me who died to bring a warning to my mother?*

Ancient Wesley's temper continued to fray. «*How should I know? Sounds like something I'd do, but it might've been one of my temporal echoes. Does it really matter?*»

I'm just trying to understand. He looked down, past the frenzied mass of Devidians, at the massive ring portal composed of ophidians linked head to tail. *What the hell is that?*

«*According to thoughts I've skimmed off the Devidians, they call it "Oblivion's Gate." It's a weapon for destroying temporal anchors and artifacts throughout the multiverse, and for collecting the neural energies released by the deaths of sentient creatures.*»

Looking down into the arena, Wesley winced as fresh bands of light shot from one Devidian to another, until the entire mob was united in a parasitic rapture.

How can they devour entire universes? Even ten billion of them can't be that hungry.

The old man's mood turned to disgust merged with grudging respect. «*Whatever they don't feast on now gets stored inside vast self-replicating batteries in the ring. And the more they take, the bigger it gets. They've got almost enough power to start breaking through barriers to stable timelines, and still have enough left over to live on for ten thousand millennia.*»

Inside the frame of Oblivion's Gate, the fire-swept debris of Bajor whipped itself apart into a spiral of dust and molten rock.

Wesley felt his hopes of salvation fading. *Is there any way we can—*

«*Reason with them? Not a chance. I've watched a dozen versions of you die trying to broker a peace. Trust me, these things aren't interested in talking.*»

A dozen versions of me? How long have you been here?

«*I can't remember. Maybe I've always been here. But this is our last rodeo, pal. Get ready to run, and don't look back.*»

Wait! I have so many questions.

«*Sorry, kid. Time's up.*» Ancient Wesley pulled a battered, tarnished Omnichron from inside his dirty coat. He lifted the small metallic cube high and focused his thoughts upon it. A tight beam of crimson energy shot from the device and slammed against an invisible barrier within the ring of Oblivion's Gate. Ripples propagated swiftly from the point of impact, washed away the image within, and terminated the river of death energy feeding the Devidians.

Violently separated from their delectable fountain, half a million Devidians turned in rage toward the source of the shot. There stood Ancient Wesley, no longer trying to hide himself. He shouted obscenities like a mad hermit at the army of phantoms.

The Devidians moved as one, surging upward toward their attacker.

The old man projected a final thought to Wesley as he fled into the shadows beyond his tunnel: «*Run, you fool!*»

Wesley tried to will himself into motion, but his feet felt as if they were rooted to the floor. His muscles refused his commands. Even as his mind pleaded for retreat, his limbs were frozen. He watched thousands of wraiths surge through the far tunnel in pursuit of the old man.

Then a wave of Devidians, translucent and luminous, rose in front of his own tunnel. In unison, they shrieked a warning—*no,* he realized, *a call to arms.*

And they charged.

He backpedaled, firing his transphasic disruptor into the mob. Roiling orbs of harsh, violet-white energy vaporized several Devidians with each shot, but the onslaught never halted or slowed. It pressed onward, preceded by chilling gusts that reeked of death and open sewers.

Wesley ceased fire, turned, and ran. He sprinted back the way he'd come, toward the free-fall windshafts. When he was close enough, he dived into the downward windshaft. Arms out in front of him, his head tucked, with his legs together and feet pointed, he turned himself into a missile, his profile optimized for speed.

He shot straight down into the black.

As for where to get out, he took his best guess.

He caught a current that pulled him out of the windshaft, and tumbled into the corridor. With agility born of necessity he rolled to his feet and resumed running.

There was no point looking back. It would only slow him down, and the cold, fetid air blowing on his back had already told him there were avatars right behind him.

There was no grace in his stride, just the mad rush of terrified flight—past dark walls lined with veinlike tubing, through arches that evoked the shape of skeletal jaws gaping wide.

One nightmarish feature after another blurred past, stoking his primal fear that some piece of the station would come to life and break free, or that the floor would crack open like a ravenous maw to devour him.

He was moving too quickly to spot landmarks, but none of what he saw looked familiar. *Dammit! I got off on the wrong level.*

An icy breeze that reeked of rotting flesh told him he couldn't double back.

He ran harder, pushed himself to put as much distance between himself and the avatars as he could. Ran until his lungs felt like they were on fire.

Just have to keep moving. Keep going 'til I—

He stopped so abruptly that he nearly fell on his face. Through an opening in the wall on his left, he saw the great expanse of the station's interior substructure, still full of roiling mists and lazy streamers of violet energy from the chroniton core.

Two levels above him, on an open causeway that linked two areas of the station, was his outrider. His Omnichron hovered beside the silver needle of a spacecraft.

Without his Traveler powers, Wesley had no way to traverse the gap between where he was and where the outrider stood parked, except to reach another set of windshafts and—

An eerie bluish-white glow brightened the curved passageway behind him. A bracing wind struck him, thick with odors of decay. He turned to press on, only to see the same gelid light gathering strength in the corridor ahead of him, coupled with the same foul air.

End of the road.

He pulled out his quantum communicator and set it for the Omnichron's frequency. "O.C., did you find the core?"

It responded over the comm in a feminine voice, *"Affirmative."*

"Good. Record this: The Devidians have a device called Oblivion's Gate. It's under the dome at one end of the station. It feeds them with energy and sends the rest to self-replicating batteries in the station's ring. Have the fleet focus on destroying the gate and the ring, to keep the Devidians busy while the strike team goes for the core. And come ready for a fight—they have tons of those avatars guarding the station. The only good news is, they can't fly inside here, probably because of all the distortion from the temporal collider. End of message. Get in the outrider and take our intel back to the *Enterprise*, now!"

"*Traveler Wesley, I can fly beneath your position, and you can jump down to—*"

"No time to argue! Take the outrider back to *Enterprise*, and tell the fleet to forget about me. They'll need their strength to back *Defiant*'s assault on Oblivion's Gate. Go!"

The Omnichron maneuvered into the outrider's cockpit, interfaced with *Smiley O'Brien*'s onboard systems, and closed the canopy. Half a second later, the impulse engine and thrusters came to life, and the dart-like ship hovered as it retracted its landing gear.

As the first ranks of cloaked-and-hooded avatars appeared in the corridor on either side of Wesley, the outrider shot away, retracing its path through the station's substructure and, Wesley hoped, back through the intertime rift to contact the fleet.

He raised his transphasic disruptor to forestall the inevitable, only to have the short rifle blasted from his hands by a pulse from an avatar's staff. His weapon—now a charred, misshapen piece of junk—clattered across the floor and came to a stop behind him.

Seconds later he was surrounded by dozens of avatars wielding rods that resembled jeweled femurs. Among the avatars were several Nagas—at three meters long, they were the smallest Wesley had seen so far, but each was still more massive than the average humanoid.

So much for "Where are the Nagas?"

He raised his hands in surrender, even as he decided to attempt diplomacy. "My name is Wesley Crusher. I am a Traveler. I am unarmed. I—"

A sharp blow to the back of his head purpled his vision and put him on his knees. Then a jolt of blue lightning from a bone staff struck his chest, and everything went black.

C.S.S. Defiant—Mirror Universe

There wasn't a single gap in the blockade. Not one blind spot. Nowhere for Ezri Dax and her crew to steer the cloaked *Defiant* past the armada of mercenary vessels guarding the mouth of the Bajoran wormhole. The mercs' tachyon grid was at full strength. If *Defiant* came within ten thousand kilometers of its invisible perimeter, the entire fleet would know it was there.

Dax folded her hands together and weighed her options. In moments such as these, she had found that the captain's chair felt more like a restraint than an elevation. Ensconced in the center of the bridge, she was reminded of how alone she felt.

It hadn't always been this way. Before her promotion, and before her Joining, during her years on *Defiant* during the Great Revolution, junior officer Ezri Tigan had been privileged to serve among friends who had come to feel like her family—and with Leeta, her still-adored late wife, who had died on this bridge during one of the revolution's most savage battles.

I'd thought I could never set foot on this ship again after I lost her. Remembering Leeta awakened all her old sorrows. That emotional injury was years old now, but it had never truly healed. Instead of psychic scar tissue, Ezri had an open wound that she did her best to hide. Most of the time she did all right. Kept her feelings under wraps. When she made the mistake of letting herself sink too deeply into the pain of Leeta's death, she remembered how her former commanding officer, Miles "Smiley" O'Brien, had persuaded her to return to duty on *Defiant*: he had asked her to serve as his number one.

It wasn't the promotion that had brought her back. It had been his declaration of how urgently he had needed her trusted counsel at his side. Leeta had been his XO before Ezri. And in those days Ezri hadn't become Dax yet—she had still been just Ezri Tigan, unjoined Trill. So to hear Smiley say that he wanted her to take Leeta's place at his side, that had felt to Ezri like an obligation she couldn't ignore. An inheritance. Or a rite of succession.

But even more than that, it had been a reminder that she was still considered part of the "family" on *Defiant*. That her membership had never been contingent upon her link to Leeta.

After the revolution had been won, and Ezri had been joined with the Dax symbiont, Smiley had retired to a quiet, rustic life on Earth. He'd recommended Dax to succeed him as the commanding officer of *Defiant*, and to her surprise, the Commonwealth Parliament had agreed.

Now she was on the verge of ordering her ship to its almost certain annihilation.

How am I supposed to break through that line without getting us all killed?

She heard the starboard-side door to the bridge slide open. With a slight swivel of her chair, she looked back to see Vedek Kira walk toward her. The Bajoran woman's rust-red hair was tousled, as if she had been roused from a troubled sleep. "Reporting as ordered, Captain."

"Thank you, Vedek." Dax got out of her chair and met Kira. She led the older woman toward the starboard-side duty stations and lowered her voice. "There's something you need to see." They stopped at the tactical console. Dax tapped the shoulder of the young, brown-haired human woman who had been monitoring the station. "Šmrhová? Some privacy, please?"

"Aye, Captain." The tactical officer stood, nodded at Dax, and then retreated to the aft console, well out of eavesdropping range.

Dax and Kira huddled close and leaned forward, toward the tactical screen. With a few quick taps on the controls, Dax called up the ship's most recent sensor data. "We arrived in the Bajor system about ten minutes ago. This is what we found."

The small screen filled with an image of Bajor wrapped in rings of fire and lightning, before breaking apart and then crumbling into dust.

Kira's eyes widened with horror. "May the Prophets have mercy . . ."

"It gets worse." Dax switched the playback to quick snippets of Bajor's moons spinning apart into dust and vapors, followed by the true catastrophe for their mission: the wormhole, appearing and disappearing, over and over again, its normally beautiful bluish-white horizon turned ghastly hues of purple and dancing with wild tentacles of green lightning.

"Everything was normal when we dropped out of warp. But less than two minutes later, the whole system started to self-destruct."

Kira shut her eyes as she cupped her hands over her mouth and nose, as if she were fighting to stifle an urge to weep. When she lowered her hands and spoke again, her voice was barely a whisper. "It's the Devidians."

"Sure looks that way." Dax summoned a fresh screen of sensor data. "Plus, the wormhole's spitting more than lightning. We're picking up chroniton surges, Hawking radiation, and crazy levels of triolic waves. Even if we could run the blockade, flying into that mess might fry us dead in a matter of minutes."

Kira opened her eyes. "If we time it right, a few minutes might be all we need."

"I'm not sure you're hearing what I'm saying. Before we got here, our best plan for getting you inside the wormhole was to create a distraction that might draw the mercs out of position. But now the whole system's ripping itself to shreds and the wormhole's gone wild. There's no distraction we can make that can top what's already going on out there—and the crazier things get, the tighter the mercs form up around the wormhole."

Kira called up a tactical scan of the mercenaries' ship positions. "Why would they retreat *toward* the wormhole when it's going berserk?"

"Because that's what they get paid to defend."

"But Bajor was the one paying them. If Bajor's gone . . . who are they sticking around for?" Suspicion tightened Kira's focus. "Is it possible the Devidians tricked the mercs into defending them?"

"Good question. But right now I'm more worried about how to make enough of a gap in their line to get you and your Orb inside that apparently malfunctioning wormhole."

Kira crossed her arms, as if she hoped to bottle up her frustration. "All right, Captain. What do you recommend?"

"Depends. If your Prophets are the kind of gods who grant miracles, I'd tell you to start praying." Dax threw a cynical look at Kira. "*Hard.*"

25

————

Temporal Disruption Base—2373, Borg Timeline

The away team scuttled like rats from one shadow to another, then huddled and squatted amid a cluster of machines whose functions Beverly Crusher was at a loss to discern.

She and the others clutched their rifles to their torsos as a squad of Borg drones marched past, just a few meters away. Motionless and paranoid, she listened and waited for the drones' steady footfalls to recede and become lost in the background noise of rumbling generators.

The last echo of marching feet faded away. Data emerged from his hiding place, but remained low, in a deep squat, as he faced the rest of the team and whispered. "The control room for the temporal disruptor is close." He indicated the direction with his hand. "Seventeen-point-four meters in that direction." He looked at Sisko. "Which would you prefer to hear first? The good news, or the bad news?"

Sisko let out a low sigh. "Good news."

"The control center appears to be a highly defensible position, with only one narrow point of ingress, and a reinforced, bunkerlike structure. Furthermore, this facility appears to have been repurposed from a previous human construction, so its physical infrastructure contains a minimal amount of Borg technology. Consequently, it is unlikely that the Borg will be able to weaponize this environment against us in the same manner that they were able to animate the interiors of their cubes."

Bashir rolled his eyes. "Thank heaven for small mercies."

Picard side-eyed Bashir. "You *should* be thankful, Doctor. Combat inside a Borg cube involves fighting the ship as much as the drones. That is a complication we *do not* need."

"Agreed," Sisko said, cutting off any further debate. "The bad news?"

Data seemed reluctant to continue. "There are several dozen Borg drones in defensive positions around the control room, more than we can overcome in direct conflict. And it is unclear what distraction, if any, would be sufficient to persuade the Collective to redeploy enough of them to make an assault viable."

The team deflated at Data's news, but something else bothered Crusher. "Data? Why do you consider the control center's defensibility an advantage? Wouldn't that be a disadvantage?"

"From the standpoint of our initial assault, yes. However, there are only a few drones inside the control room. Most of their defensive force is outside its main door."

"I still don't see how that's good for us."

"It will be vital to those who stay behind *after* we take control of the temporal disruptor."

Crusher felt as if someone had omitted a crucial detail from her pre-mission briefing. "Why would any of us need to stay behind?"

"To defend the disruptor until it can be synchronized across time with the Devidians' chroniton core, in order to undo the original divergence event that created the First Splinter timeline." Data turned a meaningful look at Sisko. "It will not take the Borg long to detect our sabotage. They will reverse our changes unless we prevent them from doing so."

"Wait." Crusher tried to wrap her head around all the time-science involved, a subject that had never been her forte. "If the original divergence event was caused by the Borg firing this disruptor thing, why can't we just blow it up and skedaddle? If it's busted, it can't fire. If it can't fire, no timeline split, right?"

Data shook his head. "It is not that simple, Doctor. Rather than undo our divergence event, we would merely cause a paradox that would generate yet another unstable alternate timeline for the Devidians to exploit. In order to truly undo the event and amputate our branch of time from the rest of the multiverse without doing further harm, we must create an interdimensional, cross-time quantum resonance using the Devidians' own technology, as well as the Orb of Time, to resolve the paradoxes that will occur as we change the past."

Everyone around Crusher nodded as if they had understood all that technobabble gobbledygook. "Really? I'm the *only* one who doesn't get how this works?"

Data put a faltering smile onto a humble expression, and did his best to sound reassuring. "Forgive me, Doctor. I did not mean to bombard you with jargon. All I can do is ask you to trust me, and to trust the calculations that Wesley and I have made."

The invocation of Crusher's firstborn son toppled her resistance. She softened her tone as she asked Data, "Wesley trusted this plan?"

"It was his idea, Doctor. His grasp of temporal dynamics is . . . extraordinary."

"I'm sure it is." She steeled herself to push on. "So . . . who'll be staying behind?"

"That is not yet clear." Data checked the power setting on his rifle before he added, "It will depend upon which of us survive the attack on the control center."

Crusher closed her eyes and sighed in dismay. "I just *had* to ask."

26

C.S.S. *Enterprise*

The glimmer of hope Luc had felt upon seeing the outrider *Smiley O'Brien* reappear on *Enterprise*'s sensors evaporated as Troi declared, "No life signs on board, Captain."

His dismay turned to vexation as René Picard stepped out of the port-side turbolift onto the bridge, spoiling for a fight. "What does she mean, 'No life signs'? Where's my brother?"

Luc glowered at the brash young man. "Why aren't you in sickbay?"

"I guess your guards don't know it has more than one entrance. Now answer *my* question: Where is my brother? He should've come back by now."

The lad's timing was inconvenient but not unwarranted. Luc cooled his temper. "We're looking into it. If you want to observe, do so quietly—and stay out of the way."

Chastised as much as he was placated, René retreated to the aft science stations and found a secluded nook in which to ensconce himself and brood.

Merde. Luc's mind went immediately to worst-case scenarios. He imagined Wesley Crusher dead in the outrider's cockpit. Or worse, only part of the earnest Traveler's body on its deck and a sheen of blood coating everything else. He considered asking Troi to scan the outrider for signs of battle damage, but he was reasonably certain she was already doing so—and he wanted to avoid saying anything that might deepen René's distress.

Doing his best to project calm, Luc folded his hands over his lap and leaned forward in his command chair. "Helm, set an intercept course for the outrider. Commander Troi, ready a tractor beam. As soon as the outrider is in range, scan it for any sign of tampering or enemy munitions. If it's clean, bring it aboard."

"Aye, sir." Troi keyed commands into her console. Luc admired the half-Betazoid woman's focus and efficiency. Though her heritage had gifted her with empathic talents, she often used them not to report on others' states of mind, but to tailor her own presentation to become what those around her most needed in order to feel safe.

On the main viewscreen, the outrider quickly grew larger as it was towed back to the *Enterprise*. Luc was wondering what his crew might find aboard the short-range vessel when Troi announced, "We're receiving a transmission from the outrider. Audio only."

"On speakers."

A feminine voice, pleasant but noticeably synthetic, issued from the bridge's overhead speakers. "*Enterprise, this is Traveler Wesley's Omnichron. As ordered by Wesley, I am transmitting to you the navigational data needed to safely cross the intertime rift. Following that will be detailed sensor data regarding the exterior and interior of the Devidians' base located inside the intertime subdimension. Several alternate routes to the station's chroniton core have been mapped: the most direct, the path of least resistance, and detour options.*"

Luc told Troi, "Open a reply channel." He waited until Troi nodded, signaling that the channel was open. "Omnichron, this is Captain Luc Picard of the free starship *Enterprise*. Is Wesley Crusher still alive?"

"*Unknown. What follows is the final message from Traveler Wesley.*"

After a brief pause, the feminine voice of the Omnichron was replaced by a recording of Wesley. "*The Devidians have a device called Oblivion's Gate. It's under the dome at one end of the station. It feeds them with energy and sends the rest to self-replicating batteries in the station's ring. Have the fleet focus on destroying the gate and the ring, to keep the Devidians busy while the strike team goes for the core. And come ready for a fight—they have tons of those avatars guarding the station. The only good news is, they can't fly inside here, probably because of all the distortion from the temporal collider.*"

Another pause, and the Omnichron's voice returned. "*Traveler Wesley's final request was for the fleet to abandon him and save its strength for the assault on Oblivion's Gate.*"

Troi looked up from her station. "We'll have the outrider aboard in thirty seconds."

Luc got out of his chair and moved toward Troi's console. "Have one of your people recover the Omnichron for analysis, immediately."

"Aye, sir."

While Troi delegated his order to her subordinates, René approached Picard at the security chief's station. "Captain? Are we going in to save Wesley?"

The question stirred Luc's long-running inner conflict between passion and reason. "It's not that simple, René. Even with the intel from the Omnichron, taking the *Enterprise* through the intertime rift—never mind the entire fleet—could be quite perilous."

They were joined by Lieutenant Perim, who apparently had overheard René's query. "I've started analyzing the outrider's sensor log. Once we cross the rift, warp drive won't function and our jaunt drive won't be able to generate new wormholes, which means we'll be limited to sublight operations. There's also a risk that quantum fluctuations inside the intertime subdimension might destabilize the synthetic singularity at the core of our jaunt drive. If that happens, any trip we make to the other side might end up being a lot shorter than we expect."

If Perim looked worried, Troi seemed outright dismayed. "I've also reviewed the outrider's sensor logs. The Devidians' station has a lot of firepower. Small ships like outriders might be able to evade their barrage, but without our jaunt drives, we and the rest of the fleet will be easy targets on the other side. Assuming we don't blow up our own singularity cores, we should expect to receive a major beating from the Devidians."

None of that appealed to Luc. "What would be the smart play, Commander?"

Troi thought it over. "Blockade the entrance to the rift, and wait for *Defiant*. That way, we save our strength and give her maximum cover for the final assault."

Luc was about to give that plan his blessing when René asked, with mounting fear and fury, "What about Wesley?"

Looking the young man in the eye left Luc feeling trapped. *What am I supposed to say? That his brother's life isn't worth jeopardizing the mission? That Wesley knew what he was getting into? How would I feel if someone said that to me about Deanna?*

Luc did his best to adopt a comforting tone. "I understand your urge to save your brother. We all do. But rushing in unprepared might do more harm than good."

Being confronted by logic only hardened René's resolve. "I don't care, he's my brother. We can't leave him there. We have to help him."

"That's exactly what Wesley told us *not* to do."

"So?"

Luc rested his hand on René's shoulder in a gesture of comfort. "If we ignore his request, we might lose everything his sacrifice gained. We mustn't let our emotions control us."

René's mien darkened with anger. "A coward's excuse."

The accusation stung Luc to his core, and he could tell from the swath of sudden angry reactions around his bridge that his senior officers hadn't appreciated René's verbal jab, either. Purely out of reflex, Luc's hand closed on the hilt of his combat knife. "What did you say?"

"You heard me." René pointed at the image of the singularity and its event horizon on the main viewscreen. "My brother went in there *alone*, and he did what he had to do to get a message out. *That* was courage. You owe him nothing less."

Tactically, it was a stupid argument. But the nodding heads all around the bridge made it clear to Luc that René had struck a deep chord of pride and honor in the hearts of his bridge crew—including within Luc himself. *Damn this lad and his silver tongue.*

Luc faced Troi. "Any word yet from Captain Tenmei?"

"Negative. *Defiant* remains out of contact in the past."

Feeling like the rope in a tug-of-war, Luc pivoted toward Perim. "How long until the Devidians unravel our cosmos?"

The slender Trill woman checked the padd in her hand. "Seventy-four minutes."

There were so many variables. Luc hated making command decisions in the face of such a plethora of unknowns. That was why he had kept K'Ehleyr so close for so long. If she were here, she'd know what to do. *But she's not. I have to choose.*

Everyone was looking at him, waiting on his next order. Right or wrong, committing to any action now would be better for their morale than watching him dither.

He moved to the center of the bridge and raised his voice.

"While I would prefer *Defiant* were here to join our assault, we must fight our battles with the forces we have—and Mister Crusher deserves a chance to stand with us until the end. Commander Troi, load the sensor data from the outrider and the Omnichron into a log buoy, and launch the buoy clear of the accretion disk, to a point near where the *Hope* will enter the system. Set it to transmit an alert beacon on an open frequency. *Hope* and *Defiant* will need that information if they're to follow us."

He felt the excitement of his officers as they parsed the implication of his statement. Resolved to face the end of time with dignity and courage, Luc settled into his command chair. With a press of a pad on the armrest, he opened a shipwide internal channel.

"All decks, this is the captain. Red alert. All hands to battle stations." He closed the internal comm channel and directed his next orders to the bridge crew. "Commander Troi, order the rest of the fleet to fall in behind us, shields up, weapons hot. Helm, as soon as the signal buoy is away and clear . . . take us into the rift." He lifted his chin. "Let's show Mister Crusher that we don't abandon our friends—and show the Devidians that we *fear no evil.*"

27

U.S.S. *Titan* NCC-80102

Every step from *Titan*'s bridge to its sickbay had been excruciating for Troi. Cursing like a madman, Riker had struggled against his security escorts the entire time. It had taken three able-bodied security officers plus the significant mass and strength of Doctor Ree to put Riker on a biobed and keep him there until he could be restrained with a force field.

Even now Riker fought like a wolf introduced to a leash. The force field kept his legs together, his arms at his sides, and his back on the biobed. His head, however, was only partially restrained. He spewed vulgarities while he thrashed in wild erratic bursts, and with such violence that Troi was terrified he might break his own neck. It left her feeling sick and hollow to watch her *imzadi* flail against a force he couldn't hope to overcome.

Riker fell abruptly still and quiet, and then he sought her out with his eyes, his face a sudden portrait of anguish and fear. "Deanna? Please let me go."

"I can't, Will. This is for your own good."

If Ree was paying attention to their conversation, he hid it well. The chief medical officer kept his eyes on the readouts above Riker's biobed and held his forked tongue.

Riker's eyes, wide with desperation, stayed fixed upon Troi's. "Deanna, you don't understand. I can't let them die, not again."

"Die *again*? Who are you talking about?"

"Thad and Kestra!" Tears fell from Riker's eyes. "Our children!"

"Will? We have *one* child, a daughter. Natasha."

He winced as if she had slapped him, and then he squeezed his eyes shut in denial. "No. No, no, no, no, no . . ." He gritted his teeth and fought to hold back gasping sobs. "We have a son! Our first child—"

Troi recoiled with bitter tears in her eyes. Painful memories overwhelmed her and left her feeling adrift and alone, as she had several years ago. She gently set her palm to her husband's bearded cheek. "Will, our first pregnancy ended in a miscarriage. Don't you remember?"

Riker wept with rage, his body paralyzed but his mind drowning in a sea of anguish that Troi felt as keenly as if it were her own. Whatever else had changed about Riker, the special empathic bond that he shared with Troi clearly remained as strong as it had ever been.

Holding a hypospray between two scaly digits, Ree reached toward Riker and pressed the device gently to the admiral's throat. With a soft hiss the hypo injected drugs into Riker's carotid artery. Riker ceased resisting the force field, and half a second later he sank into a dreamy, murmuring state of twilight sleep. Before Troi could protest, Ree held up his free hand. "Forgive me, Counselor. We need to speak, and time is short."

"I *know* time is short, Doctor. How long will he be out?"

"A minute or two at most, I promise. May I proceed?" Ree waited until he received a grudging gesture of permission from Troi, and then he continued in his rasp of a voice. "Thank you. My scans confirm your suspicions: Admiral Riker has experienced a severe case of what the *Aventine* medical staff called 'temporal multiple-personality disorder.' "

"Is there any cure?"

"There is a treatment, though it has been used only once to treat manifested TMPD. The concepts behind it were meant to serve more as a prophylactic measure."

"But there *is* a treatment, yes? How long until you can give it to Will?"

"*That* is the problem, Counselor. I already have."

"You what? Then why is he still talking about children we never had?"

"Hard to say." Ree swiveled his long reptilian head toward Riker, who stirred as he gradually regained consciousness. "There is much we do not know about TMPD. If I were to form a hypothesis based on what little we have learned here, I would surmise that any prolonged exposure to the phenomenon can cause the hyperaccelerated formation of memories and behavioral patterns in a wide range of species."

Troi understood Ree's comparison. "It's like an obsessive-compulsive behavior. Once it takes root in the brain, every time the patient succumbs to it, the disorder carves its own preferential neuropathways into the patient's brain, creating new memories and habits."

"In essence, yes. The man on this biobed might physically be the same Admiral Riker with whom you have served for so many years, but there are at least two versions of his psyche alive inside his mind: the one you know, and the one that has led us, this ship, and possibly the entire galaxy down a path to our own destruction." Ree looked up at Riker's vital signs, flicked his tongue at it, and then let a groan rattle around inside his fanged gullet. "I have done all I can, Counselor. The rest is up to you."

She reacted by reflex, training a fierce stare at Ree. "Me? What am I supposed to do?"

"You have in the past described yourself and the admiral as *imzadi*. Whatever continues to afflict Admiral Riker dwells inside his subconscious. I suspect our only hope of freeing his psyche rests in your unique capacity for reaching his mind."

Troi focused her empathic talents upon her husband. She and Riker had always enjoyed a stronger link than she'd found with most other men, of any species. If there was even a remote chance that she could find the true essence of the man she loved, her husband and the father of her child, she had to try.

Riker's eyelids fluttered weakly as she pressed her palm to his forehead. Troi opened her mind to his and concentrated with every ounce of strength she could harness, to project her thoughts into the deepest recesses of his brain.

Will? Can you hear me? Listen to my voice, Imzadi. *I'm here.*

Inside his mind there was only chaos and pain. Psychic noise, no doubt the product of two personas both struggling to be heard at once. Primal emotions flared like bursts of color in Troi's imagination. Sickly yellow fear, bloodred anger, ashen hues of guilt . . .

Then, looming over everything else inside her *imzadi's* thoughts, there was a darkness as endless as it was profound. It was *everywhere*, touching everything, darkening everything it touched, stitching the seams of Riker's consciousness with funereal colors.

It was the source of the discord inside Riker's mind.

Perhaps it was an incepted clue from Riker, or maybe just a flash of intuition, but all at once Troi understood what Riker's omnipresent darkness really was.

That's his temporal shadow—the shadow is the other him!

She pulled herself back from Riker's mind, out of the deepest fathoms of their bond, and gave herself a moment to think.

Ree leaned closer to her, his curiosity evident. "What did you find?"

"My Will Riker is in there, but I'm going to need help bringing him out."

"What sort of help?"

Troi straightened her back and infused her voice with the timbre of command. "Commander Tuvok, report to sickbay, *immediately.*"

28

Temporal Disruption Base—2373, Borg Timeline

A million whispers haunted Picard. They were too many to hear, too loud to ignore. He felt like the floodlight that bathed the southern vineyard of Château Picard on foggy nights. It drew battalions of moths that would swarm the great, fiery lamp, their wings banging and burning against its filaments as instinct drove them to their deaths, until at last they smothered it with their sheer numbers. Come the dawn, maintenance 'bots would emerge from their hiding places to clean the burnt shells of dead insects from the floodlights.

Each night the tragedy played out anew. But the moths never learned.

I am that light. No matter where I go, the voice of the Borg finds me.

All he asked of the universe was a moment's peace. A few seconds of quiet. A chance to think. But that was too great a demand, too much to hope for.

He sat on the concrete floor, his back to a wall, with the rest of the away team huddled around him in low crouches. Sisko and Bashir conferred in private, while Lal and Crusher watched the passages behind the team for any sign of pursuit. Neither his wife nor Lal looked comfortable brandishing a phaser rifle, but Picard was certain that either or both of them would shoot to kill if necessary, and without hesitation.

The team was in a narrow transverse off one of the main corridors inside the Borg's temporal-disruptor facility, waiting for Data, who had ventured ahead on his own to scout for alternative routes of attack and retreat for their imminent assault on the site's control center.

To reduce the risk of detection by the Borg, the team was obeying strict radio-silence protocols. Even the use of passive-sensing tricorders had been forbidden except in emergencies, since their ambient energy signatures might attract nearby patrols of Borg drones.

Picard had hoped that after spending some time inside the facility he might acclimate to its Borgified environment. Instead, each passing moment made it feel all the more oppressive. The heat, the humidity, and the dueling odors of ammonia and hydrocarbon lubricants all weighed upon him, nauseated him, reminded him that he was just a thinking bag of meat trespassing inside his archenemy's mechanized domain.

The whispers swelled into a storm that howled through the empty quarters of Picard's old dry brain, taunting him, mocking him, hunting him. There was no doubt now that the Collective was aware of his presence, even if it seemed uncertain of who or what, precisely, he was. It felt him moving among them, just as he sensed the thousands of drones that surrounded him and the away team. The drones moved in circles, closing barriers to partition the facility one section at a time, one floor at a time, in a cold, methodical search pattern.

It's only a matter of time until they find me. Until they find us. If they realize why we've come, all of this will have been for nothing.

His mind was playing tricks on him. He knew not to trust it. Every shade that shifted by the slightest degree made Picard want to cry wolf, to see the Borg in every corner.

If I cannot trust my own senses, I am a danger to the others.

Sisko and Bashir cut short their hushed conference and tensed with anticipation. Behind Picard, Lal and Crusher each spared a quick look over their shoulder and then resumed their watch on the team's rear flank. A few seconds later, a humanoid shape turned the corner into the transverse. The silhouette raised one hand, showing three fingers, then one, then two.

It was Data, flashing the code for "all clear."

Sisko beckoned Data back into the fold. The away team regrouped in a tight formation, everyone keen to hear Data's report.

Data sounded optimistic. "I found another way into the control room. It has an access hatch that leads to a crawl-space subbasement. We can use that to make a surprise attack on the control room. Once inside, we can seal the main door to fend off the Borg's counterattack while we reset the temporal disruptor. After the process begins, we can use the subbasement to escape this facility and return to *Defiant*."

Sisko approved with a nod. "Good work. How do we get under the floor?"

"There is an access point roughly forty-one meters from here."

"Outstanding. Lead on."

Data turned to guide the away team out of the transverse. Picard and the others stood and readied themselves for a swift but stealthy passage through the industrial maze.

Then a voice like a railroad spike slammed through Picard's mind.

«*LOCUTUS.*»

The voice felt like acid and flames, from his forehead to his cerebellum. Agony shot down his spine and robbed him of his balance. His legs buckled. Crusher and Lal caught him as he fell, sparing him what had promised to be a hard, cold landing.

They eased him to the floor.

Crusher cupped his face with her warm hands. His vision was blurred by pain; he could see Beverly in front of him, speaking to him, but he couldn't hear a word she said. All he heard was the dark chorus of the Collective, repeating in unison—

«*LOCUTUS.*»

A jolt of sharp odor hit his nostrils. He shivered, his senses sharp, his mind once more rooted in the present. In front of him Crusher discarded a popped-open dose of smelling salts.

"Thank you," he said, his voice weak and brittle.

She held him by his shoulders. "Jean-Luc? Are you all right?"

The stentorian voice of the Collective had retreated, but in the deepest recess of his mind echoed the voice of the Borg Queen: «*I will find you, Locutus.*»

He felt her fascination, her alienation, her insatiable curiosity.

And he understood then what he needed to do.

He held out his hand to Crusher. "Help me up."

She hoisted him to his feet. He steadied himself. Then he faced Sisko. "Captain, my presence has jeopardized the away team. For the sake of the mission, we must split up. You take the team to the control room, and I will lure the Borg away."

Bashir sounded skeptical. "What makes you think that will work?"

"Because I'm the one they want most, Doctor. They don't seem to know why, but now that Locutus is among them, they won't stop until they find him." He pivoted toward Sisko. "If I join the assault on the control room, every drone on Earth will converge upon us. Our defenses will never hold. I need to buy you time, any way I can." With a heavy heart, he faced Crusher. "It's the only way, Beverly."

Tears shone in her eyes. "I know." She kissed him, quickly but with passion tempered by sorrow, and then pressed her forehead against his. "I know."

Picard kissed his wife once more, and then forced himself to step away from her. There was grief and dread in her eyes as she let him go.

Picard checked his rifle, and then he nodded to Sisko. "Good luck, Captain."

"And to you, Captain."

There was no time left to waste. Picard jogged away from the team, darting alone into the deepest patches of shadow and smoke he could find, determined to give his wife and friends as much time as he could—while he did his best not to think about what lay ahead for him, as he charged toward a confrontation with the enemy he thought he'd outlived years earlier.

The Queen's voice echoed in his mind: *«Locutus . . .»*

He cast off his fear, summoned his fury, and quickened his pace.

You want me, Your Majesty? Come and get me.

C.S.S. *Enterprise*—Intertime

Luc clutched the arms of his command chair for dear life as another barrage from the station and the Devidians' armada of giant Nagas assailed *Enterprise*'s collapsing shields. His voice was hoarse from breathing hot smoke. "Damage report!"

Perim shouted over the roars of explosions, "Starboard and dorsal hulls buckling!"

"Helm! One-eighty roll to port! Boost port and ventral shields!"

Luc white-knuckled his chair's armrests again as *Enterprise* rolled over while cruising at half impulse, straining the limits of its inertial dampers and structural integrity field.

The jaunt-ships had been made for speed and maneuverability—assets they had been unable to bring to bear as they had passed, single file, through the intertime rift—directly into a dense formation of colossal spacefaring Nagas and the Devidian station's firing solutions.

Enterprise had been the first ship through the rift. Relentless salvos by the Devidians and ramming attacks by Nagas that phase-shifted adroitly past *Enterprise*'s shields had knocked it out of position in less than a minute. By then *Independence* and *Phoenix* had made it through and peeled off to *Enterprise*'s starboard, while *Terra Nova* and *Vostok* pushed clear of *Enterprise*'s port flank. With the jaunt drive useless inside intertime, and all hopes of maneuvering impeded by the continued arrival of more jaunt-ships, Luc had done the only thing that he could: he'd ordered the launch of squadrons of outriders, to harry the Nagas, draw the Devidians' fire, and, he'd hoped, offer some measure of cover for the capital ships yet to arrive.

It had proved as hopeless an effort as everything else.

Contrary to the sensor logs of the *Smiley O'Brien*, the exterior defensive systems of the Devidians' station had responded with overwhelming force, filling the space around the facility with a tempest of supercharged plasma. The jaunt-ships had been torn to pieces, several at a time, as they became caught up in the storm of destruction, while the Nagas "swam" into the outriders' attack formations, swiftly reducing them to burning, broken scrap.

Just minutes into the battle, all the jaunt-ships had crossed through the rift, but fewer than half remained in the fight. *Phoenix*, *Terra Nova*, and *Vostok* all had broken apart after enduring sustained bombardments from the station and temporal assaults by the Nagas. Burning husks were all that remained of *Independence*, *Intrepid*, *Progress*, and *Victory*.

Vasquez and *Endurance* were holding position between *Enterprise* and the station, buying Luc's crew time to make critical repairs and get back in the fight. *Excalibur* and *Kearsarge* were making daredevil-close corkscrew orbits of the Devidians' station, pummeling it with torpedoes and phasers as they went, all while suffering steady blows from pursuing pods of Nagas, all of whom were wreathed in wild flurries of temporal distortion and chroniton fire.

As *Enterprise* finished its rolling maneuver, Luc opened an internal comm channel. "Damage-control teams to the forward magazine! Get the torpedo launchers back online!" He closed the channel without waiting for an answer. They'd either get it done in the next half minute, or they'd be dead along with Luc and everyone else on the ship. "Perim! Tell *Endurance* to lead the next attack. We'll cover them with *Vasquez*."

"Aye, sir."

"Tactical! All phaser banks, suppressing fire on the station. We need to give *Endur—*"

A brutal collision knocked out the lights on the bridge and threw Luc from his command chair. He tumbled across the deck and rolled to a halt against the feet of helm officer Tolaris.

Lying on his side, Luc heard a deep and all-encompassing sound, like the monstrous bellows of the deep sea. Next came a high-pitched tone, like the buzzing of an insect, but it echoed inside his head like the whine of a drill.

His eyes fluttered open. All he saw was layer upon layer of shadows. When he tried to sit up, hot bile surged into his esophagus and his head spun.

Stunned. I must be. Maybe concussed.

Hands gripped his shoulders. Pulled him up to a sitting pose. He stared at the person holding him, but all he saw was a dim silhouette. Then a great shower of sparks rained from the overhead and bathed Troi's face in golden light. She pushed a hypospray against his throat. A fleeting sting in Luc's jugular made him wince. Then the benthic droning that had flooded his skull abated, and he heard the whoops of the red-alert siren and the groans of the dying.

Troi shone a light into his eyes. "Can you hear me, Captain?"

"Yes. Now get that out of my face. Sitrep."

She averted her palm beacon's harsh white beam. "Nagas crushed our jaunt ring. Main power offline. No weapons or shields. Subspace comms are down."

"Quantum comms?"

"Functional, but no one's answering."

"The rest of the fleet?"

"We just lost *Vasquez*. *Endurance* and *Kearsarge* are dead in space, and *Excalibur*'s making a kamikaze run at the station."

Luc knew his options were dwindling rapidly. "Do we have propulsion? Thrusters?"

"Maybe." Troi turned suspicious. "Why?"

"Activate the self-destruct, set a collision course for the station, then abandon ship."

"We can't trigger autodestruct. Both computer cores are offline."

There was no point asking if the cores could be repaired in time. If that had been an option, Troi would have told him. "Help me to my chair."

Luc let Troi stretch one of his arms across her shoulders. She lifted him off the deck and helped him limp back to the command chair. Around them lay the rest of the bridge crew, their bodies burned, bloodied, bent, and broken.

At his chair, Luc opened an internal comm channel. "All decks, this is the captain. Abandon ship. Repeat, all hands, abandon ship." He nodded at Troi. "Let's get out—"

Guilt caught him midsentence, and he looked aft, into a mass of wreckage beneath a collapsed portion of the bridge's overhead. Seeing only smoke rising from the tangled heap, Luc felt a sick foreboding at the prospect of having broken a sacred oath.

His voice fell to a haunted whisper. "René . . ."

He shrugged off Troi's arm and lurched aft. She staggered after him. She, too, had been concealing the true extent of her injuries. "Luc! We need to go! Now!"

"Not without the boy!"

Luc almost fell atop the mangled duranium and broken plates of ceramic polymer. With bare hands he pulled at sparking tangles of EPS wiring, ignoring the burns and the numbing shocks as he ripped them out and hurled them away like fistfuls of long grass.

Automated alarms chirped and shrieked from several bridge consoles as Luc and Troi struggled to clear the mound of battle damage. She noted with alarm, "We're being targeted!"

"I know! Keep digging!"

Another crushing blow rocked *Enterprise* and threw Luc and Troi to the deck. As the duo struggled to stand, two more blasts pummeled the ship. Wild torrents of sparks fell from broad fissures in the overhead, landing hot upon Luc's bald pate. He swatted away the blazing phosphors while Troi batted burning motes from her unraveled mane of black hair.

He attacked the heap of debris. "Dig!"

"Luc! It's time to go!"

He ignored her and continued heaving debris aside.

For a moment she looked ready to leave, ready to say to hell with him and flee alone to an escape pod—but then her anger melted into resignation, and she joined his frantic excavation.

Seconds later, she called out, "I see him! René, can you hear me?"

From under the mound of debris, Luc heard the young man's pained groans. "Can you reach him, Deanna?"

"I think so. Anchor me."

Luc held Troi's left hand as she extended her right down to René. From his vantage behind Troi, Luc was unable to see what was going on, but then he heard her shout, "Pull us up!"

He pulled and shifted his weight, using every bit of leverage he could muster. Seconds later Troi and René were free of the heap, both dusty and scraped but neither seriously injured.

He held the lad by his shoulders. "Are you all right?" René nodded but said nothing. Luc smiled at Troi. "Well done. Now get us out of here."

She took René's hand and led him toward the bridge's port-side escape pod. Luc limped close behind them. As Troi opened the pod's door, more alarms shrilled from the tactical console. Spooked, René looked back. "What's happening?"

Luc pushed René and Troi into the escape pod. "We're out of time." He dove into the pod, shoved past them to the control panel, and triggered the emergency launch.

The door to the bridge snapped shut.

In a fraction of a second the pod was launched clear of the ship. Its high-gravity acceleration mode pinned Luc, Troi, and René to its hatch for several seconds before the inertial dampers kicked on. René looked and sounded as if he were in shock. "Are we safe?"

Through the pod's sole viewport, Luc saw his *Enterprise* explode under a barrage of plasma fire. He smiled as its white-hot fireball consumed a giant Naga.

He rolled the pod so that the viewport faced away from the burning remnants of the jaunt-ship fleet—confronting instead the looming mass of the Devidians' station, which was picking off escape pods in every direction, showing no mercy to the vanquished. Those the guns missed, the Nagas made every attempt to swallow whole.

Luc looked back. Troi was holding René close, trying to hug the fear out of him.

Luc fired the pod's thrusters at maximum. It shot like a bullet toward a narrow gap in the station's exterior hull. He had no idea whether the pod could outrun the Nagas' maws and the Devidians' targeting sensors, but getting out of the cross fire was the only way to save René.

He patched every last drop of power he could find into the pod's engine.

Here's hoping what worked for Wesley works for us—because if it doesn't, we've all come a long way for naught.

Devidian Temporal Collider—Intertime

Wesley awoke with a shudder. He was in a numbingly cold room, bound to a dark metal frame that resembled a medieval torture device forged from the macabre technology of the Devidians' station. His arms had been fixed in place fully extended and level with his chest, and his legs had been parted so that his feet aligned beneath his shoulders. It took him a moment to recall why his stance seemed familiar.

They posed me like da Vinci's Vitruvian Man *illustration.*

Dozens of ribbed tubules protruded from the frame and pierced his arms, legs, neck, and torso, like wires binding a marionette to its controller. Through some he felt the pull of siphons; through others, the push of infusions. Via the frame he felt the steady thrumming beat of a mechanical pulse, and wondered whether it was now controlling his heart.

Must be drugging me.

Three Devidians moved about the hexagonal compartment. The tight space was packed with bizarre technologies Wesley didn't recognize. Across from him stood a roughly circular frame, almost identical to the one that held him. Like his frame, the empty one was anchored into the floor and the low, domed ceiling. Unlike his, the empty frame was wreathed in tendrils of deep green electricity—some creeping, others dancing, all of them crackling and filling the air with the scent of ozone.

That can't be good.

The tallest of the three Devidians adjusted some settings on a panel that to Wesley looked like nothing more than a jumble of burnt bones. The ghostly, luminescent creature turned and drifted over to Wesley. It stopped in front of him and leaned in to study him.

A stream of spectral light shot from the odd, tubular cavity atop its head. The beam blinded Wesley for a moment—and then he saw what the Devidian wanted him to see, and he heard the wraithlike creature's voice inside his head.

Projected into his mind was a vision of the jaunt-ship fleet shattered and aflame outside the station. Squadrons of outriders crushed and eaten by giant Nagas. Wanton slaughter.

«*Your friends are doomed. They did not heed your warning.*»

Rage and denial welled up inside Wesley. He wanted to scream, but his body was going numb. Meanwhile the vision continued, showing him more destruction.

Then he saw the battle as the Devidians did. To them it was a banquet. Hope beaten into despair. Courage reduced to terror. Pride broken down into shame. Each darkened turn of emotion a delicacy for the Devidians' refined empathic appetites.

Then came the final course, the sweetest dish of all—the agony of a consciousness going dark; the delectable nectar of death itself.

Tears of rage fell from Wesley's eyes, but his voice remained silenced.

Stop! Those are people! Sentient beings!

He felt the satisfaction of the Devidians, and their cruel derision.

«*You are all cattle. Grist for the mill. Nothing more.*»

All his life Wesley had thought of himself as a peaceful being, a decent soul. But all he felt for the Devidians was hatred. For the first time in his life, he truly wanted to kill. And not just the Devidians closest at hand, but all of them, every last one, the entire species of—

His mind blanked at what felt like a psychic punch in the face.

He had to fight to focus his mind, to bring it fully back into the present. That was when he realized the Devidians were feasting on his fury, his sorrow, and his guilt.

Damn it. I let them goad me. Gave them just what they wanted.

Across from him, the shortest of the three Devidians secured something inside the previously empty frame. When the two phantasmal humanoids between Wesley and the other frame stepped away, he saw that a cluster of ophidians—the reptilian beings the Devidians had domesticated so they could take advantage of their ability to move freely through spacetime—had been linked to the second frame in much the same manner that Wesley was bound to his.

What the hell is going on?

The tallest Devidian projected another vision into Wesley's mind—the moment of jaunt-ship *Enterprise*'s destruction. The elegant vessel erupted from within, consumed itself in one brilliant flash . . . and left behind nothing but heat and free radicals.

«*Your sibling is gone. You led him to his death.*»

It had been impossible not to feel the gloating in the Devidian's taunt.

In his imagination, Wesley dreamed of breaking free of his bonds, avenging himself on the three ghouls holding him hostage, and then bringing the entire station to a fiery end.

But all he could do was stand mute as the Devidians activated their insidious machines, marshaled their dark materials, and wreathed him in the same restless, excruciating green lightning that had begun to cocoon the ophidians in front of him.

The trio turned in unison to face him.

Wesley felt the malevolence in the leader's telepathic declaration.

«*The Traveler has come to us at last. This is the end—and the beginning.*»

Temporal Disruption Base—2373, Borg Timeline

Audacity was the key. Standing alone against an army, Picard knew he had no advantages other than sheer nerve. That alone would not be enough to stop the Borg. But that was not his design.

His footfalls were crisp on the cold cement, their echoes sharp off the cinder-block walls. The ceiling was so far overhead that it was lost in the darkness. But on level after level above Picard, Borg drones lined the walkways on either side of the corridor and watched him in silence. Hundreds of red beams converged upon him and tracked him through the narrow passage.

None of the drones had accosted him. Long before he had seen them, he had felt the collective psychic pressure of their presence. Rather than continue his attempts at hiding, he had concentrated on announcing himself, in the hope of drawing as many of the Borg inside the station to him as possible: *I am Locutus of Borg. I come bearing a message for the Queen.*

The narrow passage opened into a cavernous space with the same vertiginously high ceiling. Like the rest of the facility, it smelled of chemicals and mildewed concrete, of decay and rust. In the center of the atrium's floor was a square pit five meters across. Centuries earlier it had been ringed by waist-high railings, but that safeguard had fallen away, leaving only its corner posts. Clusters of cables anchored some-place high above dangled down into the pit.

Vapors spewed from cracks in the floor and snaked upward through a chaos of wires that drooped across the width of the atrium, crisscrossed at irregular angles and intervals. A few distant light sources bathed the atrium in a weak greenish glow.

From the encircling levels above Picard, hundreds more red beams angled downward, each one finding him until he shone like a crimson flame in the dark.

He stopped a few strides shy of the open pit, looked up, and shouted into the blackness, "I am Locutus of Borg! Show yourself, my Queen!"

Murmurs and rustlings filled the ranks of the drones. Then came a hiss of steam and the moaning hum of a generator. Plumes of vapor boiled up from the pit and climbed into the dark. Prismatic flashes illuminated the billowing steam cloud in hues of indigo and viridian.

Instead of descending from above, as Data had said she'd done aboard the *Enterprise*-E, the Borg Queen ascended from the pit—and a sickening sensation of terror overcame Picard.

The moment he saw her, he knew she was not the Queen he remem-bered.

She was a giant—nearly two and a half meters tall. Mottled greenish skin, glowing yellow eyes, and a forehead crowned with seven horns. Her legs were crossed at the ankles, her arms outstretched low and away from her sides, and a vast black cloud of what Picard surmised were airborne Borg nanites hovered around and behind her, creating the impression that the Queen possessed demonic wings of churning smoke.

A falling shower of sparks briefly lit up her head, revealing the various connection ports grafted onto the top and back of her bald pate. Floating above Picard, she regarded him with a peculiar tilt of her head. Her gaze was cold and clinical, like that of a scientist examining an unfamiliar species of insect. "Locutus."

"Yes."

He locked his eyes with hers, hoping that if he snared her attention with his gaze, she might not notice his left hand tucked inside a pocket on the thigh of his combat uniform—nor realize he was clutching a dead-man's trigger on a high-yield plasma grenade.

It was a crude plan, but it possessed the virtue of having few moving parts. When he triggered the grenade, it would vaporize most of the atrium, including the Queen and, he hoped, the majority of her drones inside the facility. It would not kill her permanently, of course. A copy of her consciousness, preserved in a distributed manner throughout the Collective, would simply be downloaded into a new vessel somewhere else. And the loss of a few hundred drones would be inconsequential to the Collective at large.

But it might sow enough chaos for a few minutes to enable Data and the others to finish sabotaging the temporal disruptor, prep the link to the Orb of Time and the Devidians' chroniton core, and make their escape.

If I can do that, at the cost of my life alone, I'll call that a victory.

The Borg Queen drifted forward, never blinking, never looking away. There was an ancient quality to her gaze that Picard found unnerving. It was like staring into the eyes of a dragon—something inhuman and eternal.

She alighted upon the hard gray floor just steps in front of Picard.

Her lips formed a crooked smile, but her eyes remained dead and merciless. "At last we meet, Locutus. Or—should I say?—we *meet again.*"

Fear hit Picard like a cold spike in his gut. He forced himself to suppress his emotions and dull his reactions. "Have we met before?"

"Not you and I. But I know of many realities. Many dimensions."

With one stride forward, she loomed over him.

She dragged a taloned finger across the front of his black tunic while circling him, a predator sizing up a potential meal. "Two drones from your reality came to mine long ago. When they shared their memories with the Collective, I saw *you*." She was behind Picard now, tracing her claw across his back. "*Locutus*. Or is it Picard?" She finished her orbit and stooped to confront him, her face close enough that he winced at her foul breath when she spoke. "Tell me how you betrayed the Collective, *Locutus*."

"You shouldn't speak of betrayal—*Sedín*."

He searched her eyes for a reaction to the name of the Caeliar whose essence had provided the basis for the first Borg. *If I can make her doubt herself, make her confront her own flawed origins . . .* Belatedly he realized something was wrong.

She tilted her head quizzically. "Why do you call me Sedín?"

"Because it's your true name. From before you were Borg."

Her face remained blank. "That name means nothing to me."

Picard's heart sank. *Damned time travel.*

The Borg had meddled with time travel once that Picard knew about. Who was to say they had not done so many times more, in countless alternate timelines? They might have generated multiple conflicting origins for themselves, mired their beginnings in paradox, or even have cross-pollinated different timelines.

He abandoned that line of verbal attack. *Best if I don't mention the Caeliar. If they exist in this or other timelines, I shouldn't give the Borg any ideas.*

The Queen cupped Picard's chin in her massive hand. "Why have you come to me?"

He arched one brow, telegraphing his irony. "To bring you a gift, Your Majesty."

He let go of the dead-man's switch on the plasma grenade.

And nothing happened.

The Queen adopted a smug expression as Picard's faded. "Do you think me a fool? Did you think we would fail to notice your concealed munition?"

He took the grenade from his pocket. When he looked at it to deduce its malfunction, it turned to metallic powder in his hand. Then his rifle disintegrated off his shoulder. *Nanites.*

She seized Picard by his throat. "I will show you fear in a handful of dust." In one easy motion she lifted him off the floor. "I know you came to sabotage our disruptor. But what are your people *waiting* for? Why don't they just *destroy* it?"

He had to choke out his reply: "Go. To. Hell."

Holding Picard by his throat, the Queen rose from the floor. He writhed and struggled in her grip while she towed him toward the pit. Her smoky black cloud enfolded him as they sank into the dark, and she whispered into his ear, her fetid breath warm upon his flesh.

"You *will* tell me, Locutus. And before I finish, you will *beg* me for assimilation, and then for *death* . . . but receive *neither.*"

29

U.S.S. Titan NCC-80102

The lights in sickbay had been dimmed to twenty percent of normal, and in the penumbral twilight Troi found Tuvok's rich voice hypnotic, and the warmth of his fingers against pressure points on her face and temple oddly soothing.

"My mind to your minds. Your minds to my mind. Your minds to each other's."

Tuvok sat between her and Riker, who remained confined to the biobed by a force field. The Vulcan man had one hand on Troi, and the other in a similar pose on the side of Riker's face. He was using his native telepathic talent to serve as a conduit for a mind-meld between Troi and Riker. Though the couple had long shared a powerful empathic bond due in part to her half-Betazoid ancestry, this effort to free Riker's mind from possession by a version of himself from a parallel timeline required talents more sophisticated than Troi alone could muster.

Through the meld she felt Riker's hidden struggle. Two sets of memories, in many ways alike but in others terribly different, vied for control of his brain and body. The intruder's psychic force was much stronger than she had expected it to be. In hindsight, she saw her error. Great pain often spurred powerful intentions. The driving power behind the alternative-Riker persona was fury and sorrow, indescribable loss, and crushing guilt. Those emotions coursed from him in dark, seemingly inexhaustible waves.

She focused her thoughts in a separate mental space so that she could confer privately with Tuvok. *Can you isolate the second Riker persona? I want to communicate with him directly.*

«I believe so. Give me a moment, Counselor.»

Whatever Tuvok was doing inside Riker's mind, Troi felt it only in the most abstract sense. Barriers were being erected. Sanctuaries of tranquillity were established, and with coaxing from Tuvok, the different expressions of Riker partitioned themselves from each other.

The conflict within Riker ceased, as if his two personas were boxers ordered by a referee to withdraw to neutral corners.

Troi heard Tuvok inside her mind. «*The other Riker is ready for you, Counselor.*»

Thank you, Tuvok. Please guide me to him.

There was no physical contact, yet the best analogy Troi had for what occurred next was that Tuvok led her, as if by holding her hand, through a maze of shadows—some made of memory, others of delusion—to a bucolic green hilltop surrounded by jagged, snow-capped mountain peaks beneath a pale blue sky. At the top of the hill, a dozen meters from her, the Will Riker who was not hers sat upon a wide tree stump, with his back to her and his head bowed.

She approached him with caution. It was hard to predict what he might do. Even if this milieu was merely a mental construct, Troi knew of evidence that being slain in such a setting could induce a shock sufficient to kill one's real body outside the simulation. That was a risk she hoped to obviate. As she drew within a few paces of him, she heard him crying. His grief was subdued, muted, reined in as best as he could manage, but true tears fell one after another from his eyes, ran along the ridge of his nose, and gathered at its bulb.

Her instinct was to lay a hand upon his shoulder, but she hesitated, unsure of how he might react. "I know you're not my Will Riker."

He snorted out a bitter laugh and shook his head. "I've been wondering how long it would take you to see through me."

Troi did her best to sound comforting and not confrontational. "You didn't make it easy. In many ways you and my Will are very much alike."

"Except he still has his family, and I don't." He regarded Troi, his eyes full of tears and his face distorted by fury and sorrow. "I had to watch them die, Deanna."

"Who?"

"*All* of them. My friends. My children. *You.*" Pain twisted him, both in flesh and spirit, and more tears ran from his closed eyes. "My entire universe died around me. Whole worlds turned to ash. We knew we were doomed—but we thought we could save others if we stopped the

Devidians before they finished us off. We were wrong." He slid forward off the stump and landed on his knees in the dew-soaked grass. His hands curled into fists, with which he punched the ground in front of him. He sobbed with rage. "They were too strong. Waiting for us. Seen us do it a thousand times before. Same bread crumbs, same trap, over and over."

"Trap? Will, what trap?"

If he had heard her, he didn't show it. "We held on as long as we could, but then they fired one last shot. A green bolt of lightning speared me as my ship blew up—and then I was here, on *Titan*." He sleeved tears from his face as he fought to push words past grief's chokehold. "But I wasn't in control. I was just a rider, watching another me make the same mistakes all over again. It was like a nightmare."

"So you took control."

He nodded, even as guilt and anguish made a wreck of him. "I had to. Our children were gone. Thaddeus. Kestra. But if I could save *this* reality, I'd still have you. And I saw so much of Kestra in Tasha—I knew I had to save her." Mania overtook him, and he grabbed Troi by her arms. "It's all happening again! We're running out of time!"

"What is?"

"The Devidians! The attack on their base in intertime! The timeline collapse!"

Though the mindspace they shared was imaginary, as was his hold upon her, because of her empathic talents she felt his distress as a tangible discomfort. "Will, you need to calm down. We're on our way to stop the Devidians. We'll do what has to be done, I promise."

"No! You don't understand! This is the end, the last chance to save this timeline! We can't let it end like this, Deanna. Not let it get erased like it never mattered!"

Tuvok, help me calm him. I need to ease this Riker into a twilight state so I can make contact with our Riker.

«I will do my best.»

At the speed of thought, Tuvok flooded the alternate Riker persona with urges to sleep, to surrender, to dream. The arctic hilltop faded away, leaving only a void. Alternate-Riker's fevered state washed away, and the dark tides of his emotions retreated.

Troi turned her focus to the other personality inside her *imzadi's* mind—the William Riker she knew and loved. His psyche had been violently suppressed. Now it felt dormant. She tried to coax it back to the fore, but his consciousness felt light-years out of reach.

Tuvok? Can you bring our Riker into an environment like the last one?

«I do not think so. The other was already active. This one is in hiding.»

Can you project thoughts from me to him? Memories? Images?

«I will try. Focus your mind upon that which you wish me to impart.»

Troi summoned all the memories she could of their daughter, Tasha.

The difficult pregnancy she and Riker had thought would end in miscarriage, as their first had. Tasha's birth on the water world they had called Droplet.

Tasha's first night at home on *Titan*.

Her first steps. Her first words.

Seeing her dance in a recital for the first time . . .

The true Riker's essence stirred.

His apparition took shape in front of Troi, at first barely visible. He looked torpid and lost. When his lips moved, ever so slightly, Troi moved closer to hear what he said:

He whispered "*Imzadi . . .*"

"I'm here, Will! Listen to my voice and follow it back to me."

The specter of Will Riker weltered like a candle's flame. "Deanna?"

Tuvok's voice resonated in Troi's thoughts. *«More good memories. Share them now.»*

She concentrated with fierce intensity, summoning her favorite memories of Will Riker.

The day they had met . . . their first kiss . . . the first time they made love . . . the day he had asked her for the great honor and privilege of being her husband . . .

Come back to me, Will.

At once the vision of Riker turned vibrant with color and rich with presence, though his eyes were closed. Troi clasped her husband's hand . . . and then his eyes opened—

In the real world, Riker woke with a start, breaking the telepathic link.

Looking into his eyes, Troi knew this was her Will Riker, conscious and back in control, but looking shell-shocked. His voice trembled as he oriented himself. "Tuvok? Deanna? You have to help me! There's another person inside my mind, another *me*—"

Troi cut him off. "We know. That mind is subdued." She nodded to Doctor Ree, who had been observing from the shadows. Noting her cue, he turned off the biobed's force field.

Riker's hands went to his face, as if he needed to prove to himself that he was real, a physical being. "I was trapped inside myself. Like a spectator. The more I fought, the deeper he buried me." He sat up, and Troi steadied him while he recovered his bearings. "He's in so much pain, Deanna. So broken and angry."

Ree moved closer and checked the readouts above the biobed. "Your vitals are all normal again, Admiral. We've purged your body of the temporal disharmony that caused this, and I've equipped you with a device that should protect you from a repeat experience."

"Thank you, Doctor." Riker nodded at Tuvok. "And also you, Tuvok."

Tuvok reciprocated Riker's nod, and then he said to Troi, "I will give you two a moment. If you need me, I will be on the bridge."

As Tuvok made his exit, Troi kissed her husband. "Welcome back, *Imzadi*."

"Good to be back."

"Are you sure you feel all right?"

He nodded. "I think so. I'm in control again, but to be honest, I can still feel the other Riker in the back of my mind. More than anything, I feel his fear—" He paused, and his face betrayed a dawning horror. "About the Devidians. The timeline. And the attack in intertime . . ." His eyes went wide, and then he seized Troi by her shoulders, overcome with desperation.

"Deanna! *Where is Jean-Luc?*"

Temporal Disruption Base—2373, Borg Timeline
Minutes after Picard had left to draw the Borg away from the control center, the drones guarding its main door departed en masse, all marching in the same direction as if summoned by a siren's song. Watching

them go, Crusher knew that her husband's plan had worked—and, not for the first time, she both celebrated his ingenuity and lamented his bravery.

How many times had he been called upon to sacrifice himself through the years? Not once had he ever refused. But why did it always need to be him? Hadn't he done enough already for the Federation? For the galaxy? The universe?

Pointless questions, she knew. Nothing was ever enough. Nothing ever would be.

Only a handful of drones were left behind to defend the entrance, and when Sisko gave the order, Data, Bashir, and Lal made short work of the slow-moving cyborgs. Precision shots with the high-power transphasic-disruption rifles vaporized the drones. All six guarding the control center were neutralized before the Collective had time to register what had happened to them, much less adapt their defenses.

Let's hope we stay this lucky.

Sisko signaled the team to advance. They emerged from concealment, rifles braced against their shoulders, and moved quickly to the control center's entrance. Data and Bashir were on point. Crusher and Lal were in the middle, with orders to watch the flanks for signs of Borg activity. Sisko brought up the rear of the formation.

Data hacked the door's electronic security swiftly and without comment. Its indicator shifted from red to green as it unlocked.

Bashir gave a thumbs-up to Sisko, the signal to advance. Using his fingers, Data gave Bashir a three-second countdown, and then he opened the door and moved inside with speed and determination. Bashir was right behind him.

Just as Crusher lost sight of them, screeches of phaser fire rang out from inside the control center. She counted six shots, maybe seven, and then all was quiet. Part of her needed to know what had happened, whether Data and Bashir were both okay. But she had her orders, so she kept her rifle braced and continued her surveillance of the open levels above them.

Nothing moved anywhere in her field of view.

A scrape of footsteps at the entrance. Bashir peeked out to beckon the team inside. Lal and Crusher slipped past Bashir. Sisko backpedaled across the open space, looking for danger in every direction until he followed them through the doorway, and then to the right, down a narrow corridor that led to the main room of the control center.

Once everyone was inside, Data closed the main door. In a matter of seconds he changed its pass code to something insanely long and complex. When he finished he said to Bashir, "We should weld the door shut as a precaution."

The doctor drew his compact phaser from his tactical vest. "I'll handle it." He went to work, fusing the thick metallic door to its steel frame.

Crusher leaned toward Sisko and kept her voice down. "Won't the Borg just beam in?"

"No. The shielding that protects the controls from being affected by the temporal disruptor also blocks transporter signals." He checked his chrono as Data passed him. "We're cutting this close."

Data seemed unconcerned. "Adjusting the disruptor's settings should not take long. Lal, will you assist me, please?" Lal moved to Data's side, and together they approached the broad console that governed the enormous temporal disruptor that filled the levels above them. Perhaps for Sisko's benefit, or maybe for that of the entire team, Data narrated his and Lal's efforts.

"Our first task is to invert the disruptor's chroniton matrix. This will negate the original divergence event, which produced the First Splinter timeline in 2373."

The two androids' hands moved faster than Crusher could track, making precision adjustments to several dozen different controls. Waveforms and other visual representations of the disruptor's output shifted into new shapes and symmetries.

"The inversion is complete. The next step is one for which we can prepare, but cannot complete until the Orb of Time is in position and we take control of the Devidians' chroniton core. Using the Orb as a calibrating beacon across dimensions and spacetime, we must establish mutually canceling subharmonic resonance frequencies here and in the Devidians' core, in order to trigger a paradox-free temporal recursion that will retroactively unmake this timeline."

Sisko absorbed that news with a grim frown. "How long will that take?"

Data arched his brow. "There's no way to know until we begin. But the sooner the rest of you return to *Defiant*, reach the Devidians' base, and initiate the process, the greater our chance of success." He nodded toward the steel hatch in the concrete floor. "That leads to the subbasement. If you proceed due south, you should find an egress point. Once outside, you can arrange a rendezvous with *Defiant*."

Lal ceased entering commands into the console and faced Data. "I will not leave here without you, Father. If you mean to stay, so will I."

Her proclamation seemed to trouble him. "Lal, the Borg will use every means they possess to retake control of this room. Even welded shut, that door will not hold for more than a few minutes. Staying here is a suicide mission."

She regarded her father with a teenager's disdain. "Father, *every* part of this plan is a suicide mission. Our best-case scenario is that our sacrifice saves others. Since I am to die, I choose to do so with you. And as it is my choice to make, I will not debate it further."

Data acquiesced with a nod. "Very well." To Sisko and Crusher, he added, "You both should start making your way back to the ship."

Crusher made her own fateful choice. "I'm not leaving without Jean-Luc."

Sisko sounded pained. "Doctor, odds are he's already gone."

"I don't believe that. I *refuse* to believe that."

"Regardless of what you believe, we don't have time to mount a search and rescue."

Fed up, Crusher strode to the floor panel, unlocked it, and pulled it open. "Fine. You go back to the ship, and I'll go find my husband. With or without you."

She felt Sisko getting ready to snap, but then Bashir returned from welding the main door. Though his enhanced hearing must have caught every word they'd said, he chose to play dumb. "So sorry, excuse me—what have I missed?"

His interruption gave Sisko time to vent his fury as an angry sigh. "Data and Lal will stay behind to guard the control room. The rest of us need to go, but Doctor Crusher won't leave without her husband."

Bashir absorbed that with aplomb. "Do we have a fix on Captain Picard's position?"

Crusher switched on her tricorder and set it to scan for Picard's com-badge transponder. "Bearing zero-eight-three, two hundred eleven meters, *z*-minus forty-one meters."

Bashir checked the charge on his rifle's power cell, and then he walked to the open hatchway. "What are we waiting for? Let's go get him." Without an order or an invitation, he descended into the sub-basement.

Crusher cast an impatient look at Sisko, who sighed in disappointment. "Mister Soong, if we're not back before *Defiant*'s ready to go, tell them to leave without us. Is that clear?"

"Perfectly, Captain."

"Good." He frowned at Crusher. "All right, Doctor. Let's go find your husband."

Picard awoke to find himself a fly caught in a web.

He was only a few meters above the floor, but he had no way to reach it. After spiriting him to the pit's nadir, the Borg Queen had coiled thick cables around his ankles and elbows and hoisted him up. She had reduced him to a pathetic marionette, a spectacle for her own twisted amusement. The last thing he had felt before plunging into a tableau of ugly nightmares had been a pair of cold stings at the nape of his neck.

He tried to turn his head but couldn't. Something had penetrated the base of his skull. He dreaded to think how deeply the Borg technology might have burrowed into his brain.

The Queen floated down out of the vaporous shadows, still enfolded by her black cloud of nanites, her yellow eyes ablaze. "Your body has hosted Borg implants before." She traced the edge of his jaw with one of her talons. Its scrape was unpleasant, but it concentrated Picard's attention. "You spoke for us to your people. The Federation."

It was true, but he refused to confirm it. He couldn't risk telling her anything—but how much had she already stolen from his mind while he was unconscious? What had she seen?

She raised her hands and pressed the tips of her claws against both sides of his face. His eyes widened in horrified anticipation, and she gazed through them into his soul.

"Someone—or some*thing*—removed your implants. Even the nanites embedded in your brain. But who? Your memories have shown us your Starfleet. It does not possess such skill."

He feigned confidence. "You would be surprised what we can do."

"I do not think so." She withdrew her hands, but then, with a flourish, she poked the bridge of his nose. "Show me who *really* freed you."

Delirium took hold of Picard like an undertow dragging a swimmer into the briny depths. He fought to resist the Borg's plumbing of his memories, tried to compel his focus back into his present moment, but the Queen's talent for excavating secrets was diabolical. His every attempt to deflect only seemed to push her deeper into his psyche and closer to the truth.

Then she tore it from his memory in flashes—

The Caeliar.

Their post-organic civilization. Their Great Work—a quest for contact with something even older and more powerful than themselves.

Then, most calamitous of all: the final report of Captain Erika Hernandez—and its revelation that the Cacliar represented both the Alpha and the Omega of the Borg.

The Queen's sinewy hand locked around Picard's throat. "Tell me everything about the Caeliar, Picard. *Everything.*"

"I will tell you *nothing.*"

"I promise, Picard—you *will.*"

Something cold surged into Picard's head through the tubules implanted in his neck. He winced as the freezing sensation hit his sinuses and made his skull feel as if it were about to crack open. Next came jolts of fiery pain deep inside his head and down his spine, into his extremities. His flesh was on fire, but his mind felt as if it were entombed in ice.

He wanted to scream, but he couldn't breathe. Gasping like a landed fish, he thrashed against his restraints, but he was trapped, suffocating, panicking . . .

The Queen smirked at his distress, and then she laughed.

"This is only the *beginning*, Picard. I can make it so much worse."

Picard resurrected his memory of a mind-meld with Ambassador Sarek, and recalled what he had learned of mental discipline from the ancient Vulcan diplomat. He closed his eyes. Imagined a single point.

Trained his thoughts upon it—and slowed his breathing. His heart slowed its wild race inside his chest, and the thudding of his pulse in his ears abated.

I raise a wall for my mind. A fortress of logic.

Her foul whisper invaded his ear. "A Vulcan mental barrier? I've broken *millions* of them, Picard. Millions created by Vulcans. Do you really think yours poses any challenge?"

He refused to be baited. *My mind is still. My logic is—*

Exquisite tortures sliced through him. Agonies came in waves, each crueler than the last. Within moments his fortress of logic fell like a house of cards in a hurricane, and all his memories of suffering became hers to control.

The tortures of Gul Madred. The ego-death of his first assimilation. Cold steel, a Nausicaan's blade, plunging into his back and erupting from his sternum. So many friends' deaths. A lifetime of wounds and losses, of injuries and regrets, engulfed him at once.

He screamed in a way he never had before, not just in pain but in horror at what he knew was soon to come, and the hopelessness of knowing he could not stop it.

Emptied of breath and vigor, he went limp in the strands of the Queen's web. Tears of despair fell from his eyes.

She was right. Part of me would give anything to make this end. Even if it meant being assimilated again. Anything to make this stop.

The side of her fist bumped under his chin and nudged his head up. When Picard opened his eyes, his vision was so blurred from pain that he could barely discern the details of the Queen's face, but he saw she was only centimeters from him, their noses almost touching. Then he noted the change in the shape of her mouth, from a scowl to an evil grin.

"You're ready now, aren't you? So tell me: How do we find the Caeliar?"

He was so tired that even filling his lungs was a labor.

The Queen wrapped one mammoth hand over Picard's bald pate. "Tell me, Picard, and I might grant you the relief of assimilation after all."

It took all the strength Picard had left to sharpen his focus on the Queen—and spit into her glowing yellow eye.

He expected her to recoil in surprise or disgust.

She didn't even blink. Made no attempt to wipe away his spittle.

"Resistance is futile. I *will* break you, Picard. It's only a matter of time."

Now he had to smile. If he'd had the strength, he might even have laughed.

"Time," he said. "The one luxury I don't have."

She seemed uninterested in his implied threat. "You possess knowledge of value to the Collective, Picard. Minutes from now, those secrets will be ours. And you"—she removed her hand from his head and unholy torments racked his entire body, as if his blood cells had been turned into a billion tiny suns—"will be my slave."

Past and present became one, all happening at once, effects preceding causes, as memories bled together in Picard's addled mind, all of them tainted and changed . . .

Rain pelted the windows of the château as young Jean-Luc struggled to make his hands find the notes on the piano. His parents' insistence on his taking lessons baffled him. *Can't they see I have no talent for this? How can I play these chords? My fingers don't reach that far!*

All he wanted was to hide in his room, power up his padd, and lose himself in true stories of ancient cultures and lost worlds. He dreamed of escaping this cold house, his father's reproach, his brother's resentment . . .

His fingers refused his commands and struck one false note after another. A flat out of place here, an unwanted sharp there. Errors compounded one another until he lost the melody and slammed his hands down on the keys in frustration. "*Merde!*"

His curse was still fresh in the air when his mother snapped from the kitchen doorway behind him, "Jean-Luc! Mind your tongue!"

Shame warmed his face. His mother was the only reason he had made any effort to try to learn the piano. No matter how sloppily he played, his efforts always seemed to make her happy. "I'm sorry, Ma-ma." He lowered the wooden lid that protected the keys, then turned to face her as he finished his thought. "It's just that I—"

The gigantic Borg Queen stared down at him, her mottled green skin draped in his mother's rustic gingham dress and white cardigan. She flashed a grin that looked like a predator's threat display. "Play me another song, Jean-Luc."

He lurched in retreat, tripped over a leg of the piano bench, and sprawled across the floor. The Queen prowled toward him. Little Jean-Luc scrambled into motion, his shoes slipping on the polished hardwood floor of the music room. Then he was up and running for his life.

He sprinted toward the open front door and launched himself out into the night—

His feet ached as he neared the last mile of the Academy Marathon. Cadet Picard saw only a handful of people ahead of him, the runners everyone considered the favorites. Even from six dozen meters behind he could see their stamina was flagging.

I can overtake them. Pass them. I can win this.

It was an audacious notion. No first-year cadet had ever won the Academy Marathon. But Jean-Luc Picard was no ordinary cadet. He had arrived in San Francisco determined to shed his old self, his childhood marked by mockery, his adolescence of loneliness, a father that treated him like an alien left in a basket on his doorstep, an older brother who reveled in all his failures. That was behind him now. Behind him like all those other runners. Like the ones in front of him soon would be. He was going to show them all. Show them he was a *winner*.

Arms close. No wasted effort. That's it.

He pushed himself forward, into third place. Then into second.

He relished the gasps of exhaustion he heard behind him.

Now his sights were set on the runner ahead of him. On first place.

The lead runner was only about ten meters ahead as he rounded a sharp curve. For the briefest moment he was beyond Picard's sight.

It's time. Picard dug deep and forced himself to quicken his pace into the turn.

He barely saw the olive blur that shot from the bushes and slammed into his left leg. It felt like a pile driver had hit him. His left femur snapped like brittle kindling, and he face-planted onto the asphalt roadway, writhing in hideous pain, howling strings of French curses.

It took him a second to master his pain enough to look around for some explanation of what had happened. Then he saw her. The Borg Queen, towering above him.

"You can't run from *me*, Picard."

Fear overcame his anger. He couldn't stand, so he dragged himself across the pavement, off the road, and into the woods, all as other runners surged past behind him.

The dirt under his hands turned to mud, and he slid headlong down a steep slope, caromed off tree trunks, and finally slammed face-first into a huge rock—

Bang! The gavel landed with a second sharp report that echoed inside the small tribunal chamber, deep within Starbase 32. Captain Sartak, the presiding judge, pointed at Picard. "Objection overruled. Captain Louvois, you may continue."

Captain Picard looked toward his prosecutor, Philippa Louvois, who by a cruel twist of fate also happened to be a former lover of his from many years earlier. The blond woman had her back to him as she reached to pick up a padd from her table.

When she turned toward the three officers who constituted the tribunal, Picard saw his father, Maurice, and older brother, Robert, both dressed in their vineyard work clothes, sitting to either side of Sartak—and that his prosecutor was really the Borg Queen.

By reflex, Picard sprang to his feet. "Objection!"

Sartak pounded his gavel against its block. "Overruled! Sit down, Captain."

"That's not Captain Louvois! That's—"

Clarity returned like a slap to his face. *Induced delusion. Memory invasion. I know these tricks. This is what the Borg did the first time they assimilated me.* He left his table and strode toward the Queen. "You don't frighten me. I know your lies."

"And I know *yours*." She waved her arm toward the judges. "Tell them how you froze in combat. How you hid your mistakes and blamed everyone but yourself for losing the *Stargazer*."

He summoned his pride and used it like armor. "I did all I could to save my ship."

The Queen put on a show of mock sympathy. "A pity they don't believe you, Picard."

Sartak, Maurice, and Robert all regarded Picard with cold contempt. One at a time, starting with the Vulcan captain, they each intoned in a voice like thunder—

"GUILTY."

"GUILTY."

"GUILTY."

Picard stole the gavel from Sartak's hand and snapped its handle. "Lies! I was acquitted for the loss of the *Stargazer*!" He flung the broken pieces of wood at the Queen. "I've been here before. You won't fool me again."

She seemed darkly amused. "Who said I was trying to *fool* you?"

The Queen grabbed her table by one of its legs. Using only one arm, she hurled it with ease at the wall behind Picard.

The wall shattered like a trompe l'oeil painted on fragile glass.

A roar of decompression struck Picard, but then his ears popped as the pressure inside the tribunal chamber dropped to vacuum.

The Queen snapped her arm toward the judges. Narrow black tubules of Borg biotech shot from three of her fingers and skewered the men's throats. In a matter of seconds, the trio began transforming into Borg drones.

Suffocating, stunned, Picard fell to his knees. He wanted desperately to disbelieve his circumstances, to break the Queen's spell over his mind, but all the willpower he possessed was no match for her gifts of mental subjugation. She was too ancient, too powerful, and her methods far crueler than anything Picard had ever known.

Yet he refused to give her what he knew she wanted most: his surrender.

His strength faltered; his vision blurred. But still he got up.

He broke off a leg of the defense's table. Carrying his improvised club, he staggered toward the Queen. Winding up to strike, he knew he would get only one clean shot at her.

Then he lost even that paltry advantage.

In the airless space, there was no sound, but something alerted the Queen. She spun to face Picard as he swung the table leg. She caught the wooden lever in her monstrous hand. Tore it from Picard's grasp. Then she kicked him in his gut and doubled him over.

He wasted half a second gasping for oxygen that wasn't there.

She took him by his throat. Lifted him over her head.

When she slammed him down onto his back, the floor shattered as the wall had before it, and then Picard was plunging, free-falling, but at least now there was air and sound. He could breathe again, and his own terrified shout trailed him into the black.

He thought the pit might really be endless until he glimpsed the jagged stones at its bottom, just before he made impact—

Jean-Luc Picard, family man and retired Starfleet officer, jolted out of a nightmare and sat up in his bed, sheets tangled around his legs. Bullets of sweat dotted his face and bald head. Cool night air caressed his perspiration-damp chest and limbs.

He searched for the source of the breeze and found the open window on Crusher's side of their bed. Outside, a full moon low on the horizon cast dappled shadows through the vineyard rows of Château Picard. Picard sighed with relief. *I'm home. Safe in La Barre.*

Still half-asleep, Crusher mumbled, "Everything all right?"

"Yes. Everything's fine. Go back to—"

Movement in the bedroom's open doorway drew Picard's eye. A small, slender shape, barefoot, shuffling wearily in from the shadowy hallway. As the silhouette sharpened, Picard recognized his son by the familiar chaos of his sleep-tousled hair. "René? What is it?"

The child took two more halting steps into the bedroom's silvery glow of moonlight—and terror consumed Picard from within.

René was a Borg drone.

"NO!" Picard struggled to free himself of the sheets that snaked around his legs, only to find them coiling tighter. He had to get up, to reach René, help him somehow.

"Beverly! Help me!"

His wife rolled over and sat up. The thing that looked back at Picard had Beverly Crusher's face, but the mottled gray flesh of a Borg, and the cold, haughty voice of the Queen. "You are *mine*, Picard. And your family soon will be."

He scuttled clumsily backward, shouting, "Never!" Then he tumbled off the foot of the bed. Landed on his back, on the hardwood floor.

In a flash of limbs the Queen was on top of him. She straddled him.

Pinned his shoulders to the floor and put her face so close to his that he smelled the metal of the implants beneath her flesh. As she held him in place, René kneeled beside Picard's head and reached out with one hand as assimilation tubules extended from his fingertips.

The Queen's satisfaction was cold and malicious.

"You have only yourself to blame, Picard. *You* gave them to me."

Tears fell from Picard's eyes as his assimilated son injected Borg nanites into his jugular. "No, no, no, no . . ."

A fireball blasted the bedroom to pieces and banished the Queen's sadistic smile.

Blistering-hot air gusted into Picard's face. The shock of it snapped him out of the Borg Queen's drug-induced fugue state, but he remained disoriented.

Orange phaser blasts flew past on either side of him, vaporizing drones in single hits.

Another detonation a dozen meters away toppled a bulky cluster of machinery—which fell and pulverized another half-dozen drones.

A steady beam of phaser energy traced an arc above Picard's head—and severed the web of black cables that had held him suspended. He fell and landed hard on his stomach, despite his best effort to use his hands to break his fall.

Lying prone, Picard searched for the best route to cover or escape. In every direction he looked, he found concrete structures, long-defunct machines, disturbingly biological-looking Borg technology, and wild flurries of phaser beams disintegrating everything in their path.

Then he saw her: the Borg Queen. Hiding behind hard cover, her back to Picard as she directed her drones like a conductor leading an orchestra.

On the grit-covered floor between him and the Queen lay a bar of rusted iron.

Picard pulled the Borg tubules from the back of his head. Cast them aside.

Liberated, he stole forward. Kept low to the ground.

He grabbed the iron bar with a light touch and nary a sound.

Gripped its lower third with both hands and prowled toward the Queen.

He was one step from striking distance when the Queen spun toward him, her arm outstretched, and shot a black cable from an implant in her palm. The cable moved with a mind of its own, dancing like a serpent, faster than Picard could track. It coiled around his neck and throttled him. He dropped the iron bar and clawed at the cable, tried to loosen its hold, but it was slippery, metallic, and stronger than he would have imagined.

He fell to his knees as the coil sprouted teeth and began sawing into his flesh.

The Queen towered over him and gloated. She raised her cable-hand and used it to make Picard's captive body dance like a marionette. "Beg for mercy and I'll take your head quickly."

The cable around Picard's savaged throat relaxed just enough to let him answer.

He coughed . . . and then he grinned.

"You should have let me use the grenade."

He savored the Queen's confused expression for nearly a full second.

A maximum-power phaser blast hit her in the chest.

The reddish-orange shot also severed her coil, which went slack around Picard's neck.

As he tore the sawtoothed garrote from his neck, the giant Borg Queen fell against a concrete wall. Her ruined but not-yet-dead body spewed smoke and fluids as she slumped to the floor.

Beverly Crusher stepped out of the shadows behind Picard, her rifle braced against her shoulder, its muzzle aimed at the twitching Queen. "Tell me if this hurts."

Her next shot lasted several seconds.

Only when the last of the Queen had become a blackened scorch on the floor did Crusher cease fire, lower her weapon, and rush to Picard's side. "Jean-Luc! Are you all right?"

"No. Most certainly *not*."

She slung her rifle over her shoulder and pulled out her medical tricorder to assess Picard. "No broken bones. Mild concussion. And a known Borg hallucinogen in your bloodstream." She put away the tricorder, opened her medkit, and pulled out a pair of hyposprays. She injected the first into Picard's jugular. "That'll neutralize the Queen's drug in a few seconds. When your head feels clear, tell me, and I'll give you a palliative to help you function until we get out of here."

"Understood."

Picard took a deep breath to restore his equilibrium. As he drew another, Sisko and Bashir arrived. The two men each dropped to one knee on either side of Picard and Crusher. They kept a watchful eye on the space around them, through the targeting sights of their rifles.

Sisko sounded anxious. "It's a good bet every Borg on Earth is heading this way."

Crusher gave the second hypospray shot to Picard as she replied, "I'm surprised they haven't adapted to our rifles yet."

There was optimism in Bashir's voice. "Starfleet never existed in this timeline. Maybe these Borg haven't seen adaptive-frequency phasers before, or transphasic disruptors."

The doctor's hopeful mood did not improve Sisko's. "Let's just hope they don't adapt *before* we finish the mission." A large cluster of new signals appeared on his rifle's targeting scanner, and then he looked at Picard. "Are you ready, Captain?"

"I think so."

"Good—because we need to *run*."

30

———◆———

Devidian Temporal Collider—Intertime

Dark energies coursed through the circular frame that held Wesley prisoner, and through its linked duplicate a few meters away. Tendrils of charged plasma crawled over his body and those of the serpentine ophidians ensnared in the other frame—all while the ghostly trio of Devidian scientists huddled over their macabre machines and conferred in sinister whispers.

The various pieces of tubing they had jammed into Wesley continued to cycle fluids through his body. The process had been running for so long that he wondered whether any of his own blood remained inside him, or if it all had been replaced with something alien and foul.

He shouted at them, "Why won't you tell me what you're doing?"

They ignored him, as they had before. The longer they worked, the more excited they seemed to become. Wesley was no expert in Devidian body language, but the three scientists acted as if they were on the verge of a breakthrough of some kind.

One of them reached for a large, bonelike lever on the main console. The other two tensed as the first grasped the control. Then all three turned to watch Wesley, who realized that their sudden undivided attention meant something truly awful was about to happen to him.

The lead scientist flipped the lever.

And Wesley's soul was ripped asunder.

A surge of power like a supernova shot through him. The instant that it hit, he felt the loss of his intuitive connection to spacetime, and a forced separation from his gift for perceiving higher dimensions and phase-shifted matter—all of the powers he had learned to master as a Traveler. Suffering beyond measure erased his thoughts. He became pain incarnate.

He knew he was screaming—he felt his vocal cords shredding—but all he heard was the crackling buzz of raw energy. There was no way to block out the pain: he felt as if he were being burned alive, yet his flesh refused to die. Instead, the agony went on and on, driving him mad.

Then it stopped.

Blessed silence. A halt to the fiery torture. Wesley's screams tapered off as his stamina failed. Still bound inside the frame, he sobbed and gasped for air. His head drooped forward, too heavy for him to hold up any longer.

In front of him, the pack of ophidians lashed to the other frame hissed and struggled as black lightning limned in violet shot through them. For a moment, there seemed to be two clusters of ophidians, then three. Wesley blinked hard, thinking that his eyes had lost focus. When he looked again, there were five clusters of ophidians, all in the same pose, all bound to the machine, all in pain—but wavering, merging and pulling apart, as if some force were trying to compel them back into unison. He stared, dumbfounded, at the sickening spectacle.

What the hell are the Devidians doing?

As soon as he had formulated the question, he heard the Devidians' telepathic reply. *«Do you not see? Or do you just not wish to?»*

Before Wesley could ask the Devidians to elaborate, they flipped the lever and plunged him back into his own private pit of hell.

The first wave of exotic energy felt strangely familiar to him, even in his compromised state. The particles' peculiar subatomic spins gave them a silvery aura when they moved as waves, and he caught their bitter aftertaste in the back of his throat: chronitons.

Then came the sour flavors and cold stings of quark changelets; the petrochemical taste of tachyons, like shards of polyester embedded in his tongue; the blinding dazzle of Higgs bosons, tannic and peppery . . .

A pulse of synchronic distortion hit Wesley like a gut-punch. In a microsecond he had been separated into seven versions of himself, each one spatially and temporally out of phase with the others by the tiniest of intervals, but enough to render them all insubstantial.

Like when I crossed the interphase barrier. Have to reunite myself.

The moment he tried to marshal his Traveler skills to put the echoes of himself back into synchronous phase, the machine punished him with a brutal shock of dark energy.

The tallest of the Devidians leaned in close to study Wesley's reactions.

«*You still do not understand.*»

Wesley forced his head to roll to his left, so he could look at the Devidians' master console. He saw two holographic figures projected above the console. The first was fully humanoid, obviously himself. The other was of the surgically fused cluster of ophidians. Both translucent images showed him and the ophidians as having been forced out of phase.

The shortest of the Devidians entered a command into the console. When he finished, the two holograms drifted toward each other. Then they *merged*.

Only then did Wesley realize what was happening. When he spoke, his phase-shifted voice created its own echoes. "You sick bastards. You made a *hybrid*?"

The tallest one moved to stand beside a large lever mounted in the floor next to the other frame. «*Now you comprehend.*» It waved toward the merging holograms. «*We vivisected your subtle body. Mapped its energies, and your thoughts. Unlocked your secrets.*»

He wished he were solid so he could spit at them. "You stole what makes me a Traveler."

The middling Devidian sounded offended. «*Duplicated.*»

The tall Devidian pulled the floor lever back the other way. «*And improved.*»

Primordial energies spun and screamed inside the bounds of the second frame, engulfing the ophidians in a growing cloud of purple smoke.

A flash blasted away the vapors to reveal, hovering in the center of the frame where the ophidians had been, a twisting mass of black and silver dust. It looked to Wesley like a presence of smoke and fury. Then it expanded and split into twin whirlwinds of shadow. The first took on an anguine form that solidified—into a Naga. Then the second resolved into a humanoid shape—

—and became one of the Devidians' terrifying, soulless avatars.

The hulking Naga slithered free of its frame. Flexed its jaw full of fangs. Cocked its exoskeleton-wrapped head and spread its cobralike hood at the sight of Wesley.

The avatar was motionless for a moment—and then it came to life, under the control of some unknown, remotely located Devidian.

«They are the first of their kind. We will make legions from these proto-
types.»

"First? What do you mean the *first?*"

A fearsome growl rattled in the Naga's throat. Then it shut its eyes—
and *vanished.*

The avatar manifested a cloud of black vapors that solidified around
it, becoming a deep-hooded holocaust cloak. Draped in its dark shroud,
the avatar left the lab in quick strides.

Only then, far too late, did Wesley understand what the Devidians
had done.

The short Devidian turned off the machine, and Wesley's body returned to a single phase. His Traveler powers remained suppressed, and
he felt expended—like an old washcloth that had been wrung dry so
many times that its weave was about to unravel. Nonetheless, he found
the strength to lift his head and project his contempt at the Devidians.

"You fused my DNA with the ophidians' to make the Nagas *and* the
avatars."

The tall Devidian sounded pleased with itself. *«Yes.»*

"That's why you didn't fire when I came to the station. And why you
let me land."

«Yes.»

He looked at the now-empty frame. "Where did it go?"

«Not where. When. *Forward and backward. To end the Travelers and
trigger the sequence of Fate. The cycle's beginning and its end are the same.»*

The short one added, *«We could not win this war without you. But you
deliver yourself willingly in every dimension. You become the instrument of
your own destruction.»*

The trio of parasites floated toward the laboratory's exit. As they departed, the tallest left Wesley with a parting thought: *«When we return,
we will make you watch your universe die, and then we will devour your
soul . . . one memory at a time.»*

Temporal Disruption Base—2373, Borg Timeline

There was no time for second-guessing, just running and gunning.
Bashir was on point, leading the way back to the loose floor grating that

led into the building's subbasement, because his nearly eidetic memory made him the only one who could remember the route through the Borg's shadowy industrial labyrinth without the use of a tricorder. Just as vital, his augmented vision meant he didn't need a palm beacon to spot Borg drones in the dark.

Crusher and Picard were right behind him. She toted her rifle in one hand, and kept the other free to assist Picard. The captain was in rough shape, but he had his wife to help him keep up. In his right hand he carried a compact phaser Crusher had given to him.

Bashir intended to make sure neither Crusher nor Picard had to use their weapons. He heard the heavy clanking steps of Borg from around the next turn well before he got there. He sprinted into the turn, firing his rifle in a tight arc. In one burst he mowed down three drones, clearing the next stretch of corridor. He looked back for Picard and Crusher, then waved for them to hurry up. "Let's go!" As they reached the corner, he resumed his run through the maze.

Sisko brought up the rear, and was falling farther behind with each minute. Bashir knew it was because his former commanding officer insisted on trying to double-time in reverse, keeping his back to the rest of the team so that he never took his eyes off their rear. It was a noble decision, but it was slowing Sisko down, and Bashir worried every time he lost sight of his captain, even for a moment.

Bashir reached the last turn before the loose grating. The way ahead was clear. He stopped and looked back. Crusher assisted the limping Picard, but there was no sign of Sisko. Bashir gestured for Picard and Crusher to continue ahead, and he whispered as they passed, "Second grating, on the left."

Crusher confirmed the instruction with a nod. "I remember."

As she and Picard hurried toward the grating, Bashir searched the dark for Sisko. *Come on. Where could he be? Please don't tell me he took a wrong—*

Sisko turned the far corner, still backpedaling.

Bashir signaled Sisko with a low, short whistle. Sisko looked over his shoulder at Bashir, who beckoned him. "Come on! I'll cover you!"

The captain hesitated for a moment, and then he turned and sprinted toward Bashir, who kept his rifle low but ready.

A bright scraping noise, the shriek of steel against concrete, turned Bashir's head. Crusher and Picard had forced the rusted grating open, and now she was helping her husband step down into the shallow sub-basement crawl space.

Bashir looked back at Sisko—and spied a drone in the corridor behind him.

"Down!"

All the captain had to do was drop to the floor, or make some attempt to duck.

To Bashir's horror, Sisko spun about-face and tried to raise his rifle—but as he aimed, the drone fired. A reddish pulse shot from the Borg's wrist-mounted energy weapon and blasted open a smoldering hole in Sisko's gut.

Shocked by the sudden, clearly mortal wound, Sisko froze for half a second that felt like forever to Bashir's adrenaline-amped enhanced senses. The captain went limp and collapsed, clearing a sight line for Bashir, who put a full-power shot of orange transphasic energy through the drone's head, disintegrating it. The drone's headless corpse dropped to its knees, smoke rising from its open neck, as Sisko landed on his back.

There were bound to be more drones coming, but Bashir no longer cared. He ran to Sisko. The captain was lying in a quickly spreading pool of his own blood, his seared viscera exposed through a large, crude wound in his abdomen. He was still alive, gasping softly, his eyes unfocused, his once majestic voice reduced to a thready rasp. "Doctor . . ."

"Hang on, Captain. I need to get you to cover."

Bashir got his hands under Sisko's shoulders and lifted him off the floor. Though he looked slight of build, Bashir's many genetic enhancements had included superior strength. Though he had once berated his father for imposing genetic resequencing upon him as a child, at this moment he was grateful for all it had given him.

He rounded the corner, dragging Sisko, whose boot heels scraped across the concrete floor. Over his shoulder he saw Crusher standing in the waist-deep crawl space, holding open the grating. He snapped in a harsh whisper, "Cover us!"

Crusher pushed the grating fully open and leaned it against a wall so she could pick up her rifle. The she and Picard crouched back-to-back in the opening, using it like a foxhole as they watched either end of the corridor, while Bashir pulled Sisko toward them.

When she hollered "Left!" he darted left, a fraction of a second ahead of a phaser shot that screamed past him and felled a drone that had seemingly emerged from a wall. Then more shots flew past him, and he heard Picard's phaser shrieking, laying down suppressing fire in the other direction. *Which means we're surrounded. Wonderful.*

Bashir laid Sisko down at the edge of the gap in the floor and hopped over him, into the subbasement. He lifted the captain with one arm under his back and the other behind his knees, and lowered him gingerly onto an open patch of floor in the crawl space.

A dry rattling sound rolled inside Sisko's throat while Bashir scrambled for his medkit. Holding a surgical multitool, he kneeled beside the captain and went through the motions of medical care even though he knew there was nothing he could do. Nothing that would make any difference now.

Crusher and Picard filled the corridor above with phaser fire, giving Bashir flashbacks to the siege of AR-558 during the Dominion War.

She shouted down to him, "They're falling back!"

"Grenades," Bashir replied. "Collapse the ends of the corridor, then weld the grating shut."

Above him, Crusher and Picard hurled plasma grenades down the corridor. Half a second later came a series of earsplitting explosions that rained dust onto Bashir and Sisko.

But all that Bashir heard now was Sisko's deteriorating respiration, and his brittle voice. "Leave . . . me."

"Never." He took Sisko's hand, clasped it in both of his.

There was no more strength in Sisko's hand. "It's time."

Hot tears stung Bashir's eyes, and he fought to keep himself from breaking down. Despite all he had suffered through the years, all the loved ones he had lost, he had always denied himself the privilege of grieving, the solace of mourning, until the death of Sarina by the machinations of Control had left him broken and trapped inside his own head. Now, with the last of his emotional armor long gone, his lifetime of buried feelings had risen to the fore.

Sisko was his captain. His comrade in war and peace. His friend, dying in his arms.

The ghost of a smile played across Sisko's face. "All these tears . . . for me?"

"For you. . . . For Sarina." Hard sobs racked Bashir's chest even as he fought to hold them back, and tears fell from his eyes, streaking through the grime on his face. "For Ezri."

Sisko coughed blood onto Bashir's hands. "This . . . is a good death." He struggled to lift his other hand and lay it atop Bashir's.

The purity of Sisko's conviction only deepened Bashir's despair. "I don't know what that means. I sacrificed all I had, everyone I ever loved, to win a war no one asked me to fight." He paused as Picard and Crusher closed the grating above them and started welding it shut.

Bashir leaned closer to Sisko and continued in a faltering voice. "I don't see the point anymore. Death is universal. Inescapable. Inevitable. Everything is doomed to entropy and oblivion. Even time itself is going to die. So why bother now? Why go on fighting?"

Sisko's eyes dimmed. "A life only has meaning . . . when we *make it* mean something." He summoned the strength to grant Bashir a smile. "So go make ours . . . *mean something*."

More tears fell from Bashir's eyes, onto his and Sisko's clasped hands. He did his best to reciprocate Sisko's encouraging smile. "Yes, sir."

"Julian . . . call me Ben."

Sisko's eyes fluttered closed as he let go of his final breath.

Bashir reverently folded the captain's hands atop his chest.

Benjamin Lafayette Sisko—decorated Starfleet officer, Bajor's revered Emissary of the Prophets, and Julian Bashir's beloved brother-in-arms— was dead.

PART III

THE MEASURE
OF A LIFE

31

"Defiant to away team. Please respond."

Hunkered in the subbasement of the Borg's temporal disruptor facility, Picard heard Worf's voice issue from his combadge and those of Crusher, Bashir, and the slain Captain Sisko. He tapped his combadge, isolating the conversation. "Picard here. Go ahead, Mister Worf."

"Commander La Forge has finished critical repairs. Defiant is airborne and cloaked, en route to your position. ETA sixty seconds."

Picard's mind raced. Nothing had gone as planned. What was he to tell Worf?

"Key assets are in position, but we'll need a few minutes to get clear of the disruptor's distortion field for transport. Can the cloaking device be trusted until then?"

"Unknown. The sooner we depart, the better."

"I see. Stand by to beam us up on our next transmission. Picard out."

The channel closed with the faintest *click*, and Picard turned to see Bashir in the steam-occluded shade of the station's plumbing and power conduits, retrieving power cells and plasma grenades from Sisko's tactical vest with clinical detachment. "We need to get back to *Defiant.*"

Bashir shook his head as he loaded the recovered grenades and power cells into pockets on his own tactical vest. "Go without me."

Crusher took hold of Bashir's arm in a gesture clearly meant to offer comfort. "Julian? Are you sure?"

The bearded, bedraggled physician cast a melancholy look at Sisko's corpse. "I'm sure." Bashir picked up his rifle and checked its readouts. "Strange as it might sound, Data is now the closest friend I have left, in this world or any other. I won't leave him."

Secretly, Picard wished he had that choice. For years it had troubled his soul that Data had sacrificed himself to save Picard's life in their final battle against Shinzon aboard the Romulan warbird *Scimitar.* There had never been a chance for Picard to suggest another course of action, or to propose that he be the one to give his life. Data had seen all the possibilities in a fraction of a second and made the decision for both of them.

After that, it had been Picard's burden to live with it.

Now it was happening again. Data had assessed the risks, evaluated the options, and once more he was stepping into the breach, offering himself up in the name of what was right. And all Picard wanted was to die by Data's side, or in his place.

But there was no time for that now. Sisko was gone, which meant Picard was once more in command. He had a duty to return, to lead the last strike against the Devidians, to see this done, no matter the cost. Words from William Shakespeare's tragedy *King Lear* haunted him: *The weight of this sad time we must obey.*

He shook Bashir's hand. "Godspeed, Doctor."

"And to you, Captain." To Crusher, Bashir said simply, "Good-bye."

Overwrought, all Crusher could do was nod in teary-eyed valediction.

Bashir scuttled away into the dark jungle of pipes and conduits. As his silhouette melted into the misty shadows, Picard took Crusher's hand. "Time to go."

U.S.S. *Defiant* NX-74205—2373, Borg Timeline

Defiant's main engineering deck was being held together as much by faith as by science. La Forge saw jury-rigged solutions everywhere he looked. An improvised articulation frame for the dilithium chamber. Handmade replacement parts for the warp reactor's magnetic antimatter injectors. More than a kilometer of wiring and cables cannibalized from other systems on the ship, all in the name of getting off the ground before the Borg tore it all to pieces.

He watched the master systems display as *Defiant* accelerated away from the Borg-infested Earth of an alternate 2373 he prayed he would never see again. They were half a minute from orbit, and if all went well, in ninety seconds they would be past the range of the Borg's surface-based antiship weapons, and also standard ship-to-away-team communications range.

He took his quantum communicator from his pocket. *Lucky I have this, then.*

Though *Defiant* was operating with a skeleton crew, La Forge found himself crowded every time he tried to find a moment of privacy. Behind the warp reactor he nearly collided with a mechanic making repairs on the warp power relays. Stepping into the corridors was no help. Every few seconds someone or other hurried by with an armful of cabling or a bunch of tools. He needed to stay close to engineering, so returning to his cabin was not an option.

At last he found a measure of peace on the upper level of engineering, in the deuterium storage compartment aft of the warp reactor. It was a tight space, with narrow catwalks between massive tanks filled with the liquefied hydrogen isotope, and dimly lit. In other words, perfect.

He shut the compartment's door behind him, then powered up his quantum comm. It took him a second to adjust it for a private channel to Data's quantum comm unit, and then he waited.

He heard the feedback tone for a signal attempt in progress. *Please answer. Please answer.*

An almost perfect hologram of Data appeared just a meter in front of La Forge, on the catwalk. Data was standing, though the transmission included no information about his surroundings. He smiled at La Forge. *"Hello, Geordi. Are you safely underway?"*

"We are. Captain Picard and Doctor Crusher beamed up just a minute ago."

"I am glad to hear that."

A profound sadness welled up inside La Forge and robbed him of his brave façade. "The captain says you and Lal aren't coming back."

He saw his sorrow mirrored in Data's eyes. *"I'm afraid that's true."*

"Did you know? Before you went down there?"

"I suspected. But I had to see things myself to be sure."

"So . . . this is good-bye." Saying the words felt like cutting out his heart.

"It would seem so. Even under the best of circumstances, whether we succeed or fail, it is likely we will never see each other again."

There were a million things La Forge needed to say to Data. Things he wished he had said long ago, some he had thought of only in the past few seconds, and they all collided inside his mind and left him at a loss for words to express his grief. "Data . . . when your first self died aboard the *Scimitar* . . ." Sorrow became a tourniquet around his throat, and in the circuits of his cybernetic eyes his tears caused faults that registered as pain. "That was the worst day of my life. Worse than the day I lost my mother." He shook his head sadly. "So many possibilities, so many destinies. All lost." He tried to dispel his mounting urge to sob by forcing out a laugh. "And then you came back! I was just figuring out how to accept that you were gone, and then there you were: standing in the *Enterprise* shuttlebay."

Data cracked an embarrassed smile. *"It was a strange experience for me, as well."*

"No doubt." La Forge sleeved tears from his cheeks. "Getting to know this new version of you, and seeing you with Lal again . . . it's been incredible, Data. I just wish we could have had more time."

"I suspect everyone feels the same when they know the end is near."

"Yeah, I guess they do."

There was no time to drag this out. Soon they both would be in the worst fights of their lives, and there was much to do before then. But so many memories cried out for reminiscence that La Forge once again found himself stumbling over his own words, his voice trembling as he did his best not to cry. "I know we'll have to cut this off in a moment, Data, but I . . . I just want to say . . . after all this time, and all we've been through . . . I just . . ."

As always, Data came to his rescue.

"I love you, too, Geordi."

Revealed in the warmest way possible, La Forge had to cry, and he had to laugh at the same time. Once upon a time, Data would not have known what to make of any of this. Now he seemed to comprehend it more deeply than La Forge ever had, and that filled him with joy.

Wonders never cease.

Through the closed door, La Forge heard the summons to general quarters. Duty called.

"I have to go. Good luck, Data."

"Good luck, Geordi."

Data closed the channel at his end, and his hologram blinked out of sight.

Alone in the dark, on a narrow catwalk flanked by fuel pods, La Forge hid his face in his hands and, for nearly a full minute, let himself howl out in anguish for the best friend anyone in that timeline had ever had, or ever would.

Then he dried his tears.

Straightened his back.

La Forge soldiered on—because he knew that his best friend would expect nothing less.

One blast after another hit *Defiant* from behind, flickering the bridge's overhead lights and control panels. A parade of warnings across the master systems display prompted Picard to confide to Worf his fear that their damaged ship couldn't endure the sustained punishment the Borg were certain to inflict before *Defiant* jumped back to the future in its native universe.

Suppressing a smile, Worf had replied, "She will be fine."

In a matter of minutes Picard had come to share Worf's confidence in this formidable vessel. It was the willow that would bend but never break. Even with two Borg cubes hectoring it with torpedo barrages as it passed Venus on its way toward Sol for its high-warp slingshot back through the temporal fracture, *Defiant* continued to accelerate.

All the same, Picard was ready to be done with the Borg, once and for all. He disguised his anxiety as a routine care of duty. "Number One: ETA to time-jump?"

Worf answered from the wraparound helm console in front of Picard. "Ninety seconds. Coordinates set. Commander La Forge is making final calibrations to the warp coils."

"Very good." Picard looked toward the tactical station, which now was occupied by Lieutenant Keeso from the ship's security team. "Tactical, we could be time-jumping home into a combat situation. Set all weapons to standby and sound general quarters."

"Weapons to standby, sound general quarters—aye, sir." Keeso armed the ship's weapons with a few fast taps on his panel, and with a final touch he triggered the red alert.

Flashing panels on the bulkheads and the wailing klaxon were almost enough to distract Picard from the soft buzzing of his quantum communicator. He had never before possessed one of the clandestine devices made by Memory Omega, so its signal of an incoming message took him partly by surprise. He retrieved the gadget from a leg pocket of his black tactical uniform and set it to deliver only the audio portion of the message. "Picard here."

Data's voice came through the quantum comm, bright and clear. *"Captain. Geordi tells me* Defiant *is safely away."*

"We are, Mister Data. Are you all right?"

"So far, yes. Doctor Bashir has returned safely. He and Lal will defend the control room while I complete the cross-dimensional calibration of the Devidians' chroniton core and the Borg's disruptor matrix. Until then, I must maintain active connections to all of the quantum comms we were issued, in order to keep them synchronized across time and universes."

"Meaning, we're all now on a very short deadline."

"Yes, sir."

"Noted." Picard paused. What he wanted to say next to Data was of a personal nature, and he felt self-conscious having such a conversation with an audience. But he chose to push those reservations aside. *We're all minutes away from erasing the last fourteen years of our lives. No one will ever know what was said here. So I might as well speak plainly.*

"Data, we haven't much time. And there's something I need to say."

"Is this about what happened on the Scimitar, *sir?"*

"Yes. There was no time for me to say it then, and I've been too embarrassed to broach the subject with you since your . . ."

Apparently, Data could tell Picard was struggling to find the right word, so he volunteered one. *"Reincarnation?"*

"Yes. Let's call it that." Picard took a second to collect himself. "I need to say thank you, Data. For saving my life that day. And for everything that followed." For a second he considered stopping there and taking his confession with him into his grave, but decided to crack on instead. "For a long time after you died, I wondered if I could have stopped you. I worried that I'd hesitated, that I'd second-guessed myself." Shame flushed his face with heat. "I was afraid that I'd let you die because part of me saw you as more of a machine than a person. I—"

"*Captain. You have no reason to doubt yourself. I took action on the* Scimitar *because, as your first officer, I was responsible for defending your life. I purposely left you no time in which to countermand my decision. Consequently, you did not let anything happen, sir.*"

Picard permitted himself a half smile. "I see that now, Data. And I want you to know that, in time, I answered my own question. And it was the same answer I found when I served as your legal counsel against Starfleet and Commander Maddox, all those years ago. You may be synthetic in form, Data . . . but you most assuredly are *not* a machine. You are, in fact, one of the finest people I have ever known. And one of the greatest friends I have ever had."

"*I promise you, sir: the feeling is mutual.*"

Worf looked over his shoulder at Picard. "Fifteen seconds to time-jump."

He nodded at Worf, who resumed monitoring the ship's helm. "I need to go, Data."

"*Bonne chance, mon capitaine.*"

"*Bon courage, mon ami.*" It took an act of will for Picard to let the moment end. "Picard out." He switched the quantum comm back into standby mode and readied himself for the hard, blood-dimmed hour that awaited them all.

On the main viewscreen, a ragged wound in spacetime, spawned by the formula from Wesley Crusher's enigmatic Omnichron, opened ahead of *Defiant*—the passage back to whatever remained of their home dimension in the First Splinter timeline.

Worf kept his hands steady above the flight controls. "Initiating time-jump."

The tactical console beside the command chair warned of a targeting lock by the pair of Borg cubes pursuing *Defiant*—and then, as the image on the screen changed to the bluish-white maelstrom of the temporal conduit, all sensor traces of the Borg vanished.

Defiant was on its way home—and also to its end.

Devidian Temporal Collider—Intertime

Wesley had given up struggling against his bonds. There was no point. His strength was nearly spent, but even if it weren't, he could not have hoped to break the restraints on his wrists or ankles. His efforts had left his body aching, and the aftereffects of the Devidians' experiment had filled his mouth with the taste of copper and bile.

Bound to a circular frame in the Devidians' laboratory of horrors, he had been plagued by the memory of the creatures they had engineered in front of him. Part ophidian, part Traveler, the Nagas and avatars were mindless abominations. Pitiless fiends the Devidians could send anywhere or anywhen, to lay waste to the Travelers and everyone like them.

And they based them on me. *They used* me *to kill my fellow Travelers.*

He harbored violent fantasies of revenge. Pictured himself blowing up the Devidians' entire station, collapsing their intertime dimension, wiping their entire accursed species out of existence not just in the present, but in the past, the future, everywhere and everywhen.

The nagging voice of his conscience reminded him that genocide was as verboten among the Travelers as it was among nearly every other culture or ethos that deserved to be called civilized. But he was shaking with anger, furious in his captivity. If anything, it was his powerlessness, his uselessness now that he was a prisoner, that fueled his rage.

From far off he heard the Devidians' eerie chanting, the rhythm of temporal energy pulsing through Oblivion's Gate to rend worlds, and the groaning winds that flowed through the station's numerous tunnels. The Devidians had convened beneath their dome once more, this time to usher in the end of the First Splinter timeline, and in so doing set the stage for their unstoppable slaughter and consumption of all sentient life in the multiverse.

And I helped them do it. Because I'm a fool.

Wesley thrashed and struggled against his bonds, to no effect.

He gave up and went limp. *Dammit. I'm gonna die here.*

The other frame, the one in which the Devidians had created the first Naga and avatar, rang with an oscillating, semimusical tone. An emerald hue surrounded the circular frame, and creepers of bright-green lightning danced and skittered along its edges. Something had woken the machine, because the space inside the circular frame filled with opaque gray vapor that flashed with white bursts of energy.

Wesley felt anything but optimistic. *With my luck, a Naga will slither out and eat me.* He tensed and held up his head, with his eyes open. If this was his moment to die, he was going to meet his end with at least a modicum of dignity.

Inside the mist formed a shadow in a humanoid shape. *An avatar?*

A foot shod in a dusty boot stepped out of the gray smoke. Then a leg wrapped in tattered rags—and at last Wesley saw his visitor. It was a man—human, Wesley supposed, and ancient. Hunched and pallid, he had a twist in his lower spine, a wild mane of bone-white hair, and a long, ragged beard to match. His eyes were rheumy and dim, and age and arthritis had curled his wrinkled hands into bony spiders. His long, shabby leather coat was falling to pieces.

He took a doddering step toward Wesley. And grinned. His voice was like the scratch of claws shredding onionskin. "I always did have a knack for finding trouble, didn't I?"

Wesley could hardly believe what he saw, but when he looked closer there was no denying the truth. This was yet another version of himself, another quantum possibility of his existence looking back at him like one might revisit a memory of one's youth.

The ancient one poked Wesley. "What's wrong? You go mute?"

"Not yet. What are you doing here?"

"Whatcha think?" Ancient Wesley reached inside his tattered trench coat and pulled out a scratched and weathered Omnichron. He held it up, thumbed some of its controls, and then closed his eyes while he concentrated.

The shackles holding Wesley into the frame unlocked, and he fell free of the machine. He was so weak that he almost landed on his face. Instead he dropped hard onto his knees. Smart enough not to attract attention by crying out, he hollered his pain into his sleeved elbow. When he finished venting, he stood and massaged his sore wrists. "Thank you."

"Save it. You won't thank me when you hear what's next."

"What're you talking about?"

The ancient one handed Wesley his Omnichron. "To replace the one you lost."

"What am I supposed to do with it?"

"Get your friends some breathing room."

"Which friends? How?"

The old one shrugged. "You'll see. They're coming. You'd better go."

"Where?"

"The place you least want to be."

An image of terror flashed in Wesley's mind. "Oblivion's Gate."

"Bingo. Take O.C. there and trigger a temporal separation."

"A *separation*? Hang on—won't that cause a *ton* of paradoxes?"

"Sure. But what doesn't, these days?"

The wizened Traveler shuffled toward the door to the main thoroughfare outside the lab, and Wesley followed at his side. "Isn't that kind of dangerous?"

"What? You think the multiverse is so fragile it can't take a paradox or two?" He dismissed the complaint with a brusque wave of his hand. "Grow up. You got work to do."

Wesley stopped in the doorway and turned to face his older parallel self. "What work? What exactly am I supposed to do?"

"Save the root of all spacetime."

"But can't *you* do that?"

"I just did." With both hands, the ancient one pushed Wesley out the doorway, into the thoroughfare. When Wesley recovered his balance, the old man smiled at him. "Good luck, kid."

His words were still in the air as he swiftly faded and then vanished.

Wesley looked at the dented, scuffed Omnichron in his hand.

I'm beginning to hate time travel.

32

U.S.S. Defiant NX-74205

Defiant emerged from the wild beauty of the temporal vortex, to the endless night of interstellar space. All at once the hull ceased its violent juddering; the spaceframe's groans of protest went quiet. Only the ship's familiar mechanical vibrations and pulses remained. From the command chair, Picard imagined he felt a subtle difference between the timeline they had left and the one to which they had returned, a sensation like a resonance inside his mind.

Worf looked over his shoulder at Picard. "We are back in our own timeline."

"Well done. How long do we have left to stop the Devidians?"

"Less than one hour."

Lieutenant Keeso spoke up from the tactical station. "Captain, the jaunt-ship *Hope* is at bearing one-three-nine mark eight, range one hundred six thousand kilometers."

A signal chirped on the communications panel. Alexander muted it and turned toward Picard. "They're hailing us, sir."

"On-screen." Picard sat forward and tugged the front of his black tunic smooth.

The image of stars on the viewscreen switched to a close shot of a human woman in her late thirties. She had East Asian features, golden brown skin, and black hair that she wore in a dramatic crown of upright, carefree spirals. *"This is Captain Prynn Tenmei, commanding the jaunt-ship* Hope.*"* She paused and tilted her head in mild surprise. *"Captain Picard? I was told Captain Sisko was in command of* Defiant.*"*

"I regret to say he was killed in action."

She mirrored Picard's sadness. *"My condolences."*

"Thank you, but we've no time to mourn. Has *Enterprise* found the Devidians' base?"

"It has. But I fear your counterpart did something both foolish and noble."

Dread's icy hands took hold of Picard's heart. "Tell me."

"The Traveler went through the rift first, as a scout. His outrider came back with his Omnichron—but without him."

Her news left Picard feeling stunned and hollow.

Tenmei continued. *"Despite a warning from the Traveler not to attempt a rescue, our Picard did exactly that. Except for my ship, he sent the entire fleet through the rift. We've had no contact with any of them since then."*

Fear washed every question but one from Picard's mind: *What about René? I left him on the* Enterprise. *If it's been destroyed . . .*

It was too upsetting a thought for him to finish.

Someone off-screen made a discreet report to Tenmei, who signaled her assent. Then she returned her attention to Picard. *"We're taking position on your starboard side for docking. How soon can you make the jaunt to Yama?"*

"Immediately. All decks are secured."

"Okay, we'll be there in thirty seconds. Transmitting docking protocols now."

Worf confirmed the receipt of the information with a look at Picard, who answered Tenmei, "Received. Initiate docking when ready. *Defiant* out." Picard closed the channel with a control pad on his chair's armrest, and then he stood. "Number One, you have the conn."

Worf and K'Ehleyr both stood and moved toward the command chair. She froze as she realized her faux pas. "Sorry, Captain. It's just . . . my Picard calls *me* 'Number One.' "

For some reason, that fact gave Picard a small measure of happiness. "Naturally." He faced his first officer. "Mister Worf, you have the conn. Commander K'Ehleyr, please transfer cloaking-device controls to tactical, and then take the helm."

K'Ehleyr accepted the revised order in stride. "Aye, sir."

Worf took his place in the command chair.

Picard strode aft, moving with haste even as he wished he didn't need to be the one to go. But there was no shirking this somber duty. It was his alone, as captain, husband, and father.

He needed to tell his wife that both of her sons were missing.

U.S.S. *Titan* NCC-80102

The hum of the turbolift was steady as it shot upward, carrying Will Riker toward a reckoning.

Expecting a cold reception and meeting one head-on were very different things. Riker knew of few experiences as awkward as having to face those one had wronged, and to know when doing it that there would never be an opportunity for true atonement. Just as unsettling was to know that one had disgraced oneself in front of friends and peers, and to feel certain that no explanation, however exculpatory, would ever wash away the blemishes of shame.

It's been less than two years since the Cytherians hijacked control of my mind, and now it's happened again. Except this time, I kind of did it to myself. Which I think makes it worse.

Those thoughts and others had discomfited him every moment of his brief walk from sickbay to the turbolift, and now on the short ride up to *Titan's* bridge.

Would it matter that Doctor Ree had made an all-decks announcement over the ship's internal comm, to explain to the crew what had happened? Would anyone believe it?

It might help, Riker figured, that *Titan's* crew had, like most Starfleet personnel, experienced some truly weird phenomena during their years of service. Alien mind-control was a documented fact, as were parallel universes.

But to Riker, there was something strange about trying to explain that he had been possessed by another reality's version of himself. That the maniacal tirades Captain Vale and her crew had endured had all been the product of *a* William Riker—just not the one they had known.

He shook his head. *It sounds ludicrous, even to me.*

Had he been more of a gambling man, he might have wagered that Captain Vale would just as soon throw him in the brig as let him back onto her bridge.

Not that anybody on this ship would be dumb enough to take that bet.

The turbolift slowed. Judgment was only seconds away.

On his left, Troi stood close, her arm coiled around his. Ree stood to Riker's right. The doctor had pulled his arms in close, forced his legs together, and wrapped his tail around his ankles, all to avoid crowding Riker and Troi inside the confined space of the lift.

Riker imagined what might await him on the bridge. Walls of turned backs and averted eyes? A gauntlet of reproach? Anxious, haunted stares?

Whatever I get, I'll deserve it.

The lift's doors opened.

The bridge's ambience of comm chatter and computer feedback tones washed over Riker as he stepped out of the turbolift, with Troi and Ree half a pace behind him.

Business on *Titan*'s bridge seemed strangely normal, in spite of the accelerating cosmic disaster that surrounded them. Riker took slow steps, still unsure whether he was welcome.

Then security chief Ranul Keru noted his arrival with a half nod and a smile. "Admiral."

Riker returned the Trill man's smile and kept walking.

Down in the command well of the bridge, first officer Sarai rose from her chair. "Admiral on the bridge!" Her voice snapped the rest of the crew to attention, and Captain Vale stood beside her. As Riker turned his steps toward them . . . the rest of the bridge crew applauded.

Where he had expected to find scowls of contempt, he saw only warm smiles.

His eyes brimmed with tears of both joy and shame. "Thank you." He nodded to his friends and fellow officers—Melora Pazlar, Tuvok, Sariel Rager, Aili Lavena, Keru, and Torvig Bu-Kar-Nguv, the ship's alpha-shift Choblik engineering liaison officer. And next to Torvig stood Doctor Ra-Havreii, the ship's iconoclastic Efrosian chief engineer.

They convinced Ra-Havreii to leave engineering? Now I really feel honored.

Riker motioned for everyone to stop clapping. As the applause abated, he regained a bit of his dignity. "Thank you, all of you. I don't deserve such a warm welcome. But I appreciate it." He faced Vale. "Captain . . . Christine. Please accept my sincerest apologies." He held up his wrist, on which he wore a temporal discriminator that Melora Pazlar and Doctor Ree had created, from specifications that had been provided, he had learned only minutes earlier, by none other than Jean-Luc Picard. "And my promise that I'm back to my true self. Scout's honor."

"Apology accepted, Admiral."

"Can you brief me on ship's status?"

Vale delegated the query to Sarai, who put the rest of the crew back to work with a single strong declaration of "Stations!" Then she faced Riker and resumed a more conversational volume. "We're still in the natural transwarp stream, en route to the singularity Yama."

Riker found that news encouraging. "Any sign of *Defiant*?"

"Its transponder just appeared on long-range sensors, in orbit of Yama. We suspect it jaunted into the system with help from one of the alternate-universe ships."

"That sounds about right." He pivoted toward Vale. "Captain, I have strong reason to think the Devidians are using the Yama singularity as their base of operations, and that *Defiant* and Captain Picard are in greater danger than they realize."

"Our current intel suggests the same, sir."

"Captain, I think you should take *Titan* to the Yama singularity and do whatever is necessary to support and assist *Defiant* in its mission against the Devidians. Do you concur?"

"Aye, sir. Just give the word, Admiral."

"The word is given."

With one look, Vale relayed the order to her first officer.

Sarai gave orders with speed and surety. "Lavena, increase to maximum warp. Rager, adjust Cochrane resonance for maximal transwarp conversion. Tuvok, energize shields and take all weapons to standby. Keru, sound general quarters, all hands to battle stations. And Torvig? Tell damage control to pick up the pace! We've got twenty minutes until the last battle we'll ever fight—and I don't plan on losing."

As the bridge team sprang into action, Riker stood and silently took in the moment. Then, without a word, Troi was beside him, holding his hand.

Through countless hardships, this crew had become his family—and in less than an hour they were all, without a doubt, going to their deaths. But they were together, united once more. And no matter what the Devidians had planned, Riker knew one thing for certain:

Titan was about to give them hell.

U.S.S. *Defiant* NX-74205

Picard shook his head in dismay. "Someone tell me this is not as bad as it looks."

K'Ehleyr couldn't hide her pessimism. "It's not. It's worse."

Defiant's senior officers surrounded the bridge's aft situation table. Picard stood alone at one end. Worf, La Forge, and K'Ehleyr stood behind the table, to Picard's left. Opposite them were Crusher, Alexander, and Keeso.

Worf scrutinized the data on the tabletop. "Is this all you found on *Enterprise's* buoy?"

On the port bulkhead, a viewscreen framed the image of Captain Tenmei, who had been listening in from the jaunt-ship *Hope*. *"Afraid so, Commander. According to its logs, the fleet passed through the cross-time rift almost forty-five minutes ago. No contact since then."*

Projected on the tabletop were overlapping schematics, maps, and sensor logs detailing what Wesley Crusher had learned about the Devidians' secret base inside the intertime subdimension, how to navigate the cross-temporal rift to reach it, and how to reach the base's chroniton core deep in the heart of the fortress, whose architecture looked to Picard like the guts of a monster conjured from a Klingon's fever dream.

Lieutenant Keeso highlighted details on the sensor models of the Devidians' station. "This thing is packed with firepower. More than we can handle."

His analysis met with doubt from La Forge. "Then why didn't they fire on Wesley?"

The security officer shrugged. "Beats me. This thing was made for a donnybrook." To Picard, Keeso added, "If we go in there, expect a red-hot welcome."

"Noted." Picard tapped the station's interior schematics and selected the highlighted paths through its labyrinth of organically twisting passages. "Wesley's Omnichron mapped these routes to the chroniton core. Upload this to every tricorder and padd. Everyone who gets inside should rendezvous there. Once on-site, set up the transphasic-field attenuators to make a defensible zone around the core. Then contact Data on a quantum comm and follow his instructions for triggering the temporal recursion, so we can undo this timeline without damaging others."

Around the table, everyone except Crusher nodded in understanding. She fixed Picard with a steely look. "What about René?"

"I hid his combadge in his pocket. Once we've reached the other side of the cross-temporal rift, we'll scan for his location."

It was clear that Crusher found his answer unsatisfactory. "And then?"

"We'll have to play it by ear. But our first priority must be to stop the Devidians."

She closed her eyes. Swallowed. Then nodded. Picard had seen the worry, the anger, and the fear in his wife's eyes. He wished he could promise her that everything would be all right. But she and everyone else would know that was a lie.

All they could do now was finish the mission, no matter the cost.

Picard took the measure of his comrades-in-arms. "Any questions?" He waited a few seconds, but no one spoke up. "Then it's time. Proceed."

Tenmei shared the *Defiant* officers' brave resolve. *"Captain, we'll lead you through the rift, and give you cover on the other side for as long as we can."*

"Thank you, Captain. Good luck. *Defiant* out." He tapped a control on the situation table and closed the channel. "Stations."

La Forge slipped out the starboard door and hurried aft to main engineering. Picard moved to the command chair. By the time he had settled in, the others were ready at their posts. Crusher had remained at the aft situation table, which she had configured for sensor control, so that she could lead the search for René.

From the comm station Alexander declared, "Captain Tenmei says *Hope* stands ready."

"Acknowledged. Mister Worf, put us one kilometer off their stern and match their speed. Mister Keeso, arm all weapons. Commander K'Ehleyr, engage the cloaking device."

The lights on the bridge shifted from dim white to bloodred as the ship's cloak rendered it invisible to both eyes and sensors. On the main viewscreen, the fiery accretion disk of the black hole Yama loomed large—and then the intertime rift opened like an exotic bloom of cerulean flames, swallowing first *Hope* and then *Defiant.*

An eerie howling resounded through the hull as a vortex of blue light twisted madly on the viewscreen. Worf called out over the chaos, "Navigational program Traveler One engaged. Ten seconds to intertime subdimension."

Picard fixed his stare on the viewscreen countdown.

5 . . . 4 . . . 3 . . .

The terminal end of the rift ripped itself open ahead of *Hope*, which sped out into the black, starless void of intertime. In the scant seconds between its emergence and that of *Defiant*, what had looked like an eternity of emptiness filled with blazing bolts of yellow energy.

Hope's shields flared and dimpled from bow to stern as a hurricane of ionized plasma pulses engulfed it. In under two seconds the ship was forced off its attack trajectory by the broadside strikes of two Nagas, which knocked *Hope* into the path of a concentrated plasma cannonade that ripped open the port side of its needle-like central hull.

Pulses caromed off *Hope*'s shields and blazed past the cloaked but unshielded *Defiant*. Picard realized how closely they had just skirted disaster—and as the maelstrom of enemy fire surrounding them grew fiercer, he realized *Defiant*'s cloaking device was now useless—and because it couldn't be used with shields, it might get them all killed.

"Helm, keep *Hope* between us and the station! Disengage cloak, raise shields!"

Retina-searing flashes momentarily washed out the main viewscreen. When the sensors recovered, Picard was shocked to see Nagas had taken three bites out of *Hope*. A sixth of its jaunt ring had been blasted into mangled, blackened scrap. One of its warp nacelles had been ruptured and was bleeding fiery plasma. And the forward quarter of its needle hull was gone.

Keeso shouted, "The station's targeting us, and two Nagas closing fast!"

"Helm, evasive roll to port—put us under *Hope*! Use her as a shield as long as we can. Comms, tell *Hope* to send all power to dorsal shields."

Picard was already formulating his next attack order when Crusher called out, "I found him! Jean-Luc, I found René!"

He looked back at Crusher. "Where!?"

Several hard blasts in quick succession rocked *Defiant*, dimming the lights and consoles as the ship automatically diverted more power to the shields. Static and slashing lines of interference filled the viewscreen for a few seconds. When it cleared, Picard felt a chill of foreboding at the sight of a long, scorched wound across the exterior of the station's hull, littered with metallic debris. It had to have been a Commonwealth jaunt-ship. Then he saw a strip of bent hull plating emblazoned with a familiar name: *Enterprise*.

Merciless fire from the Devidians' plasma cannons shredded *Hope*, which started breaking apart above *Defiant*. Explosions cracked open what was left of its jaunt ring—and Picard knew from bitter experience that those sorts of detonations would soon be followed by much larger ones.

Keeso called out, "Captain, *Hope's* losing antimatter containment!"

"Helm, get us clear! Tactical, concentrate fire on the Nagas!"

Lieutenant Scardas looked up from the engineering station. His Saurian face rarely betrayed his emotions, but his voice was pitched with alarm. "Sir! If we lose our cover, the Devidians will *shred* us."

"One disaster at a time, Lieutenant."

Crusher arrived at the command chair. She handed Picard a padd. "The signal's weak, but that's definitely René's combadge. *Inside* the station."

He saw the proof of his son's location and made his decision.

"Helm, heading three-five-five mark six! Full impulse, all power to forward shields!"

Worf looked as if he couldn't believe what he'd just heard. "Captain?"

"You heard me, Mister Worf."

"Aye, sir." The Klingon grinned. "*Ramming speed.*"

Without doubt or regret, Picard and his crew transformed *Defiant* into a spear—and plunged it into the enemy's heart.

33

C.S.S. Defiant—Mirror Universe

Valuable minutes had bled away while Kira waited for a stroke of luck that might enable *Defiant II* to take her inside the alternate universe's Celestial Temple, but Captain Dax still had no idea how to skirt the mercenary blockade.

On the main viewscreen, the wormhole was behaving more erratically by the minute. It spiraled open at seemingly random intervals, blooming like a colossal flower made of purple smoke, and spat enormous ribbons of neon-green lightning in all directions. Each time it opened, it grew larger. In the past hour, its widening event horizon had begun lashing violently through space. So far the great whip had destroyed two mercenary ships, but more than enough vessels remained to maintain the tachyon grid—the system made to detect cloaked starships such as *Defiant II*.

Standing behind the command chair, all Kira wanted to do was pace. Only her pride, and Captain Dax's polite yet alarmingly convincing warning not to do that on her bridge, had kept Kira rooted in place, biding her time even as she felt ready to explode.

Most vexing of all to Kira was how calmly Dax accepted their predicament. She sat in her command chair, reviewed new sensor reports on her padd, and seemed content to wait.

Kira fantasized about throttling her.

On the viewscreen, several mercenary vessels shifted their positions. It was the first time Kira had seen them move since the wormhole's second random destruction of one of their ships. She leaned over Dax's shoulder and pointed at the maneuvering vessels. "Something's happening. Maybe we can slip past them now, before—"

"No," Dax cut in. "They're shifting positions to clear the zones most likely to get hit by the wormhole's next tantrum. The tachyon grid is still up."

Kira was unable to mask her frustration. "Yes, the grid is up, but it's stretched thin. This might be the best chance we'll get."

"They'd light us up before we made it a hundred kilometers past their line."

"The Ezri I once knew wasn't afraid to take chances." Kira knew that was a lie, but she was desperate to find a way to goad this Dax into action.

Dax refused to be baited. "My decision to hold isn't about fear. To accomplish your mission, we need to get inside the wormhole intact, and with you alive. Getting shot up while trying to run the blockade like rank amateurs won't serve that goal."

"So we're just going to sit here instead?"

"Until a viable plan presents itself, yes." Dax gave Kira a mischievous look. "Can't do your mojo if you're dead."

"Ezri, *please*, we don't have much time left."

"I can read the chrono, Vedek."

"Then you must know that if we don't get into position soon—"

Brilliant flares of light filled the viewscreen, and the ship began to shake.

The wormhole had opened to more than twice its normal size, and now fearsome green tails of ionized plasma flailed madly in all directions.

Another mercenary ship took a direct hit and was swatted out of formation. Its running lights went dark as it tumble-rolled out of sight, lost in the endless dark of space. The rest of the mercenary fleet scrambled to evade the wormhole's growing fury, while maintaining a semblance of their original formation.

Gripping the arms of her chair, Dax snapped out commands. "Helm, reverse thrusters, pull us back half a million kilometers. Tactical, make sure there aren't any exotic particles from the wormhole messing with our cloak."

Kira was incensed. "You're retreating? When they're widening their formation?"

Dax grew visibly annoyed at Kira's questioning of her command decisions. "They could widen it another fifty percent and still see us clear as day when we hit the grid. Plus, the wormhole's spitting out strange-lets, changelets, baryons, and who-knows-what-else. Any of which can cause distortions when they hit a cloaking field."

It took all the willpower Kira had not to vent her rage in a wordless scream. She started to pace behind Dax's command chair, then stopped herself. She turned back toward Dax. "What'll it take to make you order this ship forward?"

"A bona fide miracle, a ton of backup, or both."

"Did you *request* backup?"

"Of course I did. But as you might've noticed, the entire *universe* is unraveling. I think the fleet might be stretched a bit thin right now."

"I can't believe we've come this far only to get stuck *here*."

"If you see a way past the blockade that we've missed, let us know. Otherwise, if I were you, I'd start praying to your Prophets for help."

For half a second Kira contemplated whether there was even a ghost of a chance that she could seize control of *Defiant II* and take it into the wormhole herself. But that was a fool's errand. This was Dax's ship, her crew, people who had learned to trust her through years of hard battle and bloody revolution. They would never back a mutiny, not by an outsider, especially not one who bore the face and name of one of their most-hated adversaries.

To Kira's profound chagrin, there was nothing she could do but wait—and pray to the Prophets that they had not sent their Hand to this accursed dimension in vain.

Devidian Temporal Collider—Intertime

Weapons slung low and charging like berserkers, the black-uniformed crew followed Picard out *Defiant*'s forward hatch, into a broad passageway deep inside the Devidians' station. They all had grabbed transphasic-disruption rifles, tactical vests loaded with extra power cells and grenades, and special equipment stuffed into combat packs, as much as they could carry.

Only Worf and Alexander had refused to don tactical vests. Worf had ringed his waist with power cells for his rifle so he could go into battle one last time wearing his baldric on his chest and his *bat'leth* on his back. Alexander wore his own baldric with fierce pride as he charged out of *Defiant* beside his father, a transphasic-disruption rifle in his hands.

Behind them, not much was left of the once-formidable *Defiant*. After its shields had failed, the Devidians' artillery had dealt savage blows to its ablative armor, though enough of the defensive plating had survived to protect the ship as it rammed through the station's exterior force field and hull to wedge itself into a pressurized section of the station's interior.

Sprinting beside Picard, Crusher switched her focus between the path ahead and the tricorder in her hand. The device was locked onto the signal from René's combadge, and she had superimposed the readout over the map Wesley had made of the station's interior with his Omnichron. She did her best to call out directions with sufficient warning. "Next left!"

Picard barreled into the turn at a mad run to find a trio of black-robed, staff-wielding avatars blocking the passage, several meters ahead.

He fired his rifle. The avatar on the left vanished in an orange flash.

The other two avatars hurled a storm of silvery death back at him.

Picard dodged left in front of Crusher. She moved with him, opening up the middle of the passage—which blazed with a pair of orange transphasic disruptor beams.

Shining bolts sliced through security officers Lighton and Sulok as their shots hit their targets. The avatars atomized in two brilliant flashes as the Vulcan man and human woman collapsed behind Picard, their eyes still open but their faces lifeless.

Before the afterglows of the avatars' deaths had faded, Picard had run past them.

Crusher called out behind Picard's shoulder, "Next right!"

Weapons fire and inhuman shrieks filled the passageways behind Picard and Crusher. He had no idea how many of *Defiant*'s crew would make it to the station's chroniton core. All he knew for sure was that there was no longer any time to look back.

Secretly, he was thankful that the origin of René's combadge signal was on the route to the station's core. If it were elsewhere, what would he have told Crusher? How would he have justified abandoning their son to die alone?

Of course, it likely wasn't a coincidence. Picard's counterpart Luc on the jaunt-ship *Enterprise* knew the battle plan as well as he did. In all probability, Luc or a member of his crew had led René there, in accordance with the standing order to seize control of the station's core.

Even now, in the face of annihilation, Picard clung to hope.

Please let our son be alive.

He took the next turn so fast that he nearly caromed off the far wall before regaining his balance. Crusher was barely a stride behind him, and the corridors behind her resounded with the mad percussion of running footsteps.

An avatar with a staff dropped from a gap in the ceiling, into Picard's path.

As it raised its weapon, he vaporized it with a pulse from his rifle.

Its lingering cloud dispersed as he charged through it.

Crusher called out, "Left at the fork!"

Picard poured on the speed. He stayed left as the passageway diverged into two paths, and less than ten seconds later, he rounded a curve to find the mangled, twisted, and scorched remains of what he guessed must be an escape pod.

Barely legible on its still-sealed hatch, and printed in stenciled type—

CSS ENTERPRISE • POD 01-C

Crusher nearly ran into Picard. She muttered curses for half a second until she, too, saw the crashed pod wedged into the walls ahead of them. As if she had read Picard's mind, she changed the settings on her tricorder. "Scanning for life signs." She made a quick adjustment as Worf, Alexander, and La Forge caught up to her and Picard. "Two life signs. Both human."

Picard leaped toward the pod and tried to open the hatch, only to find its exterior control panel shredded. He looked back at his friends, "Find the emergency release!"

La Forge and Picard tugged at loose panels on one side of the hatch, while Alexander and Worf prodded at the other side. Crusher scrambled to retrieve tools and medicines from the field medkit slung at her side.

They were still searching in vain for a release handle when K'Ehleyr dashed past Crusher to the pod. "It's a biometric lock." She waved her hand in front of the scuffed logo on the hatch, which unlocked with a soft gasp. She opened it with one hand, and then she stepped back. "The manual control is beneath the hatch, but this was faster."

"Well done," Picard said as he ducked inside the dark, smoke-filled pod, with Crusher pushing her way in close behind him.

Smoke stung Picard's eyes, and it burned in his lungs and racked him with hacking coughs. He waved his hands frantically, trying to clear the air.

In seconds the haze dissipated—and Picard saw three people tangled together at the far end of the pod. He and Crusher scuttled over the heaped trio and pulled them apart.

The jaunt-ship's Troi was on top, beside her captain, Luc Picard. They each were wearing an air mask, but the faceplate of hers was smashed. His was missing its air canister.

Beneath them, his face protected by an intact air mask, was René.

On the deck next to him was a discarded air canister whose gauge read EMPTY.

Crusher gathered up René, and as he regained consciousness she pulled off his mask. Holding her son with one arm, Crusher ran her tricorder scan with her free hand. "Multiple contusions. Signs of smoke inhalation."

René forced a pained smile. "I'm all right, Mom."

Picard pressed a finger to Troi's throat in search of a pulse, but found none. Her flesh was cool to the touch, her skin gone cyanotic blue gray. He looked at Crusher and shook his head.

His counterpart stirred. Luc's eyes could barely open, and his voice was a weak, rough scratch from a burned throat. "Number One?"

Picard shouted over his shoulder, "K'Ehleyr!" To Crusher he added, "Get René out."

Crusher draped one of René's arms across her shoulders and lifted him. They hobbled out of the burned pod as K'Ehleyr slipped by them to join Picard at Luc's side. As she kneeled, Picard noted Worf's *mek'leth* in an old leather sheath on her hip. She asked, "What's the plan?"

"We'll lift him together, on three. Ready? One—"

Luc took Picard's wrist in his enfeebled grasp. "Stop. Too late. Leave me."

"Nonsense. We can still—"

"I'm finished." Luc rolled his head toward K'Ehleyr. "Number One?"

She took his hand, and her eyes shone with tears as she leaned close to her dying captain. "I'm here, sir."

He put her hand in Picard's. "Serve him . . . as you served me."

She gave Luc a bittersweet smile. "I will."

Satisfied, Luc looked again at Picard. "René . . . all right?"

"Yes. Because of you."

"Gave my word." A hacking cough made him spit up blood. "Pod was hit. Fire. Plasma line burst. . . . Deanna . . . shielded him." More coughing left Luc's chin drenched in dark blood streaked with black gunk. "So much smoke. His air . . . empty." His eyes closed briefly, and then he forced them open. "Gave him mine."

There were so many things Picard knew Luc deserved to hear, but all he had time to tell him was, "Thank you."

Luc smiled, but his last words spilled out as slowly as winter molasses. "I never had children. Now, I wish I had. He's . . . a fine young man."

The last of Luc's strength left his hand, which fell from Picard's.

K'Ehleyr passed her hand over Luc's face, gently closing his eyes. She looked up at Picard, her expression one of valiantly suppressed anguish. "We should go, sir."

Picard nodded, and he followed her out of the pod.

They emerged to find Crusher and René waiting for them, backed by La Forge, Worf, and Alexander. Running footsteps in the corridor announced the arrival of security officers Keeso and Slayton, who each wore a fully stuffed combat backpack over his tactical vest.

Worf was eager to get back in motion. "To the core, Captain?"

"Yes, Number One. Lead the way. Keeso, Slayton, guard our six. Everyone else, stay close and watch one another's backs until we reach the chroniton core."

René seemed lost as he asked Picard, "And what'll we do then?"

Overcome by a fearful sensation that everything he loved was slipping away, Picard wrapped one arm around his son, hugged him, and then cupped his hand behind the boy's head.

"The only thing we *can* do, René: the *right* thing."

Temporal Disruption Base—2373, Borg Timeline

Bashir stalked the perimeter of the temporal disruptor's control room, hands locked tight around his rifle. Blunt-force strikes against the room's welded-shut main door had taken on a steady rhythm during the past few minutes. So far, the door, its metal frame, and the reinforced concrete walls around it were holding, but each strike of the Borg's battering ram rained a little more dust from the ceiling than the last.

He was certain it would be only a matter of time before the concrete would fracture, the door's frame would buckle, and the Borg would march in, single file, sacrificing one drone after another until they evolved a defense against Starfleet's transphasic-disruption rifles. Once that happened, the battle would be effectively over. And if that came to pass before Data, Kira, and La Forge did their temporal mumbo-jumbo to erase this timeline . . .

Then all of this will have been for nothing.

Strangely, Bashir found that easy to accept. What was driving him mad was the inexplicably sanguine conversation transpiring between Data and his daughter, Lal, while the lab around them quaked with apocalyptic collisions.

Data stood at the room's main console. He had set the quantum communicator on the edge of the panel in front of him. Every few seconds he reached out to fine-tune a combination of sliders, knobs, and toggles, all to maintain the delicate state of equilibrium—or was it entropy?—he had engineered inside the Borg's temporal disruptor.

Lal was off to Data's right, at a secondary panel. "Father? I am unable to establish the quantum temporal bridge to Vedek Kira, as you requested."

"Can you ascertain why the attempt failed?"

"The Orb of Time is not yet inside the alternate universe's Bajoran wormhole."

Data picked up his quantum comm. "Data to Vedek Kira. Please acknowledge."

The response was audio only, and Kira sounded incensed. *"What?"*

"We have less than twenty minutes to create the quantum link that will enable us to synchronize the temporal recursion that will safely and retroactively undo this timeline."

"I'm aware of that." Bashir knew that pitch of Kira's voice. She was furious.

"Is there a reason you have not yet moved the Orb inside the Wormhole?"

"A few hundred reasons, actually."

Lal and Data traded anxious looks, but he tried to maintain a diplomatic tone. "Vedek, it is imperative that you take the Orb inside the—"

"I know what I need to do, damn it. Now let me do it! Kira out." A tiny light on the quantum comm changed colors, indicating that Kira had muted her side of the channel.

Bashir halted his perimeter patrol beside Data, and waited to speak until after the Borg's next deafening assault on the main door. "That could have gone better."

"Agreed."

"Have we heard from Captain Picard?"

"Not yet." Data busied himself tweaking the main console's controls. "But we will. I'm sure of—"

The next strike against the main door came with an earsplitting crack. Bashir, Lal, and Data all spun toward the entrance. It remained intact, but deep fractures radiated through the concrete around it. The wall was quickly losing its integrity.

Mindful of the need to avoid panic, Bashir masked his fear with ironic understatement. "Well, *that's* not ideal."

Lal was less able to hide her terror.

"Father, if the Borg reach us . . . will they assimilate us?"

"Perhaps. But I think it more likely that they will kill us."

Bashir resumed his patrol of the room's perimeter and pretended he wasn't eavesdropping on Data and Lal—not that he could have ignored their conversation, even if he had wanted to.

"Father, are you scared to die?"

Another tooth-rattling bang of impact on the door put another dozen cracks in the wall.

"A bit. But curiously, not as much as I had expected to be."

Lal nodded. "I feel the same way." She cocked her head, as if amused. "Maybe we are less afraid because we both have died before."

"Maybe. But I don't recall my death, since my memories were uploaded to my brother's positronic net before my previous incarnation died on the *Scimitar.*"

"What about your father's memories?"

Data wore a thoughtful expression, one that seemed unperturbed by the pounding of a ponderous mass against the door just meters away. "I recall Noonian's experience of slipping into nonexistence as he surrendered this body to me. But the actual moment of his end? That remains a mystery to me." He offered Lal a beatific smile. "But if his last moments are any guide, Lal, I expect nonexistence will be merely a return to the state we occupied before achieving consciousness—and that death itself will be painless."

Bashir couldn't take any more blandly optimistic philosophy. "The *moment* of death might be painless, but I guarantee you a great many moments leading up to it will *not* be. And while I'm absolutely *tickled* that neither of you is afraid to die, *I'm* bloody terrified! The only reason I'm not losing my mind right now is that I'm hoping our deaths will *mean* something—that I'll get to die actually fighting *for* something."

Lal and Data exchanged abashed, confused looks.

She was on the verge of a reply when a new *clang* of impact counterpointed the *ka-bam* that buckled the door.

The new sound of brute force against metal was coming from under the floor. The iron panel that led into the building's subbasement rang like a bell as something slammed against it from below, raising a dent in its tarnished surface.

Bashir stood next to the floor panel. It pealed again.

"So, now our battle has *two* fronts. Splendid."

Data frowned. "My apologies, Doctor."

"Oh, it's all right, Data. We knew none of us were leaving here alive. Just pray we live long enough to finish the job."

34

Devidian Temporal Collider—Intertime

There was no time left for strategy, only tactics. Picard stayed at the front of the group, with Worf and K'Ehleyr at his sides. Knowing they were alone this deep inside the Devidians' base, Picard had ordered his team to shoot anything robed or serpentine. What's more, he had done so without remorse. The hour for diplomacy was past.

From the middle of the group, Crusher directed, "Next left, then take the center passage!"

Phaser blasts from the group's rear filled the frighteningly organic-looking corridor with piercing noise and flares of orange light. Picard didn't ask why or slow down. If his people were shooting, he assumed they had good reason. If one of them fell, someone else would tell him.

He made the next left, into a narrower passage whose walls had the look of slick black cartilage stretched taut over curved ribs of ebony. The deeper he and the others pushed into the base, the darker its passages became. Here in the bowels of the station, most of the ambient light came from violet patches of bioluminescent lichen that festooned the walls, floor, and ceiling—or from the away team's own bursts of phaser fire.

The air grew heavier, warmer, more humid. It leached bullets of sweat from Picard's bare head. He tried to keep up a fast jogging pace, but with each step he found it harder to breathe.

His strides shortened and he dropped back, behind Worf and K'Ehleyr.

Worf slowed and looked back. "Sir? Are you hurt?"

Wheezing, Picard replied, "No, Worf. Keep going. That's an order."

The Klingon looked reluctant to press ahead without Picard until Crusher interjected, "Sixteen meters to target, straight ahead."

Worf nodded at Crusher, and then he and K'Ehleyr sprinted down the sloped passage, into the shadows and then into darkness.

Crusher pulled Picard to one side while she fished in her backpack. He put his back to the wall and fought for air as La Forge and Alexander hustled past. René paused as if he meant to stay with his parents, until Crusher shot a sharp look the youth's way and said in a tone that brooked no argument, "Keep going. And stay near Worf."

Slayton and Keeso walked backward, their attention on guarding the rear. They stopped short of Crusher and Picard to guard them while she injected a hypospray into his carotid.

"Tri-ox. Should help you breathe."

It took only a few seconds for Picard to feel a sensation of relief suffuse his body. His senses sharpened, and he felt invigorated, as if he had just had a long and restful sleep. "Yes. Better. Thank you." He nodded toward the target. "We'd best join the others."

He and Crusher jogged down the passageway. It opened onto a broad, vaguely triangular landing, across from a two-meter-wide footbridge with railings set a few centimeters above his waist. The bridge extended more than seven meters to a large hexagonal platform roughly ten meters across. Two other bridges linked the platform to other passageways. Each of the three crossings was 120 degrees, or two sides of the hexagon, away from the others.

In the center of the platform was an irregular, organic-looking mass that reminded Picard of wasps' nests he had seen in the woods near his family's vineyards as a boy. The core module was thickest where it met the platform, roughly two meters in diameter, and it tapered both above and below the platform. It was surrounded by a ring of four curved, solid, waist-high structures that looked like control panels designed to be operated by persons with their backs to the core.

Ribbons of violet light snaked around the central mass, the same way that larger bands of the same hue had encircled the exterior of the station.

Yawning around the stage was a vast empty space filled with vapors and shadows. The walls were covered with the same bioluminescent lichen that was rampant in the station's corridors. As Picard followed Crusher across the bridge, he looked down and saw only blackness, no bottom to the chasm. When he looked up, he found a similar, feature-less void.

Behind him, he heard Slayton mutter to Keeso, "At least it's defensible."

Keeso replied, "Not if these bridges are the only things holding up the platform."

When Picard and Crusher reached the platform, La Forge was at the core, probing the featureless surfaces of the control banks with one hand while holding a tricorder in the other. The engineer frowned. "If this thing has any kind of user interface, I'm not seeing it."

His complaint gave Crusher an idea. "Devidians exist mostly out of phase with the physical realm. Maybe this thing's controls are out of phase, too."

La Forge looked up at the towering, twisting mass of the core, and then he nodded. "I think you may be right." To Picard he added, "I'll have the tricorder produce a phase-adjustment field and see if I can get a master panel to show itself."

"Make it so. Quickly." Picard faced Slayton and Keeso. "Set up the TFAs. One here on the platform, and one on each bridge. Go." As the security officers sprinted into action, Picard faced Worf, K'Ehleyr, and Alexander—and experienced a moment of nostalgia, seeing the three of them together as the family Worf had loved and lost so long ago. He pushed aside his maudlin reminiscence and focused on the present danger. "The field attenuators should keep the avatars and Nagas from using their temporal-disruption attacks inside our perimeter, and slow down the Nagas if they try to breach it. Since the core's distortion keeps them both trapped on the ground with us, in case the TFAs fail—"

"You want to set demolitions," K'Ehleyr cut in.

"Precisely."

She smiled and patted her tac vest, which was loaded with compact field munitions. "I'm on it."

As K'Ehleyr hurried toward the closest bridge, Alexander knitted his thick eyebrows in confusion. "Captain? What are these 'attenuators'?"

Before Picard could explain the theory behind using low-level Cochrane distortion to create zones of regulated quantum phase variance,

Worf answered for him. "They create areas where the Devidians and their monsters are forced to stay solid. So we can kill them."

"Got it."

Picard pointed at the bridges. "By putting a TFA on each bridge, and one here on the platform, we stop the enemy from shifting through spacetime to ambush us. If they want a fight, they'll have to come to us—and cross one or more of three choke points to do it."

An excited whoop from La Forge turned Picard's head. The engineer looked up at him, a broad grin on his face. "Master panel is back in phase! Creating a holographic translation overlay now." He pulled his quantum comm from his belt. "La Forge to Data. We've reached the Devidians' chroniton core. Stand by to initiate cross-temporal synchronization."

Data's voice issued clearly from the tiny device. *"Standing by, Geordi. But be advised, Vedek Kira and the Orb of Time are not yet in position."*

La Forge looked at Picard in alarm, then asked Data, "What's her ETA?"

"Unknown."

The engineer shot a desperate look at Picard. "Captain?"

"Keep going."

K'Ehleyr hurried back to Picard, Crusher, and Worf. "Charges placed and activated. Keeso has the detonator."

"Well done. We need to surround the core and find any cover we can. When the enemy comes, keep them on the far sides of those bridges for as long as possible. Understood?"

"Aye, sir." K'Ehleyr beckoned Keeso and Slayton to fall back to the core's ring of control banks, to stake out positions for the coming fight.

As René watched the men deploy, Picard drew his backup weapon, a compact phaser. "René." His son faced him. Picard handed him the weapon. "Take this. You'll need it." He pointed at its controls. "That narrows or widens the beam. That's the power level. Right now it's set for a narrow beam—and to kill."

René swallowed his fear, nodded once, but said nothing. His face blanched—a reaction Picard found entirely reasonable, under the circumstances.

Crusher leaned close to Picard and whispered, "Are you sure that's a good idea?"

He replied in a discreet hush. "Good or bad—it no longer matters, Beverly. This is our last stand. We *must* hold this ground until our task is done, or else we lose everything. Not just all *we've* had, but all that anyone, anywhere, *anywhen*, has ever had, or ever will have. Like it or not, this has all come down to we few—and that includes René."

K'Ehleyr and Worf readied their rifles and fell back to the core, accompanied by Alexander, who double-checked the settings on his type-2 phaser.

Picard pressed in close to his wife and son, all of them huddled against the core. Next to them, La Forge worked with a speed and precision born of necessity and existential terror.

Eyes wide with fear, René stared at the nearest bridge. "Maybe they won't come. There's a chance we can finish before they know we're here, right?"

Before Picard could answer his son, La Forge flipped some switch or threw some toggle—and a skull-splittingly loud alarm wailed, its shrill cries echoing throughout the station.

Picard gave his son's shoulder a paternal clasp of encouragement, even as he felt his own hopes begin to fade. "Forgive me, René. In all of history, there have been very few 'good deaths,' but a great many bad ones. I fear we're all about to share in the latter."

"You don't have to be sorry, Papa." René put his hand atop Picard's, and as Crusher looked at them both, he added, "If this has to be the end, I'm just glad we're together."

Crusher kissed René's cheek, and then Picard did the same.

He knew that soon enough Death would take this moment from him, and that if he succeeded in his mission, this moment would cease to have ever existed at all.

But for now, this fleeting moment was *his*. And in it he found his last full measure of hope—the one that he knew would sustain him . . . until the end.

Every part of Wesley hurt. Each muscle in his body, his head, his insides. Pain was all that was left of him, all that he could cling to. The

Devidians had ripped him apart at a fundamental level, beyond even subatomic particles. They had shredded his soul.

I should be dead. He pushed himself onward, a few more staggering steps. *I'm dying.*

The chanting and the wailing of the Devidians had grown louder, more atonal, and increasingly primal. Their inhuman shrieks made Wesley's innards writhe in terror and told his brain to run and find somewhere deep and dark in which to hide. Their ritual was building to a fevered pitch as time's last moments were ensnared by the power of Oblivion's Gate.

Wesley had made his way through the windshafts to the uppermost level, the tunnel that ringed the top of the vast arena in which the Devidians had gathered for their cosmic blood sacrifice. He skulked into a short, dark tunnel that led to a steep downward ramp.

The arena was packed with even more Devidians than he had seen earlier. They were at least a million strong, translucent and ghastly, jammed into tiers that surrounded the great oval of the arena's floor, where a hundred thousand more of their death-devouring kin had crowded together, undulating and weaving like drunkards. A river of death-energy poured from the ring of Oblivion's Gate and split into hundreds of ribbons, which forked into thousands and then tens of thousands more, linking all of the parasitic wights in their shared narcotic frenzy.

The sheer volume of energy rushing out of the gate was staggering to Wesley. Even from outside the Devidians' communal link, he felt its power, its seductive attraction. Its output had increased by orders of magnitude in the brief interval since he had last seen it.

Horror blanked out his thoughts when he realized what was happening.

This is it. This is the end. He checked his chrono. *They're early! We should have had more time. They must know what we're trying to—* His heart sank. *They've always known. Our alternate selves have done all this before. And failed every time.*

Wesley retreated to the middle of the tunnel, pulled his quantum comm from inside his jacket, and opened a multipath holographic channel to La Forge, Data, and Kira. His voice was a harsh whisper. "This is Wesley Crusher to anyone who can hear me. Please respond!"

Dim, translucent holograms of Data and La Forge materialized in front of Wesley.

"Data here."

La Forge replied, *"Go ahead, Wes."*

"Guys, the Devidians are dropping the hammer. Whatever you're doing, do it fast."

The reaction from La Forge was not encouraging. *"I wish we could, Wes. But Kira's not in position, and we don't know when—or if—she will be."*

Data shared La Forge's pessimism. *"I fear Geordi is correct. Without the Orb of Time as a shared reference, we will be unable to synchronize the required temporal recursion."*

A choir of catastrophe swelled within the arena, heralding the end of all things.

Panic made Wesley want to run, fight, scream, and hide, all at once. He remembered all that his Traveler mentor had taught him about controlling his fear and mastering his emotions. The fear was still there, but it no longer held him in its thrall.

"Guys, how much time do you need?"

Almost apologetic, Data said, *"There is no way to know."*

"He's right, Wes. We're holding on Kira. Until she's ready, we're stuck."

"Okay. . . . I'll buy you all the time I can."

There was no time to explain, no time to say goodbye. Wesley walked to the end of the tunnel and looked out over the arena packed with vampiric ghosts. He lifted the scratched, care-worn Omnichron he had received minutes earlier from his ancient counterpart, activated the device, and aligned its temporal and quantum frequencies with those of Oblivion's Gate.

It took only seconds for the Omnichron to lock the signal into an amplified repeating loop. Wesley mentally configured the device to initiate a temporal separation inside the gate.

A blinding beam of neural energy—the death emanations of billions or even trillions of sentient beings—was diverted from the gate to the Omnichron and then sent back again.

Snared in the middle of the loop, Wesley howled in a deeper anguish than he had ever imagined. He suffered a billion deaths every second—felt every life as it ended, felt the dreams and hopes of trillions of creatures as they were snuffed out without warning, without mercy or reason. An entire universe's flood-crush of grief and sorrow drowned him.

To be a Traveler had meant understanding that space, time, energy, and thought all were different manifestations of the same phenomenon. The greatest star system was no more or less a miracle than the tiniest being capable of understanding its own pain. Only now, as he felt the extermination of his entire reality course through him, did Wesley truly understand the burden of the Travelers.

They were the midwives of Creation.

The witnesses to History, and the undertakers of Time.

Alpha and Omega.

But the quintessence of his being that persisted on the edge of annihilation knew that his gambit had worked when the circuit of energy that linked him to Oblivion's Gate flared and then stopped, plunging the arena into perfect darkness.

Then a man-sized supernova scorched the Devidians with hellfire and white light, as Wesley Crusher's mortal body exploded.

By the time Beverly Crusher had realized what was happening, it was too late for her to stop it.

She had been focused on watching the perimeter, the bridges around the chroniton core and the dark passageways beyond, for signs of the next wave of the Devidians' attack. The sudden chatter of technobabble between La Forge and holograms of Data and her first son, Wesley, had barely seemed urgent enough to merit her attention.

And then she heard the grim finality in Wesley's voice:

"I'll buy you all the time I can."

Crusher spun toward La Forge. "What did he say?"

La Forge played dumb. "I'm not sure I—"

She grabbed the quantum comm from La Forge's hand. "Wesley! This is your mother! Whatever you're doing, stop! Wesley, can you hear me? Answer me! Wes—"

A narrow arc from a huge ring of fire surged through the holographic avatar of her son. He cried out in agony, with the voices of a billion suffering beings, his arms thrown wide and his head craned back as if the sins of the universe were surging through him.

Crusher reached for the hologram of Wesley. It didn't matter that he was just an illusion, a shadow play of photons and force fields. She wanted so badly to hold him one last time—

A spark of light formed inside his semitransparent torso. Then it detonated—and, in a blinding flash, Wesley was gone, and half of Crusher's soul vanished with him.

"NO!" Her roar of denial felt like her spirit leaving her body. Gutted, she fell to her knees and dropped her rifle. For the second time in just two weeks she had watched, helpless, as her first son died. She buried her face in her hands and screamed again, wishing she could spend her last breath on her grief. She felt Picard and René beside her, but she couldn't look at them, couldn't look at anyone. Her firstborn son, her baby, her miraculous child who had grown into a being more remarkable than she had ever imagined possible . . . was gone.

She had wept when Wesley's father, her first husband, Jack Crusher, had died. His loss had left her feeling alone, abandoned, bereft. But as much as she had loved Jack, she now knew that losing him was nothing compared with losing their boy, the last part of Jack still alive in the world. Her child who she had carried in her womb—flesh of her flesh, blood of her blood. Who she had just watched die by fire.

Why couldn't I have died first? I'd give anything not to have seen that. To not feel this.

Picard clasped her shoulder. "Beverly. I'm so sorry. I . . ."

For the first time in his life, Jean-Luc Picard ran out of words.

Crusher kept one hand over her eyes and pounded her other fist on the floor as she screamed and wept in rageful sorrow, wishing that her grief might crack heaven's vault.

If only I could hold him one last time . . .

Someone took hold of her shoulders. She lowered her hand and opened her eyes. Through her teary kaleidoscope she saw René, down on his knees with her. "Mom. Stop. *Listen.*"

"What are you—"

"Shhhh." He held a finger to his lips. "Listen."

What was he asking her to do? And why was he asking? Crusher didn't understand, but for a moment she quelled her sadness and her anger, and let herself just be still.

And then she heard Wesley's voice, like a whisper in her mind.

«Don't cry, Mom. I'm not gone. No one is ever really gone.»

Desperate tears fell from her eyes, and she had to struggle not to break down again, to keep her mind sufficiently at peace that she could hear her son's voice. "Wesley?"

René smiled as tears ran from his eyes, as well. "You hear him, too?"

Crusher nodded. "Yes!"

As René held Crusher's hands, she again heard Wesley's voice in her mind.

«I'm everywhere now. And everywhen. Always have been. Always will be.»

Her tears of fury and despair became tears of joy. "Will we see you again?"

«We'll all be together again soon. I promise.»

René brushed tears from Crusher's face as she whispered, "I'll always love you, Wesley."

«And from the dawn of time until the end, I'll always love you, Mom.»

Crusher felt Wesley's spirit withdraw. It wasn't a physical sensation, and yet she knew in her bones, in her heart, that his presence had moved beyond her reach. She pulled René to her and hugged him with all her strength. She would not let the Devidians or anything else take her second perfect son, her second beautiful boy, not while she still lived.

Picard knelt beside Crusher and embraced her and René. Enfolded in the arms of her husband and her son, Crusher wished she could make the moment last forever. She wished she had time to tell Picard that on some other plane of existence, Wesley lived on. She wished she had time to explain to her husband why, in the face of their imminent deaths, she suddenly was so full of hope, and why he should be, as well.

But time was her enemy now.

The passageways around the core rumbled with the sounds of an army on the move—and beyond the radiant blue sphere of the away team's overlapping transphasic attenuation fields, hundreds of avatars emerged from the darkness, gathering on the landings for the bridges.

These clearly were the Devidians' shock troops, an expendable infantry of deadly, disposable puppets. A swarm of wights come to feast on carnage, with a handful of Nagas as the tip of their spear.

Picard let go of Crusher and René and faced the enemy. "Stand ready!" He lifted his rifle to his shoulder. "Aim!"

The avatars raced forward, heedless of the energy fields that would neutralize their most terrifying powers. They seemed to be counting on their advantages in numbers, size, and savagery to overcome the away team's meager defenses.

Crusher parted from René, pivoted toward the bridge, and aimed her rifle. René turned sideways, minimizing his profile as he aimed the type-1 phaser Picard had given him.

The first Nagas hit the attenuation fields. The blue energy barrier flared as the creatures forced their armored heads through it, into the protected zone.

Picard's voice rang out, bright and fearless: "Fire!"

Orange beams cut through the Nagas as their avatar masters unleashed storms of eerie silver light from three directions at the strike team.

Crusher unleashed hell, though she knew it wouldn't matter how many Nagas or avatars the strike team killed. This enemy would never relent, never surrender. The strike team couldn't possibly hold the core for more than a few minutes.

What did matter now was that she spend her final moments bravely and well.

For her husband and her sons, Beverly Crusher vowed to do exactly that.

35

C.S.S. Defiant—Mirror Universe

The quantum comm in Kira's hand buzzed, announcing an incoming signal, but Ezri wasn't mentally equipped to handle more bad news. From her command chair she glared up at Kira. "Don't answer it."

Kira grew more distraught by the second, and in spite of Ezri's order she checked the slender comm unit's data readout. "It's from Wesley Crusher."

"I don't care if it's from the prime minister. Leave it."

"It might be important."

"Vedek, there's nothing he can say that'll make a gap in that blockade, or help us fool its tachyon grid. So why don't you let me enjoy the end of time in peace?"

Fuming, Kira paced behind Dax's command chair. At first Dax was committed to ignoring her, but within seconds it was clear that Kira's furious back-and-forth had drawn the attention of the rest of the bridge crew, who watched the anxious vedek out of the corners of their eyes. Dax turned her chair just far enough to let her get Kira's attention. "Do you mind?"

Kira stopped pacing. Her eyes narrowed as she looked at Dax, a warning that she was about to unleash a retort sharper than a serpent's tooth and twice as venomous.

Then her quantum comm buzzed again, interrupting what had promised to be a tirade for the history books. A creature of habit, she glanced at the device. "It's La Forge."

"Don't—"

Kira opened an audio channel. "This is Kira. Go ahead, La Forge."

"Vedek, our sensors say you aren't inside the wormhole yet. What's wrong?"

"What do you *think* is wrong, La Forge? The same thing as the last time we spoke—a blockade with a tachyon grid."

"Well, you've gotta get through! I'm at the Devidians' core, and Data's ready at the origin of the temporal fracture, but we've only got a few minutes until the Enterprise *passes through the Borg's temporal rift. If we miss that window—"*

"I know the stakes, La Forge! But we've got no way past the blockade."

From the comm came screeches of phaser fire and monstrous howls, followed by human cries of pain and frantic calls for help. La Forge sounded as if his vocal cords were being wound tighter with each passing second. *"Find one! We can't synchronize the cross-temporal bridge without the Orb inside the wormhole as a beacon! We—"*

More weapons fire and primal shrieks drowned out his last sentence.

Alerts lit up the comms console. Lieutenant Rennan Konya wrangled them into order and swiveled his chair toward Dax. "Captain! Priority signal from Director Saavik, on the jaunt-ship *Ni'Var*! Message reads: 'Stand ready. Making a path in twenty seconds.' "

Dax looked at Kira, who mirrored Dax's giddy shock.

Kira dashed to the nearest empty chair as Dax snapped out orders. "Stand by to drop cloak and raise shields! Helm, get ready to make a run for the wormhole, full impulse. Tactical, save your firepower. Clear the lane in front of us and leave the rest to our friends."

Šmrhová powered up all of the ship's many weapons with one touch on her console. "Weapons hot, aye!"

Dax checked the tactical display beside her chair. "Helm! Thrusters only, come about twelve degrees port, *z*-minus eight kilometers!"

"Thrusters only, twelve degrees port, *z*-minus eight kilometers, aye."

It was only a guess on Dax's part. The director's message hadn't said where she would try to make a safe path through the mercenaries' blockade of the increasingly chaotic Bajoran wormhole, but Dax knew exactly where she would strike if she could. And, assuming she was right, she had just positioned her ship for the greatest possible advantage.

As she counted down the seconds until the attack, worries plagued her.

I hope they don't half-ass this. One jaunt-ship might put a dent in the line, but if that's all they've got, we won't make it. Two might open a path, but won't give us enough cover. But what are the odds Saavik was able to commandeer three jaunt-ships in the middle of all this?

The main viewscreen whited out for half a second as incoming jaunt-ships' artificial wormholes flared open with brilliant surges of light.

When the lightstorm faded, the image on the viewscreen matched the data on Dax's tactical monitor: her *Defiant* was in the center of a formation of six Commonwealth jaunt-ships: *Galatea, Novara, Nautilus, Akagi, Lexington,* and Saavik's flagship, *Ni'Var.*

All cruising at flank speed toward the mercenary blockade.

"Disengage cloak, raise shields. Helm! Match their speed, keep us in the middle. Tactical, check your targets. I don't want any friendly fire."

"Aye, Captain."

The viewscreen lit up with phaser fire and torpedo detonations. The jaunt-ships didn't spend time or effort on fancy maneuvers—they were making a brute-force charge. *Defiant's* battle group was a six-vessel fist with one purpose: punching a hole through the blockade.

All six jaunt-ships took catastrophic damage in under half a minute—warp nacelles shattered, jaunt rings blasted in half, central hulls riddled with fiery scars. Clouds of burning plasma spread between them and trailed after them as enemy fire savaged their hulls.

But then Dax saw it: a clear shot at the mouth of the wormhole.

"Helm! Into the wormhole, full impulse! Tactical, angle all shields aft!"

Konya looked up from his console. "Captain! Director Saavik is hailing us!"

"On-screen."

Director Saavik's face appeared on the main viewscreen—and beside her stood the other universe's Ambassador Spock. Even though Dax knew he was not the same person who had set in motion the liberation of her universe a century earlier, it still gave her a chill of awe to see him very much alive and looking back at her.

Behind them, the bridge of the *Ni'Var* was curtained in black smoke and lit by falls of sparks from the overhead. Saavik cleared her throat before she spoke. *"Captain Dax. We will defend the mouth of the wormhole for as long as we can."*

"Understood, Director." Dax looked at Spock. "Ambassador? Thank you."

"For what, Captain?"

"For so inspiring your Captain Kirk that even his *memory* of you was enough to change our universe for the better. May we do you proud, sir."

"You already have, Captain."

Saavik nodded at Dax. *"Good luck,* Defiant. Ni'Var *out."*

The image on the main screen reverted to that of the wormhole's mouth, yawning open to devour *Defiant* whole. "Vedek? Get that Orb ready for whatever it is you do."

Kira stood and gave Dax a grateful nod. "Aye, Captain."

As Kira left the bridge, Dax pressed her back into her command chair and readied herself for the rough ride to come. "Helm—take us in, and then park us somewhere in the middle."

Defiant raced into the churning vortex of the wormhole. Wild, invisible currents and terrifying cosmic forces buffeted the ship, jolting it repeatedly as if it were running a gauntlet of a thousand blows. Within seconds consoles stuttered and devolved into gibberish, the overhead lights flickered and then failed, and it was all Dax could do to stay in her chair.

The pilot called out over the din, "Nearing the middle of the wormhole, Captain!"

"All stop."

"Answering all stop, aye."

An alert buzzed on Šmrhová's panel. She silenced it, but couldn't mask her alarm. "Captain, sensors show six Dominion vessels approaching from the far side of the wormhole. Running with shields up and weapons hot."

Dax pounded her fist on the arm of her chair. "I was afraid of that. They watch for any sign of attack from our side."

Konya tried to sound hopeful. "Maybe we can tell them we're not here to fight."

Šmrhová shook her head. "They won't believe it, Captain—not with four mercenary vessels coming up fast behind us. To the Dominion, we'll look like an attack leader."

"Then we'd better hope Kira and her friends work fast—and that our ship is really as tough as we like to say it is." Dax opened an intraship channel and did her best to sound fearless and commanding: "All decks, this is the captain. Red alert—*battle stations!*"

Some of the vedeks and kais whom Kira had known would have said that a starship's cargo bay was a poor substitute for a temple. Most would have told her that opening the tabernacle—or, in this case, removing the shroud—of a Tear of the Prophets in such a vulgar place would verge on blasphemy. But she had done so before, out of necessity, and more than once.

What needed to be done would be done, by the will of the Prophets.

The door of the cargo bay was locked; she had made certain of it.

She was alone with the Orb of Time.

In her left hand she held her quantum communicator. She had set it as Data had directed, to create an open link between herself, the Borg temporal disruptor, and the Devidians' chroniton core. Her friends all were in place, fighting to finish what they had started.

Now they were all waiting for her.

Kira knelt on the deck in front of the covered artifact. She felt its power through its shroud of thick, dark cloth. It was just as she had remembered. She had felt the awesome potential of this Orb even when it had been secured inside its original tabernacle of rare metals and leaded glass. Its true power rested within its mysterious crystalline lattices, its extradimensional layers, its energies whose sources were not of this universe.

She pinched the shroud and pulled it away.

Bathed in the magenta light of the Orb, Kira knew that any place where a person of faith contemplated a Tear of the Prophets with reverence and noble intention was, in fact, a temple.

Its eerie radiance reached through her closed eyelids and into her mind. She blocked out the noises of the ship—the straining of its engines, the groans of its hull, the shrieks of phaser fire, and the wild percussion of attacks blitzing its shields . . .

The tides of her breathing became her universe.

No expectations. No fears. No reflections.

She emptied her mind until it was quiet, until she became an island of serenity in a relentlessly moving cosmos, freed of both past and future so that she could be rooted in the omnipresent *now* . . .

And then she opened her eyes to the glory of the Prophets.

Awash in light and power, Kira knew she had entered a realm beyond normal time. She was conscious, but this dimension felt dreamlike. Around herself she saw a few details of Defiant II's *cargo bay, though most of their edges and details were obscured by halos of soft white light. She looked at her hand and saw the quantum communicator, apparently still operational.*

Before her, manifested in this special place, was the Orb of Time.

Then she heard Sisko's voice. "The Hand is in motion."

Kira turned and saw him. It looked like him, like the Benjamin Sisko she had seen only hours earlier, the Emissary of the Prophets, the human man and Starfleet officer who had been her friend for nearly two decades.

But something was missing. Something in his eyes. A glint of humor or a hint of sorrow. The spark of inspiration. The ineffable quality of his humanity.

"You're not my Benjamin Sisko."

"No."

"Is he with you?"

The Prophet circled her and the Orb of Time while pondering her question. "Part of the Sisko will always be with us. Has always been. Is."

She had learned over the years how to parse the Prophets' riddles and circular thinking. This time, she hoped she had misunderstood their meaning. "Is the Sisko . . . dead?"

"He is no longer part of your segment of linear time."

He's gone.

The news felt like a hand reaching through Kira's guts to pull out her heart.

The Emissary . . . Captain Sisko . . . her trusted friend . . . was dead.

Grief wanted to roll through her, run amok in her thoughts with free rein, wreak havoc and drive her to rail in futility against the finality of this loss—

But she knew sorrow's tricks all too well.

She had been a child refugee. A teen freedom fighter. A guerrilla soldier in the final years of a five-decade-long asymmetrical war. She understood pain and loss.

There was a time and a place to mourn. This was not it.

She cleared her mind. Locked away her grief.

Rooted in the omnipresent never, she confronted the Prophet.

"I need you to help me build a quantum bridge between past and present, to erase what should never have been, and protect all that might yet be."

The Sisko Prophet stepped forward and pressed its palms to Kira's face. "This is why the Hand exists. This is what makes the Hand unique."

Mesmerized, Kira reached up and set her palms on the Prophet's wrists, all while looking into the endless depths of the cosmos behind his irises. "I don't understand."

"Many times. Many places. Many iterations of the Kira. But only one is our Hand."

"I thought my role as your Hand ended when we avoided a war with the Ascendants."

"That was a task of the Kira. Your current point in linear time is the task of our Hand."

Kira froze. My whole life has literally been about this. All the visions, the prophecies, every riddle about me being "the Hand of the Prophets" . . . was about *this.*

"If this is my task, will you help me?"

"We already have. What must be done next . . . only our Hand can do."

"And what is that?"

"Finish the task you were given."

"The task I was given? You mean, bridging the timelines?"

The Prophet held up a wooden baseball bat—and then snapped it in half as if it had been a mere twig. "What the Hand breaks—" He pressed the splintered ends of the bat to each other, and then he slid his hands together so that his fists covered the break. When he parted them, the bat was whole again, unblemished, as if it had never broken. "—the Hand can heal."

Captain Sisko had once told her how he had used the archaic Earth sport of baseball to explain to the Prophets how beings who lived in only four dimensions perceived the passage of linear time. In that context, the Prophet's choice of a baseball bat for a symbolic demonstration of her imminent role seemed deliberate to Kira. But the notion that she had become the Hand expressly for this moment raised new questions in her mind.

"If this is my task as your Hand in this universe, what's my role as your Hand in other timelines? What's my job as the Hand in what Data calls the Prime timeline?"

"In no other branch of time is the Kira called to be our Hand."

"So in any other timeline, I'm not your Hand?"

"Only in this lone echo of time have we extended our Hand into linear matters."

"So . . . I'm special?"

The Sisko Prophet adopted a gentle, almost fatherly aspect as he cupped Kira's left ear, as if to read her pagh. His expression was benign, and imbued with a beatific quality.

"Across an infinity of possibilities, this Kira . . . is unique."

Temporal Disruption Base—2373, Borg Timeline

The numbers refused to hold. Every time Data was sure he had locked in the calculations for the temporal recursion, one variable would change, and then another, forcing him to start over. He had done the math six times in the last two milliseconds. When more of his settings slipped out of alignment, he ran a parallel analysis in his positronic matrix.

Billions of computations raced through his circuits as the Borg pressed their assault on the control room's defenses. The main door was about to buckle and rip free of its hinges, and the reinforced concrete walls around it were crumbling. With only a corner at the end of the narrow entry corridor for cover, Bashir stood ready to repel the attack on the main door.

Lal stood to one side of the iron plate in the middle of the floor, taking care to stay clear of the plasma beam the Borg were using to cut the welded panel open. More than three-quarters of the panel's edge had been reduced to a red-hot molten wound.

Both barriers would fail within seconds.

Every scenario Data had simulated in his mind told him that once the door and panel were breached, he, Lal, and Bashir would lose the control room in approximately four minutes.

In five minutes and forty-one seconds, the *Enterprise*-E of 2063 would open a temporal vortex that would be intercepted by the Borg's temporal disruptor—and when that moment came, Data needed to be ready at this console, with all of his final calculations in place, to trigger the recursion that would undo the sabotage inflicted fourteen years earlier by the Borg.

But the numbers would not hold.

His parallel analysis identified the pattern. The variables were unraveling in reverse chronological order: The future was in flux. A tempest of clashing outcomes—the number of which was shrinking rapidly, as probability-waveform collapses erased the paths not taken and locked in those that were—was triggering ripple effects backward in time, fouling his equations. The only variable that remained steady was the one being generated by the Orb of Time.

Data spoke toward his quantum comm, which rested on the console in front of him.

"Geordi, be advised that I will not be able to lock in my final calculations until just before the moment of the *Enterprise*-E's transit."

"What? Why not?"

"Temporal echoes within anti-time, caused by the changing shape of the future, are altering the variables from your side of the equation."

La Forge sounded vexed. *"How am I supposed to duplicate your calculations in a fraction of a second?"*

"Link your quantum comm and your tricorder. When I have the final equation, I will send it to your comm, which will route it to the Devidians' control panel. When you see the green pad marked 'commit,' press it."

"Then what?"

"And then . . . nothing."

It took a second for La Forge to parse the layers of meaning in Data's words—that not only would there be no further steps to take, there would be nothing at all. Just nonexistence.

"Copy that, Data. Linking the comm and tricorder now."

"Acknowl—"

An explosion cut off Data's reply. The shock wave slammed him against the master console. He rebounded off it and landed on the cement floor as smoke filled the control room.

Bashir stood at the end of the narrow entry passage that led to the main door, snapping off rapid bursts of phaser fire into the impenetrable, billowing black smoke. The mangled door and hunks of broken concrete and twisted rebar littered the floor of the passage.

A loud thud of collision was paired with a screech of metal pushed beyond its limit. Behind Data, in the middle of the room, a pair of Borg drones had used themselves as battering rams to finish the job of forcing their way through the floor panel, which stood upright and bent backward, linked to one of its hinges by a thin strip of distressed metal.

In the passageway, Borg drones dispatched by Bashir's random marksmanship piled up beneath the lingering blanket of smoke, their bodies twitching as they spat sparks and blood.

At the open floor panel, the two drones started climbing into the control room. Lal seized the first drone's head and twisted it until its cervical vertebrae shattered with a wet crunch. Next she slammed the steel panel onto the second drone with one fierce kick, breaking its back before sending it and the panel down into the subbasement.

She fired a few shots through the now uncovered opening in the floor, then shouted to Bashir, "I need a grenade!"

Bashir paused his shooting, pulled a plasma grenade from his tactical vest, and lobbed it to Lal. She caught it, armed it, and pitched it through the opening in the floor. As Bashir resumed filling the front passageway with suppressing fire, Lal retreated a few steps to avoid the blast of heat, dust, and debris that erupted from the floor opening. Then she emulated Bashir's strategy and fired her rifle into the smoking pit, peppering it with a steady barrage of short, lethal bursts.

Data stood and faced the master console. Five minutes and sixteen seconds remained until the *Enterprise*-E would begin its transit.

Behind him, Bashir and Lal persevered in their relentless defense. Their tactics were sound, even if their positions were untenable. In the interest of preserving morale, Data kept his fears to himself. But part of his positronic matrix began obsessively running simulations over and over and over, to gauge the likelihood that all of this sacrifice would not turn out to have been in vain. None yielded the result for which he hoped.

Overwhelmed by the piercing whine of phaser pulses and the booms of exploding grenades, Data became paralyzed by the arbitrary cruelty of chance.

We are all about to die for nothing.

C.S.S. Defiant—Mirror Universe

Disruptor shots grazed *Defiant's* shields from forward and aft. The ship lurched and rolled inside the twisting madness of the wormhole, like a feather caught in a cross-fire hurricane.

Sitting in the center of it all, Ezri Dax felt more like a hostage than a captain. Victory and escape were both off the table. Her only goal now was to hold her ship together.

Konya raised his voice above the clamor of battle. "Captain! The Dominion battle cruiser *Tenak'talar* orders us to turn back or be destroyed. Shall I—" He quelled another alarm on her console. "The Nausicaan mercenary frigate *Klezhka* orders us to surrender and prepare to be boarded." He turned an imploring look at Dax. "Who do I piss off first?"

"Allow me. Tactical, lock forward torpedoes on the *Tenak'talar*, aft torpedoes on the *Klezhka*. Full spreads for both. Fire at will until both ships are gone."

Šmrhová responded as she fired, "Aye, sir! Torpedoes away."

Dax watched her tactical display as both torpedo clusters sped toward their targets. On any other day, she'd have called herself mad. Starting a fight she couldn't win? Against enemies in front and behind? Outnumbered ten to one?

Today it was the only choice she had left.

Blinking icons on her tactical monitor indicated multiple torpedo hits. At tactical, Šmrhová sounded almost giddy. "*Klezhka's* shields are down! Damage to her forward weapons grid!" A moment later, her excitement was snuffed like a weak flame in a gale. "*Tenak'talar's* shields are holding. She's charging all disruptors!"

Flight-controller Sunai Moraine looked back at Dax. "Evasive maneuvers, Captain?"

Dax shook her head. "There's nowhere to run." She looked instead to the engineering liaison officer. "Ocasio! I want every drop of power we can get routed into the shields. Shut down all nonessentials: cloaking device, shuttlebay, life-support—"

"Life-support?" asked Ensign Ocasio, with a look of horror. "*All* of it?"

"*All* of it, and dump the reserves into the phasers." Dax turned back toward Šmrhová. "Aneta: launch every torpedo, and fire the phasers until they melt. Destroy *all* hostile vessels."

Before Šmrhová could answer, Moraine called out, "Incoming! Brace for impact!"

Hit after hit rocked *Defiant*, sent it rolling and tumbling. Main power hiccuped on and off, and then it failed entirely as an EPS conduit ruptured inside the bridge's overhead, blasting open the comms console and all of the starboard auxiliary duty stations behind it. One of the overhead lights exploded and rained white-hot phosphors onto the back of Dax's neck.

A two-second lull in the chaos made Dax hope she might have time to regroup.

Then the punishment resumed.

Detonations thrashed *Defiant* hard enough to shake panels off the bulkheads. The hull groaned, and then it wailed like a wounded leviathan. Doors autolocked, emergency hatches shut throughout the ship, and the master systems display was overrun by flashing red icons of distress—plasma fires, hull breaches, power failures . . .

Then the ship was hit again. And again.

Hot smoke and bitter fumes filled the bridge.

Dax clung to her chair like a castaway hugging a chunk of driftwood. She felt the breaking of her ship's keel through the deck and knew *Defiant* wouldn't last much longer.

"Aneta! Do we still have weapons? Shields?"

Šmrhová clawed her way back into her chair. "Negative. All offline."

Dax wasn't ready to give up. "Helm! Status?"

Moraine pulled herself off the deck, sleeved blood and grime from her eyes, and made a quick check of her console. "Warp and impulse offline. Thrusters only."

A grave mood settled over the bridge crew. No one said it, but Dax was sure they all were thinking the same thing she was.

We're sitting ducks.

Alerts warbled on the comms panel. Konya glumly noted them, then he faced Dax. "The Gorn mercenary cruiser *Zorzhong* orders us to prepare to be—" He muted another alert. "Captain, the *Tenak'talar* is ordering the *Zorzhong* to stand down and surrender us to their custody." He picked up an earpiece and put it into his left ear. "The captain of the *Zorzhong* is ordering the Dominion fleet to withdraw to its side of the wormhole or be fired upon."

Looks of surprise made the rounds of the bridge crew, but tactical officer Šmrhová remained worried. "Captain, *Zorzhong* and *Tenak'talar* are targeting each other!"

Moraine muttered, "Could we be this lucky?"

"Lucky?" Dax cocked an eyebrow at the helm officer. "Ensign, do I need to remind you that we're sitting directly *between* them?"

Šmrhová approached Dax's chair. "Should we abandon ship while we can?"

It was a reasonable suggestion. But not the one Dax knew was right. Not this time.

There's no point living to fight another day when this is the last day of history. "Launch the escape pods empty. It won't fool the Jem'Hadar, but it might confuse the Gorn."

Šmrhová delegated the order to Ocasio with a quick nod. "Then what, Captain?"

"Then we go down fighting. Ocasio, tell the hangar crew to spin up the warp cores inside our shuttlecraft—the Cochrane distortion will block transporter signals and keep boarding parties at bay. Aneta, the moment either of those fleets targets us, release all of our torpedo countermeasures, mess up their sensors any way you can. And Sunai? Set all thrusters to random. Put us in the wildest tumble-spin they've ever seen. Make it as hard as possible for them to lock tractor beams or try to dock."

Her officers set to work making *Defiant* the most elusive prize possible.

Konya looked up from the comms station, his face filled with doubt. "Captain, none of that will stop them from destroying us, if it comes to that."

"We don't need to *win*, Rennan. We just need to hold off defeat for a few minutes." She shot an encouraging smile at the communications officer. "Or as Smiley O'Brien used to say, 'We just gotta run out the clock.'"

36

Devidian Temporal Collider—Intertime

Sweat poured down Picard's back. Avatars' death rays flew over his head, courtesy of the brigade of figures in hooded black robes massed at the far end of the nearest bridge, from beyond the sapphire-blue energy field created by the away team's transphasic-field attenuators.

"Beverly! Cover me!"

Crusher raked the enemy with phaser blasts, giving Picard time to spring up and fire. His finger twitched against his rifle's firing stud, unleashing bursts of phaser energy that cut down two avatars as they crossed what the away team had decided to call bridge one.

Slayton darted in front of Picard. "Captain! Look out!"

A death ray struck Slayton in the face, and he fell to the floor. The avatar that had slain him conjured a stream of white light from Slayton's body—the man's very life-essence—and drew it into its skeletal hand, no doubt to feed it to the Devidian pulling its strings from afar.

Picard fired and vaporized the avatar who'd taken Slayton's life, then ducked behind the control bank as more death bolts shot past him.

Behind him to his left, Alexander Rozhenko had joined Lieutenant Keeso in defending bridge three. The two men scoured the narrow crossing with transphasic pulses, but avatars continued to pour from the passageway beyond to sacrifice themselves—and each wave pushed a little farther across the bridge. Alexander's actions were jerky, almost panicked, while Keeso's were cool and methodical—the difference between a diplomat and a soldier.

"Slow down, sir," Keeso told Alexander. "Pick your targets. Just don't let 'em off the bridge. And don't let 'em reach the TFAs, or we'll lose a lotta ground real fast."

At bridge two, behind Picard to the right, Worf and K'Ehleyr grappled with the same threat: one mindless avatar charge after another.

The gray reapers showed no fear or reluctance to advance into hostile fire. They were consummate shock troops: soulless, fearless, and deadly.

Worf and K'Ehleyr unleashed overlapping fields of phaser fire that cut the automatons down two or three at a time. Avatars' charred corpses slipped under the bridge's railings, into the chasm's misty depths, but nothing slowed the enemy's rush into the proverbial meat grinder.

Crusher remained at Picard's side, alternating shots with him to hold back the avatars' push across bridge one. Her red hair had grown dark and heavy with sweat, and her fierce determination showed in the set of her jaw and her piercing stare.

René stayed between Picard and Crusher, crouched against their low bulwark. Whenever he saw a clean shot, either at the attackers on bridge one or behind Crusher and Picard on bridge three, he snapped off a few bursts with his compact phaser. By the time the lad had picked off his third Naga, Picard had marveled at his son's keen marksmanship. But when he looked back to compliment the lad, he saw his son's eyes were wide with terror.

A death bolt's near-miss ricocheted off the core and stung Picard's face with cold sparks. He shouted to La Forge. "Geordi! How much longer?"

La Forge peeked around the reactor. "Four minutes, forty-two seconds!"

"Is the signal link ready?"

"Not yet. Another minute."

From the other side of the core, Keeso called out, "We got a problem!"

At the far end of bridge three, a squad of avatars armed with jewel-topped bone quarterstaffs were shooting at the TFA the team had placed in the middle of the bridge.

Keeso broke from cover and ran toward the bridge. "Rozhenko! Suppressing fire!"

Alexander rolled left so he could see past Keeso, and then he raked the avatars on the far side of the bridge with phaser pulses. Keeso fired his rifle in a steady orange beam as he charged, sweeping it across the enemy's front line—

Then an avatar's lucky shot blew up the TFA.

The blue orb of protective energy popped like a soap bubble—if soap bubbles were filled with hurricanes.

The shock wave threw Keeso through the air and slammed Alexander into the core. Keeso landed hard on the platform, just out of Alexander's reach. The stunned security officer tried to get up in spite of being dazed. Unsteady and confused, he staggered while reaching for his rifle—and never saw the enemy death bolt that cut a hole through his torso.

Keeso's dead body hit the platform like a sack of wet sand.

Alexander switched his phaser to pulsed fire and lit up the enemy horde pouring off bridge three, onto the platform. He shouted to Crusher as he continued firing, "Help!"

Crusher turned away from Picard to back up Alexander.

More squads of staff-armed avatars appeared at the far ends of bridges one and two, and barraged those crossings in order to land lucky shots on their respective TFAs.

Picard foresaw the catastrophe. The center could not hold.

So let's redefine where the center is.

"Worf! Push them back! René! Cover me!"

Picard advanced, rifle braced against his shoulder, firing wide beams of killing power into the heart of the avatars' formation. Protective fire from René flew past him on his left, striking avatars and their morbid weapons, reducing the hostile fire coming back at Picard.

He had almost reached bridge one when its TFA exploded.

A searing gust struck Picard and shriveled his already thinning eyebrows as a shock front swatted him backward. He rolled as he hit the platform and kept hold of his rifle.

René hectored the enemy with orange blasts as Picard retreated behind the console wall. Alexander had also fallen back to the core, to stand with Crusher.

Picard saw dozens of avatars crossing bridge one, and just as many on bridge three, while several others on the landings behind both groups of attackers rained death rays down upon the away team as cover for the assault.

Picard hollered through the din, "Alexander! Blow the bridges!"

"Keeso had the detonator!"

"*Merde.*"

Worf and K'Ehleyr had forced the enemy to abandon its attack on bridge two, but their valor would be of little value if the avatars overran the platform from its two other crossings.

Picard considered his options—sending someone to get the detonator from Keeso's body, or overloading three of the team's rifles to use as bombs to blow the bridges—when he heard a proud exclamation of "Yes!" from La Forge.

"Geordi? Is it done?"

"Signal link secure! As soon as Data sends—"

A death ray slammed into La Forge's back and threw him against the core. His face slackened as his body went limp and collapsed to the platform. Pale tendrils of neural energy snaked from his head and were pulled away and devoured by an avatar.

There was no time for Picard to call out his friend's name. No time to shout a warning or a denial. One moment La Forge had been there, and the next he was gone.

Terrifying shrieks echoed through the endless passageways of the station. Eerie, inhuman cries that sent chills up Picard's spine.

Terrified, René looked at Picard. "Papa? We're not gonna make it, are we?"

Picard steeled himself for the inevitable.

Crusher masked her fear with determination. "Here they come."

She hefted her rifle over the console and eyed its targeting sight.

A gust of rancid air from the far passageways told the away team what was coming: avatars, more of them than they had ever seen before.

Picard braced his rifle. Beside him, René quaked with dread.

Then, from the passageways beyond bridges one and three, came sounds that Picard had not expected, but which now sounded to him like the sweetest music he had ever heard:

Screeches of transphasic rifles firing at full power.

Double-kick explosions of hybrid plasma-photon grenades.

Bellicose cries of "Charge!" and "Fire!"

Brilliant flashes of orange and white banished the shadows and scattered the avatars and Nagas—all except a few who tried to flee across the bridges, toward the platform.

Picard sighted the closest charging Naga in his rifle's holographic scope—only to see it disintegrated by a massively powerful transphasic pulse from behind.

More blazing orange beams screamed out of the shadows of both tunnels, vaporizing avatars and Nagas on both compromised bridges. Then the shooters appeared from the tunnels, stepping briskly over and around the scorched bodies of the fallen:

Two security teams in Starfleet uniforms with fully loaded tactical vests.

Leading the team across bridge one . . . was Rear Admiral William T. Riker.

Just a step behind him was his ever-loyal Caitian aide, Lieutenant Ssura, for once toting a rifle instead of a padd, followed by a team of eight *Titan* security officers.

The security officers fanned out onto the platform. Behind Picard, eight more of Riker's people deployed from bridge three into defensive stances around the core.

Riker lowered his rifle as he approached Picard. He stopped in front of him, cracked his trademark boyish smile, and offered Picard his hand. "Sorry I kept you waiting, Jean-Luc."

Picard ignored Riker's proffered handshake and embraced his dear friend, pride and decorum be damned. His voice broke as he said, "Good to have you back, Will."

Their embrace was warm but short-lived. Around them, the passageways resounded with the rumblings of a new, even larger assault massing against them. Riker frowned in concern. "Sounds like they're up for a rematch. How long do we have to finish this?"

Picard checked his chrono. "Three minutes, twenty-five seconds."

"All right. You stand by to trigger the recursion. My team and I will hold the line." Riker put his rifle to his shoulder and faced bridge one. "Let's get this done."

U.S.S. *Titan* NCC-80102—Intertime

Half of *Titan*'s bridge was aflame. Another salvo from the Devidians' station pummeled the ship, raining sparks and chunks of the overhead onto Captain Christine Vale. She shook off the torrent of hot bits and looked to her first officer. "Did they make it?"

Sarai was behind Vale at the security chief's console, which had been left vacant when both Keru and his deputy chief, Lieutenant sh'Aqabaa, joined the admiral's away team to the enemy station. The first officer held up one hand to beg patience from Vale. Then her face brightened. "Affirmative! They've joined Captain Picard's team at the core." She checked the readout, then smiled with bittersweet pride. "The admiral's final order is 'Leave it all on the field.' "

At the tactical station, Tuvok was immersed in waging *Titan*'s attack on the station as well as managing the ship's defense. "Dorsal shields failing," he declared.

Vale's training kicked in: "Helm, roll hard to starboard, show them our belly! Tuvok, reroute dorsal shield power to ventral."

The image on the main viewscreen spun and pitched as Tuvok replied in confirmation, "Rerouting power—Naga inbound!"

"Brace for—!" The behemoth's high-speed collision rocked *Titan* as hard as any photon-torpedo blast and slammed Vale's guts against her bones.

On her right, the engineering station exploded, nearly tearing poor Torvig in half and scouring the bridge with glassy shrapnel. A hot chunk caromed off Vale's forehead.

Blood spilled over her brows and into her eyes.

We won't last much longer. Gotta make every second count.

Pazlar—scorched, half her exoskeleton mangled, and clutching a bloody wound on her left side—staggered from her console toward Vale. "Captain! Huge energy surge inside the station! I think the Devidians are taking Oblivion's Gate to full power—which means they're about to unravel our timeline, once and for all."

Vale marshaled every bit of courage she had left. "This is it, people! Give those bastards everything we've got—because *there is no tomorrow.*"

37

Temporal Disruption Base—2373, Borg Timeline

The rifle was overheating in Bashir's hands. He had been firing nonstop for almost two minutes, and its emitter crystal, power cell, and prefire chamber all were becoming too hot to handle.

But the Borg drones kept attacking, no matter how many Bashir vaporized, or how many he left in scorched heaps, twitching like wounded insects. Each time, the next drone in the pack was that much closer to him before being cut down by his ruthlessly perfect marksmanship.

A few more seconds, and they'll be shooting me full of nanites.

He took his right hand off the rifle's front grip and reached for the type-2 phaser pistol on his belt. The quarter of a second it took him to draw, aim, and fire a full-power, tight-beam shot was a risk, but one that paid off: the beam cut the six nearest drones in half, bisecting each of them at a shallow angle across the lower torso.

For a fraction of a second, he felt just a bit proud of himself.

Then a drone's plasma burst hit him just below his tactical vest. White-hot, more pain than he'd ever felt in his life. Like having a star pop into existence inside his gut.

The impact knocked him backward, and he pivoted with the blow, around the corner to cover. Then he looked down and wished he hadn't. A gaping wound in his abdomen sizzled with fresh heat and reeked of cooked flesh. Several of his internal organs lay exposed.

He didn't need a tricorder to know his prognosis. At best, he had half a minute before he went into shock and became a useless pile of meat on the floor.

He looked at Data, then at Lal. Both noted his wound in silence, then met his gaze.

His breaths became quick and shallow. Sweat coated his forehead. He was getting dizzy.

Only seconds left. Time to go.

His voice was hoarse and trembling. "Good luck, Data."

Data gave him a nod of thanks. Lal did the same, with tears in her eyes.

Bashir focused the willpower of his genetically enhanced brain. Forced himself to push through his pain. Ignored the burning agony in his guts. Steadied himself.

And turned the corner.

Pivoting, he fired the rifle in his left hand and the pistol phaser in his right. Shooting one and then the other, in short overlapping bursts, he felled three ranks of drones, then four, and a fifth before he reached the open doorway to the vast space outside the control room.

Bashir paused long enough to arm the last six grenades on his vest. The high-explosive charges started blinking, signaling that their countdown to detonation had begun.

He turned the last corner and stumble-jogged away from the control room, firing his weapons madly in every direction as he charged into the midst of dozens of Borg drones that had assembled in the atrium space.

The dark mass converged upon him. Mottled-gray hands seized his rifle, grabbed his pistol arm, held him fast. He was pinned, trapped, surrounded by Borg.

Time felt elastic, bordering on phantasmagoric, as the Borg smothered him. He felt dissociated from himself, as if he were witnessing his fate through another person's eyes.

Detached from his present, his thoughts turned toward the past.

Toward all those he had lost. All those he had failed or wronged.

Jadzia, who had died despite his best efforts to save her.

Ezri, whose love he had squandered, whose forgiveness he had failed to appreciate, and whose life had ended countless light-years away from his.

Sarina, whose mind and spirit had been broken by Section 31's insane master, an artificial superintelligence known as Control.

The countless innocent lives he had taken in cold blood, all in the name of duty, on the Breen world of Salavat.

And Garak—anything-but-plain-and-simple Garak.

I took his friendship for granted. He showed me the most selfless love I've ever known. I owed him so much more. So much better.

But beyond all of Bashir's innumerable regrets, he remembered his triumphs.

Giving up his career and his freedom by defying the Federation's unjust laws in order to solve the Andorian reproductive crisis and restore hope to an entire species.

Sacrificing all that he'd had, and the woman he'd loved, to expose and bring down the illegal terrorist cabal known as Section 31.

All the patients whose lives he had saved on his operating table. Preventing Section 31's attempted genocide of the Dominion's ruling species, the Founders. Risking his life to stop the release of a plague on the Romulan world of Alhaya.

He had no idea if the virtues of his life would outweigh his sins. But he knew that when called upon to make one last sacrifice, he had answered the call without protest or delay.

Hundreds of Borg assimilation tubules snaked toward him.

The grenades on his vest ceased blinking and flashed a solid cluster of red.

The last thing he heard was his own labored wheezing for air.

Julian Subatoi Bashir smiled as the explosives at his hip detonated—a flash of sound and fury that, for just one moment, signified everything.

Devidian Temporal Collider—Intertime

Defending the chroniton core was like trying to fight the ocean. One ghostly wave of avatars after another rushed from the passageways and across the unshielded bridges, becoming solid when they collided with the faltering blue sphere of energy that encompassed the hexagonal platform and everyone upon it.

Only then, at a range of five meters, could Riker's people reliably target the enemy.

He was assailed by the screeching of a dozen weapons firing at once, and the unsteady, crackling hum of the team's last transphasic-field attenuator.

If that fails, we're as good as dead.

Just inside the energy field, the platform was strewn with the smoldering corpses of Nagas and avatars, and the glassy-eyed bodies of Starfleet personnel whose neural energies the enemy had devoured. Among the dead were six of *Titan*'s best security personnel, including lieutenants Sortollo and Denken, Chief Petty Officer Dennisar, and Petty Officer Krotine. But for Riker the cruelest cut had been losing Ssura. The Caitian had been the first of *Titan*'s people to fall, when he threw himself in front of an avatar's death-pulse to save his admiral.

He honored me with his life. I won't let his sacrifice be wasted.

But there was no winning against such overwhelming numbers. No way to hold the line. The Devidians could afford to sacrifice thousands of their avatars to the attenuation field to kill just one of the people defending Picard. The enemy had the numbers to spare.

Reapers to the left of me, reapers to the right . . . and one of them has my name on it.

Riker lined up the targeting sight of his rifle and picked off three more avatars as they solidified at the platform's edge. *They'll never run out of bodies before we run out of time.*

From the right, Lieutenant sh'Aqabaa called out, "They're flanking us!"

"Blow bridge two!" Keru shouted.

Worf snapped, "The bridges support the platform!"

Before anyone could retort, the blue sphere of energy on the platform flickered and shrank to half its diameter. The away team was all but pinned against the chroniton core, with no room to strike the enemy at range before engaging them point-blank.

Picard ended the debate. "Number One! Blow the bridge!"

Worf pulled Keeso's recovered detonator from his belt and pushed the trigger.

A blinding flash coupled with a bone-jarring *boom* made Riker feel as if his innards had been put through a centrifuge. When his eyes adjusted, he saw a spreading blossom of carnelian flames littered with debris from the obliterated bridge.

A sickening groan of wrenching metal accompanied the platform's abrupt downward tilt, toward the gap left by its demolished crossing.

Half the away team tumbled across the platform or sprawled against the core. The avatars and Nagas inside the energy field rolled along with them, a jumbled chaos of bodies in motion, prisoners of gravity and momentum. Dozens of Nagas and avatars who had been closer to the platform's edge fell over it and plunged into the chasm's Stygian depths.

The first of the away team's fallen to recover her balance was sh'Aqabaa. The tall Andorian *shen* braced herself, leveled her rifle, and swiftly picked off the last few avatars left on the slumped portion of the platform. Then she turned about and snapped orders as she jogged toward Picard. "Squads! Regroup!" She grabbed up the portable TFA unit from the platform and lobbed it to Ensign Hriss. As the female Caitian caught the device, sh'Aqabaa added, "Put it there! Push our perimeter onto the last two bridges! Squads, covering fire!"

An orange firestorm of transphasic blasts blazed toward the last two bridges, buying Hriss the seconds she needed to place the failing TFA unit in a better position.

As the Caitian retreated to rejoin her comrades on the firing line, fresh waves of avatars rushed onto the two remaining bridges and ran like wildlings toward the away team.

Riker knew that detonating more of the bridges was not an option, and the TFA wouldn't last half a minute if another Naga sacrificed itself to crush the team's final defense.

We're fighting for seconds now. Time to make every one count.

A flash, a pop, and a puff of smoke from the muzzle of K'Ehleyr's rifle told her the weapon's emitter crystal had fractured under the stress of constant firing. She ejected her rifle's power cell, hurled the rest of the weapon at the nearest charging avatar, then lobbed the still half-charged power cell to one of *Titan's* security officers as she fell back behind the line.

Worf was still at the front of the line, leading the counterattack to hold bridge three, with his son Alexander at his side. Both of them snapped off shots quickly, roaring with battle rage as they fought to hold a few precious meters of ground just a few seconds longer.

Watching father and son revel in the fury of battle stirred primitive feelings in K'Ehleyr's heart; it awakened a fierce pride and a primal sense of belonging. Growing up among the scientists of Memory

Omega, she had spent her life eschewing her Klingon heritage. Now it had come alive within her, risen with a vengeance.

A fusillade of avatars' death rays slammed into the line of *Titan* officers. They fell in numbers, including their Trill commander, their life-forces rising from them in vaporous gray curls, like wisps of smoke from snuffed candles.

Alexander, Worf, and K'Ehleyr were the only ones left defending this flank.

Then a Naga lurched ahead of an avatar and chomped Worf's rifle in two.

Worf stabbed the sparking halves of his weapon into its eyes.

As the Naga shrieked in pain, Worf drew his *bat'leth* from his back.

He felled the keening beast in one stroke. And then he charged.

Worf ran to the very edge of the platform's protective energy field, to meet the enemy head-on—and Alexander charged beside him, firing his modified phaser in one hand and swinging a *d'k tahg* in the other.

K'Ehleyr drew the *mek'leth* Worf had given her and sprinted to his side.

For the first time in her life, she understood what it meant to feel Klingon.

They held the end of the bridge with steel and courage. Worf's broad curved blade, its edge enhanced with a monomolecular filament, hacked through avatars with fearsome grace.

If one of the fiends eluded Worf on his left, Alexander met it with dagger and phaser. If an enemy escaped to Worf's right, K'Ehleyr butchered it with lightning strikes of her short blade.

Then a Naga appeared all but on top of Worf and sank its fangs into his throat.

K'Ehleyr severed the serpent's head with her *mek'leth*.

The beast's jaw opened as it died, and its armored head fell from Worf's throat—leaving his savaged arteries free to sheet bright magenta blood down the front of his uniform.

Alexander phasered an avatar into dust as it reached out to steal Worf's soul.

Worf's knees buckled.

Alexander caught Worf as he fell and tried to drag him away from the bridge.

It was the act of a grieving son, not a trained soldier.

K'Ehleyr shouted, "No! Keep fighting!"

He froze at her command—and a shot from an avatar's staff struck his abdomen.

Alexander dropped Worf and fell beside him.

They lay side by side, bleeding and gasping for air.

That was enough to draw the avatars, the universe's ultimate carrion feeders. The black-robed vampires of time and memory stampeded over the now-undefended bridge. A pack of them peeled off to swarm Worf and Alexander in a frenzy to drink their souls.

K'Ehleyr took up Worf's *bat'leth* and leaped into the thick of the enemy.

"Get back!" She whipped the great blade in majestic arcs, cleaving flesh and bone, filling the air with sprays of alien blood. "You cannot have them! You filthy *petaQpu'*!"

Viscera flew from the blade's points. On her backswing, she used the sword's weight and momentum to knock a pair of avatars away from Alexander and off the platform. She swung again and tore the head off the next one that tried to dine on Worf.

"No! They're *mine*! Mine!"

This is what it means to be *Klingon.*

To savor the cries of my enemies and feel their blood on my face.

K'Ehleyr delighted in the poetry of motion, the dance of the blade. Fearless and defiant, she stood alone, a lioness defending her mate and cub with fang and claw.

My Klingon ancestors would be proud.

A paralyzing blast of pain erupted in her lower back.

Her world flashed white and then washed to scarlet.

Gravity pulled her down and stole the blade from her hands.

She landed on her back, atop Worf and Alexander.

Above her, the avatars swarmed to gorge themselves on three Klingon souls—only to be lit up by a barrage of phaser fire. Enraged, the ghouls abandoned their feast and charged away, toward whatever was left of the away team defending the chroniton core.

Avatars surged past, the dying trio seemingly forgotten.

Worf's last breath rattled in his throat.

The light faded from Alexander's eyes.

K'Ehleyr's vision dimmed as if obscured by countless falling veils.

She let go of her life, aglow with pride.

Prepare a feast, heroes of Sto-Vo-Kor—*a family of warriors is coming.*

38

———

C.S.S. Defiant—Mirror Universe

Vedek Kira looked up as Captain Dax's voice issued from the cargo bay's overhead speakers, loud and full of fear: *"Shields are gone! Multiple hull breaches! Warp core breach in—"*

Static spewed from the speaker as blasts like strikes from a god-hammer pounded *Defiant II*. The main lights had gone dark moments earlier; now the emergency lights went out.

The only light left in the cargo bay was the magenta radiance of the Orb of Time.

Kira held her quantum communicator to her ear. No one was speaking. All she heard over the channel was a din of struggle and flight. Had the mission failed?

Outside the cargo bay, some portion of *Defiant II* exploded.

The detonation's shock front hit Kira like a punch from a fifty-kilogram fist as wide as her entire body. It threw her forward in a wild somersault. She tried to drape herself over the Orb, to protect it, but she flew past it and landed hard on the cold metal deck.

As she looked up, air rushed past her like a wave receding into the sea.

It took her half a second to realize all the air was leaving the cargo bay.

There was a hull breach force fields hadn't sealed. In a matter of seconds, all the air inside *Defiant II* would be gone, vented into the transdimensional space of the wormhole.

If I die, the Orb will go dark—and the team will lose its beacon.

Around her, the bulkheads moaned with the deep, sickly voice of dense metal being deformed by the irresistible forces of nature. Fractures appeared on the high gray walls. The cracks widened, grew, split, and branched. Then the outer bulkhead—the only one that separated the cargo bay from exposure to the vacuum of space—bulged and twisted.

Kira had seen this happen to other starships, but always from the outside. In less than two seconds, whatever remained of *Defiant II* would break up into a cloud of debris and scatter itself into the churning chaos of the wormhole's interior—and her with it.

There was no time to think, only to act. She did what every vedek, every tenet of her Bajoran faith, had warned her all her life never to do, not for any reason, ever.

She seized the Orb of Time with her bare hands.

Stop. I am the Hand of the Prophets. Stop . . .

The roar of the ship's breakup deepened and distorted, like a voice underwater. It became a steady drone so low in frequency that Kira felt it like a tingling in her teeth. Around her, the buckling of the bulkheads slowed until she could count every speck of dust, and track every splinter of steel as it tumbled through the air. Above her, inside the broken panels of the overhead, sparks within a ruptured EPS conduit presaged an explosion that would vaporize the cargo bay in a flash, leaving nothing but free radicals and heat radiation.

Stop.

Around Kira, time halted.

Alone inside her own personal sphere of eternity, she felt this alternate dimension's river of time strain to break free of her will. The rest of the strike team, no longer in this dimension but split into two other parallel branches of time, were beyond Kira's reach—which was just as well, because she needed them to be free to move forward, and to reach the end.

As the cosmos tried to seduce Kira back into its embrace, she realized she wasn't holding the universe frozen—no, she had removed herself from its dominion, into her own dimension of intertime, stretching her oasis of a single irreducible monad of time into however great an island of refuge would be required to let her friends finish what they had begun.

She knew she wouldn't be able to hold herself outside of time forever, but that she would do so for as long as she needed.

The Hand of the Prophets beheld Time incarnate, in the palm of her hand.

"When this ends, I will never have existed. No one will remember me. Or what I did."

The Sisko Prophet leaned into view beside her, a visitor in her oasis. He set his hand atop hers on the Orb of Time.

"*We* remember. *Forever.*"

U.S.S. Titan NCC-80102—Intertime

The battle was over. All that was left for Dalit Sarai to do was fulfill her captain's dying wish.

Titan's bridge was aflame, its dead officers lying where they had fallen. Tuvok was draped like a shroud over his cracked, flickering console. Faunlike Torvig Bu-Kar-Nguv was behind his station, his body almost cut in half, his cybernetic eyes gone dark forever. At conn and ops, Aili Lavena and Sariel Rager had been thrown together in their last moments, and now they lay tangled for eternity like dancers frozen midstep.

At the aft stations, Doctor Ra-Havreii sat and wept beside a heap of mangled wreckage while holding the pale, fragile hand of Melora Pazlar—the only part of her he could reach.

Sarai swatted the tactical display beside her chair until its controls stuttered into view. Automated damage reports confirmed what her senses had told her: *Titan* was hobbled and defenseless. Warp and impulse engines were damaged beyond repair. Shields and weapons were offline and not coming back. The autodestruct system was offline because both of the ship's computer cores had been completely shredded by Nagas.

Casualty estimates were just as discouraging. There were no life signs in the engineering section. Sickbay had taken a direct hit minutes earlier, and there had been no response from belowdecks since then. Sarai assumed with regret that Doctor Ree and his staff were already lost.

Through the main viewscreen's hashed static she saw the Devidians' station, sections of its outer shell damaged but most of its hideous mass untouched. Floating around it like a million tiny satellites were the remains of all the starships it had destroyed in the past hour, and plowing through that were dozens of gigantic Nagas, circling for another pass at *Titan*.

Sarai looked to her captain.

Christine Vale was still upright in her command chair, her head listing toward her right shoulder, her eyes open but bereft of life. A sharp hunk of shrapnel thrown from the forward bulkhead protruded from her throat. The front of her uniform was drenched in her blood, and her face had gone gray from exsanguination.

But she had never surrendered.

Looking at her, Sarai remembered her promise to carry out Vale's last order. One final act of spite.

She stood. Limped forward, stepped over Rager's and Lavena's bodies, and took the helm. Warp and impulse were gone, but the ship's thrusters were strong enough to do what needed to be done. She plotted a course straight into the heart of the station.

I'd rather have taken out their domed arena at the top, but we'll never get there on thrusters. So this'll have to do.

The helm rejected her course request with an error message: COLLISION RISK.

She keyed in her command code and engaged the manual override.

Eight seconds to collision once I press ENGAGE.

Sarai opened a comm channel to the away team inside the station, and also an internal channel, broadcasting to all sections of *Titan* that were still intact.

"All hands, this is *Titan* XO. Brace for impact, eight seconds from my mark." Eight seconds wasn't enough time for anyone to abandon ship, but that was irrelevant. They were all long since past the point of rescue. All that was left now was the mission.

"Mark."

She pressed ENGAGE.

The delta-*v* of acceleration pressed her back into her chair.

On the viewscreen, the station's hull filled the frame.

Sarai ignored the countdown to impact.

Watching her own end rushing up to meet her, she felt transcendently light, as if she had cast off all her cares, all her desires, so she could fully be here *now*, in this moment.

She smiled the way that she would if she knew a good joke she had not yet told.

And met her end with both heart and eyes wide open.

There was no choice but to lie. It was the only merciful thing to do.

Deanna Troi hugged her daughter, Natasha Miana Riker-Troi. She curled one arm around the little girl's head to keep her from seeing the nightmare outside their quarters' slanted viewports. "Close your eyes, sweetheart."

First Officer Sarai's staticky voice issued from the overhead speaker: *"All hands, this is* Titan *XO. Brace for impact, eight seconds from my mark."*

Confusion and fear poured from six-year-old Tasha. "Mom? What's happening?"

"It'll be all right," Troi lied, thankful that her daughter didn't share her Betazoid empathic talents. "Just hang on to me."

"Where's Dad?"

"Close. We'll be together soon."

Troi calmed herself and focused on the residual empathic bond she shared with her daughter. With effort, she could impart emotions to the girl as well as read them. She blocked out the distant wailing of the red-alert siren and the rumbles of buckling hull plates, and concentrated on sending waves of peaceful calm into Tasha's mind.

Sarai's voice intoned from the ship's PA system, *"Mark."*

Eight seconds.

Troi reached out in desperation for her *imzadi*, hoping as she did that her anguish wouldn't infect Tasha.

Please hear me, Imzadi. *Will, please say you hear me.*

Riker's voice and his emotional presence manifested in Troi's mind, as tangible to her as if he were standing beside her in the flesh. «*I'm here,* Imzadi.»

Troi drew upon every lesson her mother had ever given her in order to use her empathic talent as a conduit, to link Tasha and Riker. It took all her strength to help Tasha block out the chaos around them, so that they all could sense one another.

We only have seconds, Imzadi. *We love you.*

As Troi heard Tasha's mental voice inside her thoughts, full of trepidation but perfectly earnest and pure, she shed tears of joy: «*I love you, Dad.*»

Riker's reply was fraught with the heightened emotions of battle, and the drowning sensation of unimaginable grief: «*I love you, too. I love you both so much, more than—*»

Everything around Troi and Tasha became white light, and a heat so intense and all-consuming that it didn't leave them even a millisecond in which to feel pain.

And then all that Troi and Tasha were, and all they had ever been, became nothing at all.

Devidian Temporal Collider—Intertime

. . . more than life itself.

Riker knew before he finished his thought that his wife and daughter were gone.

Then came the distant bedlam of *Titan* crashing through the station's hull. The platform quaked violently, nearly knocking Riker and his companions off their feet.

Avatars wailed and Nagas hissed, but Riker heard nothing over his own bellows, roars of rageful anguish for his *imzadi* that made Lear's great howls pale in comparison.

Riker's reason for living was gone, stolen in a crush of impact and a burst of fire.

He planted his feet, steadied himself. And swept a beam of phaser energy in a long, devastating arc through the ranks of the enemy.

Out of the corner of his eye he saw that Worf, Alexander, and— *was that K'Ehleyr?*—had fallen. Avatars were flooding over the bridge unchecked. Lieutenant sh'Aqabaa and Ensign Hriss stood shoulder to shoulder, pulverizing one rank of attackers after another, but the platform was being overrun. They could delay the inevitable only for so long.

Behind the Caitian and the Andorian, Crusher and her boy René— *when did he get so big?*—picked off any attackers they could, but Riker saw that they were out of their depth.

Riker and two *Titan* security officers were all that stood between a mad alien horde and the last three people he loved. In the name of duty, brotherhood, and friendship, Riker vowed he would not let them die before he did. He would not let them fail.

Tears streamed down his face as he obliterated another line of avatars.

For you, Imzadi. *I'll finish this for you.*

39

—•—

Temporal Disruption Base—2373, Borg Timeline

"Data! We need that equation!"

"Just a few more seconds, Captain! The *Enterprise* is entering the temporal vortex."

Over the quantum comm, Picard shouted to be heard above the pandemonium that had engulfed him and the last of the strike team. *"Now or never, Data!"*

The fury of close-quarters battle raged mere meters behind Data. Lal was at the corner of the narrow passage to the now-demolished main door. Borg drones pushed one another through the open doorway, into her line of fire, with such zeal that Data wondered if they might be acting out of a death wish as their only means of escape from the Collective.

It seemed to him that Lal's position was strong enough to hold a few seconds more—and then drones began climbing out of the pit in the middle of the room.

Lal stepped away from the corner and faced the breach in the floor.

She aimed her rifle and fired a long burst over the heads of the drones climbing from the pit. Then she walked calmly toward Data, ostensibly satisfied with her handiwork.

A massive, cylindrical iron tank—rusted, and clearly centuries past its last useful day—wobbled on the only one of its three steel supports Lal had left intact. The other two she had melted into slag. The tank fell toward the middle of the room and landed like a blow from the hand of God, crushing the drones emerging from the pit and caving in the wall of the narrow entryway, conveniently burying the main door in several tons of broken concrete and rebar.

The tank's crash and the wall's collapse filled the room with a billowing cloud of gray smoke. Listening to the patter of falling dust and shifting debris, Data noted with approval the return of something he had too long taken for granted: quiet.

Lal stood beside him and took his hand in hers.

He adjusted his eyes' frequency range to penetrate the dusty haze, so he could be sure the console was still functioning and his quantum comm channel remained open. Then, for several milliseconds, he tasked every connection in his positronic brain with finishing the final equation to undo the Borg's temporal sabotage. He entered the last variable at the precise moment when the Borg's temporal disruptor discharged—causing it this time to emit nothing but useless heat.

"Captain: original divergence event averted. Transmitting final equation."

It took a few seconds for Picard to reply, *"Received!"*

"Initiate temporal recursion!"

He expected Captain Picard to act with dispatch. Data had, perhaps, less than a second before the First Splinter timeline would curve back upon itself and retroactively prevent its own creation. Not enough time for him to say out loud all he wanted to tell his cherished daughter— but more than enough time for them to share it, one positronic mind to another, via the encrypted quantum transceivers he had created for their brains after he had resurrected her years earlier.

These are moments I did not expect us to have, Lal, but I am thankful for them.

«As am I, Father.»

The first time I lost you, I downloaded your memories, so that part of you would always stay with me. So that the unique experience of your life would not be lost.

In a flood of information, he showed her all he had done, and all that had been lost, to bring her back to life: Noonian Soong, who had cheated death by transferring his consciousness into a new android body, and later sacrificed his potentially immortal life so he could re-incarnate Data by giving his son his body to use as his own; the quest that led Data to the immortal known as Emil Vaslovik—the only person who possessed the unique set of skills and knowledge that Data had needed to bring back Lal; and the moment when, forced to choose between saving Rhea McAdams, the android woman he loved, or Emil

Vaslovik, the only man who could resurrect Lal . . . Data had let his dear, sweet Rhea die for just a chance at bringing back Lal.

The person I was when I made you would not have done that. After I brought you online, I wondered whether I would ever be able to understand, never mind feel, *parental love. But when I was reborn in this mind that my father made for himself, based on his own neural engrams, I inherited the mania that drove him to sacrifice everything to restore me. That obsession drove me to risk everything and everyone in my life . . . for you.*

Through their shared link, he felt Lal's outpouring of love, sympathy, and gratitude.

«I would never have asked you to do that, Father. But I'm glad you did.»

And I would not trade for anything a single moment of the time we have shared, Lal. Of all the wonders I have seen in my travels . . . you are the most complex and beautiful of them all.

Tachyons and antichronitons rippled through their quantum channel.

«Is this it, Father? The recursion?»

I think it is, Lal.

There was no time in the physical world for either of them to shed a tear, but they both expressed the figurative notion of doing so as they realized their remaining time would be measured in nanoseconds.

«I hope we can be together again, in one of the realities we've saved.»

I am sure we will be.

«Thank you for my life, Father. Both for making me, and for bringing me back. Though, if we had it to do over again . . .»

Yes, Lal?

«I would have liked to have had a sister.»

I will keep that in mind.

Devidian Temporal Collider—Intertime

"Captain: original divergence event averted. Transmitting final equation."

Picard could barely hear Data over the whine of phaser fire, the howling of avatars thirsting for souls less than two meters away, and the keening of the Nagas as they struck and recoiled, over and again, like barbed whips of bone and shadow.

The Caitian ensign who had arrived with Riker's team stumbled backward. As she fell, Picard saw the ragged bite a Naga had taken from her golden-furred throat. Hriss reached up, tried to stanch the bleeding with her paw, but it was too late. As Hriss's body struck the platform, sh'Aqabaa vaporized the Naga who'd killed her.

The towering Andorian *shen* was all that stood now between the unstoppable crush of the enemy and Crusher and René, whose backs, like Riker's, now were pressed up against Picard.

They've made a wall of themselves to defend me, when I should be protecting them.

The holographic interface La Forge had added to the chroniton core confirmed the relay of Data's formula from the quantum communicator. The trigger pad turned green.

"Received!"

"Initiate temporal recursion!"

It was time.

Picard reached for the holographic trigger. With one touch he would make the Devidians' own abomination undo their countless evils—but also erase the future that he and billions of others had fought and bled to create and defend.

He froze, struck by the existential horror of the moment.

René wrapped one arm around Picard's waist.

Crying, Crusher embraced Picard and their son. "Do it."

Death rained down upon Riker and sh'Aqabaa in a storm of lethal silver.

A hundred ghostly hands reached out to steal Picard's family from him.

He kissed his wife for the last time.

And he pressed the trigger.

40

Somewhen

The future disappeared into memory. History retreated into the womb of uncreated night, and the ever-elusive *now*, that four-dimensional illusion, became a fulcrum for the shifting of time.

Standing astride it all, at the still point in the center of eternity, was Jean-Luc Picard.

He watched realities crash like waves. One after another they appeared, only to fade away, their possibilities expended, their outcomes and potentials unmade. He saw all that he'd ever been, all of his possible pasts, and every iteration of what he might have become. Waveforms of quantum probability rose and fell in endless varieties, nearly all of them doomed to collapse to zero and wash away like sea-foam in an ebbing tide.

Nevertheless, an infinitesimal percentage of them persisted, even if only for a moment, before they succumbed to the insatiable appetite of entropy. Forever dwelled in those moments, in those glimmers of chance made manifest.

But as Picard watched time devour its orphans, he knew that his regrets for roads not taken had shaped his soul as much as the contentment he'd found in those he had followed.

I carry all of my possibilities within me . . . always.
I contain multitudes.

The loam is cool and sticks to five-year-old Jean-Luc's tiny fingers.

He shapes the spring-damp soil with his hands, does his best to make it match the picture in his mind. Rolling waves. Peaks and troughs.

He toils in the shade of his family's house, a grand château of brick and limestone. This field, on what he calls "the sunset side" of the house, had been empty all winter. When the snow melted, the barren patch of dirt had stretched to the nearby woods, flat and smooth.

This morning, however, Jean-Luc had woken to find the field no longer smooth, but transformed into a march of widely spaced, parallel waves. His own private ocean.

Too excited to eat breakfast, he had ignored the calls of his mother. Toting a pillowcase full of toy ships—tiny replicated models of ancient, wind-driven vessels from what the history vids called "the Age of Sail"—Jean-Luc had slipped out the back door and sprinted off to chart a course across his newfound sea.

What will I find? New lands? Dragons? The edge of the world?

Fueled by wonder, Jean-Luc orchestrates epic sea battles. He sends countless ships beyond the horizon. Some brave terrible storms. Others match wits with monsters as mysterious and as powerful as the ocean itself. Into a single morning Jean-Luc packs a lifetime's worth of adventure, a dozen tales of heroic explorers, and all the worlds they've found.

Then comes a voice like a tempest, vulgarities flashing like lightning.

Jean-Luc looks over his shoulder. All he sees is a silhouette, but that's all he needs to recognize his father, Maurice Picard. Broad shouldered and thick trunked, Papa looms over Jean-Luc like a giant. His tirade is fast and full of rage, a torrent of French profanities slurred almost to the point of incoherence. He points, shouts, and slaps the back of Jean-Luc's head.

More invective spills from Papa's mouth, but it happens too quickly for Jean-Luc to understand. He can't track his father's words, only the tone of his volcanic fury.

Papa lifts his booted foot and brings it down like Old Testament retribution upon a cluster of Jean-Luc's treasured ships. The fragile toys crunch and splinter beneath Papa's boot. Growing more enraged by the second, Papa circles Jean-Luc while meting out his mad punishment for a sin Jean-Luc doesn't understand. One crushing stomp after another reduces Jean-Luc's entire fleet to shards and splinters, scattered across the cold earth like the flotsam and jetsam of ships wrecked by Poseidon's fickle wrath.

At last, Papa exhausts himself. Still swearing under his breath, he plods away from the field of destruction. He never looks back to see the tears streaking down Jean-Luc's face.

Eyes burning, nose running with snot, Jean-Luc is still crying when his older brother Robert finds him, sitting in the dirt surrounded by the debris of his once-great armada. The teen echoes their father's pose as he towers over Jean-Luc and eyes him with contempt.

"What were you thinking? Papa just tilled this patch to plant new vines."

It is hard for Jean-Luc to rein in his tears and form words. "I—I just—"

"Never mind. As usual, I have to clean up your mess. Thanks for nothing." Robert marches past Jean-Luc and makes a point of crushing the last bits of his ships.

Like Papa, he walks away without looking back.

Unlike Papa, he laughs as he goes.

"Jean-Luc? I think we've found something over here. Could you come take a look?"

Jean-Luc Picard, PhD, sighed. There was a rhythm to his work, and he disliked being interrupted. He ceased coaxing silt off a fossil, set down his soft-bristle brush, and adjusted his eyeglasses as he looked up at his research partner. "What is it, Linus?"

"Oh, nothing big. Maybe just a clue to the location of the Iconian homeworld."

Just past forty years old, Linus Ramsey, PhD, was nearly two decades younger than Picard. Despite his relative youth, he was as accomplished an archaeologist as Picard was, and in some areas of specialty his expertise was unparalleled.

One of those specialties was Dinasian artifacts. It was Ramsey's search for the foundation of an ancient Dinasian temple that had persuaded Picard to come to Denius III.

Picard set aside his tools and got to his feet, though he had to remain hunched over inside many of the caves they had excavated. The natives of Denius III had been small of stature, so for humans and other bipeds of similar size, these prehistoric catacombs were close quarters.

He gestured toward the exit. "Lead the way, Doctor."

Ramsey led Picard through a warren of caves and lava tubes. Some they and their team had discovered intact. Others they had had Hortas excavate with care over the past few years. Those efforts had yielded hundreds of precious artifacts, including some that dated back as far as 140,000 years. Enough to guarantee Picard a tenured career in academia when he left here.

They arrived in a vast, open cavern deep beneath the planet's surface. Down here, several teams worked, each in their own demarcated zone, on the painstaking task of archaeological excavation. Even with the advantages of twenty-fourth-century technology, this kind of labor required time, patience, and the delicate touch of trained hands.

The pair made their way into the deepest portion of the excavation. All the digging machines and other personnel had been moved clear. Lamps on tall stands ringed this nadir of the dig, all of them casting harsh white light on something at the bottom.

Picard kneeled in front of the object. A curved plate of tarnished metal riddled with engraved markings, some of which were obscured by green oxidized particles.

Ramsey kneeled beside Picard. "Well? What do you think, Jean-Luc?"

He didn't want to be too quick to answer. He studied the plaque's details. Compared them against his memories of others he had exhumed during his decades as an archaeologist. Though his instinct as a scientist was to err on the side of caution, he was excited by what he saw.

"I think you might be right. Some of these markings are Dewan. Some are Iccobarian. Have you determined its age? Or its provenance?"

"All our tests confirm it's been here for at least two hundred twenty thousand years—and that it isn't native to this planet. Its alloy contains elements and isotopes not found naturally on this world." He pointed out several patterns in the markings. "I've seen fragments that had glyphs like these, but never anything like this, all in one piece."

Picard nodded, seeing the possibilities. "Yes, I see what you mean." He sighed in mild frustration. "You realize, of course, we won't be able to decipher these markings without the aid of an advanced computer— and that we can't risk this falling into the hands of the Romulans."

"Yes, Jean-Luc, I know. I'm not stupid."

"Just young," Picard said, needling Ramsey in good fun.

Ramsey grinned. "At least I still have all my hair, old man."

"I presume you've requested aid from Starfleet?"

"Naturally. They're sending one of their new *Galaxy*-class starships to pick us up: the *Yamato*. I told them we'd want to supervise any research of the artifact that occurs on the ship, and they consented to my terms."

"Good." Picard pulled out his holo-scanner and made a recording of the artifact for future study. "How long until *Yamato* arrives?"

"About ten hours. So I'd get packing if I were you."

"Noted."

Ramsey gave Picard a friendly slap on the shoulder as he headed back up the tunnel. "See you at the transport site. And keep this to yourself unless you want to suffer through a nine-hour rant from Doctor Belacqua, demanding to know how you could abandon her like this."

"Also noted."

Picard watched Ramsey leave, while concealing his own mounting excitement. The prospect of a journey aboard any Starfleet starship would fill him with gleeful anticipation, but to be welcomed aboard one of their new *Galaxy*-class ships? He had never dared to hope of such an honor.

That could have been my life.

Afflicted by an acute case of nostalgia, Picard thought back to his youth, and the two years he had spent as a cadet at Starfleet Academy. He had excelled in his studies, and in a variety of athletics . . . until one of his instructors, Professor Richard Galen, persuaded him to abandon a life of military service for one of pure scientific research and discovery.

At the time, it had seemed the logical thing to do.

Forty years had passed since that day. When Picard looked back on his life, he found it filled with wonders, with revelations his work had brought to light. He had authored several books, including a few that had revealed some of the galaxy's greatest myths to be grounded in objectively provable truth. The Preservers. The Shedai. The Tkon.

But this would eclipse them all—the Iconians!

I've lived a life of the mind, on my own terms. How many people ever truly get to say that and mean it? But when I consider how much farther

I might have journeyed as a member of Starfleet, how much more I might have seen . . . I have to wonder what kind of life I might have forged amid the stars.

Four decades. I gave Starfleet my entire adult life. For what?

Lieutenant junior-grade Picard stalked the corridors of the *Enterprise*-D, alone inside a black cloud of resentment. For him it was the end of another year of steadfast service to the astrophysics department, and once again he had failed to earn a place on the science division's promotion list. For decades it had been the same story, repeated annually. Officers half Picard's age leapfrogged past him into leadership roles, senior staff billets, and transfers to the command division. Callow youths without his experience or his desire to serve.

It's unfair. I have so much to offer, and I ask so little.

How many so-called friends had pulled away from him, time and again, when they realized he was never going to climb the ladder? His peers of old, people with whom he had attended Starfleet Academy, had long ago forgotten his name. Even some of his former lovers had pretended not to remember him, rather than indulge his longing for connection.

The best his superiors ever said of his performance was that he was "steady," or that he was "punctual." Who ever ascended to command merely by being punctual?

Each passing year added to Picard's frustration. The more fervently he pursued success, the more his desire to be recognized festered into something cold and bitter.

It was late. Picard knew he should go back to his quarters and try to get some sleep before his next duty shift in the lab, analyzing spectral data from gaseous anomalies in the Keriad Cluster. But he was too anxious, too upset by what Troi had said to him in Ten Forward when he had insisted to her and Commander Riker that he was capable of greater things:

"Hasn't that been the problem all along? Throughout your career you've had lofty goals, but you've never been willing to do what's necessary to attain them."

My dilemma, reduced to its essence.

Riker, of course, had concurred with Troi. "Get noticed," he had counseled Picard. "Stand out in a crowd." As if there were some standard Starfleet protocol for how to do that.

Where did I go wrong? When did my life veer so tragically off target?

Picard searched his memory for some kind of obvious turning point, some crossroads at which he might have made a different choice, one that could have led him to grow into a different man than the passionless, defeated functionary he had become. But he couldn't see one. As far as he could tell, at every opportunity he had made the smart choice, the rational decision.

I played by the rules. Did all they asked of me. So what went wrong?

Nagging at him from somewhere deep in his unconscious mind, a faint and distant voice suggested that the fault was not in his stars but in himself that he was an underling. That perhaps it was the safe path that had led him here because it could lead him nowhere else.

Perhaps if I had sipped from the chalice of my own mortality when I was young, I might have striven to make more of my life. But what good comes from knowing that now? How tragic is wisdom that brings no profit to the wise.

He wandered forlorn into Ten Forward and slumped into a chair beside a window.

Warp-distorted starlight streaked past in blue-shifted swirls.

Picard gazed into the endless void in search of the lost parts of himself.

I could have been so much more than this.

The air in Jean-Luc Picard's hospital room is as cold as the grave and sharp with odors of disinfectant. He blinks his eyes and lets them adjust to the dimness of his surroundings. The holographic display of vital signs above his head paints the narrow space in lime-green light and ink-black shadows.

He searches for a window. Some sign of whether it's day or night, and where he is. Through a narrow parting of the curtains, he spies a desolate landscape of gray desert dotted with craggy rock formations, all blindingly bright against a black starless sky.

I must be on Luna.

An alert chimes softly but insistently from the holo-display above him. It seems an innocent thing, but the longer it continues, the more shrill it sounds to Picard, and the more alarmed he becomes. He tries to sit up, but his body refuses to obey his desires.

Am I dying? What's wrong? What's happening? Why is no one helping?

His respiration quickens. Within seconds he lies gasping, panicking at the prospect of death by suffocation, alone in this tiny room—

A young Cardassian man hurries in. Races to Picard's side. Makes a few tweaks to the settings of the biobed, which folds to bend Picard's legs at the knees, and elevates his upper torso to ease his breathing. The gray-skinned fellow presses a hypospray to Picard's throat. With a soft hiss, state-of-the-art pain relievers flood Picard's bloodstream.

Picard cries out in desperation. "Beverly? Where are you? Where is René?"

The Cardassian presses his hand to Picard's shoulder in an apparent effort at comfort. "Admiral? Are you all right?"

"Who the hell are you?"

"I'm Nurse Eltck Teban."

"Where's Beverly? Where's René?"

Teban looks confused, shakes his head. "I don't know those names, sir."

Enraged, Picard forces Teban to remove his hand. "My wife! My son! Where are they?"

The nurse's confusion turns to pity. "Sir? Your record says you never married or had any children." Observing Picard's distress, Teban's concern deepens. "Is there someone else we can contact for you?"

"Why am I here?"

Teban holds up a holo-padd and turns it to show its display to Picard. "You're in the Starfleet Veterans Hospital, in New Berlin on Luna."

"I know I'm on Luna! I didn't ask *where* I am. I asked *why* I'm here!"

Teban highlights a segment of Picard's patient record and enlarges it to make it easier for Picard to read. "You're being treated for end-stage Irumodic Syndrome, sir."

"Irumodic Syndrome?" Picard's mind races, only to slam into one dead end after another. None of the facts in hand make sense. He shoves the holo-padd back at Teban. "Get me Riker. Or La Forge. Or Data. Someone I can talk to."

The nurse sighs. "Sir, we've explained this before. Admiral William Riker passed away over a decade ago. As did Mister La Forge. And your shipmate Commander Data died saving your life on the Romulan war-bird *Scimitar*, during the Battle of Bassen Rift."

"I know that! But Data came back! His father brought him back!"

Teban shakes his head. He looks heartbroken, as if playing out this moment over and over for months or even years has taken a crushing toll on him. "No, Admiral. He didn't. I'm sorry."

A lifetime of memory crashes onto the shores of Picard's consciousness. Awash in his own history, decades all at once, feels like drowning in emotions.

Recollection brings a grim awareness of the truth.

I've been clinging to life out of nostalgia as much as dementia. Because I'm terrified to learn what lies beyond the veil.

From the doorway comes a trepidatious knock. A woman asks Teban, "Is he awake?"

"Yes, Doctor."

A woman wearing a long white medical jacket enters, steps around the curtain, and smiles at Picard. She is Bajoran, brown skinned, with a head of playfully curly hair and large, kind eyes. She carries something tucked under her arm, a small object wrapped in a shroud.

"How are you feeling today, Admiral?"

"I don't know. Who are you?"

"My name is Doctor Feren Berzel. I'm in charge of your care." She holds up the shrouded object. "I brought what you asked for. It wasn't easy to get, but the fact that it's legally still your property helped a lot." She hands it to Picard.

He removes the delicate shroud to reveal an ornately carved, rectangular metal box. About as long and deep as his forearm, but a bit wider. Nervous, fearful of breaking something, he lifts its lid. Its interior is lined with light-purple velvet. Resting inside a pad custom cut to hold it is a slender metallic cylinder, a musical instrument.

It takes Picard several seconds to find the word for it: a flute.

Again, memories rush back like someone opening a floodgate.

The Ressikan flute. Artifact of the long-dead people of Kataan. Gifted to him after he became the living receptacle of their people's last deep-space probe, a time capsule launched before the destruction of their world by a natural calamity.

Under the influence of their probe, Picard had lived a lifetime in twenty minutes. In the years that followed, he had often found great comfort and peace from playing the flute.

With trembling hands and stiff fingers, he pries the flute from its box. Holding it leaves him overwrought with joy and bittersweet longing. "Where was it?"

"You'd loaned it to the Smithsonian Museum for Galactic Antiquities."

He nods, as if he remembers doing any such thing. "Thank you."

"It was my pleasure."

"May I . . . have a moment to myself? Please?"

Doctor Feren smiles. "Sure." She ushers Nurse Teban out of the room and follows him to the corridor. The door slides closed after them with a gentle *swish*.

Picard struggles to place his fingers over the tone holes, to purse his lips above the embouchure. It's a futile effort. He no longer has the dexterity or the breath to play.

But just holding the flute is enough. With it in his hands, he remembers its distinctive sound. He recalls every tune he ever played on it, his duets with Nella Daren.

Feeling his life slip away, he closes his eyes and loses himself in memories of music, grateful to hold the flute one last time and remember his life as it was . . .

"Go on, Jean-Luc—hold him."

Picard is still trembling from the emotional ordeal of witnessing Beverly Crusher giving birth to their son. Around them, nurses, specialists, and technicians clean the sickbay operating room under the supervision of Doctor Tropp, who is serving as the *Enterprise*-E's acting chief medical officer while Crusher remains in postdelivery recovery.

Sitting up in a biobed, Crusher is haggard, her face drawn following hours of labor, her sweat-soaked hair tangled into knots. To Picard she has never looked more beautiful.

Once more she offers him the swaddled infant in her arms. "Take him. He won't bite."

Countless fears echo inside Picard's head. *What if I'm not suited to fatherhood? What if I can't be the father the boy needs? What if he doesn't love me? What if—*

Crusher eases René into Picard's arms.

He looks down into the eyes of his perfect, innocent son.

Love and hope fill Picard as if from a wellspring. He imagines it having been within him all along, dry and untapped, an unexplained emptiness whose importance he had been unable to understand . . . until now. Looking into René's eyes, and seeing his boy gaze up at him with absolute faith and trust, changes Picard in a way he would once have called impossible.

Tenderly, he holds René to his chest. Within moments the infant drifts into a fitful sleep. Watching his son slumber in his arms, Picard is grateful for his life as it is in this moment.

"Welcome to the world, my boy." He blinks away tears of joy. "My beautiful son."

A summer wind at his back, Jean-Luc pushed himself to make his third lap around the vineyard even faster than the first two.

In less than a year he would be old enough to apply to Starfleet Academy. To take his first step toward escaping this place where hope and dreams came to die. He planned to be ready.

He was moving so fast, the sweat on his forehead dried before it could fall into his eyes. He pushed his jog into a sprint. Experience had taught him he could hold this pace for up to six minutes before his hands shook and the blood in his veins burned like acid. He liked knowing his limits—and exceeding them.

The world became a blur. He breezed past the château. Turned south. Kept his arms close. Legs pumping, he kept his eyes on the horizon.

He barely noticed his older brother along the path ahead. Robert was down on his knees in the gravel and dust, pruning some of the old-growth vines with the care of a surgeon.

Jean-Luc had no breath to spare as he raced past.

Robert, as usual, did.

"Keep running!" he shouted at Jean-Luc's back. "That's what you're *best* at, isn't it?"

After running 42.195 kilometers in one hour, fifty-eight minutes, and forty-six seconds, Cadet Picard barely heard the cheering and applause that greeted him at the finish line of the Starfleet Academy Marathon of 2323.

Three steps past the shining green laser beam that marked the end of the course, Picard slowed his pace, and then he stumbled to a halt. His heart slammed inside his chest, and his lungs were on fire. The moment he stopped moving, sweat poured from every square centimeter of his body. His legs turned to rubber, and he dropped to his knees on the asphalt outside Ferry Plaza, before turning to fall onto his back.

All Picard wanted was to lie still for a few minutes, but someone was shaking his hand with great vigor, as if they were trying to wrest his arm from his shoulder, and they were talking to him, but he couldn't hear a word they said through the pounding of his own pulse in his ears. He opened his eyes and blinked through the late-morning sun, until he recognized his friendly assailant as his friend, fellow freshman Cadet Cortin Zweller.

"Corey? What did you say?"

"I said, 'You won!' You crazy sonofabitch, you did it! First freshman ever!"

Picard wanted to laugh but he could barely breathe, so he settled for a grin and muttered to himself, "Take *that*, Robert."

"Take my hand, Jean-Luc."

Picard lifted his hand to accept Anij's invitation. It had been more than twenty years since he had last seen the Ba'ku woman, here on her adopted homeworld inside the Briar Patch. The decades between had been unkind to him, such that his hand shook until he clasped hers.

"I fear I am not the man I once was."

Her smile was subtle and mysterious. "I'm sure you are. You've only forgotten."

She led him out of her home's main room, into a small backyard encircled by tall shrubberies and ancient trees. Birdsong lilted from the boughs. Insects unseen filled the air with sawing melodies. Anij's well-tended garden was green and lush, and filled the warm twilight air with scents of mint and lavender. Sunset lurked beyond the yard's shelter of green, but nonetheless dappled the lawn and a small artificial pond with patches of honeyed light.

Anij pressed her free hand to Picard's cheek and looked into his eyes. "How long has it been since your diagnosis?"

"Just over six years."

Sadness filled her eyes. "I wish you had come back sooner."

"I came as soon as circumstance allowed."

She removed her hand from his face. "Our metaphasic radiation should halt the progression of Irumodic Syndrome, maybe even reverse it. But it might take many years."

"That's not why I've come, Anij." He had rehearsed this conversation so many times inside his head, yet he still found it awkward to continue. "It seems my . . . *condition* has produced an unexpected side effect. One my physicians can't explain."

She gestured toward a nearby bench, beside the tiny pond. "Tell me more."

They settled onto the bench. Picard collected his thoughts. "I have moments of confusion. I forget where or when I am. Or, I think I'm in another time, another place. And I've been having visions. Of my past. My future. As if my mind has come unstuck in time. Except . . ."

Anij leaned closer, intrigued. "Except?"

"There are *discontinuities*. Visions of past events that conflict with my memories. Versions of the future that conflict with one another. Which makes me wonder—am I unstuck in time? Or am I succumbing to delusion?"

Anij pondered for a moment. "Jean-Luc, do you remember what I told you the last time you were here, about the perception of time?"

He plumbed his memory. It felt like rooting through a box of dusty bric-a-brac in search of a bauble. " 'Stop reviewing what happened yesterday. . . .' "

" 'Stop planning for tomorrow.' Exactly. Whether you've become unstuck because of your condition, or for some other reason, the best thing you can do is practice grounding yourself in the now. Be *here*, in *this* moment. Exist *here*."

Picard tried to clear his mind, tried to silence the chorus of critical voices that had taken up residence in his psyche. They went quiet as he looked once more into Anij's eyes. Then he was in the past, in this same place two decades earlier, and Anij—looking exactly the same then as she did now—halted in the middle of a moonlit walk to face him.

"Have you ever experienced a perfect moment in time?"

"A perfect moment?"

"When time seemed to stop, and you could almost *live* in that moment."

He blinked at the déjà vu—and the moment was gone. He was back on the bench, in the sunset garden with Anij, but now he recalled their long-ago conversation with total clarity. "You told me that a single moment in time . . . can be a universe in itself."

Her face lit up with delight. "Exactly. You do remember."

"Yes. But I need to know more. Not just how to hold on to a moment—though that would be a good place to start."

She nodded in understanding. "You want to learn how to guide your consciousness through time. How to navigate its eddies and its rivers, forward and backward."

"Yes, that's what I need. Can you teach me that?"

"I think so. It might take a while, but the stay will do you good."

Picard sighed with relief. This was the first good news he had heard about his condition in years. "Thank you, Anij. If nothing else, I'll be happy to know which of the lives I've been seeing are real."

Anij looked amused. "Therein lies your first lesson, Jean-Luc. They're *all* real."

Dreams in progress—that was how Captain Jean-Luc Picard perceived the dozens of starship spaceframes being assembled in Mars orbit. Each one destined to travel the galaxy, discover wonders yet unknown, or earn some other measure of prestige.

He reveled in his view of the Utopia Planitia Fleet Yards from the command complex's visitors' lounge. The facility's executive director had reserved Picard a table by a broad viewport that overlooked not only the broad sprawl of the fleet yards, but also the berth where his own command, the *U.S.S. Stargazer*, was undergoing fast-tracked upgrades to its primary sensor array.

He wished he could accelerate the process, or speed up time. Sitting idle didn't agree with him, and he disliked being this close to Earth. He was an explorer.

Another day or two and we'll be on our way back to the frontier, where we belong.

Given his druthers, he would have been on the *Stargazer*, supervising the refit from its bridge. But his senior science officer, Lieutenant Jack Crusher, had implored Picard to meet him here at 1600. Not wanting to disappoint his best friend, Picard had agreed. Now he found himself entranced by the movements of robots and workers in utility suits assembling the vessels of the future in front of him, all while he savored a splendid glass of Montepulciano d'Abruzzo.

When he heard footsteps drawing near, he knew it had to be Crusher, and that it must be 1600 on the dot, because Jack was nothing if not punctual.

Picard turned to greet his friend—only to be struck speechless by the sight of Jack's companion, a statuesque woman in a Starfleet medical uniform. She had hair the color of a Martian sunset, eyes as deep and blue as the Caribbean sea, and legs as long as Picard was tall. Most captivating of all was the quality of her bearing—she radiated intelligence, confidence, and charisma.

Remembering his manners half a second late, Picard stood to greet her and Jack.

Crusher beamed with pride and infatuation. "Captain, allow me to introduce to you my fiancée, Doctor Beverly Howard. Beverly, this is my best friend and commanding officer, Captain Jean-Luc Picard."

Doctor Howard extended her hand to Picard. "Lovely to meet you, Captain."

"Likewise, Doctor." Picard hoped that neither Jack nor the ravishing Doctor Howard could tell that his artificial heart felt like it skipped a beat as he shook her hand . . .

Ensign Picard, stabbed in the back in the middle of Starbase Earhart's gaming arcade, looked down at the Nausicaan dagger jutting from his chest, dripping with his blood.

And he laughed.

"Welcome aboard the *Enterprise*-D, Captain Picard. I am Lieutenant Commander Data, senior operations officer."

Picard stepped off the transporter platform. "Thank you, Commander."

Data led Picard out of the transporter room, into a curving corridor. "Your itinerary specifies that your first order of business is to proceed to the bridge and formally assume command. Do you wish to do so now, or would you prefer to settle in to your quarters first?"

"The bridge, please."

"Very good, sir."

Picard followed Data past several junior personnel to a turbolift. The ride to the bridge was brief, and the assumption of command was a mere formality that involved the ship's main computer recognizing Picard's voiceprint and authorization code. When it was done, Picard walked to his new command chair and eased himself into it.

Around him was the most advanced technology Starfleet had to offer. One of its newest *Galaxy*-class starships, crewed by some of its most accomplished officers and specialists, as well as a large contingent of civilian scientists. This massive vessel was a triumph of engineering, created in the name of peaceful exploration and scientific discovery.

This was the kind of life for which Picard had joined Starfleet.

He relaxed into the chair. Later he would tour the ship alone, but for now he wanted to bask in the sensation of being at the center of something as beautiful as it was powerful.

What a marvel of a ship! So full of possibilities . . .

━━━━━

What a waste of a ship. So full of memories . . .

Picard surveyed the charred remains of the *Enterprise*-D's bridge and his ready room. Nearby, Commander Riker searched through the rubble and debris. He had come to help Picard find one of his heirlooms, an album of Picard family history. Picard felt certain it was somewhere beneath the wreckage and scorched furniture. He had to believe it was intact.

Sunlight and a sultry breeze spilled down through the bridge's dome, whose panes of transparent aluminum all had been shattered and lost during the saucer section's crash landing on the surface of Veridian III. The warm light and clean air contrasted with the deep shadows and lingering odors of smoke and burnt wiring that suffused the demolished command deck.

Picard picked up a bust of some alien figure whose provenance escaped him. He had almost remembered whose likeness it was meant to be when Riker asked, "Is this it?"

Riker shifted part of an overhead plate out of the way so Picard could see what he had found. The moment Picard saw his family's seal through the soot, he knew they'd succeeded.

"Yes! Yes, that's it, Number One!" He lifted the large, leather-bound tome from the ashes and dusted it off. It looked weathered, but mostly intact. "Thank you."

Riker stepped out of Picard's way and took a last, sentimental look around the bridge. "I'm gonna miss this ship. She went before her time."

That remark struck a chord inside Picard.

"Someone once told me that time was a predator that stalked us all our lives. But I'd rather believe that time is a companion who goes with us on the journey, and reminds us to cherish every moment. Because they'll never come again."

No one will tell young Jean-Luc what is wrong with Pépé Felix.

All his life, Jean-Luc has admired his grandfather, his Pépé. Strong and proud, funny and generous, Pépé filled every room with laughter. But since midwinter something has been wrong. Everyone tries to hide the truth from Jean-Luc, but he hears the whispers, catches the looks of worry. He knows that his mother, when she thinks no one is paying attention, sneaks away to the pantry to weep for Maurice's father.

Just last summer, Felix had been a titan of a man, powerful and brimming with wit and intelligence. Now he lies, a fragile wisp confined to a bed after becoming lost too many nights in a row, crying out in fear, wordless. The sound is horrifying to Jean-Luc. It's the wail of an animal, not a human being. What could turn a man into . . . *this*?

Mother and Papa confer *sotto voce* with the doctor, who has made a house call via hologram. Mother dries her eyes as the physician's projection dims and vanishes. Papa clears his throat and scowls.

Robert stands in the corner, his head bowed like a penitent's. He sniffles and pulls his shirtsleeve across his face. When he drops his arm, Jean-Luc sees Robert's tear-stained eyes.

This is the first time he has ever seen his brother cry.

Mother steps away from Pépé's bed, walks straight to the door and intercepts Jean-Luc. "Come," she says. "Let's go downstairs."

"Why? What's—"

"Time to practice."

He knows by her tone that she means piano practice. When he tries to resist, she takes hold of his shirt collar and all but drags him downstairs to the sitting room and its standing piano. Brooking no complaint, she shepherds him onto the bench, and then she sits beside him.

She opens a book of sheet music and points at the top of the left page. "Begin."

Jean-Luc is still searching for where to put his fingers when his Pépé calls out again from upstairs, his pitiable holler resounding throughout the château.

Mother drapes an arm across Jean-Luc's shoulders. "Begin."

Harboring a silent protest, Jean-Luc does his best to plink out the melody he reads from the music book. Past experience leads him to expect harsh correction whenever he hits the wrong keys, but this time his mother ignores one false note after another. She merely admonishes him, "Keep playing. That's it. *Fortissimo*, now."

She sniffs loudly, but when he turns his head to look at her, she snaps, "Eyes on the page!" But he already knows she's crying, and using his music to hide the song of her grief. Pépé is Papa's father, but Yvette seems more deeply struck by his impending death.

Filling the house with sharps and flats, Jean-Luc perceives a truth he doesn't know how to explain: that his mother weeps so bitterly for Pépé because she knows that Papa will not.

Standing in the rain beside his mother's grave, Captain Picard longed for nothing more than a moment of silence. A moment of peace in which to process his loss and confront his sorrows.

But that, it seemed, was too much to ask of Robert.

"Nice of you to finally show your face."

Picard avoided making eye contact with his brother. "Not now, Robert."

"If not now, when? Who knows when you'll favor us again with your august presence!"

Tiny streams of rainwater converged and spilled into Yvette's grave. Picard gave silent thanks for the downpour, which had so elegantly disguised his tears. Still refusing to look at Robert, he grumbled, "This is neither the time nor the place."

His protest only fueled Robert's anger. "So *you* get to decide that, do you? The prodigal son too good to come to his *father's* funeral?" Robert reached into the mound of excavated dirt beside the grave, pulled out a muddy fistful, and slapped it onto the chest of Picard's dress uniform. "Too good to drop a handful of dirt on Papa's grave?"

Picard seethed as the mud dripped down the front of his uniform. His hands clenched into fists, and his imagination flashed with fantasies of beating Robert senseless.

Then he looked upon his mother's casket and relented.

He forced his fists to open.

And without another word to Robert, he turned and walked away.

His brother called after him, "Still running, eh, Jean-Luc? Papa was right about you."

Picard let the rain wash away his anger as he left the cemetery.

I refuse to exalt him or debase myself by letting him goad me. Those days are gone.

His tears spent, Picard boarded a shuttle that would take him back to Starfleet Command in San Francisco—and away from La Barre, for what he vowed would be the last time.

Picard and his sister-in-law Marie sat together in the main hall of Château Beauregard, the estate of old family friends in Cirey, just outside La Barre. Long after the other guests had paid their respects and left, Marie and Picard still gazed with sad remembrance on the large easel-mounted portraits of his brother, Robert, and his nephew, René.

Over a month had passed since they had perished in a fire that swept through Château Picard in the small hours of the morning. Both had been buried weeks earlier with proper funerals, but Marie had kindly arranged this memorial for Picard's benefit.

What did I ever do to deserve such kindness?

As if she had heard his silent self-reproach, Marie set her hand atop his. "I'm glad you were able to come back."

"As am I."

He knew not to mention that he had time to spare. He was between commands because the *Enterprise*-D had been lost in action only a few weeks earlier—a debacle for which he was scheduled to face a routine Starfleet JAG inquiry the following month.

Picard stood and moved closer to Robert's portrait. "It seems like only yesterday when I was here last." The Borg still haunted his memories, and he had made a habit of eliding them from conversation. Regardless, he knew that Marie understood the root of his pain. "Only yesterday when Robert and I wound up thrashing in the mud like angry children. But I knew that's what I needed. And so did he."

Marie got up and stood in front of her son's portrait. "I never thanked you for all those letters you sent René. You awoke the dreamer in him. I've no idea what he might have become, but I'm fairly certain he didn't plan on being a vintner."

"I'm sure that didn't please Robert."

She pursed her lips, reluctant to reply, but then she did. "Robert was overjoyed."

"Overjoyed? *My* brother?"

"Your last visit changed him as much as it did you. After you left, he confessed something to me. Something he wanted to tell you himself, the next time you were together." She turned a wistful look at Picard. "He was prouder of you than he ever said. He kept up with all your travels, all your accomplishments. When he played bocce with his friends, he used to brag about you. He didn't think I knew, but gossip travels fast in a small town."

On its face, her revelation sounded like cause for joy.

Instead, tears streamed from Picard's eyes.

Marie put an arm around him, suddenly mortified. "Jean-Luc? What did I say?"

He fought to rein in his sorrow. "To think, Marie—we came so close. Robert and I . . . so close to healing our old wounds. To being a family. But then—" He gestured toward the portraits and the tragedy they represented. "This."

His sister-in-law hugged him and pulled his face into her shoulder. "It wasn't your fault, Jean-Luc. Robert was a stubborn man. Wedded to the old ways. Just like your father."

"I know." Picard withdrew from Marie's embrace. "But to hear that he loved me so much more than I knew? I see now that I never understood him. Not Robert, or even René." He drifted from Robert's portrait to René's. "I owed them so much more than a lifetime of absence and silence. Now it's too late for me to apologize, or be forgiven."

Marie stood beside Picard and held his hand.

"Jean-Luc, René only ever had love and respect for you—and Robert forgave you long ago. It's time for you to forgive *yourself*—and live a life that makes *you* happy."

Picard stood, still holding the metal bar with which he had impaled his youthful but hopelessly twisted clone. Shinzon was dead, and yet Picard was unable to let him go—unwilling to absolve himself for whatever part he had played in fomenting the man's genocidal madness.

The monotonal, masculine voice of the *Scimitar*'s computer echoed inside the thalaron generator control room: *"One minute to firing sequence."*

The *Enterprise*-E and her crew were in the doomsday weapon's cross-hairs. Badly damaged and all but immobilized, Picard's ship had no way to escape. That alone should have impelled him to find some way to stop the countdown, but he would never be able to decipher the Romulan computer interfaces, never mind deduce their command access codes, before the thalaron cannon reduced his entire crew to dust. All he could do was stare at his dead doppelgänger and see his future and his past, fatally intertwined.

Then came a miracle.

Data entered the control room, a phaser in his hand. Seeing Picard, he went to him—only to pause, perplexed by the spectacle of Picard holding up the impaled Shinzon. Picard offered no explanation. Data didn't ask for one. The android's confusion became grim resolve. He pushed aside Shinzon's skewered corpse, and Picard let the body fall away.

The computer voice droned, *"Thirty seconds to firing sequence."*

The throbbing pulse of the thalaron generator accelerated to a fever-ish tempo.

In less than half a minute, Shinzon's plan would come to gruesome fruition.

Picard looked at Data, ashamed of his own inaction, feeling guilty for failing to redeem his alienated other self, and confused about what Data meant to do.

Data looked back at him, seemingly torn between wrath and pity.

Without a word, Data pressed a tiny device onto Picard's chest.

Instantaneously, a transporter beam enfolded Picard in a cascade of light and sound, erasing Data and the *Scimitar* from his sight . . .

When the soft white haze of the transporter beam faded, Picard stood in a space he had seen only a few times before—the captain's ready room of the *Starship Titan*. Even more bewildering was the discovery that he was holding a squirming infant.

The familiar voice of Deanna Troi sweetly chided him, "Turn this way, Jean-Luc!"

He pivoted to see Will Riker and Deanna Troi staring at him. Riker was holding up a padd, snagging holopics for his and Troi's family album. Riker looked up from the padd's screen. "Would it *kill* you to smile? We did let you hold our firstborn child, after all."

Troi twisted her features into an absurd expression, coaxing a bright raft of giggles from the baby. The child's mirth proved infectious: before Picard knew it, a broad grin of genuine delight had broken through his veneer of dignity.

Wearing a grin of his own, Riker set down his padd. "See? Not so hard." He stepped over to Picard and eased the baby out of his hands. "Here, I'll take him."

"Him?" Picard feared he had committed a faux pas, but Riker took it as a joke.

"As far as we know. But you're right, we shouldn't limit Thad's possibilities."

Thad? I thought their first child was a daughter.

Troi hooked her arm around Picard's and walked him to the ready room's door. "I know you're a busy man these days, but can you stay for dinner?"

"I don't see why not."

"Splendid. I'll tell the officers' mess to break out the good china. It's not every day we get to wine and dine a Starfleet Command *admiral.*"

Admiral?

Picard slipped free of Troi's arm and stepped toward the nearest reflective surface he could find—the viewport behind Riker's desk. He stood in front of it and gazed in wonder at his uniform, a style he had never seen before, and the admiral's rank insignia on his collar.

He whispered to himself, "Where—*when*—am I?"

Outside the viewport, a flare of white light preceded an orbital sunrise above Earth. Its blaze was ameliorated by the reactive coating on the viewport, but it was still bright enough to make Picard wince and raise one hand to shade his eyes.

When he lowered his hand, he was back in the chroniton core of the Devidians' temporal collider hidden outside of time—but everyone and everything stood frozen like insects in amber. Silvery bolts of death energy hung in midair. Phaser beams seemed to link shooters and victims like threads on a conspiracy map.

Picard shifted to adjust his perspective on the scene, and realized only belatedly that he had stepped out of himself in the past. Now he stood apart from his earlier self, regarding himself like a spectator. Past-

Picard had his finger on the holographic trigger pad, and his eyes closed as he kissed Beverly Crusher. Between them, their son René was looking up at Picard, his expression trapped forever between love and fear. And around them all stood an army in hooded black robes, a thousand incarnations of Death.

I had no choice. To save those who could not save themselves—that was the mission.

White light bloomed from the chroniton core, slowly at first, and then it ballooned outward and engulfed Picard, overwhelming him with its brightness . . .

The blinding flash melted away to reveal the study at Château Picard. The room was dimly lit, but a fire crackling inside the hearth imbued the room with a rosy ambience.

Someone was sitting in one of the high-backed chairs in front of the fireplace, but all Picard saw of them from his vantage was the top of their head, silhouetted by firelight.

He crossed the room in measured steps, circled the sitting area, and stopped in front of the hearth. The fire's warmth on his back was comforting.

The person in the chair was Data, dressed as he had been on the *Scimitar*.

Picard sat facing Data, in the high-backed chair's matching partner.

Next to Picard's chair, a holoframe played the same peculiar vid on a loop. It showed an elaborate sand castle—crafted to perfection with towers, turrets, and crenellated battlements—overcome by one crushing wave. As the tide receded, the castle melted and collapsed, vanishing back into the beach as if it had never been. Then another wave surged ashore, and as it retreated, the castle was rebuilt, reborn perfectly intact . . . only to be erased again.

And again.

At last, he sat back and regarded Data. Neither of them said anything, yet Picard was certain that his old friend knew why he had come. Except . . . the serenity in Data's face told Picard that his journey had been misguided. His burden of guilt unnecessary.

Picard had sacrificed himself before, not just in this timeline, not just in this universe, but in many. Giving up the one for the good of the many—it was integral to who Picard was. To who he had always been. To who he would always be.

He had loved that same quality in Data.

As his old friend graced him with a gentle smile, Picard felt . . . *free.*

What once was is no more. What once had been to come now will never be. And that is all very well, but now it is time for Jean-Luc Picard to tend his own garden.

Summer has come to La Barre, and the vineyard of Château Picard is deep into its growing season. On either side of Picard, the old growth is lush and healthy. The grass is thick and yielding beneath his boots, and a breeze like a lover's whisper trembles the leaves. The morning air is rich with the perfume of petrichor from last night's rain. As he walks, his aged fingertips graze a cluster of fruit hanging heavy on the vine.

His faithful bulldog trots at his side. It stops for a second to root in the dirt, as dogs are wont to do. Picard whistles—"Number One!"—and the hound races back to his heel.

He tousles the wiry fur on the dog's head.

Panting, it looks up at him, its tongue dangling from the side of its mouth. Picard reaches into his coat pocket and fishes out a biscuit for his canine *compère.* While his dog chomps the treat to bits, Picard gives it a few hearty slaps on its flank.

The old man squints into the sun and drinks in its perfect light.

Just as Anij taught him, he finds forever in this moment.

Then comes oblivion's inevitable embrace.

The rest is silence.

A life is like a garden. Perfect moments can be had,
but not preserved, except in memory. LLAP

—Leonard Nimoy's last tweet
@TheRealNimoy
February 23, 2015

GRACE NOTE

WHAT REMAINS TO BE SEEN

New York City—September 8, 1966

Brown fingers strike dark keys on a taupe-shell Smith-Corona Sterling typewriter, filling the dusty apartment with their staccato patter. A line's end arrives with the ring of a bell. Its music is rewarded by the purr and *thunk* of the carriage being reset, and once more words are hammered into existence, letter by letter, ink smashed onto paper by imagination and steel.

Afternoon sun bakes the brownstones of West 136th Street in Harlem. It spears through crooked slats in an old set of venetian blinds, throwing shafts of golden light across a dining table packed from edge to edge with orderly stacks of paper.

Manuscripts. Dozens of them. Ranked and filed in narrative order.

It's the labor of a decade. The work of a lifetime.

Benny Russell sits at his typewriter, committing his reality to paper. To secure his release from the psychiatric hospital, he'd had to deny what he knows is true. They made him say his creations were mere fictions. Flights of fancy. Ephemera born of a troubled mind. *Lies.*

But now he's free. Free to tell his stories. To tell his truth.

No one wants to publish his saga. His novels, novellas, and short stories come back from agents and editors unread, topped with form-letter rejections, or with nothing at all.

But Benny will not stop writing them. He cannot.

His stories *need* to exist. This world he has seen, this future of infinite possibilities—it's *real.* He *knows* it in his soul, just as he knows the stars are fire.

He nears the end of a page. The end of a chapter. The end of a novel.

It's a tale of tragedy. Loss and sacrifice. But also redemption. And hope.

For these noble souls whose lives Benny has struggled to capture, it is the end of just one of many possible worlds. But though he knows there are other paths to take, and more adventures to record, he still weeps for this one as he types the novel's final line:

The rest is silence.

He pulls the paper from the typewriter with a flourish. Reads it over.

Yes. This is a fitting end to a tale of heroes. A tribute to those who would give everything to defend an ideal. Who would sacrifice their lives for a principle. Who would die for love.

He puts the last page in its place, at the bottom of a pile of paper. Taps the stacked manuscript until all its sides are tidy and uniform. He wraps a large rubber band around it, and then he sets it into its spot on the table.

This would be a fine place to end his work for the day . . . but he knows there are new stories that need to be told about these heroes. About other lives they've led in other universes, all of them no more and no less real than those he has chronicled so far.

It's time the dreamer begat a new dream.

He picks up a fresh sheet of paper. Feeds it into the Smith-Corona.

Inspiration strikes like lightning. He types with passion and precision.

When he comes to a halt, his new novel's first sentence looks back at him:

In latter days, sitting alone in his manor, pondering the events of years that preceded this self-imposed exile, trying to understand where and how it had all gone wrong, M. Jean-Luc Picard (formerly of Starfleet) would often come back to one moment.

Benny smiles. This feels right.

A new future begins here.

ACKNOWLEDGMENTS

My first thanks, as always, are to my wife, Kara. Her support and encouragement during the writing of this novel were essential. I don't know what I would do without her as my sounding board, cheerleader, and dinnertime therapist.

This is the thirty-sixth novel I have written, and my twenty-ninth for *Star Trek*. Of them all, this one has been the most difficult to write. Not just because of its content, but also the circumstances that coincided with its development and creation. Those included, but are not limited to, the global COVID-19 pandemic; the deaths of my longtime idol Neil Peart of Rush, my mother, and my friend and fellow *Star Trek* author Dave Galanter; and, last but certainly not least, a tumultuous election followed by a seditious, violent attack on the U.S. Congress.

That's not to discount the challenge presented by the material itself. The ongoing shared literary continuity of the *Star Trek* novels extends back at least to July 2001, with the publication of the *Star Trek: Deep Space Nine* novel *Avatar*, Book I, by S. D. Perry. That tome marked the beginning of the books' serialized DS9 post-finale continuity, an effort that in time expanded to encompass many of the *Star Trek* novels published by Simon & Schuster between 2003 and 2020. Over a span of nearly two decades, twenty-five authors collaborated, either directly or through the *Star Trek* books' editors, to craft this intricate shared literary continuity.

Part of what made that possible was the absence, after *Star Trek Nem-*

esis, of any new *Star Trek* feature films or television series set in the twenty-fourth century or later. Because no one—not the authors, editors, or licensing executives—expected there to be more films or series continuing the narratives of *Star Trek: The Next Generation*, *Star Trek: Deep Space Nine*, and *Star Trek: Voyager*, those of us creating the novels were afforded greater freedom to carry those series' characters' stories forward, to new developments and new adventures.

Then came *Star Trek: Picard*.

Within a few episodes, it became clear that the literary continuity we had conceived and crafted for nearly twenty years could not be reconciled with the future described in *Picard*'s backstory. One revelation after another pushed our vision of the late twenty-fourth century farther and farther out of concurrence with the newly established canon.

One of the core tenets of licensed *Star Trek* fiction is that it must make every effort to be consistent with canon as it exists at the time of each work's creation.

Knowing that there were at least two more seasons of *Star Trek: Picard* coming our way, I and several of my fellow *Star Trek* authors realized we had a problem. Either our labors of two decades would be cast aside, abandoned *in medias res*, or else we would need to find a way to bring them to a conclusion. Not wanting to see our work end on cliffhangers, and not wanting our readers to feel as if their many years of support had been for naught, James Swallow and I hatched a plan to build an epic finale for the literary continuity. Soon afterward, we enlisted fellow *Star Trek* novels veteran Dayton Ward to join our secret cabal.

This was the beginning of what Dayton dubbed "The Plan."

I should say at this point that I could not have asked for better collaborators than James and Dayton. They are as generous as they are talented. As we cooked up ideas for what became this trilogy, no one got possessive about their ideas. We eagerly pushed some of our best inspirations to one another, built upon one another's suggestions to plot out the story, and kept in mind at all times that this needed to be a team effort.

Whether *Coda* succeeds in honoring the twenty years of imagination and labor that led us to this point will be decided by critics and readers, after it's too late for any of us to fix it.

Some of the fellow *Star Trek* authors whose works have been part of this epic adventure include Una McCormack (whose *Star Trek: Picard* novel *The Last Best Hope* is referenced in this book's epilogue, aka the "Grace Note"), Christopher L. Bennett, David R. George III, S. D. Perry, Kirsten Beyer, Greg Cox, Heather Jarman, Olivia Woods, Michael A. Martin, Andy Mangels, Keith R.A. DeCandido, Geoffrey Thorne, Peter David, Michael Jan Friedman, Robert Greenberger, Kevin Dilmore, Jeffrey Lang, Andrew Robinson, J. G. Hertzler, William Leisner, David Weddle, John Jackson Miller, Paula Block, Terry Erdmann, and Robert Simpson. They are giants all, and we have been honored to stand upon their shoulders.

Our editors deserve praise for their roles in this endeavor. This crazy journey began with Marco Palmieri, who brought serial continuity to the *Deep Space Nine* books. John J. Ordover and Margaret Clark adopted it for *Star Trek: The Next Generation* and *Star Trek: Voyager*. In time, the shared continuity made it into various series, including *Star Trek: Titan*, *Star Trek: S.C.E.* (aka *Star Trek: Corps of Engineers*), edited by Keith R.A. DeCandido and John J. Ordover, and even *Star Trek: Vanguard*, which was co-created by Marco and later passed into the stewardship of Jaime Costas and then Margaret. Last but not least, senior editor Ed Schlesinger has been our ringmaster through all these years, keeping all of us on time and on budget.

None of this would have been possible, of course, without the explicit approval and support of the *Star Trek* Licensing team, who have without fail been some of our most ardent champions. At the start of this literary odyssey, that department was headed by Paula Block. For many years now, however, that role has been occupied by John Van Citters, currently Vice President of *Star Trek* Brand Development for ViacomCBS Global Franchise Management. Both Paula and John have been trusted partners in making the shared literary continuity the best it could be.

Another vital member of our team is Scott Pearson. For several years now, Scott has worked as both an author and a copy editor for the *Star Trek* books, but he and I go way back. Scott has been my drinking buddy at Shore Leave, my partner in hijinks at the *Star Trek* Original Series Set Tour, and my reliably grumpy long-distance compañero.

We're lucky to have him as our copy editor, and I am fortunate to be able to call him my friend.

As I noted earlier in these acknowledgments, one of the emotional blows I endured this year was the death of Neil Peart, percussionist and lyricist for Canadian progressive-rock trio Rush. Neil and his work have been an artistic and personal inspiration to me since I was twelve years old. I never had the privilege of meeting Neil, though we did briefly exchange emails back in 2007, after I gifted him signed copies of my first two full-length *Star Trek* novels, which featured a character named in his honor.

Consequently, when I first discussed with Dayton, a fellow die-hard Rush fan, my ideas for what would become this trilogy, I knew that it would be important to me to find a way to make this tome both a conclusion to a twenty-year, multiauthor collaboration and an homage to an artist whose works and personal ethos have been fundamental in guiding my own creative path. In time, I began to see the threads weave themselves together. The sentiments of "The Garden," the last song on *Clockwork Angels*, the final studio album by Rush, echoed in an eerie way the last words of Leonard Nimoy on Twitter, as well as bits of dialogue about time, in a number of the *Star Trek: The Next Generation* feature films.

Once I discovered that, I knew I'd found my theme.

Those who have perused the acknowledgments of my early *Star Trek* novels might recall that music—in particular, film and television soundtracks—is essential to my process when I'm writing. That has never been more true than it was while writing this book. While there were tracks from many albums and composers in the inspirational mix for this project, the work of one composer has stood out from the rest: that of Lorne Balfe. I've found his score for *Mission: Impossible— Fallout* to be some of the most exciting imagination fuel I've ever heard. But even more stirring has been his work for the first two seasons of the BBC/HBO series *His Dark Materials*. Balfe's four CDs of original compositions for that series, more than any other music in my extensive collection, helped inspire key scenes throughout the *Coda* trilogy, and many of the most important moments of this book. Thank you, Lorne.

Naturally, I thank my agent, Lucienne Diver of The Knight Agency, for vetting contracts whose verbiage I don't understand, and for tracking down royalties I would never otherwise find.

A special note of thanks is due to several persons who helped me try to add a portrait of the late, great Leonard Nimoy to the Valediction page featuring his final tweet. John Van Citters secured permission from the gracious Susan Bay Nimoy to use the text content of Leonard's tweet, and I had a photo in mind to go with it. Unfortunately, copyright law is very strict in the publishing world, so it's crucial to verify the provenance of photos—not only who created them, but who owns the rights to publish them for commercial use, such as in a book.

In the case of the photo I had set my heart on, that proved impossible to do.

We really tried. The search for the photograph's owner involved the combined efforts of John Van Citters; Dayton Ward; *Star Trek* historians Larry Nemecek and Bonnie Moss; startrek.com editors Yasmin Elachi and Ian Spelling; Leonard Nimoy's gallery representative, Richard Michelson; freelance writer Hartley Pleshaw; *Imagine* magazine publisher Carol Patton; Leonard's daughter Julie Nimoy and her husband, David Knight; and Leonard's granddaughter, Dani Nimoy Schwartz. Even though our quest ultimately proved unsuccessful, my sincere thanks go out to them, one and all, for all their help and patience.

Finally, on behalf of myself, my collaborators Dayton Ward and James Swallow, and our editors Margaret Clark and Ed Schlesinger, I send out my heartfelt gratitude to all you readers who came along with us for all or any part of this twenty-year literary adventure. We hope you'll stay with us as we set out to tell new tales of heroes and exploration in the years to come, as *Star Trek* continues to grow and evolve.

Live long and prosper, my friends.

David Mack
New York City
11 April 2021

ABOUT THE AUTHOR

David Mack is glad it happened, but sad to see it go.

Learn more on his official website:
davidmack.pro
Or follow him on Twitter:
@DavidAlanMack